LIGHTNING

Books by Bonnie S. Calhoun

STONE BRAIDE CHRONICLES △ 2

C-1

LIGHTNING

A NOVEL

BONNIE S. CALHOUN

Revell

a division of Baker Publishing Group
Grand Rapids, Michigan

© 2015 by Bonnie S. Calhoun

Published by Revell
a division of Baker Publishing Group
P.O. Box 6287, Grand Rapids, MI 49516-6287
www.revellbooks.com

Printed in the United States of America

Library of Congress Cataloging-in-Publication Data is on file at the Library of Congress, Washington, DC.

ISBN 978-0-8007-2377-4

15 16 17 18 19 20 21   7 6 5 4 3 2 1

There is nothing new under the sun,
and the more things change,
the more they stay the same.
Hindsight is twenty-twenty.

1

Day 1

A clipped sound echoed along the cavernous street as Selah Rishon raised her foot onto a stone bench. She jerked her head up to glance around the abandoned streetscape.

A groan bounced from the building facades.

Eyeing the landscape cautiously, she secured her dark mop of unruly curls that sorely needed a visit from Mother's shears and finished tightening her exercise shoe. She stretched her calf muscle. Time to get this done before the sunrise and hot temperatures took over.

She switched feet, tightened her other shoe, and stretched again as she squinted into the soft rays of the morning sun trying to climb over the horizon. Dramatic shadows sliced across the ancient brick buildings, creating elongated, one-dimensional fright-men. She shuddered and pushed off on a slow jog down the broken, weed-congested street. A shadow slid to the edge of the surrounding darkness in a doorway two building cavities away on her side of the street.

Selah stopped. Her chest constricted as her heart rate ticked up, pushing starbursts into her vision. She squinted at the different shades of black, attempting to distinguish a face among the sprinkled flashes. She deciphered the outline of a short club protruding from an overly thick hand, probably gloved. Her mouth went dry. She sniffed at the air. She could almost distinguish his smell. Sweat and vegetation mixed with musk and dirt. A male.

The black-clad figure separated from the darkness and lunged onto the uneven sidewalk. She inhaled to draw in calm and studied the shape and posture of the figure. A little taller than her five foot six. Broad at the shoulders, rectangular stance between legs and hips. Yes, it had to be a man.

Her heart pounded a staccato rhythm against her rib cage, drowning out her thoughts. *Control your breathing.*

She turned to run the other way. Adrenaline surged, prickling up the back of her neck and across her scalp. A movement whispered in front of her.

A second figure emerged from one of the numerous doorways, blocking her retreat.

How did she miss him? Not paying attention could get her hurt.

She pivoted and her back faced the street. No! Bad move. Another attack angle unprotected. She spun, positioning her back against the building. One assailant stood to her left, the other approached from the right. If she let them get close at the same time, she'd be done. Her legs trembled. She steeled herself for an attack.

A squeak. An audible click. The man to her left flicked open an auto-blade. He brandished the knife and lunged. Selah jerked her wrist up to block the attack but overswung. Her hand accidentally connected with her own chin and she bit her lip. The taste of copper heightened her senses. Selah balled her hands tight to her chest and thrust out her left leg, planting her foot in his stomach.

He doubled over as air expelled from his lungs with a grunt. The knife flew from his hand and skittered across the broken street surface. He scrambled for the weapon. Selah bounced to a defensive stance. Pivoting her hip, she kicked out to the side with her right leg, connecting with his chest. He collapsed to the road, gasping.

Emboldened that she hadn't suffered a blow, she bolted in the other man's direction. He raised his club and she assumed a fighting posture. He swung. She blocked the downward motion of his left wrist with an upward thrust of her right forearm. It rocked her core, stinging her arm. An adrenaline rush absorbed the pain.

His right fist jabbed at her head. She pulled to the right side. Her left leg shot out in a low kick and connected with the outside of his knee, knocking him off balance. As he started to fold, she maneuvered a hefty jab and shoved her fist into his nose.

Spittle flew from his mouth.

The man grabbed his face. "My nose! Why, you—" He cursed and released the club. It clattered to the ground.

She sprinted down the street, crossing to the other side. Her core buzzed with the electricity of rapid-fire movements and precision strokes. Her speed felt fluid and natural.

Pay attention. Focus. Focus, she recited until her breathing leveled off.

Stinging. She shook her hand, blew on her fingers, and examined them. Tiny smears of blood dotted the back of her hand. She had skinned two knuckles.

White AirStream at three o'clock. Someone in the pilot's seat.

This time she wasn't taking chances. She dodged behind a tree and used the street-side refuse container to hide her advance. She sprang from the hiding place, ran to the Air-Stream, and crept along its length to the front. With her back against the sleek side, she reached across her chest with her left arm and snatched the occupant out by his tunic. As his torso exited the cockpit, she jammed her right hand into the space between his left arm socket and shoulder blade. She felt his shoulder separate and he howled in pain.

Lowering his center of gravity to throw him off balance, she drove his face into the narrow grassy strip at the edge of the sidewalk and planted her knee on the back of his neck.

"All right, all right! I'm down!" With his plea muffled by the grass, the man fell limp.

"Okay, Selah," boomed the speaker mounted high on the side of a nearby building. "Your session is done, and by the looks of it, so are my men." Taraji, the head of TicCity security, chuckled over the intercom.

Selah looked up at the tiny visi-unit mounted on the street

illuminator and smiled. "Okay, Taraji. I think I may have broken Arann's nose. He zigged when he should have zagged. And Hex needs to lubricate his auto-blade. His prop has a serious squeak." She looked down the street and assessed her friendly victims.

Arann, still holding his nose, raised his hand in a thumbs-up. Selah waved and jogged back to the training zone entrance.

A black-clad form dropped in front of her. Selah recoiled as the hooded figure crouched like a jumping spider and charged. She blocked the charge and spun to the right, executing a roundhouse sweep. The figure jumped her leg and came in with fists flying. The two of them parried back and forth, blow for blow, slice for slice. Selah's comfort level with the defensive moves increased with her added speed and confidence.

A smile pulled at the corners of her lips. She felt exhilarated.

The spider figure lunged, rolled, and swept Selah's feet out from under her with one fell swoop. Selah landed on her back with a grunt as the air rushed from her lungs. The figure scrambled over her and pressed a glove-covered fist to Selah's throat.

Selah raised open palms. "Augh! I surrender."

The black-clad spider figure ripped off its hood. Taraji grinned at Selah. "Never let an opponent see your level of confidence because they will use it against you every time."

"I really thought I had you." Selah shook her head.

Taraji held out a hand and yanked Selah to her feet. "You would have, if you hadn't stopped to grin at me. It made for a perfect break in your concentration. But your increased speed is phenomenal. You're ready to move to the next level of training."

"I need to thank you for suggesting Krav Maga. It's the perfect form of exercise and self-defense." Selah wiped at her brow with the back of her arm.

"Sometimes ancient techniques are much more practical than the new." Taraji smiled and offered a wink.

Taraji could have been a twin to Mojica, the head of Mountain security, from their singular names to both of them being six feet tall and having muscular builds, long dark hair, and large smoky eyes covered with heavy lashes. The only difference was Taraji's complexion was dark like the honey Selah loved for dipping her morning bread.

The resemblance had interested her for a couple of months. No matter how silly, she had to say something. "You remind me very much of a woman I met in the Mountain."

"Who in my clan did you meet?"

"Seriously? Mojica is related to you? How come she's in there and you're out here?"

"We each have duties to complete, and for some of us that breaks our familial contacts, but it is all for the ultimate good. How is she doing these days? I haven't seen her in many years."

"She's head of security in the Mountain, and it was her mobilized force that got us and the prisoners out safely."

Taraji nodded. "That's my Moji. I'm glad she's doing well. I covet the day we'll be able to reunite as a family."

"Couldn't she just choose to leave the Mountain? I've often wondered why she went back inside."

"That is her job. She cannot leave until the Mountain does."

Selah pulled back. "What does that mean?"

Taraji reddened in the cheeks, obviously flustered at her own utterance. "It would be better if you forget that. I'll see you in tactical first thing in the morning."

"What did you mean to say then?"

"I *should* have said Mojica takes her job seriously and will gain release at the appropriate time."

Selah decided to take Taraji's change in demeanor seriously. That same look had always backed her away from pressing an issue with her stepfather. She watched the woman vault the stairs leading to the catwalk connected to her office. Gone before she could thoughtfully react. She shook her head. This whole adventure reminded her of the puzzles she used to work with Mother. All the parts were spread out on the table at the beginning, in organized chaos, with no two pieces fitting together.

Still sweaty, Selah entered the staging area on the backside of the security team training center. Her olive complexion protected her from the burning rays of the sun, but she hated being all sticky from profuse sweating. She had to remind herself that no matter how much she disliked exercise, there was a dual purpose—to rebuild the leg strength she'd found waning over the past months of lounging here seaside, and to alleviate her current predicament. She had been informed early on that walking around TicCity with knives hidden in her pants legs was completely uncivilized, so this regimen of training seemed like a great alternative to carrying kapos.

In reality, she had an ulterior motive for staying toned and lean—like love . . . regaining what had been lost.

Mindful that she didn't have to hide it here, she peeled off the vibrant blue top of her workout suit, exposing the mark hovering below her collarbone. Her narrow-strapped cotton shirt offered welcome relief from the heat. The suit top trailed behind her on the trudge across the equipment area to the ultrasonic showers as she thought about the strange conversation. It was the first time Taraji had displayed that level of firmness. If Mother had met her, she'd have said the woman was smooth as cream but tough as tree bark.

Selah smiled. She would love nothing better than for Mother to meet her new trainer.

If only she could find her mother to introduce them.

2

S elah sat in the office area of her quarters and glanced through the long expanse of glass offering a sweeping view of the blue waters of the Atlantic and exerted pressure on her thought. *One . . . two . . . three . . . release.*

Again, came the voice drifting through her consciousness.

She pictured the dart of an idea burrowing like an inchworm into the core of her subject. Treva Gilani, former child prodigy of biochemical research in the Mountain, sat on the gas rig platform called Petrol City anchored fifteen miles out at sea.

Very good, came Treva's mental response. *I like this exercise. Your thoughts are becoming solidly focused.*

Since their escape from the Mountain, they'd become fast friends, and Treva spent every opportunity helping Selah exercise her new mental abilities.

Selah tossed back a thought. *Talking about focused . . .*

I've been trying hard to research the novarium who've come before me. I need more information than Glade is offering. I get the impression he's stalling on purpose, even in the research I'm doing in the Repository. The Repository was the data file storage of the collective knowledge and actions of the Landers since their beginning at the Sorrows.

Treva's thought hit Selah's mind. *Maybe he really is busy like he says. Other than our mind-jump exercises, we haven't been able to spend a lot of time together either.*

Sometimes it irritated Selah when her friend tried to find the logic in a situation she wanted to consider chaotic. *I keep running into information holes and blocks in the Repository. There's only sketchy data on a few of the Landers in the last hundred years who've transitioned to novarium, and no files on the actual outcomes. You would think that with the transition happening to so few, they'd have every minute of data,* Selah thought.

I still have to ask. What would be Glade's motivation to stall you? Treva thought. Selah noticed a bit of force in her delivery.

I don't know, but I'm pretty sure it's him trying to discourage my efforts. Several times I've seen his name in the sign-in log at the Repository, and then mysteriously I can't find records I know I've looked at before.

Glade, in his rabid determination to find a way to the West, had relayed very little information on the meaning or consequences of being novarium, the condition that had put the bright swirling tattoo below her collarbone. Selah had taken it upon herself to search out the information, and now she felt it was being hidden from her on purpose. *Mother would say drill the well until it produces water.*

After all you've told me about her, Pasha would say stop being reckless. Hang on. Treva's thought-trail evaporated.

Selah's ComLink vibrated through the bones in her arm, tickling her elbow. She smiled and tapped the crystal. A holographic projection of Treva's head appeared above her wrist.

Selah laughed. "Sometimes it's hard to keep up with you. Why'd you break the mind-jump?" She brought her right foot up onto her chair and rested her wrist on her bent knee.

"It makes me nervous to think other Landers could mind-jump and be privy to our conversation without us knowing it," Treva said, wrinkling her nose like she'd smelled something bad.

"I did find several notations on *that* subject. Seems after the first couple of years of hearing each other's every thought, some of the Landers developed a drug concoction that deadened the ability to mind-jump, until finally a lot of them lost it altogether and didn't need the drug anymore," Selah said.

"It's sad that they thought to get freedom from the others they had to shut down the ability completely," Treva said. "They could have trained themselves to close off their minds. I've done it since I was a child. It was a hard exercise, but in the end it's been worth the peace."

"I guess they thought taking a drug was easier. Maybe someone convinced them there was no other option." Selah lifted an eyebrow. It sounded like a great start to a conspiracy.

Treva shook her head and smiled. "You could find a subversive plot under a flat stone. If I remember correctly from the stories you've told me, your past exploits don't always turn out for the best. Do I have to remind you of a certain beach? Don't go getting any ideas. I see that light in your eyes."

Selah was thinking of exploring six different file trails at one time. She had gained much Lander data, but almost nothing on novarium or the location of the special file she wanted.

Treva furrowed her brow in thought. "Now that I think about it, that drug sounds like the one used on Glade in the Mountain to keep him from communicating with the other prisoners."

Selah straightened. "They couldn't be the same, could they? That would mean there was a scheme between the Mountain and at least some of the original Landers, but which ones?" Her mind sorted through all the compatible searches she could do on the data.

Treva tapped her lip, then raised a finger. "We know there are three Protocols of Landers. The original Landers who came from the Mountain were the First Protocol. Glade is one of the venerated ones in that group. The Second Protocol are the Landers who come by sea, like Bodhi. And the Third Protocol are the lost ones Glade is seeking in the West."

"Remember, when we were in Baltimore, Glade told us about the splinter groups in the First Protocol that went renegade with their own plans. So whoever went in league with the Mountain on that drug would have to be from one of those groups." Selah pursed her lips, then pulled them tight. "I've seen that word *protocol* used as a reference all the way back to the beginning of the Lander records at the

Time of Sorrows, so somebody didn't just make it up. What's it mean?"

"It depends on if they were using *protocol* literally or figuratively. It could mean a set of rules for connecting computers, or having the same philosophy, or it could even mean a detailed research plan or a code of conduct. It's just an odd word to use for a set of people," Treva said.

Selah's thoughts had already jumped into action, crossed the quadrant, and headed for the data cubes in the Repository. Her curiosity was running rampant.

"Did you find out anything about me having Lander abilities but not a mark?" Treva didn't have clearance to use the archives at the Repository. Selah's clearance came because Glade was the original head of the TicCity Council, and even after he'd been replaced during his incarceration, his status was still solid.

"A couple of the files I cross-referenced about that have disappeared. We already knew that the original Landers were a group of regular human people who left the Mountain after the Sorrows." Selah wrinkled her forehead, thinking of what she knew. "And their marks didn't show up until they left the Mountain."

Treva nodded. "And apparently that's when the longevity came about also. They were adult men and women of various ages who started out with the mark across their forehead and down the left temple. So if they intermarried inside the group, those children also had the mark. When they or their children married outside the group, the mark didn't transfer and it created a whole new generation of Landers with no mark."

"What I get from those records is there are as many types of Landers as there are nationalities of people. And not all Landers are created equal. There is a reference to some kind of test for proliferation. I didn't find what that term meant, and the specifics on the test are missing. It was deleted on purpose, because parts of the file were in different sectors of the data cube and all those locations are now empty," Selah said.

"But they are *human*! The original Landers were ordinary *human* people from the Mountain! I lived there my whole life, and granted, twenty years isn't a lot, but I've never heard anything remotely close to talk about Landers being normal people!" Treva's nostrils flared.

"But I can't find anything about what happened to turn them *into* Landers. Some of those same people could still be alive, as is Glade."

Treva started to laugh. "And why are they called Landers? I always thought they were just the ones who came by sea and landed on our shores. But after meeting Glade and the others, I've realized there are a lot more Landers who were here originally and never came by sea."

"That's a good question. Another is, how long will we hybrids live?" Selah felt her face warming. There. She had finally said it. She didn't understand why asking it made her feel selfish when it was a legitimate question.

Treva gritted her teeth. "The more we know, the more there is to find out."

"I just don't understand why Glade won't open up. He's frustrating me. A lot of this includes me, so I'd like to be prepared for what's coming." Selah had played with that question for weeks. She now had several abilities like mind-jumping and increased physical stamina, and new dreams and the flashes were becoming common.

"Glade says he doesn't remember anything from before they left the Mountain." Treva looked behind her, then back toward Selah.

"Frankly, I don't believe him anymore. That's why I'm investigating on my own. There's something he doesn't want me to find out." Selah was pretty sure from reading his body-speak, and having grown up around three males, that he was concealing something.

"You're getting as paranoid as Cleon. It's his idea that we've landed in the middle of a huge conspiracy." Treva smiled. "And please don't get me started on what your brother thinks. He's driving me crazy about this trip."

Selah tipped her head. "What trip?"

"Didn't I tell you? Must have forgotten. I'm going to the Mountain. I've thought long and hard, and there are just some things I have to get. I don't know why, but it's been bothering me a lot lately, and I have to go." Treva dropped her gaze.

Selah froze. It had taken a few weeks for her to stop having nightmares about the Mountain. *I don't want to go back there.* Her hands shook at the thought of being shot at again.

Easy, girl! Go back to speaking words. Treva's thoughts came in a soothing tone, then she spoke. "I don't need you to go. Cleon said he'd accompany me. Besides, I'm also going to see how my uncle is coming with his settlement of Stone Braide. If he didn't run into problems, they should be a thriving colony by now. Getting into my private lab won't take much extra effort. I should have brought all my data out with me anyhow. I can be in and out in a day."

"I don't want you or Cleon going back to that dangerous place." Months ago Selah had been driven by a burning desire to find her real father. But now the craziness of such a foolish venture made her feel reckless. Dragging her stepbrother Cleon and the others into danger had caused her several delayed bouts of anxiety.

The Mountain night terrors had finally faded. Now they were replaced by streaking flashes of lightning and exploding fireballs. It seemed that since she'd turned novarium, her mind never rested.

"Enough about my plans. You didn't tell me you're having nightmares." Treva's eyebrows pinched together and she frowned. "Why didn't you say something before?"

Selah realized just how much she'd left her thoughts open in the last few minutes. Some things she just wanted kept to herself. It was an acquired skill she hadn't mastered yet. She looked at the floor, trying to think of how much to say.

"You haven't answered me," Treva said.

"Don't worry. I had some of these dreams even before changing to a novarium."

"Apparently some dreams are new and they've scared you."

"At least when I had the tsunami nightmare I knew it came from the Time of Sorrows. These new dreams have water images that I don't understand, and it frightens me." Selah knew there was more meaning to them, but apprehension kept her from exploring. They felt dangerous.

"When I get back from the Mountain, we'll work on them together," Treva said.

The word *Mountain* brought instant dread. Selah measured her words to not sound as panicked as she felt. "How do you think you can get into the Mountain and back out without being caught?"

"That's not a common concern. People are perfectly able to come and go from the Mountain. No one living there is a prisoner. It's just that a portion of them, mainly older citizens, have been brainwashed into fearing the outside world."

"Did you ever spend time outside the Mountain when you lived in there?" Selah relaxed. She hadn't thought about people in the Mountain having personal freedom.

"Hundreds of times! Some of the compounds I created are from plant life outside the Mountain."

"But don't you worry about radiation or contaminated animals?"

"No, not at all. A hundred years ago the Science Consortium verified that the radiation from the nuclear explosions in Washington, DC, had been scrubbed from the land by the tsunami, and the air particulates were made inert by some strange interaction with the ash from the super volcano eruption."

"So the later disasters negated the original attack."

Treva smiled. "It was quite a bit of fortune for the country that the other two happened. This land could have been a dead zone for hundreds of years."

"Sooo, there were rabbits in our Borough we always thought were poisoned with radiation. Are you telling me they weren't?"

"I remember reading that study when I was thirteen. They surmised something in the rabbits' genetic code was damaged by the original radiation. The change was known to cause several kinds of abnormal cell growth akin to cancer for those who are susceptible. The rabbits aren't actually contaminated, just *changed*, and some people are allergic to the genetic change like some people are allergic to fruit."

"So why do people stay inside the Mountain?"

"Look around! Other than this Lander colony, there's not a lot of modern conveniences out here. People don't want to give up their technology for some real sky and bug bites. Me personally, I love being out in the fresh, non-manufactured air."

"So why can't you recreate your compounds without going back in the Mountain?" Selah feared something would go wrong and she'd never see Treva or her brother again.

"Because my formulas took a lot of trial and error. I need my notes, or I'd be starting the process from scratch. Believe me, there are many ways in and out of the Mountain for ordinary citizens that don't involve security. Only outsiders are subject to security checks."

"I just don't like it. Maybe you'll go for nothing. Maybe someone already found your lab and confiscated everything. Maybe—"

"Trust me. No one has found my lab. I've worked in it since I was nine. I lived with Uncle Charles, and he has some very special quarters. Besides, I doubt anyone even knows I've left the Mountain. I never had time for much social interaction, so no friends to miss me. The people I was closest to were Glade, Dr. Everling, and Drace Stemple. Glade's with us, and the other two are . . . of no consequence anymore."

Selah's heartbeat calmed. It all seemed logical. Treva always seemed able to effect that change in her. "When will you leave?"

"I'll be back on the mainland in about a half hour to forty-five minutes. The next available rig comes up in three hours, so we'll leave as soon as we pack the gear. I have to finish the notes for the teacher handling my classes while I'm gone. Can you imagine? Ten-year-old kids learning about refined oil products. What kind of world is this up here in the north?"

"What kind of world indeed. A place where the father I'd never known to exist is now found, and the mother I'd always known is now lost. And Amaryllis, the child I reluctantly bonded to, is now bonded with someone else." Selah gulped down the knot forming in her throat. Losing the child had caused an intense emotional reaction that she hadn't expected. It still grabbed her chest like a tight fist.

"Are you sorry you let her go? I thought you made the right decision, you know."

"Don't get me wrong. When we arrived here I was happy Glade helped place her with a family. I was even encouraged that she instantly connected with the mother. Amaryllis said the woman resembled her dead mother. I was happy to be relieved of the responsibility." Selah dropped her head. "But it hurt when she deserted me so fast."

"I can feel your emotion. Should I pretend everything is fine, or do you want to talk?"

Selah raised her head to the ceiling and closed her eyes.

This adulthood thing felt like being thrown into the horse training pond without knowing how to swim. There were still times she needed parental advice and a shoulder for support. Glade didn't have the experience, and it made him as uncomfortable as her when she tried to make a connection. "I want peace. I thought finding Glade and coming north would solve my problems, but it just seems to have created more." She sat up straight. "I'd be real happy to find my family, but I think I have to find the peace within myself."

"Is there any expectation you can locate your mother and stepfather?"

Selah hoped so. She was confident that if there came an opportunity to explain herself to her stepfather, she could regain his love and respect. Mother had to be wrong about how he'd feel finding out she was part Lander. After all, he'd been the only father she'd known for her whole eighteen years of life. And she and Cleon had even come to a plausible explanation for Raza's death that didn't include his vitriolic rant about her and Mother, or that fateful fight.

"Not yet. Glade sent my navigator, Jaenen Malik, to find them. Hopefully he can get word to Mother that I'm safe here."

"By the way, why are you calling your father by his given name?"

"After I spent so many years calling Varro Chavez 'Father,' Glade told me to call him whatever felt comfortable. So I call him by his name."

"In time you'll find the peace to call him 'Father.' I'm sure he'd be pleased."

Selah's fear that Glade might leave her again fed her insecurity, and she hated that feeling. She knew Glade loved her, but since he was head of the Archaeological Department at the Institute of Higher Learning, his mandate was research and archaeological discoveries of what lay hidden by the volcanic ash beyond the Appalachian Mountains. That was his real love, regardless of her birthright. She resented feeling inferior to a mountain range.

"Will I see you and Cleon before you leave?" Selah leaned her head against the high back of her chair.

"Yes, I'll call you when I get in. I need to finish my notes before the shuttle leaves. Bye."

The ComLink disconnected.

Selah lowered her arm, swiveled away from the window, and reached across the desk to finger a glass vase overflowing with Mother's favorite cornflowers. Beyond the vase, a panorama of the same rich blue flowers covered the three interior walls of this large area in her living suite. The area doubled as a sitting room and office, and the wall decor used full-length photo-plate cells she could change at will. Selah pressed a pad on her desk console. Cornflowers turned to sand and the peaceful blue waves of the sea outside. It complemented the tan floor covering and black molded furniture.

At the moment, she didn't want to see more cornflowers. The color reminded her of the multicolored blue flecks in Bodhi's eyes. Pinpricks of frustration and anger bubbled in her chest. Why did it have to be so complicated? They'd started out fine when they first arrived here, but over the months his attention had waned. She hadn't seen much of him in the last few weeks.

She'd never had a relationship before Bodhi, and she didn't know what she'd done wrong. Mother would know what to do. Maybe if she changed her hair or got clothes like the city girls here. She pressed her lips tight. She wanted him back.

Selah strolled across the room and leaned against the long expanse of glass overlooking the remnant-strewn beach and the Atlantic. This modern world of TicCity was strangely out of sync with the life she'd known in Dominion Borough. At home, the ancient cities were completely abandoned and mostly reclaimed by the environment, but here in the north, the old and new existed side by side. The tsunami during the Sorrows had destroyed most of this city and the huge three-dimensional sign bearing the name Atlantic City, New Jersey. All that remained, protruding from the sea sand like a giant finger, was "tic City."

The name had stuck. Personally, she found it distasteful. It sounded like some vermin that would suck the life from one of her farm animals, but that wasn't the only strangeness around here. She was never quite sure what to expect.

She found comfort in pressing her cheek against the silky smooth surface of the glass. There wasn't much real glass back home, but she missed being there. Her emotions betrayed her with constant turmoil, and her thoughts were sometimes an incoherent jumble. The other day she had cried watching a calf being born at Cleon's farm. A calf! She'd seen dozens of calves born in Dominion. It was nothing to cry about.

And the flashes. Tremors and thunders had turned to bright flashes of lightning and an anticipation of what was to come.

A tear slid down her cheek and married itself to the glass as it continued toward the floor.

A tinkling vibration.

Glass against glass.

She pushed off from the window and turned.

Nothing looked out of place, although the water in the glass vase on her desk shimmered in concentric circles, then stilled. Light radiated through the colored glass beads that filled half the container.

A knock sounded.

Selah walked to the door and swiped her hand over the entrance lock.

The door swung wide to admit Jaenen Malik. When they'd passed through Baltimore on the way here from the Mountain, Glade had been convinced to hire Jaenen as security for Selah when they traveled, and he had proved worthy by saving her from attack in his very first hours on the job. Apparently being a novarium could start a war.

Jaenen hoisted a pack from his shoulder. Not only was he excellent at security and investigating missing people, he was just plain good to look at. Standing five feet nine, he had hair so dark it looked black until the sun showed the auburn highlights. His claim to fame was a crooked, easy smile set in a solid jaw that always needed a shave, and dark eyes with lashes so thick they created their own air current. Jaenen was effective at his job because of his charm, especially with women. But Selah had lived with brothers for many years—she was immune.

"And how is Selah doing on this fine day?" The quick flash of his smile lightened her sour mood. Since he had saved her in Baltimore, Selah believed he was mostly sincere and had no ulterior motives, other than the large sums of bio-coin that Glade was paying him. And she considered him an ally—after all, he'd given her a location for a secret Repository file that should shed light on Bodhi's condition.

"I'd be much better if you could tell me you've spoken with my mother," Selah said. A caravan of merchants had passed through Dominion Borough going south two months ago, and again on their way back north last month. No one had been able to contact her mother.

He searched his bag but didn't speak. Not a good sign.

"I'm sorry. None of your family was there. Only these people." He set a quartz data cube on the desk and pressed the top. A holographic image projected above the cube.

"Maybe a neighbor knows if something happened." Selah peered at the image of two men with bulky muscles leaning on field rakes near a barn. Her family's barn! Her throat tightened.

"The neighbors at the homesteads on either side said the same thing. One day your family was there, and the next day they were gone. No goodbye. Nothing."

She pointed at the bare arm of the man on the right. "Can you enlarge this?"

Jaenen manipulated the cube to increase the image size. "The word from these men was that the family would be gone for an extended period of time—"

"No!" A lightning charge surged up her spine, exploding inside her head with a burst of color that pulled a scream from her lips. Tears puddled her eyes, but still she stared.

A Waterside Borough tattoo, a sword laced with a lightning bolt, covered the man's upper arm. Her head swam. Selah's world faded to a blur as her knees buckled and she dropped to the floor.

Jaenen grabbed her under the arms before she hit, lifting her back to her feet. She collapsed against his chest. Her worst fears had borne fruit. *The drums of petrol in the barn* . . . Her stepfather must have gotten a large dowry for her marriage to the Waterside Borough leader's son. A marriage that did not happen. Now—repayment.

The door slammed against the wall. "Selah, I heard—" Bodhi stopped at the sight of Selah leaning against Jaenen. A storm cloud furrowed his brow.

Selah raised her head. "My mother, stepfather, and little brother are gone. It's all my fault."

Bodhi folded his arms across his chest. "What's he doing here?"

Jaenen released Selah and picked up the data cube, flicking off the visual.

"I could ask why you think you have the right to barge in here. Didn't you hear me? My family is missing!" Selah set her jaw and wiped her eyes. Her world was falling apart, and all he cared about was some kind of male bravado.

Bodhi stared daggers at the back of Jaenen's head as the man returned the cube to his bag. "I thought Glade hired a different navigator to search for your family. This one's supposed to be your security detail."

Selah made a face. "I'm safe here in TicCity. I wanted Jaenen, so that's who he hired. You don't seem to have the least bit of compassion for my loss. What's wrong with you?" Irritation grew in her like an exploding milkweed pod.

"I'll give you the rest of my report when you're not busy." Jaenen didn't look at Selah. He slung the bag back over his shoulder, edged around Bodhi, and went out the door.

Selah knew there was no use protesting his leaving. Bodhi and Jaenen had developed a ragged past of mutual confrontation, and Bodhi usually wound up with the upper hand.

He glared at the retreating man, then slammed the door as Jaenen exited the threshold. He turned on Selah. "He's got quite a reputation with the ladies."

Selah's eyes narrowed to slits. She stormed forward and poked him in the chest. "It figures. I tell you my family is missing and you make everything about what you don't like. Listen, you sea slug. I've seen you about a half dozen times in the last month." A finger poke punctuated each sentence. "I'm a grown woman, and you're no more my keeper than my stepfather is anymore. So you get no say in who I hire to do anything. Got that?"

Bodhi flashed a grin. "I'm back to being a sea slug?" She had called him that the first moment they met on the beach.

Selah's mouth opened in frustration. Her fingers spread into claws and then clenched into fists. She closed her eyes and shook with anger. "You're making me crazy. And I'm pretty much immune to your cuteness now. This is serious. Glade is so busy with his research that I rarely see him, and I don't even have you for sanity support. That leaves me with Treva and Cleon. Thanks."

Bodhi pressed his lips together. "I heard you about your

family. I didn't expect this report to be different from the caravan report last month. I just figured it would take time for you to come to terms with the outcome." He hesitated. "We can't be together right now. I have things to work out."

Her first real love . . . and now his rejection. She just didn't understand men and wished her mother were here for advice.

"On a daily basis, I have no one to talk to about the physical and mental changes I'm going through. You deserted me. You don't even mind-jump with me anymore." Selah's eyes filled with tears. Things he had to work out—indeed. She blinked back the moisture, refusing to allow herself pity at the coldness of his betrayal.

Bodhi dropped his head and muttered something.

Selah tipped her head to look in his downcast eyes. An errant tear splashed her cheek. She roughly brushed it away with the back of her hand. "What did you say?"

Bodhi's lip curled and he gritted his teeth. "I said I can't hear you anymore."

"That's ridiculous. I'm not blocking you."

"I've lost it. I can't hear Lander thoughts. It's as though I've turned human."

"But you are—" Selah reined in her tongue. *Shouldn't he already know he's human?* Wait. He had given her an explanation once before. Did that mean Second Protocol Landers weren't human, or did they just not know they were human? She needed to find out if being human meant the same thing for all Protocols of Landers. Could she bring it up with Glade? Or would he take away her privileges in the Repository for delving into things she shouldn't?

She leaned over and swept back the hair from his forehead. "I don't believe you. It's not possible. You still have the mark."

But she did believe him, and it was all her fault. Transitioning her into a novarium had done something to his body chemistry. Jaenen had tried to explain that Bodhi was going to have a dramatic decline in his abilities, but she didn't completely understand. If Bodhi wouldn't come out and say anything about it, Selah didn't want to embarrass him by letting on she knew.

The look in his eyes softened to longing. He quickly recovered and pushed her hand away. "Do you think I'd lie to you about something that important?"

"Well, no. I didn't mean to accuse you of any dishonesty. It's just that I don't understand how this could happen. Glade still has his abilities and so do the rest of the Landers who were in the prison with him." Selah ran a hand through her hair. "Are you sure you're not just stressed or something? Did you visit the healer?" Maybe Jaenen was wrong about Bodhi's condition.

"I don't want those people near me." Bodhi's cheeks reddened.

Selah raised both hands. "Then I can't help you, or you won't *let* me help you."

Bodhi jerked back. "I can take care of my own problems."

"Same goes for me. You don't get to make choices for me. We don't have a bond anymore." Selah squared her shoulders, opened the door, and gestured him out.

He stared at her, searching her eyes. For a moment she thought he was going to pull her close. Then his shoulders slumped. He hung his head and left.

34

She leaned her head against the door. Why wouldn't he go see the healer? He was suffering the loss of his abilities because of her. He had probably pulled away because he resented her.

The dam burst. Anger bubbled up in her.

The tinkling vibration from earlier grew in intensity.

Smash!

Selah spun to face the noise.

Her glass vase lay in pieces at the base of the photo-plate cell wall, water dripping down the image of an ocean wave.

3

Selah carefully gathered the shards of glass and deposited them in the waste chute. She turned to survey the area again. How did the vase travel six feet across an open space to smash into the wall? She gathered the scattered, broken flowers and added them to the trash. Another beloved thing lost.

Her ComLink vibrated. Treva's icon flashed green.

Selah bit her lip and answered. Treva's frantic face popped onto the screen.

"What in the world is going on? I felt such a mental rush from you it nearly drove me to the deck as I was getting on the shuttle. I must say, having an educator stumbling around looking drunk is not a desirable characteristic."

Selah looked at her friend with wide eyes. "I'm sorry. It's my fault! I'm mad, hurt, and scared all at the same time. My family, Bodhi, even my beautiful cornflowers—"

"Stop! I don't want to know about them. I want to know about you! What was that? You sent so much energy at me it felt like an explosion."

"I-I don't know. All I remember is a flash . . . and my flowers exploded against the wall." Selah blinked a few times. Light-headedness overtook her for a second, then subsided.

Treva tipped her head to the side. "How did your flowers get destroyed? In a flash, like lightning or something?"

"No . . . yes . . . maybe . . . I think the flash was only in my head. But the vase smashed against a wall six feet from my desk."

"This is not good. Have you noticed any other changes, vibrations in your extremities, shifts or rippling in your vision, or anything like a blackout?"

"Just the flashes, and the return of the tremors. And my head lightening, like I'm floating on a wave." She shuddered, then frowned. Where did the shudder come from? "Do you think I should report this to Glade?"

"No! You listen to me very carefully. We're going to keep this to ourselves for the time being. Do you hear me? No one gets to know about this, not Glade, or Bodhi."

Selah frowned. "What are you worried about?"

"It's just intuition. Too many people are leaving us in the dark about what abilities and functions a novarium is supposed to manifest. I don't think we should be sharing your progress."

"I know you're right, but I'm a jumble of raw emotions. I feel a little crazy sometimes. My head is trying to go in ten directions at one time." A flash burst before her eyes. Selah blinked and squinted. Her heart thumped rapidly.

"Whoa, I felt that! Are you all right?"

"Yeah, I think so. Just these strange lights keep popping up." Her heart rate subsided.

"I need to study this, and you need a rest from all these distractions. Are you sure I can't talk you into coming with me and Cleon? We're taking a wagon in case Cleon spots any interesting vegetation and wants to gather samples. There's plenty of room to bring your navigator for security, and the ride will give you time to relax."

Selah glowered. She didn't want security following her everywhere she went. That was why she had a trainer. Her new speed and agility made her competent to take care of herself. "Jaenen Malik is busy looking for my mother. I don't need security. I'm beginning to think it was just a coincidence that we talked about security in Baltimore and then I needed it. I haven't so much as had anyone look at me funny since I've been here."

"So then you'll come?"

"I don't think so. Stone Braide is too close to the Mountain, and I really want to get back in the Repository. I've added at least a dozen questions to my search. It's not all about me as a novarium. Now it's a lot more about Landers in general, and how they acquired these abilities, and how many Landers there could be with no marks."

"All right, but the offer stands. This shuttle is moving away from the Petrol City platform. I should land in TicCity in about twenty minutes or so. Bye." Treva's link disconnected.

Selah leaned against the glass wall again and looked out over the water at the gas rig platform, Petrol City, anchored fifteen miles out at sea. Its geodesic dome encompassed a circular mile of self-governed real estate and grew from the ocean like a ripe pimple on an otherwise harmonious seascape. It didn't appear threatening, but sometimes she felt strange vibrations coming from there when she and Treva mind-jumped.

⬨

Selah exited the left arm of the sprawling six-story, U-shaped complex and turned west to the bottom of the U where the Institute for Higher Learning was located. She stopped. The lure was too great. She turned back east, to her beloved sea, and strolled to the edge, mindful not to leave the walkway. Stepping on sand provoked the dreams.

She inhaled the briny taste of the salt air. The sea mist sparkled on her face as she glanced to the right, over petrified wooden remains jutting from the water like tipsy soldiers. To the left, shoreside amusements were driven deeply into the sand with only horseshoe-shaped metal skeletons exposed to 150 years of elements. The ancient tsunami had scrubbed most buildings from the landscape, leaving only a single remnant—a huge wedge of rusting metal with the word *ball* partially buried by the shifting sands at the water's edge.

She turned back. The enormous building complex that housed her, most of the local Landers, and the university and Repository had risen in her level of curiosity. Even as far back as one hundred years before the Sorrows, this was called the Dennis Hotel and rumored to be the original home of a Lander.

The U opening faced the sea and the ends had been scrubbed off by the tsunami, then later replaced with two conical glass-composite fronts that extended above the building as solar collectors. The part Selah liked—the Repository—was rumored to have secret levels.

A sudden flash. Her knees buckled. She reached out, first missing then catching the post at the end of the walkway. Selah steadied herself and took a long breath. This one came without warning. Usually she felt a tingle first. The flashes were getting closer together. She gripped the post with both hands. The feeling passed. About five seconds later, she felt as though it had never happened. Selah wondered if these little events were actually happening or whether her subconscious was driving her. Maybe she had more guilt than she'd realized over Bodhi's loss of abilities.

She turned back and followed the pale composite pathway that wound through groupings of trees and grassy areas in the courtyard of the tall glass-and-stone complex. Up ahead, a group of several well-dressed young women milled about on the grass and benches outside the archaeological studies section.

Selah vaulted the steps at the front and hurried inside. The cool air was a refreshing welcome to the heat radiating from her face. Lately, every time she went to see Glade, she started to sweat. If she had to read her own body-speak, she'd say she was scared. She knew how he'd been lately, trying to discourage her from prying into the past. But he hadn't rescinded her Repository access, so that was a plus. She needed more details to refine her searches through the millions of files.

She brushed sweat from her cheeks and peeked in Glade's office. Empty. Her crepe-soled shoes padded silently across the mosaic-tiled floor to the third door. She grabbed the handle of the heavy mahogany door with both hands and pulled, then entered the teaching theater.

Class was not in session, but she saw Glade's notations on the digital boards spread across the front of the room, and him sitting at a desk in the center. As usual he was engrossed in maps and manuscripts spread across the large surface in front of him. She stopped. Her shoulders tightened.

Bodhi sat across from Glade at another table off to the right. He must have heard the door closing behind her and looked up. He lowered the data cube from his vision. A smile crossed his face, then disappeared as she moved closer.

Selah sauntered down the long length of stairs, staring back at Bodhi as she descended to the front of the funnel-shaped room. He seemed a little thinner, or was it her imagination? She'd seen him a half hour ago, but his gauntness hadn't made an impression. His blond hair was forever in need of a major trim, his mark showing between the loose curls blocking part of his face. His eyes were still clear multi-hues of blue . . . but his cheeks had started to contract. She wanted to walk to him, but she stopped at her father's desk.

"Glade, I haven't seen you in a few days. Have you been holed up here the whole time?"

No answer. The documents possessed his full concentration. She knocked on the table surface.

He flinched, and a shock of dark hair slid from behind his right ear and obscured his face. He pushed the hair back in

42

place and looked up. For being at least 150, Glade looked no older than forty. With his olive complexion and green eyes, he was a stunning example of a middle-aged man, but he had no interest in a social life—to the distress of a certain local woman who had tried to invite Selah and him to dinner.

"Oh, it's about time you got here. I thought I told Bodhi to tell you to hurry." He turned back to the map.

Selah jerked her head in Bodhi's direction and scowled. "He didn't—"

"I didn't have a chance to tell her—"

"Before he had to leave!" Selah pursed her lips and narrowed her eyes at Bodhi.

Glade looked up again. "Bodhi, I would like to talk to my daughter alone. Meanwhile, check on our travel arrangements, please."

Bodhi rose from the table and ambled close as he moved toward the door at the other end of the digital boards. He looked down at her as he passed. She felt his breath on her face . . . and then he was gone. Her breath caught.

She looked back at Glade, who was again absorbed in studying a map. She slid onto the stool beside his desk and sneaked a glance at the old maps and charts in front of him, wrinkling her nose at their musty smell. She decided to play along. "What did you want me for? Why didn't you just mind-jump with me?"

Glade pressed his index finger to the yellowed map and looked up. "Please don't connect with me through thoughts. It unnerves me to feel someone probing my mind after so many years of having the ability suppressed while I was in the Mountain. But I needed to tell you that Bodhi is going with me on this trip, and so is Taraji as our navigator. So you won't have training sessions for a few days."

Selah straightened and lifted her chin. "I've passed my training and moved on to the next phase of individual sets, so I don't have a defined schedule. I'm self-directed." Selah waved a finger. "Why are you taking Bodhi? And don't think you got away with sneaking in a *trip announcement* that way. Where are you going?"

"Bodhi has decided he has no other destination, and all men need jobs to live. He understands it's in his best interest to help me in helping you. I have maintained 150 years of funds that are more than sufficient to pay his worth," Glade said.

Selah's heart pounded against her ribs. She worked hard at containing her joy of Bodhi staying in TicCity, but she worried about his emotional state. Neither Glade nor Bodhi liked the other all that much, so it surprised her to think they could work together without coming to blows. She hesitated to comment, only to preserve Glade's almost pleasant mood. "You left off the trip part of my question. Do you really think it's possible after all these years to find passage to the West? Wasn't anyone looking while you were in captivity?"

For a moment, Glade's forehead glistened as though he might start to sweat. He brushed a hand across his brow. "Getting to the West and finding the Third Protocol—that last important set of Landers—is paramount now that you've been transitioned to a novarium. I had hoped to have more years to explore the data before you became of age, but it didn't work out that way. No one looked while I was gone because there are very few First Protocols left here. TicCity has become mostly newer Lander generations that don't have the commitment to old ways they've grown to consider myth and fallacy. The few marked Landers who were prisoners in the Mountain with me are just about all of the originals in our northern group who have survived this long."

"So that's why I don't see head markings among these people other than you, Bodhi, and the random stranger passing through."

Glade nodded. "Most of these Landers are a second generation of intermarriage. They actually place Bodhi and me higher up on the authority scale because we are among the two Protocols of originals."

Selah tipped her head. "How can people tell the difference between a First Protocol Lander like you and a Second Protocol Lander like Bodhi?"

Glade smiled. "Have you ever really looked at our head markings? They are quite different to the knowledgeable observer."

Selah filed it in her list of things to do. She leaned back on the stool, maintaining a perfect balance, just shy of touching the digital board. She felt a sudden surge of energy and her extremities warmed. "How come you're talking all of a sudden? This is more than you've told me about Landers since I arrived here."

"I've spent so many years lying and covering our tracks that it's almost part of me now. I even find myself doing it with you, and I don't want that kind of relationship. We've gotten off on the wrong foot lately, and I think if I'm more forthcoming with you, then you won't need to waste all your time ensconced in the Repository."

There it was! Call it cynicism, but Selah knew there was a reason for his sudden change—to get her to give up on her file searches. But she loved him as her father, so she decided graciousness was the better answer. "I'm glad you're willing to open up. Where are you going on this search and how long will you be gone?"

Glade looked over his magnifying tool. "We're headed into what used to be New York. Probably three or four days. We're trying to match symbols, so the longest part will be the trip there and back, but we've got the Council's fast transportation at our disposal since this is so important."

"How do the Appalachians or getting to the West help me? The truth this time." She had to take a couple of good breaths to stop the grin trying to overtake her face. First Bodhi was staying, and now they were all going to be out of the city at the same time. She could explore all she wanted in the Repository.

Glade removed his reading lenses and pinched the bridge of his nose. "The Appalachian Mountain range is very important, my princess. During the Sorrows, it protected the eastern coastal plains from the ravages of the Yellowstone super volcano. We're looking for the opening to the West. Documents tell us there will be an opening. In my time I've searched from here all the way to the northern end of this safe zone. We'll finish the search of the northern end as we cross into the tiny strip that's the only place left in New York."

"Why do you care? The rest of New York and North America are covered yards deep in ash. The land is barren and uninhabitable." Selah swept her hand over the maps, trying secretly to get a sideways look at them. Every time she showed interest, Glade rolled them up, which just piqued her curiosity more.

Glade rubbed his brow. "It's time to tell you, but to say I don't have all the facts sounds like sheer lunacy."

"Tell me what?" Selah straightened.

He looked down. "When Bodhi transitioned you to a novarium, it started a chain reaction that needs to be completed by you connecting with a Third Protocol Lander, who we can only find in the West."

Selah started to laugh. "You really had me going. I thought you were going to be serious this time."

Glade sat stone-faced. "I am serious. Much of the data and even the reasoning for this process have been lost and sometimes deliberately sabotaged to misdirect the searches. I've got bits and pieces of a very long story that I don't have time to go into."

Selah stood. "So that's all you're going to tell me?" She blinked hard. Her head felt light from standing so fast.

"I don't know any more that would really help you at the moment."

"So what's this *process* happening to me?"

Glade shook his head. "I don't know. We were subjected to mind-altering drugs before we left the Mountain 150 years ago. They gave us a folder afterward telling us our basic information and showing us a video where we all agreed to do this. To protect the integrity of the operation, we won't get to fill in all the blanks until we find the Third Protocol and the process is finished."

Selah took that opportunity to look over the map. There were several dotted lines coming from the sea that converged in the area of Dominion. Another map blocked her from seeing their origin. She wanted to study the map, but he'd eventually look up if she didn't keep talking.

Selah played with the corner of the offending map, rolling and unrolling the edge. "Then what does *novarium* mean?"

"It means you are the *new one*. The one who holds the keys to the kingdom."

Selah knit her eyebrows together. "Riddles, you're talking in riddles."

Glade looked at her like he was having second thoughts about sharing. "That's all you need to understand right now. And no, to answer your question before you ask, other Landers don't know more about being novarium than you do. They're guessing and perpetuating myths that have grown up in the absence of facts."

Selah's fingers stopped in mid-roll. "But historical accounts said the four states positioned in the ring of the volcano caldera were blown to pieces. No one could have survived. You think there are people alive for us to find, on the other side of the country?"

Glade sighed. "At this point, our existence depends on it."

Instead of raising her voice at another of his riddles, she bit her lip and took a deep breath. "Then at least explain why you won't help me find data on how to get Bodhi help with his lost abilities." Selah hoped his generous mood might extend a little longer.

"You've only known him for the three months since your Birth Remembrance. Why do you want him? He came here as a Second Protocol Lander. There are at least half a dozen young men in this community who are the third and fourth generation of our First Protocol. They are more in line with the type of man you should be with."

"I love Bodhi." Selah felt the words stick like a heavy lump in her throat.

Glade looked over at her. "What do you know of love? You're too young."

"I know how I feel when I'm with him. I know how my insides get all jumbled up and that I feel flushed." Selah cringed at opening up that way to her father, but she had to make him understand.

"And how do you know that wasn't just the changes of turning novarium coming over you? The reorganization of nerve fibers and biometric connections?"

Selah opened her mouth to speak and then closed it. How ironic that she was being asked not to trust her feelings for a man she'd known only three months . . . by another man she'd known only three months. Then again, Glade was the only other person who could help her with the cryptic file code Jaenen had given her.

And how *did* she know the difference between love and turning novarium? She was willing to take the chance on it really being love, but she wasn't willing to gamble that the file detailing the condition affecting Bodhi would still be available if she asked Glade to help her get it. She decided to stay silent.

Glade averted his eyes again and ran his hand across his chin. He mumbled something she couldn't hear.

"What did you say?" Selah continued to absorb details from the map.

"I said Bodhi is useless to you now. You need someone who still has their abilities to help protect you. There's a long journey ahead to the West, and there are going to be many trying to stop you from reaching the Third Protocol." Glade's voice came out agitated and abrupt. "I'm your father and I will guide your path on this."

Selah's head snapped up. She shook with anger. "You forfeited the right to guide my path the day you walked away."

Glade went back to his work. "Bodhi didn't come here with the mandate I've been given. His job is done. My remaining purpose is to get you on the other side of the mountains to the Third Protocol. That has to succeed above all else. Lives—a thousand years of lives—depend upon my completion of this task. I've been thwarted for the last eighteen years. Time is running out, and I make no apologies."

"So no one or nothing is more important than your plans." She glanced at him one more time. His eyes suddenly appeared tired, and he looked like he was aging before her eyes.

Selah stormed up the stairs and pushed her way through the heavy door. She wanted to slam it so the sound would echo, so it would make her feel better, but with the restrictors that closed it slowly, all she could manage was a soft thud. Not at all satisfying.

Just as she reached the outside, her ComLink sounded. She punched the key, missed it the first time, and dug her fingernail into her arm.

She winced and tried again. Treva's face popped onto the screen, large and close. "Listen," she said in almost a whisper. "I couldn't talk freely before. Don't go near MedTec, and meet me at the transport. I have to tell you what I just found out."

4

Bodhi watched Selah leave. The look of anger on her face was unmistakable. He crossed the hall to the teaching theater and pulled open the door, aware of his diminishing strength. A week ago he'd have barely noticed the weight of the thick wooden door.

Glade was still sitting down at the front, bent over a slew of old maps. Bodhi rushed down the stairs and over to the table attached to Glade's desk.

"I don't know what you said to your daughter, but you have to stop treating her like that."

Seemingly unfazed by Bodhi's outburst, Glade peered over the magnifying lenses, then back down at his work.

"Selah looked like she was angry and ready to cry when she left here."

"And what business is that of yours? Need I remind you that I've ordered you away from my daughter?"

Bodhi leaned forward and rested his palms on the tabletop.

"I made a bad deal, and I'm going to back out of it. I love your daughter, and I'm going to be with her whether you like it or not."

Glade leaned back in his chair and tented his fingers together. "Is that so? Tell me, what do you still remember of your past? Keep in mind that I run this community, so where are you going to take her to live? And while I'm on the subject of living, how long do you think your life will be now that your abilities are waning?"

Bodhi's bluster faded. He froze, momentarily overwhelmed, not able to give satisfactory answers to any of those questions. "But I love her."

Glade smiled wryly. "Love is never enough. Now, I would like to think this will be the last time we have this unpleasantness. I was serious when I said you're to be my right hand and confidant on this project. I need your undivided attention, and that is why there's no room for romancing my daughter."

Bodhi straightened his shoulders. "How can you have so much trust in me when you know I don't like you for holding the rest of my life hostage?"

"Because, my friend—"

"Don't call me your friend," Bodhi said, disgust in his voice. "I'm no friend of yours."

"But you are in love with my daughter, and her safety is the reason for all of this."

Bodhi glared daggers at Glade. If there was ever a time he wished another man harm, it was surely now. "I can't believe you'd have the audacity to bring that up after the litany of intimidation you just laid on me."

Glade waved a hand over the maps. "This project is about finding the way to the West."

"And I care about your project why?"

"Because it's important to Selah as a novarium."

"Why should I believe you?"

Glade pointed a finger at him. "Because you're the one who transitioned her. You're the one who set her on this path, and you're the one who is going to help me carry it through." He frowned and ran his finger back over a section to find his place.

Bodhi's heart pounded against his chest. He took the stool next to the table. "Are you saying that just to undercut my attitude about you?"

"It's time we talk seriously, and no more of this male posturing. If I agree to that, will you?" Glade stood and held out a hand.

Bodhi hesitated. If he made peace with Glade, that was the end of it. There was no turning back on a bond. There hadn't been an opportunity to feel any spirit of kinship, other than when they first left the Mountain. That sense quickly faded in Baltimore when Glade took up a fast friendship with Jaenen Malik. Bodhi had a bad feeling about that guy. But could he trust this man?

He took a deep breath, exhaled, and stood up. He stuck out his hand and gripped Glade above the wrist, arm to arm, pulse to pulse. They pumped a shake. Bonded forever, however long that was fated to be.

Bodhi held on until he felt Glade's grip relax. He didn't want it to seem that he didn't know the customs involved in making a bond. They parted and Glade motioned him to take a seat.

"Can I get some answers now?" Bodhi's desire to understand this place competed with the knowledge that as his memories faded, his past moved into oblivion.

"Yes, we're going to spend a lot of time together, so you might as well get some answers now so I can have your full concentration on the work at hand."

"Already I can't remember home or what precipitated my coming here. How much of my memory will I lose?" Bodhi laced his fingers on the table, knuckles turning white, waiting for the sentence.

"What's it been now? Three months? The Protocol has gone inert. You should have lost just about all the memory and abilities you're going to lose. It's interesting that you ask about memories rather than the strengthened abilities you gained coming here."

Bodhi shook his head. "My past is more important than those. When you forget your mistakes, you're doomed to make them again. What about longevity? Do I lose that also?"

"I truly can't say. I've never known one of you long enough to find out."

Bodhi tensed. "What do you mean?"

"Eventually the other Second Protocols like you left the community and never returned," Glade said, turning away from Bodhi.

He felt the slight. There was something wrong in the way Glade said that. Was it painful for him to admit? Should he ask? Better still, did he want to know the answer?

"Why did they leave?"

Glade busied himself with reshuffling the maps. "That's something to be discussed later."

Bodhi understood the tone. He should drop the subject for now. But he made a mental note to ask about it again when the time presented itself. "When did you come here?"

Glade made a notation on his halo-tablet and looked up. "To TicCity?"

"No, I mean to this place, this country. You haven't lost any abilities, and you only seem to have gained. I can't believe your Protocol is the same as ours. We're all prepared for some ability loss regardless of a transition."

For a minute there was dead air, then Glade cleared his throat and spoke in a soft tone. "I could have stopped it from happening. The Sorrows were my fault."

"You're one of the *originals*? I thought you were just a progeny of that first generation." Bodhi didn't want to believe he was sitting with the catalyst of historic destruction.

"I could have stopped the nuclear explosions that set off the chain reaction." Glade looked almost passive at the moment.

"You were here?" Some of Bodhi's bluster dissolved as he looked at the pain on the man's face. He couldn't imagine bearing that much agony for eternity.

"Yes." Glade spread his hands out over the map.

"You can't expect me to believe you let a whole country be destroyed just because you could. There has to be another reason that makes more sense than this craziness. Why would you let this happen?"

Bodhi watched as Glade's countenance changed. His

shoulders drooped, then quaked as though he was being wracked with sobs, but there were no sounds. He stared off into the distance.

"Sometimes groanings are necessary for rebirth."

"That's more crazy talk!" Bodhi forgot the bond he'd just made and slammed his hand on the table. A disorganized group of old documents dislodged from a mountainous pile and fluttered to the floor like fall leaves, pulling a rolled map with them. The map bounced upon hitting the floor, the tie holding it strung open, and the map unrolled.

Bodhi wanted to rage about the logic of destroying a society and millions of people, but the look on Glade's face said he'd better pick up the documents first. He ground his teeth and bent over to retrieve the pages and map. Slow, steady breath. He picked up the map with shaking hands and began to reroll it. A small image caught his eye. He rolled past it, then stopped. He unrolled the map and spread it out on the table.

His eyes widened and his heartbeat began to race. "What is this map for?"

"These are the only clues we have to finding the way to the West. The Third Protocol left behind detailed instructions, but warring factions over the last hundred years have destroyed the data in an effort to keep us from finding the key. This is all that's left," Glade said.

"Have you noticed this?" Bodhi pointed with shaky fingers at the drawn image. This had to be something. It was too much of a coincidence.

Glade looked. "I don't see what interests you."

Bodhi twisted the map around to Glade so that the image drawn into the land topography became noticeable. He pressed his finger to the spot, tracing the ovals. "This is the symbol of Treva's uncle—his settlement, Stone Braide."

Glade's eyes lit up. "I knew you'd be an asset!" He shuffled through documents. Papers scattered everywhere.

Bodhi screwed up his lip at the disorganized chaos. Before coming here, he didn't even remember paper as a medium. "Can all of this be scanned into a halo-tablet or bio-computer?"

"No, no," Glade said, obviously distracted and excited by the revelation. "Subtle nuances will be lost by scanning. I never saw that symbol, and I've looked at that map a hundred times." He scrambled to the pile on the floor and shuffled through the pages, grabbing specific sheets. "This is the first solid clue I've had since before I went away. My boy, you have redeemed yourself. Change of plans. Reschedule our departure for as soon as possible and inform Taraji of the change in plans. We're going to Stone Braide."

Bodhi gulped, not sure how helpful it was heading back to Stone Braide. He didn't want to leave Selah, at least while Jaenen Malik was still in TicCity. And he definitely didn't want to go back in the direction of that Mountain. "Is it necessary for me to accompany you on this trip? Are there other things I could do here to aid your research?"

"There's nothing more important than this trip. It's the first lead in years, and it comes at a very important time."

"But there must be—"

"As a novarium, Selah is in danger."

Bodhi narrowed his eyes. "So if being a novarium put her

life in danger, why did you leave her and her mother? After all, you were in captivity for eighteen years. If I hadn't come along you might still be there."

Glade shook his head. "I wasn't supposed to be there that long."

"You knew how long you'd be in jail? Forgive me if I don't believe you." Bodhi would need to know a lot of details before believing this story.

"Actually, I owe you a lot of answers. You've been the fated answer to most of this." Glade's tone softened considerably, not just with sadness but with actual signs of friendship. "Do you really love my daughter?"

"Of course I do. You already know that." Bodhi would follow that woman across the earth, regardless of her father's plan, but the closer he could stay to her, the better.

"Then you'll help me. You'll dedicate yourself to the completion of this project. And my goals will become your goals—for Selah."

"What specifically does this have to do with Selah?" Bodhi asked.

Glade looked him straight in the eye. "If I haven't found the key to the West, and the Third Protocol, in nine months, then like all of the novarium before her, Selah will fragment."

5

elah stood on the composite plank walkway leading out to the docking pier. The Petrol City shuttle lumbered toward shore, reminding her of a giant futuristic version of a riverboat like they had at home. Only half the circumference of the circular structure was visible above water, and the whole outside revolved like a paddle wheel while the suspended core floated along on the water. She'd heard the shuttles could travel underwater to work on Petrol City's underside, but she hadn't seen them submerged.

She craned her neck to spot Treva. Why wasn't she supposed to go to the MedTec Unit? The healers had always been more than helpful, and she considered them experts in care compared to the sometimes inept medicine handlers at home. The lead healer set her at ease the first time they'd met in the MTU. A fluttering gripped her belly.

Selah glanced over the disembarking throng. Treva, dressed

smartly in the dark blue environmentals teaching uniform of a long tunic and slacks, her auburn locks twisted into a tight bun at the nape of her neck, worked her way out of the crowded doorway and down the ramp. She waved to catch Selah's attention.

Treva whispered as they hugged, "Don't look now, but the woman who just passed us in the dark green teaching uniform is the one who told me about the MTU."

Selah defied the instant urge to look as they moved in that direction to return to the complex. She kept her arm around Treva's shoulder so their heads remained close. "What does someone who teaches earth sciences know about the MTU?" She watched as the woman blended in with the other returning teachers and disappeared into the crowd.

"She's a normal, and apparently she was in love with a Lander who vanished about a year ago. She said a lot of Landers who go to the MTU disappear, but the Committee always seems to have a reasonable explanation."

"How can people just disappear? That sounds a little strange. I think others would be talking if it really happened. Give me something better than that." Selah squinted in the bright sunshine, her mind still trying to digest all Glade had just shared. He was head of the Committee, similar to the Borough elders back home. She recalled some of the underhanded things the Borough had done in the name of progress. Could this be the same?

"Better than that—" Treva stopped short and turned to face her. "Are you all right? You feel like a bag of nervous tension. Are you having flashes again?"

"No." Selah breathed a heavy sigh and her shoulders slumped. "I was just with Glade. Every time I talk to him it seems like I just learn more things I don't want to know. It's becoming overwhelming."

"When you're ready, I'm a friendly ear."

Selah squeezed her friend's shoulder, thankful for an anchor.

"As I was saying, the woman said it's mostly couples without children who disappear, and she said the healers are responsible for people going crazy."

Selah stopped mid-stride. "Can she prove it? It must be a city scare, a legend. It would mean the existence of this whole place is some kind of well-placed plot."

Treva raised an eyebrow. "You want to talk plots, remember where I just came from."

"Well, I need more substantial evidence before I ask Glade questions."

"How about this—the healers do extensive testing, but only on specific Landers, and they don't say what they're looking for."

"What did they say we were being tested for when we first came here?"

"I wasn't going to say anything until we understood what was going on here, but I wasn't happy with those blood and tissue samples the healers took from us when we arrived. There was no reason for them, especially using core needles— at least no reason that matched up with the explanation they gave me."

Selah's insides clenched at the memory of the needles. "Did you tell them about your biotech background?"

"That's the last bit of information I'd give away. I like keeping them off guard—you'd be surprised the tidbits I've learned."

"I've been dealing with the healers on an almost daily basis. I've probably made mistakes there too." She thought of those she normally talked to when walking through Med-Tec to the Repository. None of the instances seemed out of place.

"Hopefully not, but it's cautionary, so we can be mindful of everything we see or hear," Treva said. "I'm stopping to get my gear and I'll meet Cleon at the depot. So I'm giving you a last chance to come with us."

⬧

Selah slid back into the station assigned to her on the main level of the Repository. She had first gotten the data file location from Jaenen Malik while they were in Baltimore. He said this particular file would help alleviate Bodhi's diminishing abilities caused by the process of transitioning her to a novarium. Among her other data searches, she finally had deciphered enough file language to be able to locate the data glass holding the file.

When she first came to TicCity, most of the people she spoke to didn't know there *was* a Repository. Many suggested it might be a part of the university, or part of MedTec. In reality, the Repository belonged to the Lander Council that ran TicCity. It was a government entity that held the collective knowledge and details of the Landers since the very beginning—and most of the Landers living here didn't even know it existed. She continued to face multiple questions every time she got one answer.

She held the data glass tightly in her hand, as though protecting it. But there was no one around to interrupt her, and her next thought was to ease up on the glass before she shattered it. The excitement of holding it made her breath quicken. Might she really be able to help Bodhi? His self-worth would return with his abilities, she was sure of it. Sadly, he just didn't understand. He didn't need his abilities to hold her affection.

She poised her hand in front of her reader. In the next few minutes she was going to read a secret file that had to be at least one hundred years old, maybe more. If this file could actually help Second Protocol Landers like Bodhi regain their strengths and abilities, why hadn't it been used before?

Selah's fingers shook. She finally rested them on the table edge, data glass still between her thumb and forefinger.

She inhaled sharply and inserted the glass in her reader. A couple of commands and she'd opened the right file. Her eyes skimmed line by line as she scrolled through the pages looking for the cure. A lot of the file appeared redacted, but someone had inadvertently left a code key open. She tried to restore the missing data.

Her reader glitched. The pages jumped, resizing at will. Her eyes began to water from trying to follow the jerky movement. The screen blinked in and out, followed by more fits of scrolling. She carefully tried to alter the settings and lines of text disappeared. She frowned and tapped on the workstation, trying to nudge the reader without smacking it. Nothing. She got up and paced. Most of what she'd learned in two years of technology at Dominion had to do with coding and not the machines. She didn't know where she could get another reader right away. She rubbed her forehead and sat back down. If only Treva were here. Her skill with computer hardware would have been useful.

Selah made a face at the screen, as though it would help, and smacked at the area of the halo-keyboard, disrupting its digital stream. For a second, a blinking line of text solidified with missing spaces. *Varro Chav . . . Bethan Everli . . .* The line fragmented again.

She leaned forward. "What was that?" She banged on the keys. The screen glitched and the word *Mountain* appeared. Her fist whacked the desk. The whole data entry reappeared, scrolling by at a furious pace. She tried to stop the scroll, to no avail.

Selah rushed to copy the file onto her data glass. The machine made a strange noise. If she could copy the file, she could look at it in her quarters where she had another reader, hopefully in better condition. Yes, it was against the rules to remove data from the Repository, but if this was really the remedy for Bodhi's lost abilities, she wasn't going to take a chance on the file not being there when she came back with another reader.

Selah's mouth went dry. Why were her stepfather, Bethany Everling, and the Mountain named in a data file that was supposed to be about latent and restorable Lander abilities? This file had to have been altered recently. Wherever her step-father was, her mother and little brother would also be, and if her family was in the Mountain, she had to go.

She took a deep breath. Her personal fear was not an option. She felt strangely calm.

She reached for her water cup and stopped. The water's surface vibrated in miniscule waves. She pulled back her hand as she glanced around.

A rumble came from deep within the bowels of the earth, working its way up, growing in intensity as it climbed closer to the surface. She turned, thinking she'd be able to see the source of the growl. Earth tremors were frequent in Dominion Borough, but she didn't know how often they had them in TicCity. Mother had taught her and her brother Dane to press themselves into the sturdy arch of a doorway when they occurred. Slipping from her seat, Selah hurried toward the doorway of an adjoining office, hoping by the time she reached the old stone arch, the shaking would subside.

The still noon air exploded. A shock wave rolled through the Repository with a deafening roar. Selah jerked and raised both hands to shield herself as data glass and bio-computer units jolted off ancient wooden shelves. The sounds mixed together—metal crashed, shards of glass cascaded to the floor, and the roar continued.

Sharp-toned sirens screamed to life, punctuating the rumble with an irregular rhythm. The sirens, reminiscent of those in the Mountain when she'd escaped, unnerved her. Her muscles tensed. She wanted to cover her ears and block the sound, but she needed to run.

The old-fashioned black-and-white checkered tiles erupted as the ceramic floor twisted like a rope in slow motion. Selah froze, not knowing which way was safe.

Her feet finally caught up to her brain's urge to run. She hopscotched over heaving sections of tile and sprinted for the front door at the other end of the long, narrow Repository. Dust floated down from vibrating ancient beams.

The earth groaned, punctuated by a tremendous grinding of splintered wood. The equipment rack opposite Selah jack-hammered itself loose from the anchor bolts and hung precariously at a forty-five-degree angle.

"My data glass!" She stopped short before the front door and darted back down the aisle toward her station. Between the piercing shrieks of the siren, she heard intermittent shouts. People were yelling to evacuate the building. Adrenaline surged to her limbs as she vaulted the debris.

Behind her, the equipment rack she'd just passed crashed across the aisle, blocking her way back to the front door. With pounding chest, she spun to it, thrusting out open palms. "No!" she shouted.

The rack exploded. Equipment smashed to the floor. Old knobs and dials scattered under the desk and rolled across the aisle. Momentarily stunned at the energy radiating from her hands, Selah stumbled, trying to regain her balance. Why were her hands throbbing?

Part of a five-foot light fixture swung down from its mooring on the ceiling. She jumped out of the way before it smacked her in the head. It crashed to the floor. Still attached by wires to the ceiling, the light arced and danced like a marionette in the trembling room. The acrid smell of the sparking current drifted from the smashed end of the fixture.

The files were still loading. She frantically watched the

download ticking from forty-five to fifty percent. There wasn't time to capture everything.

"Come on, come on!" Seconds ticked like minutes. She pounded on the desk in frustration, grabbed the glass from the device, and shoved it into her pocket.

The ceiling buckled. Another light fixture smashed to the floor. Shards of something sharp slid across the floor and hurled into other objects.

She ran toward a toppled bookcase blocking the path to the door. A cracking sound marched along the length of the room. Welds on the roofing sections snapped as the rafters twisted free.

Her arms felt like weights, but Selah dove under the canted bookcase blocking the doorway and crawled through the debris of data glass and musty, disintegrating paper books. Emerging painfully on the other side with shredded palms, she scrambled for the open door. The ceiling roared down behind her. A billowing cloud of dust trailed her out the door.

Hugging the wall, she felt her way down the long, darkened hallway. Her perception of where the front door stood was skewed by the fallen partitions and debris. She hadn't been in this section of the complex before.

Selah coughed and wheezed, gasping for air. To keep from inhaling the grit, she shoved her face into her shirtsleeve, her lungs filtering only small wisps of oxygen from the enveloping dust cloud.

She tripped and lurched forward, arms spread out to cushion the fall. Her palms skidded across the rubble-strewn floor and her chest slammed into the hard surface, knocking the precious little wind from her.

The shaking subsided. Selah lay on the debris-strewn floor, disoriented, her brain fogging from lack of oxygen. She tried to think, but it had happened too fast. She labored to push herself to her knees. Panting, she rose on shaking legs. Her palms were bleeding and raw. An explosion of pain tore through her right ankle as she limped out of the crumbling building.

She coughed a few times, clearing the dust from her lungs and the gritty taste from her throat as she brushed the hair from her forehead and raised her eyes.

Shaking her head a few times, she tried to make her brain understand what she was seeing in the courtyard in front of her.

6

Selah gaped. She glanced right to where a bunch of girls sat on the benches around an oasis of grass among the stone walkways. Off to her left two educators stood comparing notes on halo-tablets. The ocean air was still crisp and clean—nothing appeared out of place, no screaming mobs, no damage. Selah clutched at her throat where it had hurt a few seconds ago. It now felt fine. She stopped and stared down at her hands—both hands. She turned them over and back again, inspecting every surface. No damage. No grit, blood, or shredded skin, just perfect, soft, clean hands.

Her heart raced.

What manner of craziness had gripped her mind? She spun to face the Repository. The debris-clogged doorway she'd just escaped stood there pristine and clean with no signs of the disaster she had just experienced. Blood pounded in her head, filling her vision with micro-stars that floated before her eyes.

She felt faint. She extended her hands to steady herself.

She glanced into the Repository hallway. Every surface was in order. No dangling fixtures or dirt on the shiny floors.

The data glass! She scrambled to locate the contents of her pocket. Her hand found the small chip. She clutched it in her fingers and shut her eyes. A sigh of relief crossed her lips. She wasn't completely crazy. What manner of deception was this? Did she do it to herself, or did someone do it to her?

Selah carefully descended the few stairs to the stone pathway. Her balance returned and her head cleared by the time she reached the bottom.

She took off running across the quadrant to her quarters and scurried into the lift. She leaned back against the wall and was breathing hard as the vehicle rose to the sixth floor. Her pounding heart threatened to blow out her ribs. She squeezed her arms tight across her chest. She'd never felt so confused or scared in her life.

Was this her imagination? Was she asleep and in some weird dream? No, she felt awake. She pinched her arm. She yelped, then snickered as a single tear escaped her eye and rolled down her cheek. *What a stupid thing to do*. She looked at her arm. That was going to leave a mark.

The lift doors slid open and she hurried down the hall. With a palm identification, she was in. She slid onto her seat and inserted the data glass in her other reader sitting on the corner of the desk. This part was real. She was holding the glass. What could explain the rest?

Her machine made the same strange noise as the one in the Repository. She ejected the data glass, inspected the reader, and reinstalled the glass. The noise returned. The file had reverted to squiggly, incomprehensible lines on top of each other. Missing words, empty spaces, fragmented sections. Her hopes dropped as she scrolled.

Wait! There it was.

She stopped and moved back up a page. The lines separated. The sentence she was looking for was gibberish with large spaces between word fragments, but parts were still there— *Varro Chav . . . Everli . . . Moun . . .* The additional missing letters let her know that if there was anything recoverable on this glass, she'd better get it fast before it all became corrupted.

Did this mean her family could be in the Mountain? And who could she show it to who wouldn't get her in trouble for removing Repository property?

Her jaw clenched. The Mountain was *not* going to claim any more of her family. She felt the urge to scream. She tried to stand but her legs went weak. She raised her arm and with shaking fingers punched the access for Treva on her ComLink.

Her friend's image popped onto the screen. "Hey, girl! We're just getting ready to leave. I'm glad you called before we got out of Link range. I've been thinking long and hard—" She frowned. "What's the matter? You look terrible."

"I don't know where to start, but I'm coming with you," Selah said. The fear now gripping her brain was urging her to action.

"What changed your mind, and why do you look scared?"

"I just have to get away from here for a while, and I had a strange incident at the Repository you'll have to help me figure out." It was going to be a balancing act figuring out when to say anything. There had been something in that file about Landers that might help Bodhi, but she feared if she mentioned the possibility of her family being in the Mountain, Treva and Cleon would get Glade involved, and he would forbid her to go. He would try to take her data glass, and she wasn't letting it out of her sight. This might be her only chance to help Bodhi.

Cleon's face pushed into the frame. His blond hair fell across his big brown eyes. If Mother saw that shaggy hair, she'd chastise him for sure. "What are you talking about, Sissy? What happened?"

"Nothing . . . I don't know. I'm coming with you. I can't stay here. Wait for me. I have to grab a few things." She'd have to plan this right and not tell them everything until they were far enough from home that they couldn't bring her back or contact Glade. Hopefully he would be far enough north as they went south that there'd be no communications.

Treva pushed Cleon out of the way. "We're loading the wagon with supplies. Come over to the Security Travel Depot when you're ready. It will take us about a half hour, so hurry. We want to get to a campsite before dark."

Selah rushed around her quarters, throwing clothes and essentials into her backpack. She hadn't pulled the pack out of the closet since she got to TicCity. It brought back memories of stuffing it this fast for her fateful trip when she had to leave her home and family. Now she found herself stuffing it with hopes of running *to* her family. She wished with all her might that this trip could give her the answers she sought, but at the same time every bit of matter in her brain screamed not to go back in that place. She was lucky once, but would she be again?

She cringed. This time she would have to go without Bodhi. He'd be another one who would never consent to letting her go back there.

She carefully wrapped the data glass and reader in a cloth, shoved them in a leather pouch, and deposited it in a side pocket. Grabbing up the pack, she thought about contacting Glade, but then dismissed that idea.

First she'd have to explain how she'd found the file while looking for information to help Bodhi get his abilities back—which would make Glade livid. Then she'd have to explain a trip to the Mountain that he would . . . To say he would not condone it was definitely too mild a statement. He'd probably rant and rave and stick her in irons. In the end, she figured it would be easier to beg his forgiveness later than to ask for permission now.

She laced up her trekking boots, grabbed her backpack, and headed for the depot, hoping all the way that she wouldn't run into Bodhi or Glade leaving.

⚛

Selah made it to the depot with time to spare. She hunted up and down the supply stations for horses and a wagon to no avail. Her heart sank. She walked back toward the front. Why would they leave her behind? It had to be Cleon trying to protect her. Maybe Treva had gotten scared and contacted Glade. Maybe—

"Hey, Sissy, over here!" Cleon waved both arms to get her attention.

Selah cringed. Someday she was going to teach him to stop calling her that. "I thought you two left me." She trotted around land skiffs and storage containers, slowly approaching the big thing Cleon was standing in. It looked like a flat-bottom boat with high sides and a clear visi-screen on the top front. "Where're the horses and wagon?"

Cleon laughed. "That's Dominion Borough talk, Sissy girl. This is the way we travel now." He beamed proudly as he spread his arms.

"This looks like a boat. How do you propose we navigate over land? There's more land than water between here and Stone Braide."

"It's an AirWagon. It floats on its own current like a Mountain AirStream." Treva came around the side and hoisted an odd-shaped bundle to Cleon, who stowed it under the backside of the front seat. "It's not practical to use horses. They take too long and we'd have a hard time crossing the waters."

"What waters? We didn't cross water coming up here," Selah said.

Cleon returned and bent down to nuzzle Treva's neck. She playfully swatted him and laughed. "That's because we didn't have a boat, so we had to follow the land route that most other people take up to the north. With the AirWagon we can shoot in an almost straight line to Stone Braide. The two routes are about the same in miles, but with us floating above the road, it cuts off a lot of time."

It amused Selah that Cleon and Treva were a couple. Treva

was a child prodigy of biotech sciences, and Cleon . . . he was lucky to have finished school. Mother was sure right when she said opposites attract.

"Well, I decided stress was making strange things happen to me," Selah said. "I need a rest. When we get going I'll tell you the bizarre thing that happened earlier today." There'd be plenty of time to tell the truth—much later.

"Cleon and I talked about this trip while we were working. We're going to do it smart. I can get in the Mountain without raising any alarms. You two are going to hide out in Stone Braide with my uncle till I get my records and find out what's been going on." Treva, hands on her hips, looked to Selah for agreement.

Selah chewed on her upper lip. She felt terrible for lying to the two people closest to her. She'd done that once to Mother, and it gnawed at her until she admitted the truth. She just hoped she could hold out till they got far enough away.

"Come on, Sissy. If we're going to do this, we have to be together on the plan . . . all of us." Cleon hopped down out of the wagon and walked toward her. "I know that look. You're up to something. I don't know what you're planning, but if anything happens to you, Glade will skin me alive."

Ugh. Cleon knew her too well to get away with this for long. He'd always been the brother she confided her plans to, though, so hopefully he wouldn't give her away.

"He would probably end both of our miserable existences if we let anything happen to you," Treva said. "I don't suppose Glade or Bodhi are aware of your little trip, are they?"

Selah lowered her eyes. "They're headed north for a few

days to do some exploring, so I couldn't tell them." She ended the conversation by placing her backpack up in the wagon and grabbing some packages of dried meat and fruit to help stow. Cleon went back inside the depot and came out carrying a high-tech-looking crossbow, a compound bow, and several quivers of arrows.

"Wow! Those are pretty nice-looking weapons," Selah said. "I'm a little jealous. I've been learning hand-to-hand combat, but I sure miss my kapos."

Cleon grinned broadly, laid the weapons in the wagon, and reached behind him to pull a soft leather case from the waistband of his pants. He held it out to Selah. She looked at him and furrowed her brow.

"Open it." Cleon shoved it in her hand and dropped his fists to his hips. "It's not going to open itself."

She slipped the flap open and started to laugh as she pulled out a half dozen of her favorite throwing knives. "Have I told you how much I love you, my brother?"

Cleon smiled. "I love you too, Sissy, and I knew you'd be happy to be reunited with your beloved kapos. When you gave them up, I secretly took them for safekeeping."

Selah nodded. "And here I thought all this time it was Glade keeping me from carrying them in town."

"We may do some hunting between here and there. Tenderizing is one thing, but I didn't want you to use any of that hand-chopping stuff on unsuspecting animals."

They both laughed. Cleon was used to making trips in these areas to trade livestock and seed bundles. He knew all the easiest routes, the best places to camp and catch game.

It amused her that since coming north, he had started eating meat, thanks to Treva. She was good for him.

Treva exited the depot with the last of the supplies and stowed them and the bows in their respective compartments in the sides of the wagon. Selah looked around. It was pretty exciting to use a vehicle like this. There was a canopy, retracted at the moment, that would protect them from inclement weather and provide sleeping quarters at night. They had bedrolls, a built-in water purifier, and even navigational equipment.

"Are we ready to go? I'm kind of anxious to get started," Selah said. In her mind she had already found and rescued her parents and her brother Dane and was planning what to say to her stepfather to smooth over the disaster she'd created for them. After all, she had fumbled through and fixed a lot since leaving home.

"We're only waiting for one more person. We got a navigator so we didn't have to wait for the caravan that leaves this afternoon. Besides, they're taking the land-only route to go the long way around," Treva said.

Selah didn't trust the look on her friend's face, but there was no reading her mind-thoughts. They didn't do that to each other without permission.

She furrowed her brow and folded her hands behind her back. "Okay, if it will save us time, but you didn't mention anyone else." She didn't want anyone else going with them. This was private family business, and she was sure they could traverse the shortcut without help. Coming north hadn't been too hard. "Who are we waiting for?"

"Me," a voice said.

Selah turned, prepared to rebuff the interloper and send him packing to seek another ride. Jaenen Malik strolled across the lot, crossbow slung over his back and a travel bag in his right hand. Her feelings moved from irritation to acceptance in an instant as she watched Cleon and Treva duck out of sight.

"Jaenen, what are you doing here?" Selah's insides fluttered. He was good-looking, and there was no way for her *not* to notice. But she could enjoy his good looks without falling victim to his charms. Besides, she could use his help. She casually pressed her hands to her sides.

"I told you I'd be going back on the road to find your family. Glade pays me well to continue the search. I'm heading south to meet up with a caravan. I put in a request for shared transportation to save on costs, and here I am. I'll be your navigator." He held out both hands and smiled broadly.

Selah brightened at his dedication to finding her family and was glad to have an ally. He would definitely take her side in any discussions with Treva and Cleon about going into the Mountain. "I'm surprised and encouraged all at the same time. Please keep this between me and you, but I found something that may give a clue to my family's whereabouts."

"You aren't trying to do my job, are you?" Jaenen chucked his bag into the wagon and locked his crossbow into the weapons holder inside the wagon side panel.

Selah moved closer and lowered her voice. "No, but that file number and location you gave me led me to this clue. I've got a data glass with a fragmented info file about the Mountain in my bag. It mentions my stepfather's name. I wasn't supposed to take it out of the Repository—"

"Don't you two look cozy with your heads together," Treva said from behind them.

Jaenen and Selah separated. Selah felt her face warm. Treva strolled over carrying an energy stick and bit off a hunk.

"Neither of you going to say anything?" Treva looked back and forth between them. Selah couldn't think of anything to say that wouldn't incriminate herself, so she opted for silence. Mother had once said something about silence being worth gold, whatever that meant.

Treva waved the energy stick as though it were a laser pointer. "You two are planning something. I can taste it." She stared down at the stick, then back at them. "Trust me. I'll figure it out."

"Do you think we'd deprive you of anything that sounds like fun?" Jaenen flashed his lady-killer smile and batted those thick lashes.

Treva softened. "No, I guess not." She started to walk away but turned back. "You just remember to invite us when you find something fun to do." With that, she sashayed off.

Selah screwed up her face and looked at Jaenen with wide eyes. "What was that? I've heard you have hypnotic power over women, but I've never seen it in action. I can't believe it. Treva's in love *and* betrothed to my brother, and with one bat of your eyelashes, you had her acting like a silly schoolgirl."

"What can I say. I'm afflicted with an exceptional power of persuasion." Jaenen shrugged.

Selah waved a finger in his face. "Yeah, don't try that eyelash-batting thing on me or I'll take a torch and singe the flapping little things off."

"Yes, ma'am," Jaenen said with a wink and a grin.

"When we set up camp for the night, I'll show you what I found. It's a garbled notation and the data is corrupted. The second time I opened it the file size appeared to have shrunk."

"That's how I work best. I take pinpricks of information and turn them into full-scale tapestries. I've worked on other partial Repository files. Maybe I can decrypt enough of it to get a legible clue."

Selah brightened. "You really think so? That would be a step forward in my search to find a cure for Bodhi's abilities." Her eyes narrowed. "Wait a minute! File numbers are one thing, but how have you gotten access to Repository files with the kind of security the healers have on them? You not being a Lander would automatically disqualify you from access to that area."

Jaenen smirked and wiggled his eyebrows. "That's why I'm considered a top-notch navigator. I've never taken on an investigation that I didn't wind up solving to the satisfaction of my customer."

Selah felt like hugging him, her hopes soaring. And he hadn't berated her for coming along on a trip that could wind up being dangerous. Finally, someone who considered her capable. She wondered if he could help her with the part of the file that had to do with Bodhi, but then she had second thoughts. Bodhi hadn't been very polite to him at her quarters. Maybe she'd better save that request till after she saw what he could retrieve from the file. No sense in making him ornery if it wasn't going to profit her trip.

7

odhi stowed his gear in the JetTrans cargo area and listened to Glade's conversation with the pilot. Having a Lander at the helm of a JetTrans on the way to Wilmington had worked to their advantage. They'd arrived early at the depot to load with a horse and wagon caravan, but because of Glade's Council status, the pilot offered them a much faster airborne ride. He also informed Glade of the latest operations of the splinter groups, since word of Selah's transition had spread like fire in dry hay.

Glade strolled from the pilot's bay to the center passenger area and slid into a seat beside Bodhi. "We were fortunate to cross paths with my old friend. It will save multiple hours of travel to Wilmington, and I've already made contact to get us booked on the earlier caravan leaving there for Baltimore later on this afternoon."

"Good. If we took a caravan from here, we'd have gotten

there too late for the early connection. Waiting until tomorrow to leave Wilmington would have definitely slowed our journey," Bodhi said.

Taraji swung her lithe six-foot frame up into the seating area by way of the open cargo door instead of taking the stairs. Her long black hair, tied tightly in a high ponytail, swished over her shoulder as she moved forward and pointed to the back section. "This JetTrans is a Council transport. There's a conference area in the back where we can talk unhindered."

Bodhi frowned. "Why do we need that?" He wasn't thrilled with the unbalanced feeling he'd been getting every time he flew in a JetTrans lately. Add to that a stuffy, closed room, and the queasy sensations were certainly counterproductive. He didn't want Glade to see his distress since it would reinforce his opinion of Bodhi as a less than ideal mate for his daughter.

"I've got some serious updates to go over." Taraji, dressed in a black, one-piece, high-tech fiber uniform, openly displayed her tactical readiness equipment and weapons. Since passengers traveling by military JetTrans were accustomed to security and navigator personnel, it didn't raise any concerns.

"I received a similar update from the pilot. We need to compare in private," Glade said.

"We've got Council authorization to use the area," Taraji said. She turned to glance at the passengers toward the front, taking note of each individual before turning back. "Some old enemies have heard of your return, and they're pretty anxious to get hold of your research materials—and Selah."

Glade firmed his jaw and pulled the satchel closer. "How could they know this fast?"

"Baltimore. There are open-end contracts for blood hunter information. People are willing to trade information for bio-coin every day of the week." Taraji continued to watch the incoming crowd and note where they sat. Bodhi wondered if she actually remembered each citizen.

"I'd be a lot happier if we could move to the back before it gets too full in here." Taraji motioned them toward the doorway.

Bodhi relented. His eagerness to know about any danger directed at Selah overrode his desire for his own physical comfort. He followed Glade. Taraji closed the doors behind them, which activated lights and air filtration. Bodhi welcomed the rush of fresh air.

The fusion jets cycled up from a roar to a high-pitched whine and then beyond the scope of human hearing. A soft hum radiated throughout the cabin. Bodhi closed his eyes and tried to hide his death grip on the chair, waiting for a repeat of the recently familiar occurrence of telescoping vision and light-headedness.

Liftoff. The JetTrans leveled off and shot forward. Nothing. Relieved to have no out-of-control senses, Bodhi opened his eyes and glanced around.

Taraji stared at him. She turned away and rested her right boot on the lower rung of the closest chair. "There's good news and bad news. Good news is we're fortunate that we're not taking the route to the south across the Delaware Bay waters. Travelers going that way have had increasing hostile encounters with marauding bands. Since most TicCity travel has abandoned the route, there's little to no security enforcement patrolling that way."

Bodhi frowned. That route had been his first choice several times, but thankfully Glade had outvoted him.

"I knew that before, but it's good to get confirmation on the point." Glade was rummaging in his satchel while holding a single rolled map under his chin. Bodhi felt the punch of his comment.

Taraji continued. "The bad news is the recent proximity of both splinter groups along this northern route. We're going to run into them on this and any subsequent trips. I guess the only thing that could make it worse would be if we had Selah along for the ride."

Bodhi looked at Glade. "Where is Selah? The last I saw she was storming from your teaching theater."

Glade smiled. "She's so engrossed in Repository files, I can count on her being fused to that building for the foreseeable future."

"If she's in greater danger, shouldn't Jaenen Malik be guarding her as you hired him to do, rather than searching for her family?" Bodhi didn't like the idea of Malik spending more time around Selah, but the alternative of her being kidnapped or hurt was even less likable.

"I spoke with Jaenen while you were collecting our supplies," Glade said. "He'll stay in TicCity to keep an eye on Selah until we return."

Bodhi rolled his shoulders and locked his hands together to stretch. After the briefing, Taraji had returned to the passenger area as a first defender if trouble appeared. He'd survived working on the map anomalies with Glade for the last half hour, and even in the same room, they hadn't come to blows. Progress.

"This packet from Treva's uncle Charles is a treasure of historical information, but some of it doesn't make sense. It would be helpful if you actually told me what we're looking for," Bodhi said.

"You'll know it when you see it. Ganston was thorough, so he must know the answers are there. His journal is written in a code for those who understand, but to everyone else it appears as gibberish." Glade continued working the magnifying glass, studying minute details in the mountains of an old linen map. "I can make out the Stone Braide symbol in this same mountain range on three of these maps."

Bodhi shifted in his seat. "That's where Treva's uncle built his colony. He found a stone symbol at that location. Remember, we saw it there on our way north."

"It lines up with these maps. They were drawn more than a hundred years ago," Glade said. "But there's still a missing code to decipher the symbols correctly. If we can find it, we'll have the answers to the West."

"What do we do when we get to Stone Braide?" Bodhi knew there were no cities there, just forests and rock. Glade was being secretive again.

"I've got a plan to triangulate these maps. Once we have

the location . . . I hope we've figured out what to do by then," Glade said.

Bodhi stared at him. He suddenly understood. Glade wasn't being secretive—he didn't know the answers. That angered Bodhi even more. Glade should at least be honest with him.

From sitting on the hard chair so long, the backs of both his legs had gone numb. Bodhi struggled to stand up, making the blood rush back to his extremities. "What time do we arrive?"

Glade looked at his ComLink. "About fifteen minutes."

Bodhi straightened. He hadn't noticed any instability or queasiness during the flight. Maybe he'd beat whatever Glade and the others thought was going to befall him. His body could be healing itself because his head had cleared, even about the future. "I want to take a shift protecting Selah."

"You're not agile enough to be on her detail, and you're not good enough for her as a man." Glade spoke matter-of-factly and didn't even lift his attention from the map.

"Who do you think you are?" Bodhi began to pace. Heat rose across his torso and down his arms. "What gives you the right to dictate the rest of her life after being a missing father for eighteen years?"

"Because I sacrificed everything for her." Glade's face reddened as quickly as his glance hardened.

Bodhi stood in front of Glade. "From what I hear, you sacrificed *nothing*. You spent eighteen years in the Mountain, deserted Pasha, and left Selah to be raised by another man."

Glade rose from his seat and stared down his nose. "You'd do much better to mind your manners, or else—"

"Or else what?" Dark brooding colors swirled before his eyes. Anger tried to overtake him. Bodhi could see it happening, and he fought to overcome the colors. Just like before. Some of his sordid past remained crystal clear in the particles of his fading memories. If he concentrated on them, he could keep them from dimming. He couldn't afford to *not* remember.

Glade's fist came up. It hung in the air for a moment.

Bodhi refused to flinch. He was not going to be under this man's command. They were going to be equals or enemies.

Glade looked at his raised fist as though he didn't recognize it. He pounded the table, then swept the surface clean of maps and charts. "I can't fail at this. I've failed at the most important times of my existence, and I can't fail at this!"

"Is this another ploy to manipulate me away from Selah? After all, you're Glade. The oldest and best, the almighty ruler of the—"

"The man ruined because of love," Glade said. "You should be glad I'm relieving you of that burden sooner rather than two failures later."

Bodhi glared. "How were you ruined because of love? You weren't there. I'd say if anyone was ruined, from the stories Selah told me, it would be Pasha."

"I'm 150 years old. Do you think Pasha's the only woman I ever loved?"

Taraji burst into the room and Bodhi jerked his head in her direction. She talked rapidly with her right hand held to the ComLink in her ear. "Tell Wilmington Council to send a squad and hope you find them before we land. With all the citizens in here, if we have to engage, it could be a bloodbath." In her other hand she carried a pair of laser darts and leg harnesses. She motioned to Bodhi and tossed them to him as she continued the animated conversation with her earpiece.

Bodhi and Glade scrambled into the equipment, both checking the loads and arming the weapons. The JetTrans thrusters whined. Forward motion ceased, and the transport moved toward the ground as Glade snatched up the maps and loaded them securely in his satchel.

Taraji tapped off her ear com. "Dispatch is thinking it's too much of a coincidence that the security team for this depot had to be siphoned off for actions in other areas of the city not normally considered criminal hot spots." She checked the load on her weapon. "Your bags are outside this door. I suggest we exit by the cargo door in the back and keep any activity away from citizens."

To punctuate her sentence, the JetTrans touched down. The vibration of the opening cargo door rattled the wall panel. Bodhi moved toward the door with Glade behind him.

Taraji, hand on her holstered weapon, stepped in front of him and smiled. "I'm your navigator for this trip, so I get to go first." She slid open the door and looked left and right, then at the civilian seating. Citizens rose and gathered their belongings. Taraji motioned Bodhi and Glade out of the room to the cargo door on the left of the meeting area.

Bodhi hooked his pack across his shoulders and quickly

canvassed the outside area. Not waiting for Taraji, he grabbed the frame and swung himself down from the JetTrans onto the rocrete surface of the landing station. The noontime sun lent its angled rays to ordinary items, making them look sinister. His heart fist-pounded his chest. He crouched, moving left, allowing the JetTrans wing to give him extra cover.

Taraji and Glade dropped down beside him. On his next sweep of the landscape, Bodhi glanced at Taraji. Her posturing was stern, but he saw the smile in her eyes. "I've instructed the pilot to take the civilians out the other side and away from this transport to the storage units. We need to get to the second building on the other side of this landing area. It's the security center they had to leave unmanned because of the last outbreak fifteen minutes ago. A security team will pick us up and get us to the caravan depot on time."

Bodhi followed the gesture of her hand, but just past her head, a bush pulled to the side. He motioned to Taraji and Glade. They ducked behind a tall rocrete wind barrier and drew their weapons.

The bush sprang back into place, and several seconds later four men turned the far corner and approached using the pathway directly in front of the bushes. They continued to walk past the transport in the opposite direction. Bodhi's chest started to unclench.

A sound caught his attention.

Bodhi and Taraji spun at the same instant. With the sun momentarily in his eyes, a laser zipped past Bodhi's head. He jerked and spun around in a lower position, firing several heated exchanges with two additional men. Bodhi dropped one of them with a shot that exploded into several starbursts, indicating the man had been carrying explosives. He dodged and fired at the other man, who ducked behind a tree along the walkway as Taraji shot one man hiding on the left. Another man shot at her but missed. Glade swung around the other side of the barrier, aimed, and shot the one firing at Taraji. A laser shot deflected from the wind barrier and blasted Glade's weapon from his hand.

"We need to make a run for the building," Taraji yelled to Bodhi over the laser fire. She wrapped a quick pouch bandage on Glade's bleeding, burnt hand.

"Glade needs to go between us, and we can tag-team, running and firing," Bodhi said. Taraji nodded.

They stayed low behind the wind barrier and snaked their way among the trees and across the landing pad to the edge of the first building. A minute passed with no laser fire. Bodhi breathed easier.

Two more shots blazed from a man to their right, one deflecting off the edge of the building, the other striking a tree, leaving a smoldering fist-sized mark. Streaking along the side of the building, Bodhi followed the traces from the other weapon and got a direct sight on the assailant. He charged to a stop, took aim, and downed the enemy with a laser to the knee. The man rolled a couple of times and came to rest against a tree, his leg smoldering.

Taraji followed the one who had wounded Glade as he ducked around the second building. She slipped around the side, with Glade and Bodhi bringing up the rear. Taraji dropped the man with two shots. They turned in time to hear the other one running away across the landing pad. Bodhi, Glade, and Taraji stormed into the security building and sealed the door.

Bodhi leaned against the wall after the door closed. The right side of his face, still warm from the close laser miss, reminded him of his mortality.

Was this level of danger going to be a regular part of his life from now on?

His insides felt odd, like a clock was ticking . . .

8

Selah rode in silence for the first hour, still trying to understand the earthquake. It had felt and tasted real, from the glass embedded in her hands to the grit in her throat. But she kept silent, fearful Treva or Cleon would think she was ill and not allow her to continue. She'd have to talk about it sooner or later, but how would she explain something with no evidence? Maybe she was going crazy. After all, she thought she'd moved an equipment rack by yelling at it. And then there was that weird throbbing in her hands. Did all this strangeness have something to do with the lightning flashes?

She looked up from fiddling with her fingers. Treva stared at her from the front seat. "Are you all right? You seem a little too deep in thought. There's all this beautiful scenery going by and you're missing it."

"I'm fine, just tired. I got up too early this morning." Selah feigned a yawn.

She glanced at her surroundings, mostly forest on both sides with a few grassy clearings scattered about. They followed a worn hard-pack road. The AirWagon traveled on an energy current about three feet above the surface, which turned out to be a good thing because they'd recently passed a few spots with trees fallen across the road or boulders obstructing their passage. If this were an ordinary horse-drawn wagon, they'd surely have had to stop and clear the obstacles.

A ways back, off in the distance, she'd seen the scarred, overgrown remnants of high-rise buildings, places old folks once called concrete jungles. This haggard road probably served as the main artery between those dead cities. She peered over Cleon's shoulder at the navigational compass. With its bio-computer map overlays, she thought it might tell what cities they had once been.

Cleon glanced back at her and smiled. He had a natural ability with this kind of machine since he used slightly smaller Mountain AirStreams on his farm outside TicCity. "This kind of high-tech equipment could increase the production on my farm," he said.

Selah snickered. "And it doesn't hurt that it has comfortable seats and a magnetic force field that keeps the wind from whipping our hair around, which is a decidedly good thing since you're traveling close to forty miles an hour."

Jaenen leaned over to tap Cleon's shoulder. "Folks, I think we have a problem." He turned in his seat to look behind them.

"What's wrong?" Cleon glanced about in quick succession.

"Those two tree blockages we just passed weren't natural. I saw fresh chop marks on one, and the other wasn't rotted or hit by lightning. No reason it fell without help." Jaenen swiveled his seat to face the side panel that stowed their weapons. "And the boulder—there wasn't any spot on that hillside where it could have come from. It was rolled here from elsewhere."

"What do you think we should do?" Treva's glance skittered over every tree and bush.

"We're probably going to have a fight. We should arm ourselves." Jaenen reached for the panel.

Cleon cycled down the thruster, and the AirWagon slowed and drifted to the ground.

"No! Don't stop!" Jaenen lunged to push the controls forward.

From trees on both sides of the road, multiple bodies swung out in front of them on ropes and twisted vines. Selah yelped and grabbed onto her seat, assessing the number of attackers.

"It's an ambush. Punch it!" Treva yelled as Cleon scrambled to get the thruster reengaged. Doing an instant stop-start had created a magnetic mislock. The thrusters revved but refused to engage.

A grubby male with unkempt hair and horridly dirty fingernails, his smell preceding him, clawed his way over the side of the AirWagon next to Selah and raised an old-fashioned wood-handled grip rifle, pointing it at Cleon. "I would raise my hands in the air if I were you, boy."

Cleon hunched his shoulders and slowly raised his hands from the controls.

The man spoke in a heavy Southern drawl Selah didn't

recognize, but her immediate concern was moving away from the rancid smell before she lost the lunch they had eaten awhile back. She edged closer to Jaenen on the other side.

Another bandit with a patch on his right eye reached over the side and grabbed her, his fingers entwining her hair. "Where you goin', pretty lady?"

Selah screamed and clawed at his hand. Her training kicked in and her mind blocked the sensation of pain. She planted her feet and turned her body, preparing to give him a sharp blow to the throat.

Jaenen shot from his seat and punched the guy in the face. Spittle and blood flew from the man's mouth and nose as his head jerked back. He released Selah and fell to the ground, clutching his nose.

Adrenaline coursed through her body. Selah dropped to the floor of the AirWagon and scrambled away from the partition, knowing she could easily be caught again.

Jaenen reached down, pulled her to her feet, and enveloped her in his arms, glaring at the bandits. "Leave the girl alone. Take our supplies."

The others, all men and equally as dirty, laughed at Eye Patch writhing on the ground, clutching his face. He jumped to his feet, cursing, and scrambled back over the side. Jaenen pushed Selah away from the danger and assumed a fighting stance.

Her lip trembled, but she refused to show these men that she feared them. She lowered herself to the floor behind Jaenen and moved just her eyes to search for the leather bag of kapos. They weren't her first thought for self-defense, but she would feel more secure knowing exactly where they lay if she needed them.

Treva and Cleon were circled on three sides with rifles pointed at their faces. Cleon kept his hands high. "What do you want? We don't have anything worth stealing."

"I think we'll take this here fancy wagon of yours." Dirty Nails had been chewing something, and now he spit, leaving a trail of brown slime on the floor of the AirWagon near the seat Selah had just vacated.

Another man with a dark green rag tied around his head climbed up on the side wall and leaned in. "This ain't gonna rightly do us any good. I told you we shoulda let them pass by. This machine needs to be charged. How you think we're gonna do that after it runs out?"

Selah took mental notes. They didn't come from a town or community with fusion power sources.

A raggedy man with leather ties holding his pants to his worn boots climbed over the side near Dirty Nails and pointed at the console in front of Cleon. "And that's got one of those bio-print controls. Only his hand will run the thing."

Selah perked up. She didn't know that. How did these guys? They looked like they didn't know what water was, let alone technology.

"Then we take his hand," Eye Patch sneered.

Selah's chest clutched at the thought of losing her brother in such a vicious way for a meaningless theft. Her breathing shallowed. She would fight to the end to save Cleon.

"That won't work, you dumb knot. It's a bio-computer.

The hand needs to be alive. And we ain't even takin' another mouth with us to feed," Leather Ties said.

"Ain't you just mister smart britches," Dirty Nails said. "Then what do you propose we do? We gotta get something out of this." He ogled Treva and Selah.

Selah raised her chin in defiance. *Try it and I'll detach your body parts*, she thought. Treva's head snapped in her direction. A hint of a nervous smile crossed her lips. She must have heard Selah's thought.

"Take our supplies." Jaenen gestured to the neatly stacked packages. "We have a lot of food."

Selah noted he didn't offer up their hidden weapons. Her heart pounded. She hadn't prepared for a battle. She needed focus, not fear. She pulled in a few long breaths to calm her quivering extremities. A flash popped before her eyes. She squeezed them tight. *Not now!*

Dirty Nails and Eye Patch herded Selah and the group out of the AirWagon and onto the side of the road. Leather Ties held them at gunpoint while the AirWagon was stripped of belongings, and several of the bandits moved off into the woods with the majority of the booty.

Selah cringed watching the supplies disappear. One of the bandits noticed her leather bag. He poured the kapos out on the ground and picked one up by the blade using two fingers.

"What would anybody want with this baby pig sticker?" He threw his head back and laughed.

"You could probably give them to Lys to clean his nails," another answered.

Dirty Nails growled his displeasure at being the butt of

their jokes and fired off a round, just missing the ear of the one who'd last spoken. Everyone scrambled from the vicinity, leaving the man standing there motionless as a tree, still holding Selah's knife.

"You don't have to get so ornery about it. I was just joking." The man threw the knife to the ground with the others, walked over the bunch, and ground them into the soft forest floor at the edge of the road.

Selah tried to make eye contact with Treva to keep her friend calm. She thought any show of emotion might give the bandits further provocation, and Treva appeared on the verge of tears. Cleon and Jaenen took up positions in front of the girls as a shield.

Dirty Nails grabbed Selah's backpack from the remaining pile and dumped it out. He kicked through her clothing and other items, then felt over the bag and ripped open the side pocket, exposing the wrapped cloth. She tensed.

He dropped the bag and unfolded the cloth, discarded the data glass pack, and turned the reader over in his hand. "Does everything you people use take some kind of power? You're all slaves to the order." He tossed the reader on the bag.

Selah squeezed her lips tight, hoping the reader and data glass hadn't broken.

"We need something more to give you passage through our land. How much money you people got to go with this bounty?" Dirty Nails walked the line of them, stopping near Selah. Her stomach lurched. She forced down her gag reflex at the rancid smell emanating from him. How could one person possess such a vile odor?

"We've got very little, but I don't think it will work for you." Cleon held out his ComLink and opened the bio-coin interface.

Dirty Nails slapped his arm away. "I mean real money! Gold, silver, stones?"

Selah jerked her head around. She hadn't heard anyone talk of stones since she was little. He meant diamonds, the stones of barter in the wild lands. Very few people she knew dealt in any physical currencies—too bulky, and easily lost or stolen.

Cleon shook his head. "No. We don't use metals or stones, only virtual coin."

Selah knew just what he was thinking. If they spent virtual coin it could be traced.

Dirty Nails grabbed Treva by the arm. Cleon reached to stop him. Two rifles drew down on him. He raised his arms in surrender as he backed away.

"I think we may need to take these here women with us as the rest of the payment." Dirty Nails sneered at Cleon and turned to face Jaenen. "You had something to say about my friend touching your woman before. What you got to say now?"

Jaenen opened his mouth.

"I'm not his woman." Selah put fists to hips. "You talk to *me* if you have something to say *about* me." Suddenly she realized how stupid that sounded, but there was no taking it back. She stuck out her chin and glared at Dirty Nails.

The bandits howled, making snide comments about Dirty Nails' lack of ability to control one little woman. His hand shot out and he slapped Selah across the face.

She saw it coming as if in slow motion. She flinched, turning with the slap to lessen the blow. Fear dissolved. She licked her lip, looking for blood, then cracked her neck from side to side. Her nails dug into the palms of her hands. Pain heightened her sense of fear.

Jaenen lurched to her defense. A rifle barrel intercepted him. He retreated, hands raised, forehead bloody.

Selah's eyes narrowed. What manner of craziness was this? Everything was moving in singular frames of time. She glared at Dirty Nails again, wishing she could shoot flames from her eyes.

The smile left his face. He threw his rifle to the side and grabbed the front of her shirt with both hands, drawing her into his putrid smell. She gagged and recoiled. He yanked her forward again to stand nose to nose, snapping her head back.

A guttural roar burst from her chest. "Nooo!" Selah thrust out both palms to push him away. Dirty Nails lifted from the ground and slammed into the top side of the AirWagon. He dropped to the ground with legs and arms splayed.

The remaining bandits turned and ran, leaving Dirty Nails to flop around on the ground. The sound of horses galloping away into the forest punctuated his curses as he gained his footing and snatched up his discarded rifle. He spit and scrambled after his men. At the end of the forest he turned back. "What kind of freak are you, lady?"

Selah stumbled back, extending her arms to steady herself. Cleon and Jaenen stood rooted.

Treva rushed to her side. "What was that?"

"I don't have a clue." Selah held up her hands and scanned

both palms. They vibrated again like this morning. Fear and wonder consumed her at the same time. Was this part of being novarium?

"I guess you won't have a use for these." Cleon gathered up her scattered kapos and dropped them back in the leather pouch.

"Are you going to tell us what's going on, or do we just pretend we didn't see you make that guy fly through the air?" Jaenen stood his ground, noticeably farther away.

Selah winced, though Treva didn't appear intimidated.

"How long has that been happening?" Treva rested her hand on Selah's arm.

"I don't know. I think I first noticed it this morning." Selah continued to stare at her hands as though some invisible text would pop up with a warning label and directions.

"Can you do it again?" Cleon closed the pouch.

"I don't know. I'll try." Selah extended her hands. She didn't know how to turn on whatever it was that made the energy burst. She tensed her muscles, then jerked her hands forward. Nothing happened.

Treva jumped back. "Hold on! I think you need a focal point and I don't want to be it."

"Me either!" Cleon and Jaenen spoke in unison.

"Maybe it's an emotional reaction, and you need to be upset or something," Treva said.

"I was angry about being slapped, and his smell made my stomach lurch." Selah rubbed at her hands.

Jaenen shook his head. "We came out of that a lot better than I expected. This is why a caravan is always the safest bet through this part of the country. You two women were very brave."

"I wasn't scared like this morning in the earthquake," Selah said.

"Earthquake? What earthquake?" Cleon slowly approached.

"When I was in the Repository."

Treva waved a finger back and forth. "We're going to have to work on improving our communication, 'cause I don't remember you saying a single word about anything like an earthquake."

Selah hung her head. "I thought you'd make me stay home if I told you I was seeing things."

"Ladies, how about we continue this conversation on the road and get out of here before our company decides to return?" Jaenen snatched up Selah's bag and stuffed the contents back inside, including the reader and data glass holder. He started to toss it into the wagon, but Selah caught his arm and gently relieved him of the bag.

The four scrambled into the AirWagon. Cleon rubbed the control panel and encouraged it to start, using sweet cooing sounds like Selah heard him use when talking to his cows. She and Treva traded glances and giggles, but when the AirWagon fired up, they both cheered. Cleon threw it in forward, and they shot up the road at close to the max of forty miles an hour.

No one spoke. The silence was almost a group signal for "don't break the good fortune by talking until we're completely safe." Fifteen minutes later they let out a collective sigh of relief as the waters of the Delaware Bay appeared.

"How long will it take to cross the water?" Already glistening with sweat, Selah rubbed her hands down her pant legs. Thinking about one of those large-finned monsters chomping down on a leg and dragging her out to sea had kept her on land since the age of ten, when she'd witnessed a shark attack that left the waters churning red with blood. She loved the ocean smell and the hypnotic motion of the waves, but that was as close as she wanted to get even though she could swim well. Mother said swimming was like riding a horse—you never forgot how.

"Maybe fifteen minutes," Cleon said. "I'll keep it at top speed. I know your love of the water."

Treva turned. "Oh, you like to swim too! I love—"

"I hate it. He was being sarcastic," Selah said.

Jaenen reached over and patted her arm. Selah grabbed his hand, turning her knuckles white with the strength of her death grip. Jaenen grimaced but lifted the left side of his mouth in a tortured half smile. Selah appreciated his sacrifice as she restricted the blood flow to his hand.

She needed something to alleviate her fear of the Air-Wagon pitching and dumping her in the water at any second. She took a few quick looks at the waves sliding along the bay. Her chest squeezed. Small whitecaps dotted the peaks on the surface, and an occasional gull dove for fish. For the most part, she kept her eyes closed, content to smell the seaweed and brine in the air. That was as close as she wanted to get.

She bit her lip raw until they safely edged onto shore at the other side, then expelled the breath it seemed she'd held since they started across.

"How soon can we get to the Mountain?" Selah said without thinking.

"The Mountain?" Treva turned to face her. "What do you, of all people, want with the Mountain?"

Selah slid her hand from Jaenen's. He looked at her apologetically. "You might as well tell them. It's now or never."

Cleon cycled down the AirWagon and it drifted to the ground. "Tell us what?" He looked at Jaenen. "Apparently you knew about this?"

Jaenen bristled. "Listen, my job is to find your—"

"It's not Jaenen's fault. I didn't tell him the whole story." Selah looked around. "Are we safe to stop here? I don't want to get attacked just for the sake of conversation."

"We're on the safe side of the bay. We'll be camping a few miles farther up the road near WoodHaven. Tell me what's going on." Cleon swiveled his seat around to face her.

"Please don't be mad." Her voice dropped to a whisper. "I went to the healer, and she let me . . ."

"What?" Cleon leaned down to look into Selah's downcast eyes.

"I've been to the Repository looking for information on novarium who've gone before me." She just couldn't talk anymore about Bodhi's loss. It was his private business, and she didn't think it was right to be discussing it in a group setting. As it stood, Bodhi would be livid Jaenen was on this trip.

"Okay, so what does that have to do with the Mountain? Please tell me they don't have novarium trapped in there too." Treva's forehead wrinkled with worry lines.

"No, nothing like that. But I did find a corrupted Mountain file with part of my stepfather's name."

Cleon jumped to his feet, banging his hip on the control levers. He winced. "Father's in the Mountain? How is that possible? Are Mother and Dane with him?"

Selah shook her head. "I don't know anything else."

Cleon pointed a finger at her. "We have to go there, but you're going back home. You're their main target, and I don't want you in that kind of danger."

"No, I'm not going home. It's my information, and if I don't get to go, you can't have it." She would give it to him anyway if there was a chance their parents were somehow trapped there, but making threats at the moment might work in her favor.

Treva attempted to smooth things over. "Wait, you two. We need to think logically of the best and safest plan."

Jaenen silently watched the exchange, then raised a hand. "Since I'm the navigator Glade hired for this family retrieval operation, I think I get a say. Selah has the data glass, so I say she gets to come. Cleon, they're your parents too, so you get to come. Treva . . ." Jaenen threw up his hands. "It's your Mountain—join the party."

Relief washed over Selah as she tried to stifle a grin. After Jaenen evoked Glade's name, there was nothing Cleon or Treva could say to make her go home. She'd won this round. That was another one she owed Jaenen.

Cleon sputtered and gritted his teeth but voiced no further protest. He turned back to the controls. "Since we don't have any food, we need to get to the camp area so we can hunt for dinner before it gets dark. But first, Sissy, I want to know about the earthquake you said you felt this morning."

"I'll tell you on the way. I'd feel more comfortable off the ground and moving," Selah said.

He fired up the AirWagon and they headed west toward the rusted skeletal remains of the city called Dove. The name made Selah think of peace—something she could really learn to appreciate at the moment.

9

Bodhi, Glade, and Taraji met with the commander of Lander security for Wilmington. His sparsely furnished field office at the landing pad consisted of a desk and chair, a computer link, and a couple of basic seats in a dusty brown room—a classic example of the quality of security Bodhi had seen in Wilmington on a number of occasions in the past. Most crime on this trail could be attributed to bio-coin payoffs of the local officials along the way. Unfortunately, corruption was also prevalent in Lander security in the larger cities like Wilmington and Baltimore.

"You three have certainly put a dent in the criminal element around this substation," the commander said. He'd arrived five minutes after they slammed the security door shut.

"Do we know if these are your ordinary malcontents or one of the splinter groups?" Bodhi chose to lean against the wall instead of taking an uncomfortable-looking metal chair.

"We picked up two bodies and captured both of the wounded trying to get away. They're splinters all right. They're all marked," the commander said.

"What kind of marks?" Bodhi looked at Glade. He hadn't heard of this before. There were more Landers with marks on their heads?

Glade shook his head. "Not like you'd think of Landers. Both splinter groups lost their Lander head markings with intermarriage of the first generation. They're still of Lander blood, but from the second generation forward, they were changed."

Taraji leaned forward on her chair. "They fought against the original Lander mission, so they intermarried on purpose to wipe out the head marks, then created their own marks."

"One group has a tattoo of a bird, and the other group has a sword," the commander said as he fingered the halo-keyboard. He tilted the screen so they could see illustrations of the two marks.

Bodhi stared at an image of a slender bird with long tail feathers that started near the fingers of the right hand and extended up the arm to the shoulder. The other image showed a sword laced with a lightning bolt on the upper arm.

"So it's easy to see who they are," the commander added.

Bodhi looked back and forth between Glade and Taraji. "You know who they are and what they look like. How long can this go on? Who protects Selah? Who protects us against this threat?"

The commander leaned back in his chair. "Like always. The violence ends when this novarium cycle ends."

Bodhi jerked from the wall. "You sound like you already know the outcome but aren't willing to help us."

Glade stood to grasp Bodhi's shoulder. "This is why I need you. When you look at the Lander population of the north, it's half splinter groups and half First Protocol Landers. Out of the Protocol group, about half of those are newer generation—"

"The newer generations, even of First Protocol Landers, are worthless," Taraji said. "They don't care about the old ways and ignore the novarium process whenever it starts. Their logic is, ignore it and it will go away and not ruin their perfect little lives, and that eventually happens. There are even Landers with head marks who hide them with makeup to fit in with everyone else." She screwed up her nose in disgust.

The commander sighed and leaned forward on his desk. He looked at Bodhi. "I'm sorry I seem disinterested, but the facts of life for us are that *both* splinter groups want the code from novarium blood. They act like crazy savages whenever the process starts. People come. People go. Our lives stay the same. We have to preserve that, and make no apologies."

Bodhi wanted to argue Selah's worth and the need to protect her, but Taraji stepped forward. "We need a medic for Glade's hand. He was—"

"Not to worry," Glade said as he unwrapped the field bandage. "It's just a scratch and nothing that would slow us down." The end of the bandage slipped off to expose unmarked flesh. Glade turned his palm up and then down. Front and back clean. "Just a scratch. All better now."

Taraji and Bodhi looked at his hand.

Bodhi looked hard into Glade's eyes. "You still have all of your abilities."

Glade averted his eyes.

The commander jumped to his feet and tapped his ear com. He held up a hand for quiet. "I think it's time to get you on your way to the safety of your caravan. It seems someone has come looking for their missing comrades."

⟡

Bodhi, Glade, and Taraji grabbed their weapons from the charging station.

"The only reason I allowed you three to stay armed in Wilmington is because you're moving on right away. But when you get to Baltimore, they'll confiscate those until you leave the city," the commander said. He led the way to the waiting security unit transporting them to the depot.

Glade and Taraji took the right wall seat behind an armed agent, and Bodhi piled in on the left with the commander, who positioned himself right behind the driver. The security unit sped off to the west side of town down a dusty road laced with random trees and numerous industrial storage buildings.

Surprised that only two security agents were in the unit, and neither heavily armed, Bodhi questioned the move. "Commander, is another unit going to meet us? This isn't much firepower if we encounter splinters."

Glade and Taraji leaned over to hear his answer above the whine of the engine.

The commander grinned wryly and gave a shrug. "We don't have the resources to protect every novarium-class offense—"

"How many cases are you talking?" Bodhi remained grim, counteracting the commander's misplaced smile.

"Every Lander girl in any of the colonies, as she turns eighteen," the commander said. "That could be as high as several dozen some years. I don't know how the splinters keep track of them, but it reminds me of a shark feeding frenzy when they smell blood in the water." He shook his head.

Bodhi blinked hard. Dozens? None of them made it to transitioning? What had happened to all of these girls?

The unit accelerated suddenly and jerked to the side to miss a stand of trees, causing them all to grab on for stability.

"Sir, we've got a surveillance pod following us, and communications caught several hostile units plotting an intercept course in the section on this side of the depot," the driver said. He increased the speed again, watching the S-pod on his scanner.

The commander cursed under his breath and tapped his ear com. "Get me a tactical battle squad, and they'd better be at the section handoff when we get there." He turned to the group. "Once I get you people to caravan security, my job is done. We were doing fine until you started this up again. I don't need to be in the middle of this."

"Middle of this?" Bodhi fumed as he held the side strap to keep from shifting into the commander's lap. "You're the head of Lander security for this city. I'd think you—"

"Don't be mad at him." Taraji shook her head. "It's standard procedure coming directly from the Council bosses. I've contacted the caravan. They're sending an extra unit to follow us."

Bodhi balled his hands into fists. He wanted to rage, but he noticed Glade was often his most controlled and calm during hectic times like this. He reined himself in and tried to follow that example but wondered how Glade was doing it.

A pulse cannon fired at the road in front of the security unit. Rocking with the percussion, the unit veered to the left, scraped the ground, and bounced up to regain its two-foot hover height.

Bodhi and Glade steadied themselves and drew their weapons.

"We don't have a pulse cannon to return fire. Our best course of action is to resist engaging." The commander's weapon remained holstered.

Taraji hadn't drawn her weapon either. "We need to be out in the open before anyone engages in return fire so we know who or what we're shooting. I want the three of us staying together." She made a point of staring at Bodhi. He understood.

The unit bucked and sputtered, dipping to the ground again and back into the air after a glancing blow off a tree.

"Sir, I've got a problem with the forward thrusters. I think they sucked in debris. We need to set down," the driver said.

The commander cursed again, and Bodhi flinched at the venom of his words.

Glade anchored himself using a side strap. "How far are we from the caravan?"

"We're in for a sprint. It's about a section and a half from here," Taraji said as she took note of the landscape. Bodhi marveled at how she keyed her ComLink and maintained her balance at the same time with just her feet pressed to the floor.

"You're actually much closer than that," the commander said. "We wouldn't leave you in the middle of nowhere. I'll give you directions."

Taraji kept her head low but moved her eyes toward Bodhi. He understood her look right away. The commander was lying. Bodhi passed the glance to Glade, who gave an imperceptible acknowledgment with his eyes.

Bodhi had readied himself to fight with splinters, not Lander security. "We're supposed to be on the same side, but it seems you're not offering any protections once we leave this vehicle. Is that correct?"

The commander's eyes shifted rapidly before they calmed and he spoke. "I—we aren't authorized for street skirmishes. We have the responsibility of transporting you from one venue to the other." The security unit bucked again, threatening to put them all on the floor.

Bodhi felt his insides coil. "Where is your allegiance—"

"We're glad that you helped us get this far, Commander," Glade said. "Thank you for directions, but I think we have that taken care of—Taraji?"

Taraji nodded. The commander's expression darkened.

The security unit dropped hard, skidding another hundred feet up the road. It came to a halting stop as the tail hooked on a low tree branch and spun them sideways.

The pilot and front seat agent had been knocked out by hitting the windscreen. The commander actually looked scared. There was nothing more for Bodhi to say.

He stepped out of the unit last this time, giving the lead to Taraji. She understood the way these people thought better than he did. He had expected all Landers to be on the same side. Why did he think that when he came here? Was it something he knew from before?

Taraji nudged his elbow and pointed back down the road behind them.

He saw it right away. The surveillance pod sent by the splinters was zooming closer. Bodhi stared at it, calculating the speed and wind. He withdrew his laser dart, dialed the setting for distance, reduced the beam width, raised his weapon with both hands, and fired.

The S-pod exploded into a hundred pieces.

Glade came forward slowly. "How did you do that?"

Bodhi stayed silent as he interpreted what just happened. He was an expert marksman. And neither the fierceness of the situation nor the enemy engagement had instilled fear in him. In fact, they had emboldened him.

He looked at Taraji. "You pointed the S-pod out. You knew I could do it. How?"

"I had the first clue watching the way you strapped on the laser dart. But when I saw you dial the load for distance I knew—the field assassin style," Taraji said.

Bodhi looked to Glade, lifted his shoulders once. "I don't know, but it felt natural."

"Let's get out of here before the other splinters catch up to the last location of that S-pod." Taraji motioned in the direction of a two-story stone building up a slight incline on the right. "There's an opening to the road on top of the hill behind that building. It cuts off a half mile of snaking around the hill and puts us mere buildings from the meeting spot."

Bodhi and Glade scrambled to keep up with the six-foot woman. Her nimble frame seemed to bound over the landscape as though she wore springs. Bodhi envied her ease of movement through the brush and up the hill. He hoped his stamina might return someday, but at least he was keeping up with Glade.

They reached the ridge. Bodhi inhaled a great gulp of air, expanding his chest and stretching the muscles that had tightened on the climb.

A laser burst exploded at the edge of the road. All three of them dove back over the rise, sliding onto the hillside.

Laser fire shot up at them from the bottom of the hill. Two shots ricocheted off the top edge of the boulder below them. One shot went left, the other, right. Bodhi fired right, Glade fired left. They concealed themselves behind trees on the slope.

Taraji was far enough up the hill that she was covered in the treetops. She slid up to the edge of the road and fired off a couple of tracer shots to get the direction of the shooter.

Bodhi tried to watch for movement below him and analyze why he knew what defensive moves Taraji would make.

Movement in the bushes below. Bodhi aimed ahead of the object, waiting for it to move into his range. He fired. A loud thump. No further movement.

The other laser below started firing wildly. Glade engaged, moving down the hill tree by tree as the target moved away but still returned fire.

Bodhi, hearing more than one weapon firing at Taraji, scrambled up the hill to her position. Just as he reached her, she ducked. He ducked. Two shots. Opposite directions. Taraji looked at him. He nodded. Back to back, they rose firing at the same time. For Bodhi, it only took two shots for him to zero in on his target. The laser hit center mass on the man's chest, and his feet jerked up as he sailed through the air and skidded to a stop in the center of the road.

Taraji hit her assailant, exploding the weapon in his hands. The dark-clad man held his arm and fled down the road toward the caravan depot.

"Clear," Bodhi called as he stooped over the downed man.

"Clear," Taraji yelled as she walked back up the road.

"Clear," Glade shouted. His head appeared at the top of the hill.

Bodhi and Taraji swept the area around them. He watched Glade come over the hill just as Taraji whistled.

Bodhi and Glade turned. A bubble-topped security unit from the caravan depot hummed above the road. It pulled up beside them, lowering to the road. The side door swished open, and a female agent with close-cropped hair and wearing a beige flight suit and headset leaned out. "Would you folks be the Rishon party we're supposed to escort away from these local malcontents?"

If Bodhi hadn't felt so tired, that would have made him laugh out loud. As it was, he could just manage a smile and a nod. They piled into the well-shielded security unit, and the agent handed them each a water flask. Bodhi felt comfortable for the first time today.

"By the way, our second unit picked up the two wounded men trying to get away. I've called Wilmington security to pick up that body back there. At least they can do that much work, since they'll just let the wounded guys go in a couple of days after you've cleared out."

"They'll be let go?" Glade seemed to lose his calm. "The Wilmington Lander Council won't charge any of them for a capital offense against a novarium? That used to be against the law."

"Any of them?" The agent pushed her headset off her ears.

"These two and the ones captured from the attack when we landed," Taraji said. "I saw them drive away in the commander's vehicle while we were talking. They were seated in the back, but they weren't in restraints."

"Hmm, forget them. They never got logged in at the Castle. And I'm sorry, sir, but novarium aren't a protected class anymore. Any crime that could befall a novarium could befall a regular person, so those offenses were already covered by laws," the agent said. She turned to speak to their driver in the secured front section, which contained a plascine-domed turret area for a laser cannon.

Bodhi looked at Taraji. "Did you actually see the commander call for backup?"

Taraji tilted her head for a moment, then looked up and smiled. "No, I didn't. That's a good catch. And I must say I'm impressed at your prowess with a weapon."

"So am I," Glade said. He patted Bodhi on the back. "You've surprised me."

Bodhi jerked. His heart pounded. Acceptance at last.

The agent turned back to the group. "We're all set to go. Could you imagine being stuck in this craziness all night?"

Bodhi wondered how bad it would be in Baltimore overnight tonight. They'd arrive there just about dark, and the caravan wouldn't leave until five in the morning. It would head south to Richmond, and they'd get off in Stone Braide.

"So what's the Castle?" Bodhi leaned back against the seat wall, the hum of the engines soothing.

"The Council building is one of those gothic castles from mythology. It's a couple of hundred years old, a dark gray stone building. It's massive. There are places inside that monstrosity that people are reported to have never seen," the agent said. They pulled into the depot, and the security vehicle lowered to the ground.

Taraji stepped out and looked around before she let Glade or Bodhi descend. She nodded. Glade stepped out.

A barrel-chested man in a blue tunic rushed over. He had to huff and puff several times before he could get enough air to speak.

"Glade Rishon! We are so glad to see you again, old friend." He and Glade clasped elbows, then pulled each other in for a back-slapping hug.

Bodhi was a little taken back by Glade's display of camaraderie. Glade, always so tightly reserved, had even smiled at the man.

"Come, your accommodations are all prepared, and we leave right on time in fifteen minutes." The man led the way.

Glade talked to their caravan master while Bodhi sidled up to Taraji, leery after the events of the day. "Is there any way for us to get a communication back to TicCity?"

Taraji shook her head. "No way unless someone travels

there. They've been trying for years to get the towns along the route to band together and create a string communication for the whole line, but they could never get all of them to cooperate."

"I'm seriously worried about Selah's safety. These splinters seem deranged." Bodhi felt helpless to keep her safe at this distance. Why had he let Glade talk him into coming?

Taraji stopped walking and fisted a hand to her hip. "Selah is in the safest place she could possibly be. TicCity is a security fortress and I'm in charge of it, remember?"

Bodhi felt his face warm as he realized the words that had slipped from his mouth. "I'm sorry. I didn't mean to insult you. I'm just worried."

Taraji smiled softly. "I understand your concern, but TicCity *is* the safest place for her to be while we're gone. Jaenen Malik will ensure her safety."

10

Selah tried to watch the scenery, but her mind kept drifting—to the people she loved, the earthquake she couldn't explain, this new ability. As soon as she rationalized one situation, the next would take its place. If she could just—

Lightning burst, colored stars radiating before her eyes. Just what she needed right now. She needed to sleep—for days.

Cleon reduced speed and the magnetic force field kicked in to make for a pleasant ride. For as much as she could concentrate, the landscape intrigued her. At home in Dominion, large multi-acre sections were cleared to cultivate crops and to use for herds of livestock. Here the forests went on forever, with very few clearings and impossibly tall and wide-based trees. At the road edge she noticed wires strung between poles shaped like tall letter T's. Her heartbeat quickened.

She pointed up to the wires. "What are those for? Is this another trap?"

"No, this land between the two waters is controlled by a regent who has embraced the old technologies from before the Sorrows. She has an energy source that generates electricity the old way," Cleon said. "Those wires carry power to the homes. I've heard they're even experimenting with communicating through the wires."

"That sounds a little backward if you ask me," Selah said.

"Yes, but you must remember your Borough always bought technology from the Mountain," Treva said. "And the Lander communities—I'm not sure where they get their technology, because they've got applications far beyond Mountain capabilities."

"True on both counts," Selah said. "And farther south in Waterside, they use petrol-powered energy sources more than we do in Dominion because they produce their own petrol."

"So in this land they must have extended amounts of fossil fuels, or extreme sources of it," Cleon added. "I never thought about it, but I've never seen any mining or reclamation operations, so I don't know where they'd be around here."

He navigated off the road and into a small clearing, following the field around a stand of large trees and then into another clearing of long grass and wildflowers. Obscured by the tall forest to the west, the sun drew long shadows on the field. Selah could guess the time. It would be dark in a few hours. She hadn't slept under the stars since traveling from the Mountain. It brought back memories and a shiver, causing her teeth to momentarily chatter.

As they entered the field, Selah picked up on a low continuous rumble hard to describe. She had nothing to reference it by—maybe horses. It sounded like thundering horses. The farther they traveled into the open area, the greater the sound grew in intensity. The air felt heavy, moist. Selah felt a misting on her face. The AirWagon drifted to the ground. The roar vibrated through the earth, making Selah tingle.

"What's causing the vibration?" Selah said in a voice loud enough to be heard over the rumble.

"Where is it?" Treva yelled to Cleon. He pointed to the right.

Treva took Selah by the hand and said into her ear, "Come see this. You'll love it."

Jaenen stayed behind with Cleon to get their weapons out for hunting. Selah reached in the AirWagon, grabbed her bag of kapos, and stuck them in a lower pocket of her pants. They banged against her calf, but the feeling gave her a sense of security. Treva motioned impatiently. Selah picked up her gait and trailed her around the next grove of trees.

The roar was deafening. Selah stopped and gaped, and her breaths quickened to short, labored bursts. It was beyond anything she'd ever seen. Water. A lot of water. Pure power.

The water cascaded over the top of a narrow rock cliff at least three hundred feet high, dropped to another ledge a hundred feet below, then cascaded another hundred feet or so into a large natural pool surrounded by enormous jagged boulders. The torrents of water moved over the rocks so swiftly and with such force they churned white—a waterfall of milk that regained its clarity as it poured into the crystal-clear pool.

The mountain and cliffs on either side of the falls were covered with trees and bushes, moss and vines with beautiful large blossoms of yellow flowers clinging to the ledges and trailing to hang over the sides in long, colorful tendrils. Selah stared in wonder, not having words to describe the beauty.

"So what do you think?" Treva asked.

"I think I want to stay forever," Selah said with a contented smile.

Treva chuckled. "I think a whole bunch of people would have something to say about you living in the wilds."

"I wouldn't care. I think it's the most beautiful thing I've ever seen. We have nothing to compare with this in Dominion," Selah said. She could imagine hiding away here with Bodhi forever.

"We have artificial waterfalls in the Mountain, so I recognized the sound," Treva said. "But we don't have anything like this. The volume of the sound alone would drive them crazy in the Mountain. They'd demand a hologram falls where they could turn off or dull the sound."

Selah dropped to the grassy slope and wrapped her hands around her knees. The roaring sound evoked peace, drowning out all the other things trying to talk in her head. Her whole body seemed to relax. She dropped her head to her knees and shut her eyes to rest for just a few minutes.

"Hey!" Cleon said as he nudged Selah in the shoulder. She jumped. Had she fallen asleep? She looked at the shadows. They hadn't lengthened much. She'd only been out minutes, but it was enough to refresh her.

"I need to do some hunting. Do you want to come?" Cleon asked.

Selah squinted her eyes, awakening her dormant thoughts and shaking off the sleep. "I heard you say that before, but I thought it was a joke. When did you start hunting?"

"After we came to TicCity. Treva convinced me the game was safe to eat."

"Oh, excuse me—I try for years to get you to eat meat, and your lady love does it in a couple of months. Oh, my heart." Selah clutched at her chest and laughed out loud. "So much for being able to have an influence on someone."

Cleon grinned, holding out a crossbow and a heavyweight compound. "Do you want either of these?"

"I'll let you take down the big game. This I've got to see. I'll do small stuff with these." Selah pulled out her kapos. She could peg a rabbit at twenty feet with one of them, and with her newfound strength she was pretty sure her range had increased exponentially. She tested the knife weight in her hand. It felt natural and familiar.

Cleon walked back to the AirWagon and deposited the compound. He slung the crossbow, cocked and loaded, across his shoulder, the quiver mounted lengthwise along his forearm.

"No one else coming?" Selah fell in step beside her brother. It felt good to be walking in the woods with him again. It made the time and distance from home melt away.

"Treva's going to set up the AirWagon for sleeping. We were lucky those bandits didn't realize we had side compartments."

"Too bad we didn't have the food in there," Selah said. They trudged away from the waterfall.

"That would have posed worse problems. If we didn't have something for them to steal, someone might have gotten hurt or killed."

"What are we hunting for here?" She followed Cleon down a path that looked worn and traveled.

"The last time I was in this area, I got a wild pig, and one of the guys in our party got a deer."

Selah stopped and looked at him. "Who are you and where is my brother, the fish and clam eater?"

Cleon shook his head, snorting with soft laughter. He held up a hand and pointed through the trees. About twenty yards away in a small clearing, three very large rabbits grazed outside a three-burrow warren dug into the hillside. As fate would have it, the breeze was blowing in the rabbits' direction.

One rabbit jerked up its head, put its nose to the air, and thumped its hind leg. The other two jerked to attention and started to dart away. Cleon swung his crossbow around front and fired at the same time Selah threw a kapo.

The rabbit on the left skidded back a few inches and fell with an arrow piercing its side. The kapo skewered the rabbit on the right, while the one in the middle escaped death by scampering into the warren and disappearing before they could shoot again.

"Two should feed the four of us tonight," Cleon said. He leaned the crossbow against a tree and moved to retrieve the game.

Selah followed behind, shaking her head at his accuracy with the bow. Cleon removed the arrow, wiped it off, and returned it to his quiver, then proceeded to try to clean and gut the dead prey. Selah watched with amusement. He hadn't quite got the hang of dressing game, and a few times he gagged trying to lop off the head. After all the years of abuse her brothers had given her about hunting, she almost enjoyed watching him retch. But Cleon was all she had left at the moment, and she did love her brother.

She reached over, stopped his hand, and gave a give-me gesture. "You go dig a hole to bury the entrails and skin," she said. She figured that was the better of the two options, rather than watching Cleon continue to make a mess hacking at the meat.

Cleon, sweat beaded on his forehead, looked relieved. He eagerly handed over the kill and moved about five feet away to stab at the soft forest floor. The dirt moved easily while Selah made short work of stripping and gutting both rabbits. She laid the rabbit meat on a large flat rock and scooped up the entrails, skin, and heads and moved them to the waiting hole. She and Cleon pushed the dirt in to cover the detritus and wiped the blood from their hands.

Selah did a little extra tamping down of the soil. She always felt like she was completing a grave and owed the animal some small measure of respect for being her sustenance—for maintaining her life—even though she was going to enjoy the meal.

Cleon turned away from the hole. "Selah," he said in barely a whisper.

"What?" She continued to tamp in a few errant clumps.

"Selah! Turn around slowly." Cleon seemed to force out the words, still in a whisper.

"What?" Selah spun to face him.

Cleon was frozen in midstride, facing down half a dozen of the largest coyotes she had ever seen. They easily weighed a hundred pounds each, which was unheard of in the south. Their large black eyes and wide, sharp teeth garnered her instant attention. She tried to remain calm so as not to excite them further. The freshly killed rabbits were doing an excellent job of that. Three of the mangy animals stood poised between them and the crossbow, ready to charge. One other circled to their left, and the last two sniffed at the rabbits.

Selah eyed each one. With every particle of her being she wanted to flee. Not practical. Coyotes could run at forty miles an hour. *Even breaths.* One of the group of three curled its lip and bared its teeth, then took a step closer. Selah averted her eyes to the ground. No panic attacks. Calm—when she wanted to scream. The animal stopped.

She ever so slowly lowered herself to the ground. Watching the animals in her peripheral vision, she groped for the knife she'd laid down while burying the remnants. Letting out a breath, she slowly rose to stand beside Cleon. He had a knife in hand as well, ready to fight.

"How are we going to take six of them?" Selah felt her shoulders tighten. Her knees tried to shake but she willed the fear away. She would be an asset to Cleon, not a liability that could cause his death.

"I don't know." Cleon's voice cracked with fear. "Can we scare them? You've spent more time in the woods than I have."

"But I've never had to face down a coyote, especially ones this big. What should we try?"

"Hey, get away!" Cleon shouted and waved his arms suddenly.

The two animals sniffing around the rabbits startled at his voice and jumped over the rock, taking up tensed positions closer to their right.

"Well, I guess that didn't work," Selah whispered. "Let's try to back away. On my mark."

They began backing toward the trees on the other side of the clearing. For every step they took, the animals moved a tentative step closer. Now they had begun to growl among themselves, as though discussing who was going to eat whom.

Selah began to sweat. The coyote closest to her sniffed the air as though it could smell her. Lowering its head, the mangy animal bared its teeth and emitted a gurgled growl. It moved toward her slowly at first, then it began to gallop. Selah stepped back and into the middle burrow of the rabbit warren.

Pain shot through her ankle as it twisted, and she fell, her backside smacking against a pointed rock to the left of the burrow. She yelped in pain. Cleon turned to grab her. Their movement broke the standoff spell.

With a vicious growl, the lead coyote leapt toward her. The rest of the pack charged.

Selah screamed and raised her hands to fend off the attack.

Cleon threw himself on top of her.

11

An arrow cut through the air, sinking into the chest of the leaping coyote. It fell dead on top of Cleon, who yelled, pushed it away, and repeatedly stabbed at it, probably not realizing that it was dead. Selah, her breathing out of control, scrambled away as another arrow shot from the trees, felling another coyote. The force of the strike drove it into the animal beside it, which yelped and, with the other three, ran off in the opposite direction.

"Are you hurt?" Selah grabbed her brother and hugged him so hard that for a second she thought her arms had locked up. Tremors rolled along her extremities, making her hands shake uncontrollably.

"I'm okay. Did you get bit or anything?" Cleon snorted out deep breaths, trying to get himself under control as he looked over Selah.

"No." Selah stared at the dead animals and looked around. "Who did this?"

"I did." A voice came out of a tree.

Selah peered at the tree, thinking it had to be her imagination. Cleon put his arm protectively around her shoulder. The underbrush rattled, then separated, and a suntanned woman with long, cascading golden curls fluidly worked her way through the branches. Just her movements impressed Selah, because not a single tendril of the woman's hair got hung up in the branches, where Selah had to keep her own pulled back or it constantly snagged.

"Thank you for saving us. Who are you? Where did you come from just in time?" Selah asked as she and Cleon scrambled to stand.

"Mari Kief, Regent of WoodHaven." Mari navigated the last of the tree limbs and stood eye to eye with Selah. Carrying a vicious-looking crossbow, dressed in tanned buckskin from her shoulders to the heavy boots on her feet, she sported a leather quiver on her left forearm and looked completely natural in the wild.

Selah held out her hand. "I'm Selah Chav—Rishon, and this is my brother Cleon Chavez. Thank you again."

Mari looked down at Selah's hand, hesitated a moment, then shook. "I don't like killing animals when we don't need the meat, but you're welcome. You didn't have much of a chance after they smelled those rabbits. That's why we hunt and trap in parties."

"Is this your land we were hunting on?" Selah looked down, shame filling her. At home, upsetting another's food source was a major offense. She didn't think Cleon realized this was someone's land.

"Yes, but you didn't know. We rarely interact with passing travelers, for safety reasons." Mari looked directly into Selah's eyes, searching them till Selah felt self-conscious. "But I'd like to invite you back to our community for the evening meal."

Selah relaxed. Mari was looking for something, the way she drilled a stare into her—some recognition, or truth maybe. Apparently she found what she was looking for.

"Oh, no. We couldn't be a bother to you and your folks. We have two rabbits that will feed the four of us for dinner," Cleon said.

Mari pointed behind him. "No, I think your dinner gathering has been canceled."

Selah and Cleon spun. The rock sat empty. The coyotes had relieved them of the kill in their speedy retreat.

Selah's shoulders slumped. They would never catch another rabbit tonight. Not after all the noise they'd made. "I think it would be wise of us to take her up on her offer," she said to Cleon.

He nodded his agreement. "I'd better go back and get the others. We have an—"

"AirWagon, yes, I know," Mari said. "I will send a couple of my men to help you navigate through our secret access points to the colony."

"How do you know about an AirWagon? And how did you know about ours?" Mari seemed to know major details about Selah's group, but she knew nothing of this woman.

"I traveled widely to the Lander settlement at TicCity and south to the Mountain before and since my father disappeared. I have an exact memory for details and sounds. I recognized yours right away."

Selah liked Mari's mannerisms and her soft-spoken ways. She appeared regal with her flowing mane, and if Selah wasn't mistaken, the term *regent* meant someone standing in for a monarch. Mari's father must have been the king or something. Funny to think of that term in this country, but since ancient times, many things had changed. People with their own kingdoms didn't seem outlandish.

Selah looked at Cleon and nodded. It would be all right—she sensed nothing devious. "How long will we have to wait for your men?" she asked Mari.

"Oh, they're right here," Mari said. She raised her arm and whistled a sharp, loud call. Four men materialized silently from the forest, all moving just as quickly as Mari had and carrying weapons just as deadly. One bald man, clad in a dark green-and-brown-splotched one-piece with a knife sheath belt, wielded a wide blade about two feet long. A shaggy-haired man dressed in faded black carried an old-fashioned rifle. The last two men with short dark hair, one in buckskin like Mari and the other in dark green, carried crossbows.

Selah took note. She'd seen more rifles in the last day than she'd seen in all her years in Dominion. Curious.

"You two go with this gentleman and help him navigate his AirWagon and the others to the colony," Mari said to the dark-haired men.

Selah tensed. Had she said she was going along with this

woman? What if it was some weird kind of plan to separate them? She didn't want to offend her new host. Cleon saw her indecision and looked like he didn't want to leave her behind.

"I'd rather you came back to camp with me. Are you sure this is the best plan, Sissy?" Cleon frowned, his eyebrows drawing together.

Selah thought for a second. Her instincts about women were pretty good. Men . . . not so much. As fate would have it, she'd instantly liked this woman's demeanor. "Yes, I'm sure."

Cleon and the two men walked off toward the waterfall and camp. Selah looked around at the two dead coyotes. "I'm sorry. We didn't mean to upset the balance. I should probably tell our security to inform people traveling this way to be mindful that these lands are claimed."

"Actually, I'm sure they already know, but it's not something that we want advertised," Mari said as she made a hand signal to the man with the blade. "It might bring unwanted intrusions."

"Can anything be done with them?" Selah pointed at the carcasses, noting the long fangs in the open mouths. She shuddered at the damage they could have inflicted had it not been for Mari.

"Yes, my man is going to field-dress them. I'll send a wagon back for him and the meat." Mari pointed in the direction they were going to travel.

Selah's stomach flopped. "But you're leaving one man alone with only a knife. What if the pack comes back? I don't want someone else hurt because of us."

Mari touched her wrist. "Raif, secure the site."

The man pushed up his left sleeve and fingered the screen of a wide black band encircling his arm.

Selah flinched, quickly putting her hands over her ears to shield them from the piercing sound. Neither Mari nor the man reacted to the high-pitched screech.

Mari looked at Selah. "Does that bother you? It should pass in a few seconds."

Selah nodded. The sound had already started to dissipate. It felt like her ears were going to pop. She opened and closed her mouth several times, working her jaw against the pressure. Slowly it eased. "What in the world was that?"

"It's an ultrasonic short-range security system we developed for personal safety. It's very odd that it affected you. The shortwave, high-frequency sound waves are too high-pitched to be heard by humans, but the coyotes and other large prey animals avoid them at all costs."

Selah perked up. That was a device that would be truly innovative in Dominion. "Where did you get technology like that out here in the woods? How is it made? Can others get them?"

Mari shook her head. "Sorry, our colony has a law against sharing technology that could be used against us. Years ago, before I was born, my people took components from TicCity and technology from the Mountain and developed the device ourselves. And in recent years we were able to add upgrades to the program to be able to tweak the settings for intensity. We are not backward country melons."

Selah realized her question had been taken as an insult. "I didn't mean—"

"I'm sorry. As soon as I snapped at you, I knew from the look on your face that you didn't mean any harm." Mari motioned for Selah to follow her. "It's just that people look at the way we live and automatically assume we sit on logs all day drinking corn mash alcohol when our technology could rival what they have in the Mountain or TicCity."

Every once in a while Selah glanced around to see if any animals were following them as she traipsed through the forest, staying close to Mari. It was a very tall forest with wide trees. If she had to guess, they were thirty feet around and maybe 160 feet tall. True to her nature, more than once she got her hair snagged on a branch even though it was secured in a ponytail. Mari noticed her distress and pulled out a tiny mesh bag from her pocket.

"Here, use this. I brought it with me just in case it got windy."

Selah took it, spreading the loosely woven springy net between her fingers. "What do I do with it?"

Mari showed her how to wind up her ponytail in a little bun and put the mesh over it to secure it in place. "We will wait at my home for your friends to arrive before we go to the community lodge for the meal."

Selah could see around the huge trees for a distance into the woods but saw no houses or huts. Her spirits deflated. It was going to be a long walk to this community. "How long before we get there?"

"We're here." Mari laughed softly.

141

Selah glanced left and right, squinted, and planted both hands on her hips. "Where's here? There's nothing anywhere." She gestured around. "Oh no! Do you live underground?"

Mari chuckled. "No, up there." She pointed up.

Selah's gaze followed her finger up into the tree they stood beside. Her jaw went slack. A whole house, thirty feet in the air! With porch and railing all the way around, glass windows, and even little dormers set in separate sections of a neat wooden-shingled roof.

The base of the tree had grown from the ground up as three separate trunks, and the house nestled neatly in and around the growing tripod. A long straight tree pole, with steps winding up and around it like a bristle brush, provided entrance to the sky domain.

"What do you think?" Mari asked.

"I think I'm speechless for the first time in a very long time. This is built in the style wealthy families use in our Borough, but in a tree! I can't believe you live in a tree! My brother will go absolutely dog-eared over this."

Mari led the way up the circular stairs, showing Selah how to hold the pole as they rose. At the top they stepped onto the porch, and Mari led her around the outside of the house. "You can see for a good distance up here in the wintertime when all the leaves are gone, but the founding fathers added a lot of evergreens in the forest and at the perimeter of the colony to make it harder for outsiders to spot."

"How? Why? I would never in two lifetimes think of living in a tree." Selah followed Mari inside. The house was furnished and as comfortable as her family home, with a large living space, a kitchen and eating area, and two doors that she assumed led to a bedroom and toilet chamber.

"It was how they survived the flood 150 years ago."

"The flood? Oh, you mean the waves from the tsunami." Selah nodded.

"Yes, it's part of our history. The water washed away everything on the land. And the seas rose many feet. Only the people who managed to make it to the forest and climb trees survived the deluge." Mari motioned Selah to sit on a long cushioned seat against a wall.

Selah had never entertained the thought of people escaping the tsunami. She'd only had dreams of death and destruction, not survival. She made herself comfortable on furniture that felt like it was stuffed with goose down and asked, "But the trees back then couldn't have been as big as this, were they?"

"No. There weren't as many large ones as there are now. It's against the law to cut trees in this forest. We must travel many miles to bring back wood to build homes when necessary." Mari puttered in the kitchen area and returned with a plate of cheeses and meats cut in finger-sized chunks.

Selah looked at the meat. She really didn't want to eat coyote. "Can I ask what kind of meat that is?"

Mari looked down at it, a question enveloping her face. Then she brightened. "Oh, no, it's not coyote." She threw her head back and laughed. "This is the summer sausage my family is famous for. It's a mix of pork and venison seasoned with mustard seeds, pepper, salt, and sugar. We make it dried or smoked. The dried sausages last all winter, and we eat the smoked now."

Selah expelled her breath. "Now that I can deal with."

They ate and talked for about twenty minutes. It amazed Selah how easily they meshed, laughing at the same things and making the same gestures. She actually felt more comfortable with Mari than she did with Treva. The thought gave her a lump in her throat.

As they laughed at a story Mari told about a rambunctious squirrel that insisted on living inside the tree near her bedroom wall, a group of voices drifted up from the ground. Mari held up her hand for quiet. Selah tensed. Did they have problems with bandits here?

Mari went to the door and looked over the railing. "Welcome to my home. Come on up!" She motioned to her men. "See you at the evening meal. Thanks for bringing them. Take the wagon out to Raif and help him take the coyotes to old man Rumen. He'll think it's his birthday. He won't have to hunt all winter."

Selah rose from her comfortable seat, wishing she could rest here for days but feeling the urgency of her mission pulling through her weariness. One by one Treva, Cleon, and Jaenen poked their heads up over the porch, big smiles on their faces and wonder in their eyes.

"Can you believe this house! In a tree!" Cleon seemed beside himself with joy. He scampered about the porch, checking how the house was put together and what held each part in place. Running his hands across objects as though committing them to memory, he looked up from what appeared to be a pipe. "Water! How do you get water in and out of here?"

Mari smiled and pointed up. "Look near the top of the tree. There's a water collection tank up there. It's gravity-fed to here by those green pipes, and gravity-fed to the ground in the brown pipes. The brown pipes drain into tanks underground that lead the water away from the tree."

Cleon bolted around the outside to inspect all the applications.

Selah grinned at Mari. "Is this house strong enough for all of us, especially energy boy over there?"

Mari nodded. "No problems at all. We could have four or five others before I'd get concerned. This house is made to last through my lifetime and a few others."

"This is like a beautiful dream. Now my only problem is going to be convincing your brother to keep our marriage home on the ground," Treva said as she explored the inside and walked to the closed doors. Mari nodded her permission.

Selah didn't want to appear nosy, so she stayed in place even though her feet were itching to see the other rooms Treva explored.

She looked at Jaenen. He hadn't said a word since he came in. She tried to get his attention, but he seemed preoccupied in looking out the window on the side where Mari had said the colony stood. Cleon had suddenly become babble boy. He had a hundred questions for Mari about the construction of the house, and he wanted detailed explanations. Selah felt sorry for her but wasn't going to rescue her yet because something about Jaenen's manner concerned her.

She walked over and touched his shoulder. He tensed. She yanked back her hand.

"Is something the matter? You're awfully quiet. You didn't even say hello when you came upstairs," Selah said.

He turned. Either his eyelids had shrunk or his eyes were bulging as though something were pushing on them from inside his head.

Selah gasped and pulled back to a safer distance. What was happening here?

12

Bodhi moved away from the second-floor window and glanced around the small, cramped hotel room. The low light didn't hide the fact that the floors were grimy and the walls were dingy and scraped occasionally by narrow streaks that looked to be squashed bugs. He grimaced at the idea of sleeping here for the night, while—

"What's the matter?" Glade asked. "You've been acting angry since we arrived in Baltimore. Considering that was around seven and it's now almost midnight, I'd say whatever's bothering you hasn't gone away." He leaned back in his seat, and it telescoped into a reclining position.

Rapid weapon fire ricocheted off the outside corner of the stone building. Bodhi flinched, scrambling away from the window area. Raucous laughter and playful screams and giggles echoed between the buildings. A few more weapons went off, but this time maybe up in the air since Bodhi didn't hear an impact.

He pressed his mouth together, then bit his lip. The metallic taste told him to control himself. "This is beyond belief. Look at this place. This hotel isn't fit for barn animals to live in, let alone people."

Running in the hall. A frantic knock.

Bodhi opened the door and Taraji stormed in. "Are you both all right? I saw the weapons fire hit the building."

"It was the outside corner. Didn't come in here," Bodhi said.

"But it did move him out of window range." Glade smiled, remaining reclined.

Taraji looked relieved. "Celebrating absolutely nothing is the favorite pastime of people in this part of town. They do a lot of gambling and ingesting of drinks that dull the senses, and thus they think it's pure fun to shoot up buildings full of sleeping people." She frowned and shook her head.

Her attempt at sarcasm made Bodhi almost smile. At least smiling would help tamp down some of his negative emotions.

Glade moved his chair to an upright position. "That kind of society evolves when education and the principles of your people are forgotten."

Weapons cracked outside, and again the outside stone wall deflected the shots. Everyone flinched. Bodhi stormed over to the doorway near Taraji.

"Why is there a city ban on weapons and they take ours, but there's an army out there? Do you have backup downstairs with you?"

"Yes, from security." Taraji put her hand on her holstered weapon. "Why?"

"Well, I could say that I'd feel safer with you and a weapon here." Bodhi tipped his head to listen for another shot. "I'm listening to the shots and calculating their trajectory by the sound of deflection—"

"Whoa. Short version, please," Glade said.

"Someone is purposely standing in the same spot shooting, to create a sense of a random pattern."

Taraji nodded. "So that if a round entered this room, it could be deemed a revelry accident. I'm on it!" She scrambled out the door, and running footsteps faded into the distance.

"So stay away from the window and continue your answer," Glade said.

Bodhi looked back toward the window and grimaced. He moved to take a seat near Glade. "We were here three months ago, in the best part of town with Lander security. We even stayed in the Town Center building with Council members. And now we're relegated to this?"

"Get used to it," Glade said. "It looks like we may need to go into hiding if this trip to Stone Braide doesn't net workable results."

"This is insanity! Selah is to be protected and cherished. She's the future for us all."

Glade stared at him, not moving.

"What's wrong? Did I say something wrong?" Bodhi asked. "I don't care anymore. I just want to go home and protect Selah."

"I've never before heard this level of passion in your voice when you spoke about protecting my daughter." Glade nodded. "I believe you now."

Screams. Bodhi tensed. He heard laughter and then giggling screams. Glade lifted one corner of his mouth in a half smile.

"How come this isn't making you nervous?" Bodhi was jumping like a frog at every crazy sound. He wanted to know what Glade did to keep from reacting.

"This is strangely like the last eighteen years I spent in the Mountain. Nights of screams mixed with laughter, weapons fire, and all sorts of things that don't normally happen in civilized society."

"And there was no respect there for a novarium at all, not even from her own people?" Bodhi didn't remember being taught how or why novarium were important, but he knew it deep inside.

"It wasn't this bad before I went into the Mountain, but they were traveling this path, toward indifference and lack of respect. Now I'm jaded to it. As I said, the last eighteen years have changed me."

"You told me love ruined you, so which is it?" Bodhi had been looking for a way to get back to that conversation, and this seemed a good time.

Glade looked down, silent for a full minute. Bodhi feared speaking further. Had he crossed a boundary?

"My wife died giving birth to my daughter. I killed her," Glade said softly.

"What do you mean? Pasha isn't dead."

Glade lifted his head. His eyes appeared moist. "I was the ruler there from the beginning—"

"Ruler!" Bodhi laughed. "You mean like a king? Oh, this is bio-coin rich."

"They'd had their fill of *president* and *governor* and were looking for something that didn't have a bad connotation. *Ruler* won." Glade shrugged. "I didn't care."

"How did you get them to follow you so fast at the beginning?"

"I saved many of them from the tsunami flood in the Sorrows. They said I made a natural leader. Anyhow, I outlived two wives over the first ninety years. I loved both of them dearly and grieved deeply because neither union produced children."

"Did you do that 'remaining within the First Protocol' thing and only marry other First Protocol Landers?" Bodhi asked.

"Yes, sixty years ago I fell in love with the daughter of a second-generation Lander, of the First Protocol. As husband and wife, we ruled together for thirty years without a child and then she conceived. Despite a few reservations, it was pretty laughable that it took us so long."

Loud music blasted in the hallway. Glade and Bodhi flinched.

A loud knock at the door. "Hey, do you want to come and have a party with us?" a woman yelled above the sound of the music. Her tiny footsteps moved away.

Glade shook his head. Bodhi nodded. They both remained silent.

A loud pounding on the door. The frame rattled. "We're having a party. Bring your bio-coin and we can buy more drinks," a male voice yelled. He banged on the door harder.

Bodhi and Glade reached to unholster weapons that weren't there.

"Rolly, come on! The party's starting," the guy yelled. He banged on the door again.

Bodhi heard the woman return. "This isn't Rolly's door. He's the next one over there." Their footsteps faded away.

Bodhi sidled up to the window to watch them exit the building while Glade listened at the door to be sure they had left the floor.

Bodhi looked back at Glade. "So you and your wife had a baby?"

"The baby lived but my wife died. I listened to the medico." Glade's countenance fell. "I should have known better."

"Medico?"

"In this part of the country that's what they call a healer, a doctor type. Apparently before the flood, the medico's father had been the mayor. His family claimed the town as theirs, but the citizens hated their family. So granted, I did save the citizens from the flood, but I think they chose me as the leader just to spite the medico's family."

"So 120 years later, revenge is still the driving force for the medico's family? And this doctor gave you bad information?" Bodhi's pulse had quickened—either from the loud constant noise or from fear for Glade's other child.

Glade, visibly shaken, clutched at his chest and fingered a silver chain Bodhi hadn't noticed before. "They said my wife contracted a blood disease and she and the baby would die before the due date. The medico insisted on a treatment that I knew was wrong."

Bodhi shut his eyes and his voice softened. "What happened?"

"My wife delivered our daughter and died an hour later."

"I'm sorry for your wife. What happened to your daughter?"

"I devoted myself to her, but I couldn't take it. She looked exactly like her mother, even had the same mannerisms." Glade's voice choked.

Bodhi had never seen Glade vulnerable, and it unnerved him. He felt like he shouldn't be looking.

Pain etched itself on Glade's face. "The longer I was around my daughter, the more I wanted to end my existence. I missed my wife so much. So twenty years ago, when the pain became too great, I ran away and never went back."

"You left your daughter behind? Where is she? Is she still there?"

"Yes, she was nine at the time. It was better for her to stay at the colony. I will never interfere or contact her." He sighed. "She and Selah must never meet, for their own safety. And I mean life or death."

"I understand. Just the idea that the splinters might get an opportunity to capture your daughters would be enough to send them into a frenzy. The girls should never be together. Are you giving me a directive to keep this secret from Selah?"

"If you want to keep both my daughters out of danger, yes."

"When did Pasha come into the picture?"

"I met Pasha because she was my assignment. We did things a little differently back then. It was my job to make sure she met up with the Lander coming by sea who would transition her. But I fell in love with her."

"What does that mean? What happened to the Lander

from the sea?" Bodhi wondered who was supposed to have protected him when he arrived.

A series of shots rang out. All in the air. Bodhi didn't flinch this time. Were enemies lurking outside waiting for him to get used to the sounds and let his guard down?

Glade shook his head. "I loved her so much I couldn't stand losing her to the life of a novarium."

"You haven't told us about a novarium's life yet." Bodhi already knew Selah was special, but he believed that partly because he loved her so much.

"I would tell you if I knew."

"So how do you know what kind of life you'd have been losing her to, if you don't know what a novarium does?"

"The only thing I do know is a novarium has one year from the time of her transitioning to connect with the Third Protocol, or the novarium fractures—her brain and physical functions fall apart. I couldn't risk Pasha. We hadn't found the keys."

Novarium fractures. Novarium fractures. Bodhi felt a wave of guilt smothering him. If they didn't find the keys, it would be his fault that Selah would . . . He didn't want to even think that word again. "How much of this does Selah know? I can understand not telling her about your other family, but have you told her that her mom was a Lander child or that she was originally supposed to be transitioned also?"

"I choked. I couldn't explain how much I loved her mother without showing my vulnerability. So I lied. Selah thinks I'm a coward."

"So you're really not going to tell her she has a sister?

What do you think will happen later if, and I assume *when*, she finds out?"

"You know how she is. Nothing would stop her from finding her sister, and to have both of my children together . . ." Glade shook his head. "It would put both of their lives in danger of death or a lifetime of being imprisoned for experimentation. The splinters will stop at nothing to get biological samples from two of my children."

"But if Landers can sense each other, how does your daughter hide?"

"Like Pasha, who wasn't transitioned at eighteen, my daughter's gene also went dormant. I put a system in place that would thwart other Landers from finding her or the colony. And I found another effective way of using the same technology to upgrade the colony's security so it will serve them for many lifetimes." Glade sagged back in his seat. "An endless life can be very cruel."

Bodhi felt a lump rise in his throat. It had never occurred to him how many times Glade would have to bury loved ones. "What happened to Pasha's Lander from the sea?"

Glade dropped his head again, his shoulders slumping. "I led him to be captured by people hunting Landers. He fought them, and they killed him on the way to the Mountain where they were going to sell him."

Shots from a laser dart drilled through the window and struck the wall a foot to the right of Bodhi's shoulder, leaving a charred circle. Bodhi dove in Glade's direction. Another laser dart. This one burst into the room. The assailants were shooting from a building across the street.

Bodhi and Glade retreated to the far corner, where the steep angle to the window would restrict the size and strength of the beam if they were hit. A breath of quiet. A shot. It hit Bodhi across his right bicep like a sharp needle. He jerked away just as the door blew open and Taraji and two Baltimore security stormed the room.

They battled the splinters until a secondary security unit took over the fight at a closer distance.

Glade had both his hands pressed tightly over Bodhi's arm. Taraji stood by, dismissing the other two with her thanks.

Bodhi felt the fire in his arm receding. He watched Glade's face turn pale. He'd had that feeling himself with Selah's waif Amaryllis.

Glade released his arm. Other than a shirt with a burn design on the right sleeve, nothing looked out of place.

Glade looked at Bodhi and Taraji. "I'm afraid if we don't find answers at Stone Braide, we're going to have to take Selah into hiding. The splinters are worse than I've ever seen them."

"You've just never had this much invested with a novarium. They've all been this bad, and many were much worse," Taraji said.

Loud metallic music blasted from the horn on top of a passing SandRun. Bodhi remembered the SandRun sound from the first day he met Selah and saved her from being kidnapped by those hoodlums—

Their tattoos. Why didn't he remember that before?

A sword laced with a lightning bolt.

Splinters.

13

Selah moved farther away, trying to understand Jaenen's wild, bulging eyes. He clenched his jaw and crossed his arms tightly over his chest, exposing the tip of a lightning bolt on his arm. Her newly heightened reasoning ticked off scenarios that would produce this kind of crazed response from him. Nothing this horrifying came to mind. He had the least emotions of anyone she knew.

"We should not stay here. Something is wrong. I can't put my finger on it, but it's not good. I feel it." Jaenen clutched at his head. His eyes jerked across the landscape, looking, searching. But Selah couldn't tell for what.

She peered over the banister, trying to spot anything unusual. "Give me a clue, anything to go on. I haven't seen any signs to make me think we're in danger."

Jaenen lashed out. "We need to go. Now!" He pushed

past her, arms flailing. She stumbled back. His steps faltered, his legs turned wormy, and he fell facedown, unconscious.

Selah lifted his shoulder, turning his head. His eyelids lay partially open. His eyes—she screamed and let go.

Mari ran to her side. "What happened?"

Selah's whole body shook. Her eyes widened as she touched Mari for support. "I don't know. He just collapsed, ranting about something being wrong and we had to go. His eyes, they've turned white!"

Mari rolled him onto his back, checked his pulse, then used both her thumbs to raise his eyelids.

Selah's heart pounded against her ribs. No pupils, and both eyes had gone bloodshot in a matter of seconds.

Mari sat back on her haunches. "His eyes rolled up in his head, but he's got a strong pulse and is just unconscious. Has he eaten anything here in the forest today?"

Selah turned to Treva, who shook her head. "No, nothing. We were waiting for you and Cleon to come back. He had some water, but that was from our reclamation unit."

"Tell me about his eyes. Were they making sudden movements? Was he sweating?" Mari pulled down on his chin to open his mouth.

"No sweating." Selah stood up. "But his eyes darted around like a sand flea. That's when he collapsed."

"Oh, bugs and beetles!" Mari jumped to her feet and ran to a wooden panel near the front door. Loosening the latch, she swung the little door open, and a bizarre contrast of raw tree bark and high-tech electronics greeted her with several flashing lights. She pulled on a handle, turned a dial on the panel to the left, then returned the handle to its locked position. She shut the door and leaned back against it.

"He should be all right in a few seconds."

As she spoke, Jaenen's eyes fluttered open, clear of the milky whiteness. He sat up. "What happened? It felt like my head exploded."

"You scared the breath right out of me," Selah said, bending over him.

Treva and Cleon grabbed his arms to help him stand. Selah led him to the long seat against the wall. He sat blinking and stretching his eyes as he worked the muscles in his jaw. Selah had had the same need to relieve the pressure in her ears.

"Is your animal control affecting him like it did me?" Selah asked.

Mari nodded. "I'm afraid so. It's so unusual that two strangers in one day would be affected the same way."

Cleon joined them on the seat. "What kind of animal control would affect him like that?"

Mari pursed her lips. "Shortwave, high-frequency—it's an animal *deterrent* actually. We have the systems built into our homes in addition to carrying portable devices. Selah experienced activation of a portable device around the coyote kill area, and Jaenen just experienced the colony-wide home systems activating for the night."

Cleon opened his mouth, but Selah put her hand on his knee and shook her head. She knew his next question. "No, they don't share technology."

"Sadly, I understand." He nodded. "I often fear that the

technology in TicCity is going to fall into the wrong hands someday."

A loud vibrating hum drifted through the air, filling the room. Mari walked to the wall, picked up a handle attached by a wire, and spoke into it. Selah hadn't noticed the crude device hanging on the other side of the panel box, but she recalled that kind of communications from the history data glass. She could barely make out someone answering back.

Mari hung the device back on the wall. "We are being requested at the evening meal."

Six pinpoints of light blinked on, bathing the darkening room in a soft white glow.

"How'd you do that?" Selah glanced around at the tiny lights no bigger than her pinky nail.

"Night lighting is on a timer." Mari pointed. "Go out and look over the railing."

The four of them walked to the porch. Treva oohed and aahed. It looked as though the stars had descended to earth. All through the forest tiny lights brightened the path.

Jaenen frowned. "Isn't that dangerous? Won't outsiders find you faster with that level of illumination?"

"No, this is another shortwave development. The light doesn't carry that far. When you're out of range, you don't see them. Notice you can only see light for a short distance on the path. The lights are on all the way to the center of the colony, but shortwave doesn't travel that far."

"I like this place more and more every minute," Selah said. She finally admitted to herself the country was more to her liking than TicCity. She'd tried to live that city life, but it didn't give her the same peace she felt here. Maybe she should think of moving out of town near Cleon.

"Come, join us for the evening meal and meet our people." Mari led them down the stairs and along a winding stone path between trees. The sounds of another waterfall drifted closer. The tree house, lights, and waterfalls enchanted Selah like the memory of Mother's stories of fairies and wood sprites.

The path opened into a wide clearing with deeply trodden grass, stone seats, and what looked to be a wide stone well rising from the center of the clearing.

Cleon nudged her arm. She glanced at him and he pointed up. She turned and turned until she had taken in the complete circle. Her hand went to her mouth and she stared, mesmerized.

The colony square was more of a circle about two hundred feet in diameter. Ringing the circle were pairs of trees so huge Selah couldn't guess at their height or girth. She suddenly felt very tiny. If there had been a hundred people holding hands, they might not have reached around a pair.

Some tree pairs were connected at the base because they had encroached on each other's space a long time ago. And some had spaces between the two trees. But they all had one thing in common—the houses built against their trunks at random levels and with various designs. Stairs and walkways connected the houses and the trees. Each tree pair had between twenty and thirty homes dotting their sides, with new buildings under construction. The lowest house to the ground was still twenty feet high, and each had lights, adding a strange downward glow to the trees.

"How does something like this happen?" Selah stared in awe. "I've never seen . . . I keep saying that, but it's true! What manner of trees are these?"

Mari shrugged. "They're just plain old hemlock trees, and I mean the old part literally. The ones in this circle are the only remaining trees of the forest that saved our people from the deluge. The tsunami 150 years ago carved out a C-shaped piece of land with these trees in the center, and the accompanying earthquake heaved the land behind, turning soft hills into big hills. We are naturally protected on three—"

An arrow zipped by them. Selah concentrated on the next approaching sound and pushed Cleon away from the trajectory. The arrow thunked into the ground to the right of them. Another followed closely behind, clipping Selah in the left arm. Instant slicing pain. She cried out and grabbed her arm. Blood oozed between her fingers and ran to her wrist. Treva and Jaenen dove to the ground and pulled her down.

Selah winced in pain. Strangely, the only sound she heard was a waterfall crashing to the rocks and children's voices.

Mari stood her ground. "Whoever is doing this, you are disrespecting *my* guests. Do you hear me! *My guests.*" Anger filled her once calm voice.

"They're the danger the fathers foretold. Letting them come here will bring death for our disobedience," a voice yelled, echoing in the circle.

"Jaris, I know your voice. I've heard it every day of my life since I can remember. The full weight of the realm is going to land on your head for this disrespect."

"Get down!" Selah pulled at Mari's arm, trailing a bloody

streak from her hand down the arm of the woman's buckskin shirt. With no real cover, the only option was running from the circle and creating an even bigger target.

"You're disrespecting the will of the forefathers," Jaris yelled. He was busier talking than aiming as he fired another arrow, and it missed its target.

Mari wrested her arm free from Selah's grip and straightened her shirt. "I am not. I am regent." She tapped a few keys on her wristband. "Everyone has their individual fletching on arrows." She reached over and snatched up the three arrows from where they had found purchase in the dirt and waved them at the tree colony in front of her. "I will find you! You can't hide from me, Jaris."

Three of Mari's men came running across the landing and down the stairs on the pair of trees closest to them. They hurried over to her. She thrust the arrows into the first man's hand.

Selah could see the raging anger on Mari's face. She wanted to tell her to just let him be. They'd be leaving in the morning, and these people had a right to their superstitions. Besides, she could feel the wound healing, though she couldn't tell Mari how easily her body had begun healing itself in the last couple of months.

Splash! Selah glanced around. Where did the sound come from?

The man looked at the arrows, examining the feathers on the ends. "These two belong to Jaris, and this to Dumas," he said as he held up the arrows.

"As I thought. Bring them to my colony chamber." Mari moved to Selah's side.

Selah kept her hand over the torn sleeve to hide the fact that her arm was no longer bleeding.

Splash! Screaming. "Help!"

Selah's head snapped in the direction of the sound. "Someone's in trouble."

"Where?" Mari glanced around the circle, empty except for them.

Cleon dusted himself off. "I don't hear anything."

Treva and Jaenen glanced around, looking up at the tree homes.

"Help!"

Selah gasped at the suffocation. Someone was drowning. Her heart pumped harder. She pushed past the four of them and sprinted for the sound of the waterfall on the other side of the far trees. The others rushed behind her.

The closer she got, the more she smelled salt water. Chills mixed with her sweat.

She skidded into the clearing at the base of the pool below the waterfall. Off to the right a girl flailed in the water, while above her a boy and another girl tried to maintain a grip on moss-covered rocks as they edged their way over to the trees and safety.

"Is someone going to save her?" Selah yelled to Mari over the sound of rushing water. Her heart flip-flopped. The sea was the source of this waterfall. She paced back and forth, waiting for someone to jump in, and wrung her hands. There couldn't be sea monsters in a pool. Could there? *Somebody jump in, please!*

Mari shook her head. "No one here swims. We haven't

since the Sorrows. The sea is a curse. The children know that."

"So you're going to let her drown?" Selah's breath came in short, jagged gulps. She hated salt water. She couldn't do it. Why did it seem to be chasing her? *Somebody, please!*

"It happens on occasion." Mari's face displayed resignation. "That girl's father is the one who shot you. I'd think you'd be less than charitable."

Panic seemed to overwhelm Selah. She went toward the water, then backed up, then went forward again.

Treva, having lived her life inside the Mountain, didn't swim, but Cleon and Jaenen scrambled to get their boots off. Cleon wasn't a strong swimmer, and Selah could see how a fighting girl could pull him under.

She touched Jaenen's shoulder on the way to the water. "You shouldn't be in the water so soon after that seizure. I'll do it."

Jaenen looked concerned. He grabbed her arm. "Are you sure? You were just shot and you panicked when we passed over salt water."

A gurgling scream was drowned out by water. The child slipped below the surface.

Selah wrenched free. "I have to. There's no one else, and I don't care about her father. She's a child." Selah ran to the edge, slipped off her leather boots, took a couple of deep breaths, and jumped into the pool opposite the base of the waterfall. Ice-cold water greeted her like a slap in the face, freezing her muscles and turning them into instant sludge. She gasped and swallowed a mouthful of salt water.

Coughing, she swept the hair from her eyes and gained her bearings.

The child's flailing arms beat at the surface to her left. She gurgled and slipped under the water again. Her body went limp and floated to the surface facedown. Selah's powerful strokes brought her in range in a matter of seconds. She grabbed the child, flipped her over. No time to start her breathing there.

Selah wasn't sure how long she could force herself to stay calm in the water as the fear closed in on her and tightened her throat. She struggled for air. Her fear was irrational—there were no creatures with large teeth waiting to rip her to shreds. She labored to breathe and pull the girl to shore by the back of her tunic.

Cleon reached for the child while Jaenen reached down, grabbed Selah's arm, and yanked her up. On hands and knees, she crawled along the grass, dry heaving once or twice and spitting out salt water. Falling to the ground and rolling on her back, Selah inhaled deeply. Still salty air, but she'd made it. Had she conquered the fear for good? Only time would tell.

Cleon pumped on the child's chest while Treva blew into her lungs. Finally she regurgitated a spray of water, gasped for air, and began to cry.

Mari punched a few buttons on her wristband, spoke, and then looked down at Selah.

Jaenen helped Selah to her feet. "You're shivering enough to break a tooth. I don't have a coat, but I've got arms. Let me warm you." He wrapped his arms around her, trying to ward off the shivers wracking her body.

Selah was grateful. Her teeth clacked so hard it was making her ears hurt. Between tremors she leaned into Jaenen's warmth and watched Mari standing there, staring at her.

"Why are you looking at me like that?" Selah asked through chattering teeth.

"I'm trying to figure out what and who you are." Mari came closer and examined the tear from the arrow in Selah's shirt. Selah looked down at it. Blood had saturated the tear earlier, but the water had cleaned the material.

Selah's arms and legs felt as weak as dandelion stalks. She just didn't have enough extra energy to lie. She tried to wrap her hand over the spot, but Mari gently moved her hand away.

"You aren't bleeding anymore," Mari said, fingering the material.

Selah gave a nervous half smile. "It was just a scratch. I'll be fine."

"It bled, yet there's no torn skin, or even a mark that there was bleeding." Mari looked from the sleeve into Selah's eyes. "Who are you?"

Selah pushed the wet hair back from her face. "I'm just a traveler trying to get to the Mountain."

Colony people began to gather at the water's edge.

Mari let out a sigh. "I think we'd better forgo a community meal. I'm having my men bring dinner to my place. You need dry clothes, and I'd like to get you out of my colony before something else happens."

Selah nodded with a teeth-chattering smile. "At least we broke that curse and no one died."

Mari motioned for them to follow her back to her home. "You haven't left yet."

167

14

Day 2

Selah disliked saying goodbye to Mari. They'd gotten along like sisters. It would have been nice if Mari lived closer or traveled more, but she didn't. So much for another friendship.

Now Selah had a new dilemma. Since they'd left Wood-Haven, Treva had not been acting like her normal bubbly self.

Selah touched her shoulder. "Did you eat something that didn't agree with you?" She worried that maybe something about WoodHaven's security system could be having a latent effect on her.

"No, though I did have more of that crusty bread and apple slices dipped in honey before we left," Treva said without turning. "Why do you ask?"

"You seem unusually quiet. We've been on the road for almost four hours and you haven't complained about anything."

Treva had a penchant for an orderly world, but it just didn't work that way outside the Mountain. So she dealt with a constant source of things that could be organized better if they were done her way.

"Do you think Mari will ever wind up being queen or whatever term they use for their ruler?" Treva wrinkled her nose when she spoke Mari's name, and Selah caught the subconscious action.

"I think Mari's happy being regent. She still expects her father to return someday. Why?"

"I was just wondering what kind of governing structure Uncle Charles is using in Stone Braide."

Selah smiled. "Are you expecting to be crowned or something?"

"It never hurts to explore a girl's options. I could be great at—"

"Get to exploring those options, because we're here," Cleon announced.

Selah and Treva turned to look ahead. Several buildings in the process of being plotted by a massive 3-D printing press swung into view as he made the turn, but all was idle. Stone Braide looked abandoned. Cleon cycled over a stone slab and brought the AirWagon down to rest.

Both girls stepped down. Jaenen and Cleon opened the side panels and retrieved their weapons.

"Where is everyone?" Cleon hopped down with his crossbow. "I don't like the looks of this. You girls stay near the AirWagon."

Jaenen strapped on the sling for his crossbow and mounted it across his back. He gathered up his things, stowing gear in his pack, seemingly uninterested in the lack of activity where there should have been a community. Selah started to say something about his indifference but figured he'd take it as additional hostility over his assessment of the Repository file. It had degraded further and erased the evidence she'd found, so he declared it insufficient to mount any kind of search.

"I'm sure it's fine. Uncle Charles must be here somewhere. Maybe they're on a break or something. Selah, will you help me look?" Treva asked as she walked away.

"No, I don't think so," Cleon said. "There's dust all over those machines. They haven't cycled in quite some time. Treva, come back here and wait." He nocked an arrow into his bow.

Treva waved him off and continued to walk, peeking in the empty shell of each partially constructed building.

Jaenen glanced at the barren countryside, then shrugged. "Looks like everybody got smart and went back inside the Mountain. I consider that a good call. It's pretty desolate out here."

"It didn't look like this the last time we were here." Selah, eyes wide with amazement, took in the desolate landscape. "There were a lot of trees and bushes, and the surrounding hillsides were like forests. And grass . . . all of this was covered in grass. What happened here?"

Cleon wandered over to what appeared to have once been a tree stump but now sat bleached and petrified. "If I didn't know better, I'd say this tree suffered an extended pulse blast. I remember trees looking like this when our Borough brought in that Mountain security team."

Selah nodded. "They dealt with those bandits squatting

on the homestead outside Dominion. But why would all of this land be destroyed?"

Jaenen touched her arm. "It's been a very interesting trip, but I need to meet with my caravan up the road a piece. I'm already late and I don't want them to leave without me," he said.

Selah's eyes narrowed. "But why? You can't leave—"

"I told you. That file you have is too corrupt to get more from it. I'm sorry, but it's not enough to derail the solid lead I have on your family. There must be a good explanation for your stepfather's and Everling's names being there. Or maybe the file was so corrupt that it just appeared to be their names. In any case, that's a lead for another day. You mind yourself and stay out of the Mountain." Jaenen pulled on his leather gloves and wound the pack strap around his hand before hoisting it onto his shoulder.

Selah frowned. "I won't go in the Mountain . . ."

Jaenen nodded to Selah and waved to Cleon and Treva.

She watched him walk around the bend and out of view. ". . . Until you've gone on down the road to your caravan." Something about the way he acted nagged at her. Not only had he exhibited no real interest in the file, but this scene of utter devastation aroused no curiosity in him. Should she worry that the seizure episode at WoodHaven had done some kind of brain waste on him?

"Hey you guys, come see this!" Cleon yelled. Selah and Treva trotted over.

He stood near a cream-and-tan-hued building that looked to be one of the few structures in the settlement made from actual stone. The charred interior of the empty shell had scorched tendrils snaking out of empty holes that appeared to have been poly-laminate windowpanes but were now solidified blobs at the base of the openings.

Treva gasped. A strangled sob pushed from her chest. "What could have happened here? Where's Uncle Charles?"

"This building was occupied." Selah slowed as she entered. The ash formations were consistent with furniture being instantly incinerated. A flashback to the cell where she thought Glade had died in the Mountain played in her mind. She instantly looked for telltale signs of bodies.

"This is what I wanted you to see." Cleon motioned them outside. Off to the right of the building were several white charred sticks and a blackish residue splattered on the wall of the one-story structure.

"That's dried blood. Someone died here." Selah squeezed her eyes shut. *Please don't let it be Treva's uncle.*

"The bandit hideout," Selah and Cleon said at the same time.

Treva looked between the two of them with tears running down her cheeks. "Are you saying bandits did this? That my uncle Charles may be dead?"

Selah shook her head, hands on hips. "No, we're saying this is the mark of the Mountain security private force that gets hired out to quell Borough problems. This is what their scene cleanup looks like. They don't carry away their victims."

"They incinerate them." Cleon bowed his head, as though paying respects to whoever died here.

"Why would they—" Treva stopped. A look of horror

crossed her face. "Do you think they made the connection to us and arrested him? Could he have tried to fight back?"

"Whoa, wait. We don't know anything yet. Stop making assumptions," Cleon said.

Selah noticed a flash in her peripheral vision. She turned to the left. In the distance sat a now barren hillside with all the grass dried to crispy sticks. The dried pines reminded her of the bristle brushes Mother had made to clean her precious canning jars.

She pointed in the direction she wanted to go. Cleon nodded but Treva started to question. Selah raised a finger to her lips. Treva brushed away the tears and followed her.

Selah crept up to the opening. It appeared to be a cave carved into the hillside. At one time, the now dead trees had camouflaged the entrance. Now it was quite noticeable from a distance. As she approached, a figure peeked out, then ducked back inside. All she caught sight of was a multicolored, flowing fabric on an unkempt, white-haired old man.

"Stop! Wait!" Selah darted to the opening and grabbed the man's arm.

He rapidly slapped her hands away. She grabbed faster than he could slap.

"Let me go. Let me go. I'm no good to you. I don't know anything. I'm an old man." He tried to squirm from her grasp.

Treva and Cleon caught up, but neither approached.

"Could I get some help here?" Selah inhaled his musty odor and wondered if the old guy could have some sickness because of how dirty he appeared.

Cleon grimaced. "I think you have it under control, Sissy."

"I think I know him." Treva moved closer. "Are you the man who used to take Wednesday evening meals with Charles Ganston and the Gilani family?"

The old man stopped struggling and displayed a toothless grin. "Yes, that would be me. And who might you be, young lady?"

"I'm Charles Ganston's niece, Treva Gilani."

The old man gasped. Both hands went to his mouth and his fingers began to shake. He reached out and took Treva's hand in both of his. "My sweet princess." He touched the back of her hand to his forehead.

Treva turned red and stared at Cleon and Selah with eyes wide, shaking her head slowly. Her mouth formed the words *I have no idea*.

Selah shrugged. She hadn't observed the old man enough to know if he had a full orchard or whether his fruit lay rotting on the ground. Only watching him would tell. Maybe he meant *princess* as a term of endearment.

"Why would you call me that?" Treva didn't pull completely away but discreetly removed her hand from the man's ratty-haired forehead.

The old man looked as though she had spoken gibberish. His eyes blinked rapidly. "Because you are the heir, of course. Your parents were the Keepers of the Stone. Your uncle took over when they died. Didn't he ever tell you any of this?"

Treva shook her head. "Keepers of what stone, and where did you hear such a silly story?"

"Are you talking about that Stone Braide symbol he was going to use for the main building?" Selah pointed toward where she had watched her father trace his fingers over the object he called a remnant of a very sad time—a circle superimposed over the three entwined narrow pointed ovals.

"Yes, yes, that is the one." The old man smiled his toothless grin at Treva. "Once it was unearthed we were sure it would be just a matter of time. I hear tell there's even a novarium."

Selah's eyes darted from Treva to Cleon. Should she say something? Both shook their heads. She should keep it quiet for now. Still, if the little old man from nowhere knew there was a novarium, letting him know it was her didn't seem wrong or hazardous.

"Not that I don't believe you, but I need to talk to my uncle first. What would be 'just a matter of time'?" Treva bit her lip.

"Finding the clues to unlocking the secret of the Third Protocol, which is necessary for completing a full cycle," the old man said matter-of-factly.

Selah ran the words through her head. A shudder jerked her arms. If he knew of the Protocols . . . Who was this old man?

Treva stepped forward. "Completing a—"

Selah grabbed Treva's arm, then shook her head. She would tell her later about Glade's discussion, but not in front of a stranger, no matter how much he knew on his own. *Use what you are given, volunteer no information.* Words of her mother. In what context had that been a lesson? Selah couldn't recall.

Treva's breathing grew shallow. Her brow pinched as she looked from the old man to Selah. "Those data packages I gave to Glade. They must have been the clues. Even so, my uncle never told me anything about my parents, except that they were murdered. Why am I learning about this from some old man?"

"Charles told me you knew the whole story of your parents, and that he gave you the clues when you left the Mountain with the novarium and her father, Glade."

She turned back to the old man. "If this is true, why was Uncle Charles giving me stupid clues instead of just coming out and telling me?"

"He will have to tell the story of your parents. I only know pieces. But I do know Charles was trying to save you from the evil," the old man said. "The clues had to be masked so only the worthy could unfold them."

Selah looked closer at the old man. He was suddenly speaking a little strange, even for an old guy. His language choices sounded like ancient dialogue, not normal words.

"What are the clues for anyhow? I should have read all the pages in that packet before I gave it to Glade." Treva wrung her hands.

"If I remember correctly, you didn't read *any* of them." Cleon looked at the old man. "Maybe she's not the worthy one."

"I've got to find my uncle." Treva turned toward the buildings.

"They dragged him away," the old man said.

"Away? Where did they take him?" Treva's legs seemed to go weak. She clutched Selah's arm for support. And Selah knew in the pit of her stomach right where Charles Ganston had been taken. All she could hope for was Mojica. She'd had an allegiance to Ganston—hopefully it had survived.

The old man bobbed his head a few times, rubbed a hand across his chin, and stared off into the sky. "Back to the

Mountain. It will always keep going 'round, till the Keeper of the Stone brings it down." He turned his head to look at Treva. "Yes, it will just keep going 'round."

Selah told Cleon to watch the old man and pulled Treva off to the side. "Listen, I'm not sure what's going on here, but that old guy isn't playing with all his straws. He's talking a little crazy. Maybe his perception of what happened to your uncle is a little skewed. We can't storm in there until we know what's going on. We have to play it close to the vest. I think our best bet is to try to locate Mojica. She'd know about your uncle."

Treva sucked in a deep breath. "I know you're right, but what if—"

"We don't have time for *what-ifs*. We have to find Mojica, to find your uncle, to understand the rest of the old man's babble." Even though Selah worried about Charles Ganston's safety, she worried more about Bethany Everling. That crazy scientist would be the only person concerned with anyone in this group.

With Treva's help, Glade had pulled together a sinister picture of the barbaric and evil experiments Bethany and her husband, Noah, had performed on a captive Lander population. Selah would always hold it against her that she tried to have Selah's transport shot out of the air as they escaped the Mountain the last time. Not a good start. But she wanted to search for more information on her parents. Helping Treva presented the opportunity but was probably dangerous.

"I guess that means you're coming?" Treva looked unsure of whether to agree. Selah knew her reluctance centered on her fear of being chastised by Glade should something happen to Selah.

"Do you want to consider how much trouble I could get into if forced to stay here to my own devices?"

Treva shook her head. "I've already shuddered enough for a lifetime—don't make me start a second time around." She turned and motioned Cleon over. "Did you get anything else out of him? Is there another way to find the clues? What will they accomplish, in words I can understand?"

"Just, 'Only they who understand can read the clues. To the rest it is nonsense.'" Cleon hunched his shoulders and released them with a huff. "I don't have *any* idea what that means."

"It's five miles to the Mountain. It should take us ten minutes," Treva said.

"What do we do with him?" Cleon hiked a thumb over his shoulder.

Selah stared at the old man for a few seconds. "We can check on him on our way back. He's survived without help all this time, so I don't think he needs any now. He was as strong as a piglet when I tried to corral him. And I think if we tried to take him, he'd make us regret it."

"I wasn't prepared to let you talk me into going back in there. I thought you were just going to sneak in and get some papers," Cleon said to Treva.

She looked down at her hands, then back at him. "I didn't plan on my uncle being missing. I've been supportive of your family being gone, and I just assumed you'd feel the same about mine. Was I wrong?"

Cleon lifted her chin with his hand and gently brushed his lips across hers. "Wherever you go, I go."

The love between them warmed Selah's heart. Treva was the medicine Cleon needed to heal from the guilt he still felt about causing their brother's death. Treva's patience was returning his joy for life.

Cleon gestured toward the AirWagon and the three of them piled in. He turned it toward the hillside and followed Treva's directions.

Selah rode silently for five minutes, thinking of possible ways to gather information about her family. It had been her suggestion, and now she hoped they'd be able to find Mojica. She'd give them the advantage of a powerful Mountain ally.

"Whoa! I never knew this was back here." Cleon reduced speed and stared ahead.

Selah unwound herself from her thoughts. The Mountain range on this side looked nothing like the austere, unfriendly range facing the southern, populated part of the country. Two waterfalls, spilling from dizzying heights of the Mountain, fed the lush vegetation on the north-facing slope with the enormous mist fanning out to spray the range.

"I'm falling in love with waterfalls," Selah said. Another strange sensation of peace washed over her. She shook off the shiver rolling from the back of her head and down and out her extremities.

Treva pointed. "Those are what we have to watch out for." JetTrans landed on a platform connected to the front of a circular building that telescoped from the Mountain and came to rest on a natural peak jutting up from the mountain range floor.

"How do we get in?" Selah rubbed her hands on her pants. She was sweating just being this close to the Mountain, but she had become wiser and stronger since the last encounter, thanks to Taraji.

"Cleon, bring us down near the other AirWagons." Treva pointed to an area littered with all manner of transportation, from wagons pulled by horses to SandRuns, like at home. Cleon set down near other air vehicles.

"Now I understand the fence on the front of the Mountain. It keeps locals from knowing about this area. I don't get it. What are these for?" Selah glanced at the assortment of vehicles.

Treva chuckled and hopped down. "You didn't think everyone lives a sterile life inside the Mountain, did you? Many people spend a lot of time outside. This is where they store personal transportation since Mountain law doesn't permit them to bring the vehicles inside. The old law says they could carry some strange, hidden contamination." Treva started toward a large set of doors. "Regardless of the fact that most everyone buys and eats food from the outside, along with any other product they so desire."

"So what's the plan?" Selah asked as she and Cleon caught up to Treva. "How do we find Mojica?"

"I figured we'd get my files first, in case anything goes wrong early," Treva said. "At least then we'd get out with something important. Then to Uncle Charles's office as if nothing is wrong. Like I said before, since I had no friends my age and I'd just started at Everling's lab, there was only Uncle Charles to miss me. So I don't know if anyone noticed I was even gone. If not, that gives us another advantage."

They approached the set of heavy metal doors. She turned to face them. "Follow me in and don't talk to anyone. Just act like you're average citizens coming home from the Wilds."

"The Wilds?" Cleon looked disgusted. "Is that what they call where we normal people live? Figures. They were always so nose-up when we came here with Father to trade. But then they would overwhelm him with their demands to buy Mother's textiles."

Selah could understand both sides. How each was taught, and thus the way they grew up.

"Don't get upset. You have to pass for a citizen. Being all red in the face is going to garner a closer look. They may think you're smuggling contraband. Calm down." Treva rubbed his arm.

Selah looked closely. Was he smiling?

"So this is your plan?" she whispered. "It's not much of a plan. I thought—"

"You thought what?" Treva stopped before the opening. "This is the best we've got. Just walk in and take our chances. Anything actually subversive would take too much planning, and we need answers now."

Treva turned and trotted through the doors with Selah and Cleon close behind. They passed a couple groups of people on the way in and then approached the security zone. Treva turned her head away from the station and walked by. Selah passed next, then Cleon.

"Halt there," came the voice of the security guard.

15

Selah and Treva slowly turned to face Cleon. He'd stopped right where he was. His face went crimson, and he looked like he was ready to panic and run. Selah gave him the eye to calm down, give them a chance to help.

The guard strolled over to Cleon. "How are you today, citizen?"

"Fine," Cleon answered, trying to keep his voice calm. Selah started to ask Treva whether there was some pat response to a greeting here that they should know, but the guard continued.

"And I'm sure you know the rules by now, right?" The guard smirked.

Selah couldn't read his expression, but she figured he must think Cleon lived there or he wouldn't have phrased the question like that. She decided to gamble. Deep breath.

She scurried over to Cleon playfully. "Of course he knows the rules. Which one do you want me to impress upon him?"

She batted her eyelashes at the guard. For a moment he seemed more interested in Selah than Cleon, but he quickly regained his composure.

The guard pointed down. "He needs to clean his shoes on the bio-remover so he doesn't bring that contaminant inside."

Selah looked down at the clump of weeds caught in the tread of Cleon's boots. He was dragging it behind him. She looked at the guard. "All men need a mother figure now and then to keep them on track." She pushed Cleon toward the bio-remover near the doors and stepped on the weed to disconnect it from his shoe. Her heart slowed its staccato beat and she wondered if her ribs would hurt tomorrow.

⬩

Selah and Treva rushed Cleon down several halls and through a few corridors before Treva stopped to lean against a wall and catch her breath. Selah didn't even feel winded yet. Lately, her body seemed to ache for exercise.

"We did it. I can't believe we made it in here with no problem," Treva said.

Selah's mouth opened. "Are you telling me you didn't think it would work? That we could have gotten caught?" Suddenly she didn't feel a little brave, she felt a lot brave. They'd done it. First time around. *Please let this work.*

"I wasn't sure. They're only trained to look—"

"Save the explanations for later. Let's get what we need and get out of here. I'm getting a bad feeling about this again." Cleon's upper lip formed droplets of sweat. "Easiest to hardest is the order of the day. Let's move it."

"Easiest are my files. This way to my quarters. If our luck holds, my access will still work." Treva hurried down the hall and around numerous turns.

All the corridors were the same. Slightly different shades of pastels, but all the same size, the same bareness, and very few people. Where were all the people? Selah remembered the directions for the first few turns but quickly gave up. Directions in the woods were easier to remember than bundles of nondescript halls. But she was certain Treva would be there to lead them out. Her logic may not have been sound, but it was the only thing she had at the moment.

The last corridor led to Treva's quarters. Treva reached for the door but pulled back her hand.

"What's wrong now? These are your quarters, right?" Selah asked while searching for an occupant plate.

"Yes, but what if they've been given to someone else and the code is changed? I could set off the alarm for this whole section."

"This is not the time to worry. Code in your access and let's get inside or start running. Those are our only two options," Cleon said. He shifted from foot to foot and peered around the corner of the next hallway. Selah knew from experience that his nervousness would keep him alert. He'd be a huge asset to their safety.

Treva shut her eyes briefly, then gnawed on her lip. She coded her access and laid her palm to the door panel. Selah would later remember this as the three of them waited, primed and ready to sprint down the hall. They tensed for the shrill alert of the warning horn.

The lock hummed and the door swooshed open. Cleon let out a huge breath and rested his head against the door frame, motioning them in. "We've got the grease."

Selah smiled, even as nervous as she was. It had been quite awhile since she'd heard him make mechanical references like he and their brother Raza used to.

Treva marched through the quarters with Selah following. Cleon remained near the door as security. Selah marveled at how neat and orderly the quarters were. It did lend credence to Treva's assertion she'd always had compulsive, orderly behavior. Selah noticed a row of long-dead potted plants. Each were in the same size pot on the same size saucer, and they were the same distance from each other and from the edge of the sun shelf. Selah fought the urge to move a couple just to see if Treva would notice.

She strolled into Treva's bedroom. That was why Cleon wouldn't come back here. He knew it was her bedroom. His gentlemanly qualities were sometimes a pleasant surprise.

Treva had swung open a bookcase unit to expose a doorway and a hidden room. Selah stepped into the long room. "Okay, how is something like this hidden in the Mountain?"

Treva gathered up data glasses and a few halo-tablets, stuffing them into a pouch slung over her back. "When I walked in here just now, it became clear to me I've had the clues all my life, but they were just normal circumstances to me. How many other kids have a secret room in their bedroom? I bet none." She shook her head.

"Now that you're tuned to it, what else in your life felt normal but there was no reason for it?" Selah wondered how many of those instances she had missed in her own life in Dominion. Many small things she'd found odd about her mother's teachings were becoming meaningful, like learning about computers when no one used them in Dominion, or the survival techniques that had come in so handy.

Treva spun, glancing around the room. Her face brightened. She rushed to a narrow cabinet at the back wall and carefully slid open the second drawer from the top. "This was a special present from my father when I was little. He taught me a poem to go with it. He wouldn't let me have it until I could recite the poem from memory." Treva held out a necklace. On the end dangled a triangular shape, with the point bent outward at the bottom. The pendant held an ivory insert. Selah recognized it because an antique shoehorn her mother owned had a handle made of ivory. She watched as the triangle spun back and forth on the chain. The golden-colored metal seemed to glow in the bright light of the room.

"I hear people coming down the hall. It sounds like more than one," Cleon called in a stage whisper.

Treva crammed the necklace in her pocket and they scrambled out of the room. The two of them leaned into the swinging bookcase to push it back into place. Treva directed them out a back door into another corridor.

"I didn't wait to see if they were coming to your place," Cleon said. "If they were just passing by, we'd have been safe to head back the other way. I recognized that last turn. It led to where we met your uncle before."

Selah lowered her head and let out a sigh. She'd been hoping to get a connection to Mojica next. If anyone knew whether her family was in the Mountain, Mojica would be the one.

"We can take a shortcut through this section." Treva turned right and trotted to the corner. Footsteps sounded. She peeked around the corner and hurried back to their position, motioning them faster down the hall in the other direction. "There's a two-man patrol coming this way."

They darted to the corner, skidding to a stop at the echo of more approaching feet. Selah's adrenaline pumped hard, trying to scramble her thoughts, but she pushed the feeling away and pointed to the corridor they'd originally exited. "Back to Treva's apartment."

She scrambled to the doorway and slapped the entrance button like she'd seen Treva do. It asked for a handprint. She turned to make sure Treva and Cleon were catching up. When she pivoted back to the doorway, it had opened from the inside and two pulse disruptor weapons were aimed at the center of her chest. She glanced down at the green and blue laser dots bobbing over her heart and yelped.

Cleon and Treva ran into her from behind. The momentum left the three of them sprawled at the feet of the two guards holding weapons. A third pair of shiny heeled boots walked into view. Selah looked up.

The woman stared down at her. "Did you really think with the technology at my disposal you'd get back in this Mountain without me knowing about it?"

Even though the woman acted like she knew her, Selah didn't recognize her. The only person she knew inside was Mojica, and this blonde, middle-aged woman with pale green eyes certainly wasn't her. The guards backed away at the woman's hand gesture, allowing the three of them to scramble from the floor. With Cleon standing in the center, the weapons found their marks on Selah and Treva. Selah was sure the woman had been talking to her, but Treva answered as though the statements were meant for herself, playing it as though she'd done nothing wrong.

"Dr. Everling, I'm not sure I understand your need to have weapons trained on my chest."

Selah marveled at the calm demeanor Treva presented. Not a tremble to her words, complete confidence. But would it be enough to bluff a move with this woman? The name Everling brought a chilled tremble to Selah's back even though sweat ran down the sides of her neck. This was the woman from the experiments on Landers. Every part of her wanted to scream at this woman's evil, but she had to remain calm if they were to get out of here.

"Oh please, Treva. Do you think I haven't noticed you haven't reported to work in months or picked up any of your compensation? Or"—Bethany Everling lowered her chin with a half smile on her lips—"come to see your uncle on his deathbed?"

Treva stumbled back. Cleon caught her and held her upright. "What have you done to Uncle Charles? He was fine until you dragged him back here."

"So you were in that preposterous community of his? I just don't see the lure of that dirty, uncivilized world."

"No, I wasn't in Stone Braide, but I'm sure you already know that. We saw the destruction." Treva spit out the words.

"I don't know what you could be talking about. Must have been bandits. They can be so barbaric."

Selah watched the woman's body-speak. Deception. One of the first exercises for Krav Maga that Selah had rated highly in was reading body-speak. Her mouth went dry. It had been different interpreting the movements when there were no distractions like emotions to color her judgment.

"Your uncle was fine when he came back inside for a meeting. It was during the preliminary settings that he had a massive stroke. I'm so happy you're here. People have been asking about you." Bethany's smile showed perfect teeth, her voice dripping with sweetness.

"Take me to him now!" Treva's voice rose to the tenor of a command.

Selah hadn't been prepared for such a forceful display from the always mild and calm Treva. And the Everling woman's reaction! Maybe she read Bethany wrong, but she actually seemed sorry for Charles. But was she sorry for his condition or that he was still alive?

Bethany put her hands on her hips. "I'm more than certain you know where the hospital unit is located. You should probably go see him while there is still time. The guards will accompany you there, and later we'll discuss why you returned here and brought these people."

"I want them to come with me," Treva said as the guards tried to separate her from the others. "They know my uncle. They want to see him too."

Selah and Cleon nodded.

The woman relented and directed the guards to take the

three. She went off in another direction, her heels tapping out a strong gait.

Selah's insides were screaming to run, but there was no place to go that didn't include getting shot with a pulse disruptor. The woman appeared harmless enough. Her bodyspeak was still deceptive, but it didn't appear aggressive. Concern for strangers in her facility was warranted. The next question would come if she checked their identities in the system.

At the moment, coming into the Mountain seemed like the stupidest plan in the world. But it was too late for regrets now. With Treva occupied with a dying uncle, it was up to Selah to think of a way out.

For a moment, Selah forgot the peril and reveled in the technology. They left the maze of corridors she thought were typical of the Mountain and moved onto streets with buildings and trees and people traveling about. Her senses swayed but were not fooled by the holographic sky and sunshine that stretched across the massive inside roof of the Mountain. The air smelled funny, not clean as outside but heavy with something chemical masked by a floral scent—maybe several flowers mixed together. She wondered if Treva noticed the smell after being outside for several months.

As they crossed the street, she noticed it seemed to go on forever before curving to the right about a mile down the road and disappearing around a bend. A living replica of an ancient destroyed city. They were ushered into a multistory building. At home, Dominion's buildings were one or two stories at most because there were a lot of empty acres for expansion. These cities seemed to run out of open acres before they ran out of buildings to put on them.

They traveled up to a floor that needed the guard's handprint for access. Every time he used a bio-access panel, Selah felt sicker and more trapped. Even if she thought of something to do, she didn't know how to get out, and she hadn't been able to get a signal from Treva. Were they being held, or could they leave after she saw her uncle?

They stepped into a softly lit hospital room. A flash streaked across Selah's vision. She blinked rapidly a few times, knowing it happened in her head because no one else reacted to the bright flash.

On the med-bed unit lay Charles Ganston, motionless and barely breathing. A mask and tube extending from the headboard were secured over his mouth and nose. The rhythmic breathing pump signaled the rise and fall of his chest.

Hooked to machines by numerous sensors placed on bare areas of his chest and arms, he appeared pale and small—nothing like the robust man Selah had met a few months ago. She wanted to cry, but Treva would need her as a strong support. Charles's skin had developed the translucent quality of death. Selah slid her arm across Treva's back as the girl leaned in and cried softly on her shoulder. No words . . . too much pain.

The outer door slid open and Bethany Everling, now wearing rubber-soled shoes and the white slacks and long jacket of a scientist, entered the large room. Selah wondered how a person could do the evil things this woman was known for, yet appear calm and benevolent. Her loose blonde hair was now tied back in a severe bun, matching her demeanor.

"I suppose I should offer you some reasonable explanation after you've cooperated so fully in bringing yourselves into my specific domain without creating a scene and requiring me to deal with Politico fallout like the last time." Bethany, arms crossed and feet firmly planted, stood next to the guard who'd followed her in.

Selah and Treva turned to face her. Cleon moved to Treva's side. Bethany knew they had been part of the original Lander escape. Selah worked to appear calm as her mind screamed about the stupidity of coming into this Mountain *again*. Still, finding out more about her parents overrode her caution.

"Since I don't understand what you're talking about, I want to know what's being done for Uncle Charles? What does the doctor have to say?" Treva imitated Bethany by crossing her arms over her chest and staring back. Selah hid her look of surprise by running a hand over her face. She'd never seen this stern side of Treva before.

"The irony is probably lost on you, my child, but this is the same room that I myself lay dying in several months ago," Bethany sneered. Selah felt Bethany's scorn and hostility slam into her like a rolled boulder, and she gasped. It was more than a sensation from reading her body-speak. She registered a physical effect from this woman's hostility.

"I'm glad you survived, and hopefully my uncle will too." Treva's lip curled up ever so slightly.

"Do you want to know *why* I was in that bed?" Hands behind her back, Bethany began to pace. "I was poisoned in some last-ditch effort to stop my husband's—" She stopped and wheeled to face them. Her mouth puckered tight as though ready to spit. Selah's stomach clenched. The woman's rage enveloped her in its cloud.

Cleon's realization of what was coming next changed his expression to horror. Selah felt bubbles of anxiety creeping up her chest. Bethany shouldn't be the one to tell Treva about the rabbits.

"I hope they caught the person responsible. That's a terrible thing to do to another person." Treva shook her head.

Selah watched Cleon's countenance shrinking. Her heart cried for her brother. He'd be a broken man when his part came to light.

Bethany smiled. "Yes, I caught him." She spun on her heels and faced the bed. "Meet the man who poisoned me—Charles Ganston." She glared at Treva.

Selah's knees trembled. A bead of sweat ran down her back between her shoulder blades, making her shiver. This couldn't get much worse, and the subject hadn't even got around to her yet.

Treva shook her head back and forth. "No, I don't believe you. You're just angry because of . . . well, you're just angry."

Selah held her breath. *Don't give anything away.* She stood rooted. She knew the truth of this story and couldn't fake surprise. Treva would know she had kept it from her. No one was going to like this ending. But why the diversion? What did Bethany have planned? Selah wished she had asked more about this woman. She didn't know her enemy at all, and that could be a fatal mistake. Lesson learned.

"No, there's more. Seems your new boyfriend here, Cleon Chavez, is the market man for the contraband rabbits used by your uncle to poison me."

Treva turned to face Cleon. "Tell me she's lying, that you didn't have any part of this. Because you would have told me before now, right?" she demanded. "Tell me she's making this up just to cover up trying to kill my uncle."

Cleon shrank down to the chair beside the bed. His head went into his hands. "I was only my brother's helper a couple of times."

"Oh, certainly that makes it all right then!" Treva threw up her hands and turned on Selah.

She couldn't lie to her friend. It betrayed every trust they had. Words stuck in Selah's throat as her tongue turned to sand.

"No, don't say you knew this and didn't tell me either," Treva yelled at Selah, who shrunk back.

What was there to say? She had only tried to protect their relationship by not telling, and now it looked like that would be what destroyed it.

Selah shook her head. "I'm so sorry. It's not like it sounds. You have to hear the whole story." Her eyes darted to Bethany and back to Treva. "But not now. When we get home."

Bethany glared at her. Selah could easily read her body-speak. The woman knew the rabbits hadn't poisoned her. She was using it as an excuse.

"You seem to have misunderstood, young lady. Or should

I call you Selah? You're not leaving here." Bethany returned to stand by the guard.

Selah stiffened. There was no longer a need for pretense. "So you know who we are. That and a bunch of bio-coin will buy you a quart of cooking oil. A lot of people know we're in here, and they'll come looking for us. They know her uncle is in here. What are you planning on doing with us?"

Bethany smirked. "All I'll have to say is that he died. I'm going to make that true very soon. But you're not too bright for a novarium, young lady. If anyone, including your father, knew you were coming into this Mountain, he would have literally moved the Mountain to keep that from happening. You came here on your own."

Selah remained unresponsive, arms trembling. The bread and apples she'd eaten that morning churned in her stomach. How could Bethany possibly know this much about her? "I ask again. What do you want with us?"

"I don't want anything with *them*. It's you I've been trying to get my hands on, and here you walk into my Mountain as nice as you please. My great-grandmother used to say, 'Good things come to those who wait.' I think I believe her now." Bethany unfolded her arms and walked over to stand in front of Selah.

At the moment Selah would have preferred talking to Bethany rather than face the ire Treva was projecting. But she had to face her friend sooner or later. She took a breath and turned away from Bethany to Treva. "Please give us a chance to explain."

The hurt on Treva's face dug into Selah's heart. Treva

looked to Cleon, who hadn't lifted his head. "I don't want to hear it from either of you. To think you would kill a man, over what? You didn't know anything about him at the time that would justify such evil." Her face reddened the more she talked.

Cleon stood and touched her arms. He opened his mouth and a squeak came out. He cleared his throat. "I just knew we delivered the rabbits to that man. I didn't know what he intended to do with them."

Treva's eyes bulged and she pushed him away. "But you thought the rabbits were poisoned and still sold them to someone who wanted them."

Cleon collapsed back to the chair.

"But Treva, you said yourself, the rabbits weren't really poisoned," Selah said. If they weren't poisoned after all, then Cleon hadn't hurt Bethany.

"Not poisoned, but a genetic malformation. When introduced to an immune system as weak as ours after 150 years in this Mountain, it caused cancer like I had. It also caused the heart muscle degradation that killed my husband's father," Bethany said.

Selah tried to touch Treva's shoulder but she pulled away. "You are not the people I thought you were. I think I need some time to myself."

"What are you talking about? You're going to let one thing ruin our friendship and your engagement to my brother?" Selah looked to Cleon. "Say something!" He wouldn't lift his head. She looked at Treva, pleading. "Where are you going? You're going to leave us here?"

"After what you did—"

"I didn't do anything. Cleon came with Raza, but he didn't do anything either."

Treva's contempt felt like an ax to her chest. "Yes you did. You kept it from me."

Selah recoiled. She had broken their friendship. She wanted to cry, but she wouldn't give Bethany the satisfaction.

"Treva will be escorted back to her quarters, where she will stay under section arrest to greet the many family friends and Politicos who will want to give their condolences about the passing of her uncle when he dies." Bethany motioned to the guard, who opened the door and admitted another pair of guards with weapons.

"And what if I don't cooperate?" Treva's chin came up in defiance. Selah relaxed a little. That sounded more like the Treva she knew.

"Your uncle will die faster, and I can dispose of you sooner." Bethany narrowed her eyes.

Selah held out a hand. "Treva—"

"I'm not ready to talk to you two yet." Treva's look morphed to stone. No emotion. Flat features. Dark eyes. She turned on her heels and left the room, followed closely by the two new guards.

16

Selah clenched her hands to contain her fear, but her nails dug into her palms. Bethany had successfully turned Treva against them, and now their chances of getting out of the Mountain dwindled by the minute. Sorry would come later. Right now survival depended on a better focus. How to buy time with this woman, to be able to think? Maybe seeing what Bethany wanted would help Selah understand what to do next.

There were too many things in her head. Another flash. She winced and shook it away.

"I know, I shake my head too. That girl is not like us. She doesn't understand what's at stake here," Bethany said. Selah sensed curiosity coming from her.

"What do you think you're going to gain by having me here?" Selah figured as long as she kept her talking, the woman's interest might ward off disagreeable surprises.

Bethany looked from Selah to Cleon to Charles Ganston's shell. "I know he's not going to wake up. But . . ." Bethany shrugged her shoulders. "I did, so just in case he can hear me, let's move this discussion to a more private setting." She motioned to the guards, who hustled Selah and Cleon from the room.

☖

Selah and Cleon tried to walk together, but a guard stepped between, pushing them apart. At one point they were back in the city street, and Selah could sense Cleon had the urge to run. She'd thought about it herself. But they'd still be trapped in the Mountain, and the chance of getting a pulse rifle shot in the back was almost a hundred percent. She gave him the *no* look when he glanced up. He scowled but didn't bolt.

After passing through enough corridors to make her dizzy and up a ramp, they stopped at a double-wide plascine wall. The guard hand-palmed a door. It swished open and he pushed Selah and Cleon in and closed it. Selah scrambled to find a way to open the door. The controls were either remote or only on the outside. Her hopes sank, but she refused to admit it was over. Could she connect with Treva mentally? She pulled Cleon down beside her on the long bench and began to concentrate. Nothing. She squeezed Cleon's arm so tight he yelped. She released her grasp but went back to concentrating.

The far door slid into its wall. Bethany strolled in. "Don't bother trying to do that mind communications stuff. These rooms are shielded to that frequency of your brain. Glade taught me that."

"What do you want from me?" Selah tried to keep control of the discussion, especially now that Cleon was a broken man. The last time he'd been this despondent was at Raza's death.

"Direct. I like that. I want your blood, and if you give it to me, then I won't prosecute your brother. He actually did me a favor," Bethany said without blinking an eye.

If she sacrificed herself, it could save Cleon. But could she trust Bethany to keep her word? The only thing she knew of this woman and her husband was their search for immortality.

"Why do you want my blood?" Selah knew the answer, but she hoped to buy time to find an escape route or maybe a way to reach Mojica. Hopefully she was still around.

"There is an ancient document about novarium. It says—"

"Where would you find an ancient document about Landers? I don't think that's possible. You must be lying. What do you take me for, a child?"

Bethany smirked. "I probably know more about you than you do. Did you know the ancient books say the novarium will bring new life?"

Selah faltered. She hadn't heard that. But then again, up to this point, Glade had controlled everything she learned about novarium. Should she pretend she knew that tidbit and gamble the woman wasn't making it up to trick her, or admit she didn't know? *Answer a question with a question.* "What makes you think a statement like that is really true?"

"Because I'm a gambler, and I'll take the odds that your

blood will change me and correct this Mountain's genetic problem forever."

Selah tried a bluff of her own. "And what if I don't want to give you my blood? One thing I do know is Landers can mentally keep you from getting their blood."

Bethany hesitated. "I'm sure Glade informed you of the drugs we used on him to gain his compliance."

"Don't even try them on me. Novarium are immune to your original drug concoction, and you've never had any novarium for testing a new formula."

Bethany didn't know that was an outright falsehood. She didn't seem as well versed in novarium as she'd let on, which made Selah all the more relieved. This vile woman didn't have the advantage.

"Then you will doom this whole society and your brother to death," Bethany said.

Selah's heart rate ticked up. "I didn't think you'd let me or my brother go anyhow. But why would you kill all these people because of me? This is your community."

Bethany's facade dissolved. There was no more benevolence. Selah sensed the woman's madness, and it brought a cold shiver and another flash. This woman's emotions were raw and savage, and they threatened to overwhelm her.

"Thought you might try to say no, so I've already begun the inoculations." She looked down at the ComTex on her arm. "In four hours the cycle will be complete, and if you don't give me your blood, the people will die."

"*I* will die if I do that."

"No, we'll take it slowly over the course of a couple of

weeks. Your body will replace what I take. You, as novarium, have an exceptional bio-compensation system."

"You still haven't told me why you need my blood. I know you're trying to gain immortality, and my father said it doesn't work that way."

Bethany nodded. "Ah, Glade. I'd say send my regards, but you won't be seeing him again. We're very close to achieving the Third Protocol on our own. You will give us the needed boost to overcome the cellular degradation."

Selah stopped. Bethany knew about the Third Protocol. How? Maybe less cooperation would get her answers just out of spite. "I'm not giving you anything. These are your people. The responsibility for their deaths is on you."

"I'm sure Cleon would not agree with you if it were his life on the line."

"Leave me out of it!" Cleon yelled. "You've already ruined my life, so a death sentence would end the pain. Go on, do it. Selah, don't you dare give her your blood to save me, or I'll kill my own self." Cleon heaved several large breaths and pounded on the wall with a fist. She saw a tear in the corner of his eye before he turned away.

"I guess you heard my brother. He's willing to be a sacrifice. You've got nothing." Selah gagged on the words. They were going to die.

"I was hoping *not* to need to do this, but I really hate being pushed." Bethany keyed her ComTex. "Show him in."

Selah glanced between the door in front of her and the one behind her. Had she caused danger to Treva just to show she could stand up to Bethany? Her heart pounded and her mouth went dry. She didn't want to think. She clutched Cleon's hand.

The door Bethany had entered swished open.

A dark-clad figure with a week's worth of beard growth and shaggy hair entered. Selah stared for a moment, then gasped. She let go of Cleon's hand.

"Father!" Selah ran to Varro Chavez and threw her arms around his neck. Other than the beard and longish hair, he looked normal. Her heart soared. It would be all right now. "I'm so relieved to see you. Where are Mother and Dane? How did you know I'd be here?"

Selah felt a slight hesitation in his grip. She pulled back to look in his face.

"I'm happy you're safe. We've been worried since you left," Varro said, averting his eyes. He lightly patted Selah's back.

Cleon watched from about ten feet away. Selah motioned him over. He shook his head.

"Chavez, tell her why she needs to cooperate with me." Bethany grinned.

Selah glanced from her stepfather to Bethany. That was the first honest grin the woman had given all morning. Selah wondered why she seemed familiar with Father.

"Selah, my daughter, I need you to cooperate with Dr. Beverly," he said. His lips twitched, and his body-speak indicated he was tightened in knots. Selah jerked away. It was unsettling to feel her stepfather's unmasked emotions when his outward appearance showed the opposite.

"Father, I can't work with that woman, but I'm sorry I left. We didn't think you'd understand. Where are Mother and Dane? I've missed them so much." The words rolled out in disorganized thoughts and fragmented sentences, but she had so much to say. This could still be fixed. She knew surely he'd understand if she explained and said she was sorry.

"Your mother and Dane are taken care of for now. You need to cooperate," Varro said, his voice changing slightly in pitch.

Selah tried to smile. It felt wrong. She reached out to Cleon. "Come here. Say hello."

Cleon shook his head, moving closer to the other doorway blocked by a guard. "I'm not going near him. I know that look. He's not telling the truth. Something's wrong. He knows."

Selah winced. She tipped her head to the side. "Father, what did you mean about Mother and Dane being taken care of *for now*?"

Varro reached out to take her arm. "You need to do the small favor the Mountain needs and it will be over quickly."

She slowly pushed away his hand. "It's not a small favor! You have no idea what this woman is capable of doing. She just threatened to kill this whole community if I don't cooperate."

Selah searched his eyes for some recognition. They were the same as always, only now she was listening to his body-speak and not his words. He remained as calm as he'd been the day on the beach when Raza killed the Lander. The realization hit her hard and she staggered. She didn't know this man.

Varro seemed to be counting unseen numbers, then turned to Bethany. "You started the inoculations already? That's cutting it close. We need time to prep her."

"Wait! No one's prepping me for anything."

"This thing is going to make me a wealthy man and help me pay one very large debt. Now, you wouldn't deny me that, would you? It's such a minor thing for you, and besides, you owe me for that dowry. Your body will recover from the blood loss." Varro ran his hand through blond hair that came almost to his shoulders. Why hadn't Mother cut that raggedness off?

"Father, please tell me this is a joke. I've got a lot to tell you, and I know you'll be proud of me when you see how it worked out." She had no doubt this wasn't a joke, but she needed every extra second to think. Stupid questions took up time.

"Of course I'm proud, but this is no joke. There's no time to get the Protocol matchup verified," Varro said without emotion.

Selah's mind screeched to a halt so fast she would later remember that she was on autopilot from the moment Varro Chavez said the word *Protocol*.

She turned to Cleon and started to back away. Her father—no, her stepfather—was hiding something. His emotions came through strong and simple. Deception. "Where are Mother and Dane?"

Varro moved forward and grabbed her arm. "Listen, Selah, we don't have a lot of time. We can discuss this—"

"No!" Selah screamed, holding up a palm and wrenching her arm free from the attack as her training had taught her to do. The force from her palm sent Varro reeling backward into Bethany.

The door next to Selah slid open. A guard rushed in and

they collided. As the guard started to fall, he thrust out his weapon. Selah snatched it. The unexpected weight pulled her down on top of him. She struggled to stand and keep possession.

Cleon bolted out the door as Bethany and Varro lunged forward.

Selah squeezed the trigger. Energy pulses burst from the barrel, forcing the weapon to jerk back and forth, peppering the walls and floor with smoldering burnt streaks.

Varro, Bethany, and the guard ducked for cover.

From behind, a pair of hands clasped Selah's. Cleon. Relief flooded her stomach. She released the weapon to him and scrambled away from the fallen guard, charging out the door with Cleon close behind.

As he exited, Cleon spun and trained the weapon on the door until it closed. He fired several rounds at the palm pad. It exploded, the fried circuits black and crackling.

"Will that blast disable the door permanently?" Selah asked as they ran.

"I don't know, but it will buy us time," Cleon said.

Selah charged to a door opening. "In here! I think the color of this hall is familiar." Her exceptional memory matched the colors with the configuration of door openings. Every time she stopped to think *how* she was doing it, it stopped working. Another novarium trait surfacing. She kept her concentration until they reached the city street. She snatched the pulse rifle from Cleon, shoved it under her tunic, then tightened her belt to keep it in place.

Relief flooded her. She knew the way to Treva's from here.

Cleon pulled on her arm. "Hold it. Are we going to Treva's? She hates us."

"Where else can we go? Answer fast before we draw attention or the guards catch up."

"Ganston's office. Maybe that skinny guy Jax is still there. He can find Mojica." Cleon was looking more confident now. Selah wanted to argue Jax probably wouldn't have the job anymore, but she couldn't say for sure.

"Do you remember the way? I recall several instances of the same color hall and same number of doorways, just different configurations. It might take too long to figure out the right one."

"Yes, I know the way." Cleon navigated the halls like a rat Selah had once seen in a maze race. Or maybe she was projecting how crisscrossed her brain felt. In any case, he executed every turn perfectly, and in less than a minute they stood before Charles Ganston's office.

Selah lifted her fingers to the door pad. Her hand lingered just out of sensor range. Should they trust another person from the Mountain? Cleon smacked the panel, pushed her inside, and waved the door closed behind them. Jax averted his eyes from the large wall monitor and turned to glance in their direction. His eyes widened.

Selah leaned over the front of the desk. "Do you remember me, Jax? Treva and Mr. Charles helped me get my father out the last time I was here."

Jax's head bobbed up and down. He backed away as his lips pressed to a thin line. "Yes, I remember you troubled children. It caused quite a stir here, yes sir, quite a stir."

"Where or how can I find Mojica? We need her help right away," Selah said.

"Yes, yes, I know exactly how to help. You hide in the inner office, out of sight, and I'll make the call," Jax said. He ushered them into Ganston's office and closed the door.

"What are you doing? How do you know we can trust him?" Cleon pulled the pulse rifle from the back of Selah's tunic.

"It was your idea to come here. Why did you suggest it if you weren't sure?"

Cleon laid the rifle across Ganston's desk and raised both hands to his head, running sweat back across his hair. "I don't know. I panicked. After seeing Father . . ."

Selah shook her head. Her knees started to tremble as she began to weep. "That wasn't real. There's a reasonable explanation. They must be holding Mother and Dane hostage to make Father act like that. They must—"

Cleon grabbed her by both arms. "Stop. Listen to me!" The pressure of his fingers made her wince. She wanted to pull away but he wouldn't let go. "I tried to tell you that day with Raza. What you saw today was my real father."

"No! I don't believe you. He was mean and cruel and—"

"That's the man he's always been. I've watched you since we were young, trying to make him acknowledge you as a daughter." Cleon hung his head. "When he swore me and Raza to secrecy about you not being his child, I felt a certain smugness, probably some stupid sibling rivalry, because he said he could never love a child not his own. I'm sorry. I've always known your love for every one of us had no such conditions."

It had been one thing to listen to Raza's outburst before his death, but she never believed the picture he'd painted of Father. In her mind, anything could be fixed. Reality didn't agree. "I thought if I just explained—"

"Nothing you could say to him would help. I often thought he was only nice as a gesture for Mother's sake. The man I saw today, that's who he is."

Selah slumped against the desk, dazed. *It can't be fixed.* She'd seen him and pleaded with him, and his countenance had never changed. "What happened to Mother and Dane?"

"I don't know, but I think I made a mistake bringing us here. There's just something I didn't like about the way Jax looked at us."

"I was too numb to concentrate on his—"

The door to the outer office slid open.

Selah snatched up the pulse rifle and turned. Two guards rushed in to take up positions on either side of the door. Bethany strolled into the room. Cleon grabbed the weapon from Selah and aimed.

Bethany raised a hand. "Don't bother, I had the pulse deactivated by remote as soon as you left my building."

Cleon pulled the trigger. Nothing happened. He hit the charger and pulled on the trigger again. Nothing. He raised it by the barrel as a club.

Bethany shook her head as she motioned a guard to retrieve the weapon. "Turn it over. I'm sure Pasha and Dane will thank you."

Selah gasped. Where were they holding her mother and little brother? She had to get them someplace safe.

Cleon slowly lowered the weapon and handed it over. His shoulders slumped.

"Check them for other weapons." Bethany walked toward the outer room.

Selah stood for the search, noting Bethany's change in attitude. She hoped Treva had hidden the files she carried rather than trust Bethany.

Jax rushed over to Bethany. "I hope you'll continue to consider me for this position, especially after I've proven to be of additional value to you."

"I do believe you're correct. Telling me of Charles Ganston's original treachery was not worthy of such a lofty position as head of Historical Archaeology, but this new information does give you a boost beyond the threshold I desire of my candidates." Bethany continued out the front door. "Our decision will be finalized when Ganston dies."

17

Bodhi spent most of the trip from Baltimore to Stone Braide trying to figure out how to keep Selah safe when he returned home. He had also learned a lot about Glade's life. It had kept him tossing and turning on one of those chair loungers last night. Granted, having unauthorized weapons discharging at all hours, accompanied by screaming and loud music, probably contributed to his discomfort this morning. Bodhi didn't want to feel sorry for Glade's chaotic failure at life . . . but he did. And that, in turn, muddled his perception of whether Glade was really doing him a favor or keeping him from Selah out of spite.

"You've been especially quiet this trip. I prepared for your arguing the whole way," Glade said. He sat erect. Bodhi noticed he rarely presented himself as slumped or defeated in public.

Bodhi still needed to think without lying. He avoided

the question. "If you're correct in your translation of those documents, and the key is discovered here, then the trip was worthwhile." Suddenly Bodhi's chest felt strange. He took a deep breath to relieve the pressure. Was he feeling excitement or dread? After listening to him for a full two days, he realized Glade's true dedication was beginning to sink in among his doubts.

The land wagons stopped at a deserted site of several partially erected buildings. The sandy, scorched earth showed little vegetation with barely a living tree in sight. Bodhi took a long, concentrated look. Was this the right place? Impossible. He left here a few months ago, passing through a living, vibrant forest.

Taraji hopped down first, slowly moving away from the caravan with her pack slung over one shoulder and her other hand resting on her holstered weapon.

Bodhi slowly stepped down from the wagon and grabbed his bag. Glade spoke to a few seated travelers before hopping down, then watched as the land wagons pulled away and the three security units flying guard flew by.

Glade joined Bodhi and Taraji. He pointed at the dead trees. "Do you see what I see?"

"Yes, but what—"

"That's pulse and laser damage," Taraji said.

Glade shook his head. "We may be too late. If only I'd caught on earlier. I should have known. My years buried under Noah Everling's drugs have dulled my senses and made me forget important facts."

Bodhi felt like adding, *That happens when you're 150.*

But he didn't think Glade would appreciate the humor, so he just nodded.

Off to the left, closest to the mountains, a cave entrance with a flash of colored cloth caught Bodhi's attention. He motioned Glade and darted for the opening.

An old man strolled from the cave sporting disheveled silver-gray hair and a multicolored tattered robe. He stopped in front of the opening and crossed his arms over his chest. "You come seeking the wisdom of the ages."

Bodhi looked to Glade, who dipped his head in thought. Taraji held her ground.

"You come seeking the wisdom of the ages," the old man repeated, his face contorted in a scowl.

A look of recognition passed over Glade's eyes. He raised a finger then dug into his backpack, pulling out a leather satchel of yellowed papers. He leafed through the pile and separated out the correct one. "And the wisdom of the ages is fleeting."

"You're the one." The old man's face lit with a pleasure that threatened to crack his wrinkles. "Please tell me you've gathered all the documents."

Glade nodded. He dropped the backpack and held out the leather satchel. The old man reached out a shaky, leathered hand and touched it. He displayed a toothless grin and rushed into the cave with Glade following behind, both chattering like best friends.

Taraji looked at Bodhi. "Do we stay out here or go in?"

"I'm not sure what these two could do in a cave in the wilderness to help anything." Bodhi's belief was still riddled with doubt. Was Selah really going to fracture in nine months if they didn't find the key? No one had shown him any evidence of that, but maybe it was just wishful thinking on his part. There had never been anyone like Selah in his life, that much he remembered. He wanted to be the best for her.

He'd never known how to act around women, especially with love involved, but now he was learning. Until Glade said to end it. Agreeing to that demand tore at his heart in a way Glade should understand.

He wished he had stopped to see her before he left yesterday. She'd been so angry the last time they met. Still, he'd never admit he feared her father. Or did he fear more what he might become with the physical changes he was enduring?

"Bodhi, I need your help with these new data points he's added to our diagram." Glade motioned them in.

Taraji let Bodhi go first and she brought up the rear.

Bodhi prepared for smoky lanterns and a bunch of cave-moldy maps and charts. He trudged behind Glade. After several seconds, it dawned on him that they were moving through an eastward maze of fresh-air tunnels. Glade had closed doors across several of the passageways they passed through. Where was the old guy? How would they find their way out of here? And how did Glade know where he was going? Just as Bodhi caught up to him, they walked into the opening.

It wasn't an overly tall cavern. Taraji could have jumped and hit the roof. One wall had several spherical grottos cut into the smooth, milled surface.

Bodhi took a quick look around. This was a solid limestone cave with some sort of illumination that appeared to be coming from the cave ceiling. He moved underneath one of the lit areas and looked up.

"Help me input our data. Between our two sets of documents, we have the full number of points. It's real this time," Glade said. He seemed genuinely thrilled. That made Bodhi excited and scared at the same time. If Glade was right about the key, then he must also be right about Selah.

"Go ahead—I'll go back out to the mouth of the cave and keep watch in case we've got any tagalongs from the caravan." Taraji nodded to Glade and retreated back into the tunnels.

"We have the three sets together—yours, mine, and the Keepers'," the old man said as he walked to the table and patted Glade on the back.

"Are you telling me that this key—this wonderful, great, *important* key—was counting on three old, worn papers to make it to the same spot at the same time?" Bodhi stared at the two men.

Glade and the old man looked at each other, then at Bodhi. "No matter how it got here, we have the way now," Glade said.

Bodhi ran his hands through his hair. If all this data produced the key to the West, then the faster he could help them so Selah could live, but the faster she'd leave him forever to do whatever it was she had to do. Or if this wasn't the answer, then Selah would . . . He just couldn't think or say that word. Reality hit him like a bolt of lightning splitting a tree. Either way, his job—his reason for coming here—was completed, and there was no going back. Would he expire?

Bodhi shivered, brushing off the feeling as a reaction to the dampness in the caves.

The old man waved his hand over a long, flat stone and the wall in front of him lit with random dots creating a familiar pattern.

Bodhi moved closer and rolled the image over in his mind a few times. "With more points filled in, that could be a Stone Braide pattern."

"You are correct," Glade said. "Because we recognized the symbol, it gave us a good reference for where to place the rest of the points to complete the pattern. With the documents I had, the Keeper journals from Charles Ganston, and what this man has, we can fill in all of these points." His smile radiated satisfaction.

"How is this possible? How is any of this possible?" Bodhi swept his hand around the room. "Up the road, people live technologically superior lives in a biospheric Mountain, yet here in a cave, in a land where horses are used for transportation, the equipment is more advanced. How? How does this happen?"

The old man shuffled over to where Bodhi still stood under the illumination. "My boy, there were great technological societies 150 years ago. They were the cause of this mess in the first place. So there are many remnants that have survived—just some that shouldn't have."

"I still don't understand—why now? How can you be sure that the way to the Third Protocol should be discovered at this very time and not fifty or a hundred years from now?" Bodhi was clutching at anything. Maybe Selah had more than nine months. There had been novarium who left TicCity, and no one knew if they had fractured.

"Why do you think I was standing at the entrance expecting you? All the parts have arrived. The ancient documents say that shortly after the transition, the novarium will come and the key will bring the lightning that illuminates the future," the old man said.

"That's not correct. The novarium isn't here," Bodhi said.

"But she is. She went into the Mountain with the Keepers' child and another boy." The old man sat down and started shuffling through the documents from Glade.

Glade and Bodhi spun to face him.

"When was my daughter here? Why didn't you say so before?" Glade stormed toward the old man, but Bodhi jostled his way in between and used an arm to restrain him.

"You can't stop this, or it will take another 150 years for the Mountain to complete the cycle again," the old man said matter-of-factly.

Glade slumped into a chair. "I don't think I could endure that much more. I'm tired."

Bodhi squeezed Glade's shoulder and backed toward the cavern opening. "Which way did she go? We've got to get her. After the things they did to Glade . . . That is a very evil place."

"She has to be here." Glade's voice sounded strangled.

Bodhi stopped. His fists clenched as his temper rose. Glade seemed old and resigned. Not at all like the fierce one who'd steered him from Selah just a few short months ago. "If that doctor catches her in there, we'll never see her again. Do you want to risk that?"

"No, I don't, but I also don't want to draw attention to the fact that she's in there. If they don't know, we may lead them straight to her," Glade said. He seemed to be recovering from his initial shock.

"Neither of you seems to have read the Keepers' documents." The old man threw up his hands, seeming exasperated. "The order of the cycle is very specific. Apparently you've stumbled upon the steps by some grace. But now you must retrieve her so that she is on time."

"On time for what?" Bodhi and Glade asked in unison.

The old man shrugged and looked at Glade. "The end of the cycle you started when you began adding additional data to the map."

"End of the cycle? Why didn't you tell me I would start a countdown?" Sweat popped out on Glade's upper lip. Bodhi felt more panic from seeing that than he did about the situation.

"Because I didn't think it was an accident that you all showed up at the same time. In twenty-four hours everything will be done." The old man continued to look at the map.

"This could have been delayed—if I hadn't added data?" Glade's expression crashed.

"But then Selah would not have the key and she'd go mad," Bodhi said, trying to center Glade.

The old man stood up. "Do you know what it's like to live in a cave for 150 years?" He looked at each of them, holding their gaze for several seconds. "No. I didn't think so. I'm tired. My job needs to be completed."

"I only have twenty-four hours to get her back here." Bodhi

looked to Glade. "I know you don't want me near her, but you're not going to stop me."

Glade nodded once. Bodhi darted for the tunnel.

"Wait! Not that way." The old man hurried to a limestone panel on the far side of the cave. "Use these tunnels. The distance is much shorter. Always stay to your right going there, and to your left on the way back." He used a holographic keypad to swing the door open. "After being inside, she may act a little disoriented. Bring her back here to me and Glade."

"This is your fault, old man. You knew she was the novarium and you let her go back in that Mountain to be captured. If she's harmed, I will haunt your dreams till the end of time." Bodhi surprised even himself with the ferocity of his response.

The old man shrugged as though he didn't notice. "She had to go in there. The chemical compound she needs to inhale is the very thing that has been degrading the DNA in those people for the last 150 years. It's very ironic—what gives her life hastens their death."

18

The rear guards pushed Selah and Cleon behind Bethany. Two more guards fell in line outside the doors to the Historical Antiquities Department. With no possibility of escape, Selah focused her thoughts on seeing her mother and finding a way to free her and Dane, but her plans were tempered with fear for Treva's safety. Would this evil woman make Treva suffer for Selah's actions?

This time Selah recognized the halls back to Bethany's building. Committing them to memory gave her an exit plan if they got free again and a mental exercise that helped calm the chaos within her.

The time from the department to Bethany's offices took exactly five minutes and seven seconds. Selah sucked in a breath when the scorched palm pad came into view. They bypassed that door and turned to another corridor on the right.

Selah stopped short. She knew this doorway and so should Cleon. This lab had held Glade during his incarceration. Here they'd found the unconscious form of Bethany's husband, Noah Everling, and the burnt remains of the man who'd worked for him.

The guard tried to push her forward, but she resisted. What had happened to Noah, the doctor who'd tormented Glade? Selah had only seen his wife since she'd been here.

She got a whiff of that floral scent again. If she lived here and had to smell that every day, it might drive her nuts. A lightning flash crossed her vision. Her mind struggled to focus.

The guard pushed Selah harder. She contained the urge to turn on him since it might endanger her mother, and instead let him push her through the open door.

On the right sat the cell where she'd cried when viewing what she thought were Glade's burnt remains. She hesitated to look in that direction. A banging sound filtered into range. She looked over. Behind the transparent plascine wall, her nine-year-old brother, Dane, his brown eyes wild-looking beneath the darkening mop of blond hair, pounded on the wall with both fists.

Selah's heart beat to bursting. She ran to the wall. "Mother! Dane! Are you all right?" This was the room where fire burst from the walls. She tried to find the control to open the doorway.

Pasha Rishon, in her quiet elegance, strode to the wall and calmly placed her hands flat on the clear plascine, her flowing mane of dark hair set against green eyes and her lean frame dressed in gray slacks and tunic. She smiled softly. Selah instantly remembered a time when Father had playfully threatened to cut Mother's hair so the horse he was showing at Farm Competition could have an impressive tail.

Selah moved to the spot and placed her hands against her mother's. She barely felt her warmth through the wall. Yet the connection, no matter how slight, brought her a flood of peace. She'd found her mother and little brother at last. She turned to Cleon. A guard held him back with a weapon pressed to his chest.

"Let Cleon come over here," Selah said, trying to force courage and composure into her voice, though it sounded strangled. She had to remain calm for Cleon and Dane.

Bethany didn't move, and neither did the guards. Selah spun to face them. "Mrs. Everling, if you want me to—"

"*Dr.* Everling is my official title," Bethany said with arms crossed.

Selah pressed her lips together. Her defiance bubbled up. "*Bethany*, let my brother come see our family. If you want me to cooperate, let's see you do some of the same." She fisted her hands on her hips. Where the brashness came from, she didn't know, but she felt like a weight had lifted from her chest.

She turned back to her mother. They communicated with their eyes, and Mother gave her strength.

Bethany shrugged off the demand but directed the guard to let Cleon go to the wall. He hurried over to reach out to Mother and Dane.

"I want time with my mother and brothers." Selah rubbed Cleon's shoulder and turned back to face Bethany.

"And why do you think you rate special treatment? You've already assaulted me, Chavez, and my guards."

"Because I've got what you want, and it would go a lot easier for you if I were happy while I was doing it. You wouldn't like me angry." Selah glared at her.

Bethany turned away to face a console. Selah figured the demand hadn't worked. She'd better get in any greetings before her family disappeared. But as long as she cooperated, their safety would be ensured, and she'd demand proof of it.

Bethany cleared her throat. "Okay, I agree. You can have an hour with your family."

"And a noontime meal for us?" Selah asked, wanting to stretch the time.

"You don't get that long. A meal will be sent. Immediately afterward we start the extraction."

A chill crawled down her back. Selah shuddered involuntarily. The feeling came so swiftly it tingled her toes. Did she really hear a humming in her head? She looked around. It sounded like a machine had started, but no one else reacted to the sound.

⬡

Selah hugged her mother and brother, then hugged them some more as they ate the meager meal of fruit and bread. She watched Cleon being smothered in little brother giggles and mother kisses. She'd been silently hoping for this day, but at what cost? Knowing the disregard her stepfather had already exhibited, she couldn't think of a single circumstance where this could have turned out differently. Even Varro's mandate—

She stopped. She had just thought of her stepfather as Varro. Did that seem right? This was the man who had raised her since birth.

Dane grabbed Selah around the neck and gave her a big hug. "I missed you something fierce. You left without saying goodbye. Mother said you had important business to attend. Are you coming home now?"

She smiled and tousled his hair, then looked over his head at Mother hugging Cleon, motioning that they needed to talk.

Mother nodded and whispered to Cleon, who turned to Dane. "Hey, shrimp, I missed you. Let's see if you remember the wrestling moves I taught you."

Cleon and Dane moved off into the back corner, and Mother scooted over to Selah.

With her mother's arms resting around her shoulders, Selah felt a new sense of responsibility. She had to protect them from Bethany . . . and from Varro.

"Mother, what happened after I left? How did you get here?" Selah pressed her head to her mother's shoulder. The familiar herb scent of her special soap comforted her.

Mother didn't answer. Selah sat up. "What's the matter?"

"I'm sorry." Mother closed her eyes and shook her head. "I dreaded the day I'd have to tell you. I've played it over in my mind a hundred times, and I still don't understand any of this. I don't know why or how long he knew, but Varro and his friends from Waterside were trying to keep you from becoming novarium. They wanted some kind of Protocol to pass from you to your offspring with Jericho Kingston."

Selah grabbed her mother's hands. "What do you know about the Protocol?"

"Nothing. I've just heard Varro use the term numerous times in his conversations with Simeon Kingston. The man was quite upset about not getting back the dowry he paid for you."

Selah wanted to blurt out that Varro and Simeon had been part of a murder, but that knowledge might become a bargaining chip if it were truly a secret. "How much did Var—Fa—" Selah squeezed her eyes shut with a sigh and dropped her head.

Mother rubbed the back of Selah's hand. "You can call him Varro. I heard you found Glade, and I'm so happy you did. I'm sure you've decided to call him Father."

"I hear the caring in your voice when you say his name."

Mother's eyes moistened. She turned her gaze and took on a faraway look.

Selah smiled softly. At that moment she knew what she wanted to do. "How much did Varro owe for my dowry?" She figured even a reasonable amount could be dealt with. Repayment would smooth all this over.

"Apparently it was a million bio-coin. Varro spent most of it on land and extravagant high-tech farm equipment. He brought us here and made a deal with that evil woman for all the coin he owed plus a bonus."

Selah gulped in air. There was no reasonable amount anywhere close to that value. The reality of the deal had become clear. This wasn't clan. This was commerce. Dowries were payment. She had come close to being married off to cement a neighboring clan relationship. But in reality, she was being sold into some strange slavery. How often had that happened to other girls in Dominion?

Bethany swept into the room, followed by four guards. "Okay, your time is up. We have to get you to prep."

Selah stood in the doorway between their weapons and her family. Cleon moved to her side and put his hand on her shoulder.

Bethany motioned her out.

"Will my family be safe?" Selah stared at Bethany, reading her body-speak.

"As long as you cooperate and don't do anything funny to your blood, we've got an agreement." Bethany's posture verified she spoke the truth. It also told Selah that Bethany believed her story about being able to manipulate her blood. Bethany's knowledge of novarium was an act. Selah needed more time to create a plan.

"Let's get started." Selah moved through the doorway. Cleon followed.

Bethany pointed at Cleon. "Not you. Stay in there with your family."

He started to object.

"It'll be all right." Selah pushed him back in with Mother and Dane.

⟁

It'll be all right echoed in Selah's head. The sound stretched and vibrated, each word repeating multiple times, ebbing and flowing like the ocean. Selah tried to concentrate on the surface where she lay. A dizzying wave kept pulling her mind away. Her stomach lurched. She fought to swallow what little moisture she had in her mouth. *Focus!* Fighting her way back, she latched onto the wave, bringing feeling in her arms until they became solid. Her palms pressed to the cold metal beneath her. She moved her fingers.

Voices talked around her, but the echo made them impossible to understand. *Focus!* She fought frame by frame to quiet the sounds in her head. The only thing that could cause this kind of disorientation was a drug. Selah tried not to panic, and the sense was so dull she almost laughed. That would not be good. They'd know she was conscious.

Feeling returned to her feet. Slight moves of her toes. Now her brain. *One. Two. Three. Say them faster, faster . . .* Her head cleared. She remained unresponsive, hoping to hear something useful.

"I've got you hooked to bio-machines. I know when you're awake, Selah," Bethany said from a distance of about five feet.

Selah figured it was now or never. She lunged, straining against the straps holding her arms, legs, and torso to the table. Her eyes flew open. She felt rage . . . but it was too dull and flat to pull a forceful response. Her body betrayed her.

"That's more like it. As you can see, I sort of lied. The liquids you received to replace the blood loss were a drug cocktail I developed for the next generation of clones, which you were also responsible for me losing. So I decided to try it out on you." Bethany snorted with laughter. "And guess what? It worked. Not like I wanted, but you've been out for an hour, which was more than enough time to get a good harvest of your blood. My team is at work in the lab as we speak."

Stark white walls and floor prevented Selah from locking on a focal point other than the wires and tubes attached to her arms and legs. She was dressed in white shorts and a T-shirt. She could hear rhythmic clicking from the machine behind her head, but trying to focus on the sound made her head reel.

"An hour!" That was what she wanted to say, but the words came out slurred. She tried to sit up, but the restraint on her chest held her down. She sank back to the table. She checked the tubes and apparatuses connected to her body. Blood leaving in one place—her right arm. Fluids coming into her body in one place—her left ankle. She had to concentrate on restricting flow to those areas.

"Hmm, look at that." Bethany studied her screen and waved her hand over a halo-button.

A shriek of pain burst from Selah's lips as unbelievable white-hot pain seared her brain. Her body convulsed and her back arched, straining her chest against the strap. *Stop!* Dots of sweat burst on her forehead and ran down her temples in lazy rivulets that ended puddled in her ears.

The pain disappeared. No lingering sensation. Gone. Selah shuddered. Her breath came in great heaving gulps. "Water! Please give me—"

"Now we make a new deal. You keep the blood flowing, and I won't introduce you to any more of my new forms of persuasion." Bethany didn't wait for an answer. She turned away from Selah, poured a cup of water into a squeeze bottle, then turned back to loom over Selah's face. "Open up."

Selah set her jaw. She tried to glare, but her eyes were still drifting in and out.

"I hope you don't think I'm going to untie you to let you drink. Open up."

Selah reluctantly opened her mouth. The spray bounced off her lips and she closed her eyes. Refreshing. The water washed away some of the fog in her head. Her tongue wasn't stuck to her mouth. Maybe she could earn a little sympathy by showing compassion. "Are your people safe?"

"Yes, all of the people have been given your blood as an inoculation. They are safe." Bethany waited with another douse of the squeeze bottle. Selah shook her head and Bethany straightened.

"I don't believe you. I don't know much about science, but I do know you can't just give someone's blood to another person unless they're the same type. And I doubt this whole Mountain is the same blood type."

"You're correct," Bethany said. "But your blood has no antigens, making you a universal donor. We have already started the extraction of the DNA booster."

"Other than being a universal donor, what's so special about my blood?" Selah felt like a cow at the slaughterhouse. It was odd to see her blood flowing out but not feel physical loss or weakness other than dizziness from the drug.

"I wasn't actually sure until I examined it myself, but there are components to your hybrid blood that I've never seen before. I don't know how they work, but I know one of the results. Longevity. Despite our high technical skills, we still don't have the equipment powerful enough to unlock your secrets. But with your help, I may be able to stay around long enough to accomplish it."

Selah watched Bethany gently touch the smooth skin of her cheek as she stared at her own reflection in the plascine panel. It was creepy to know this woman wanted to use Selah's blood to live longer.

"What is a DNA booster?"

"Our closed society's DNA has degraded over the past century and a half to the place where the people will all be sterile in another two generations if there isn't a fix. My husband found a fix with your father's blood, but we needed yours—a hybrid—to have the necessary bonding properties." Her smile trembled. "My husband was right about using a Lander child. He would be proud of my accomplishment."

Selah decided against the snide remark she wanted to hurl. Her mind cleared and her muscles responded. There would come a point when she'd be able to break the straps, but she needed to be patient and wait for an opportunity when she was alone. "Where is your husband?"

"Unfortunately my husband will be a vegetable for the rest of his life, which I would never seek to prolong."

"I'm sorry." Selah could feel the woman's pain for her husband. She watched her eyes brim with tears, then Bethany bolted from the room, leaving her chair spinning.

Selah tested the straps. Still not much give in them. She needed to restrict the flow of that drug into her ankle, and hope her strength increased.

She closed her eyes, resting her head from the chorus of lightning permeating her vision.

Just then the door at the other end of the room slid open.

The sound caught Selah's attention. She tipped her head to the side and squinted at the figure coming fast.

Treva shook her arm. "Selah, wake up!" She scrambled to loosen her restraints.

Selah soared with happiness. "Where'd you come from? I'm really sorry I made you angry. I saw my mother." The fog dissipated from her brain, but she still seemed to ramble. She clamped her lips shut so as not to look sillier.

"I wasn't really angry. I already knew about Cleon and the rabbits." Treva's nimble fingers pulled the torso strap through the table loops and threw it to the floor. She hauled Selah off the table and stood her on her feet.

Relief flooded over Selah. She had her friend back. She wobbled but managed to grab the table edge. "But how did you know?"

Treva swiftly pulled Selah's clothing from a drawer. "I read the first two pages of my uncle's letter. He noticed I liked Cleon and he didn't want his reputation sullied. He admitted it was all his fault and Cleon only came one time and didn't know anything."

"But you've never mentioned a word to either of us." Selah squinted at Treva, trying to make the three images of her meld into one.

Treva slid her boots over. "I figured he was too embarrassed but would say something one day. I love him enough to wait."

Selah slid out the needles and pulled the sensors from her body. As soon as the clear drip ceased, her stamina returned. "So you were fooling with us when you pretended to be angry."

Treva stripped the sensors from her back. "How else was I supposed to get out of there and try to get help? Besides, I had to hide my parents' papers again."

"Help! You got help? Did you find Mojica?"

"No, not yet, but I got your mom and Dane free and Cleon is leading them out. So we don't have a lot of time before security is alerted. Let's go." Treva hurriedly helped her dress.

"How did you know my family was here?" Selah squinted, trying to focus. Finally she just jammed her feet into the boots and wiggled them on.

"The secret room in my quarters is on the tip of a very old internal network. I heard Bethany talking to a man called Varro. I've heard that name enough times from Cleon to have it imprinted behind my eyeballs." Treva grabbed her by the hand and dashed for the door.

19

At first Bodhi walked cautiously through the smooth-sided tunnels. It looked like giant worms had bored through solid limestone to build this maze wonder. A horizontal column of illumination from the ceiling traveled with him, stretching from so many feet behind to that same distance ahead. He tested it. No matter how slow or fast he traveled, it remained centered over him. He found a comfortable jogging speed and his breathing evened as his brain absorbed the chemicals from running. He calmed. Logic returned, overcoming his breakneck dash to be Selah's protector. He needed an actual plan to find her and then escape without the shootout of last time.

The air never changed. There was none of the dampness or musty smell he remembered from other caves. He kept to the corridors on the right but felt the narrow chamber curve to the west before straightening out. Strange. He smelled flowers, and the hum of a loud machine vibrated in his head, making him wince as he approached what appeared to be the end of the tunnel. He slowed.

Bodhi felt a cool flush as the blood drained from his sweaty face. He strode to the wall and ran his hands over the full width of the smooth, cool limestone surface. What was this? There was no opening. He searched more of the wall surface. Why would the old man send him out like a dog chasing its tail? His chest started to tighten. Glade could be in danger. He swallowed hard. Selah could be in danger. He stared at the wall, trying to will it open.

He breathed hard, pacing back and forth. He ran a hand through his hair. What were his options? It was a long way back. If his internal clock still functioned, he figured he'd been in the tunnels for an hour. That was another hour back to the cavern and then traveling five miles by land to the Mountain. But he had no way of getting in. How had Selah gotten inside?

Bodhi turned to head back up the tunnel. A scraping rumble filled the space, vibrating the floor. He thought of running, but he'd be seen for quite a distance. He couldn't outrun a weapon. He turned in time to see a seamless door swing open at the end of the tunnel. He steeled himself for a fight.

The first woman through the door had to bend over through the opening. A long, dark ponytail dropped over her shoulder as she raised her head.

"Mojica!" Bodhi had never been so happy to see such a beautiful familiar face. If he hadn't been in love with Selah, this was the kind of woman he'd have been attracted to—smoky eyes, high cheekbones, and great lips.

Mojica straightened to her six-foot stature, and her black beret missed the top of the circular tunnel by about four inches. Three more of her tactical force entered, clad in dark one-piece uniforms. Bodhi got to wear one of those high-tech uniforms when they'd carried out the rescue of the Landers.

"I have to admit that you're the last person I expected to find gracing this passageway," Mojica said. Her hands fisted on her hips. "But I *was* waiting for you to show up pounding on the front door." She motioned him to follow and went back through the doorway. Her forces brought up the rear.

Mojica led him through several corridors that looked to be made of Mountain stone on one side and a composite on the other. He hurried to keep up with her long stride. "You've got to help me—"

"Yes, Selah's here. I knew where she was up until about a half hour ago."

Bodhi grabbed her by the arm and spun her around. "If you knew she was here, why didn't you save her?"

Mojica shook her head and calmly pried Bodhi's fingers from her arm. "Selah walked in here of her own accord. I have special sensors that alert me the moment a Lander or progeny gets near the Mountain. It is not my place to stop her from anything. It is my domain to be of help when asked, and not until."

Bodhi winced as they walked out into bright daylight.

"I'm asking! Help me get Selah safely out of here, please!" He shielded his eyes and looked up. A lazy blue sky appeared, with clouds and a brilliant orb streaming faux sunshine that gave off warmth.

"It's going to be a little difficult at the moment. Treva has apparently taken her into the Keepers' old tunnel system. They could pop up anywhere within the numerous miles of communities in the Mountain. I've got most of my TFs working on another operation at the moment." Mojica led him into an area covered in sand and cactuses. Were they cactuses? Yes. How did he know that?

Mojica walked to the front of a flat-roofed mud-brick building.

"Not acceptable to me. I'll find her myself. I thought you were friendly to her cause, but I must be mistaken." Bodhi turned away from the door opening.

Mojica yelled to a TF, "Stop him!"

The dark-clad tactical force member turned out to be another Amazon-like woman mirroring Mojica's stature. She stepped into Bodhi's path with her right hand on her hip weapon and her left palm out to stop him.

Bodhi glared at her and turned back to Mojica. "You're going to stop me? What is wrong with you? You helped save her father, and now you're going to let her be harmed?"

Mojica strode to his position in three long-legged steps. Standing toe-to-toe with her, Bodhi recognized her intimidating act of looking down her nose at him. He didn't feel threatened. In the past, he'd used the tactic himself.

"If you run around skittering like a protective boyfriend,

that's the fastest way to get her hurt. Have you noticed there are no sirens or alerts? Bethany Everling got her slacks handed to her the last time her private security force ran roughshod over the Mountain terrain, and she knows better than to raise an alarm that would bring the Politicos down on her again. With her husband turned into a head of cabbage, her influence is limited to the Science Consortium, not general governing."

"I think you're just saying anything to placate me so I won't go look. But that's not going to be the case. And I don't skitter," Bodhi said. He wanted to bluff her, but it was hard not having any idea where he was in the Mountain or how to find Selah.

Mojica let out a deep sigh and waved away the last of her TFs. "Technically, I'm the only one available to help you."

Bodhi opened his mouth to protest. But protest what? He'd better settle for the help he could get, not what he wanted, even though he had the impression this woman didn't like him much. His internal clock was losing hours.

The humming in his head dropped a few decibels. He let out a sigh of relief.

Mojica looked at him sideways. "Did you feel that?"

"Yes," Bodhi said. "It gave me a headache when I first encountered it in the tunnels. I got used to the vibration, but to have it cycle down is a relief. What is it?"

Mojica shook her head. "Nothing for you to worry about. I just didn't know that you as a transitioned Lander would be able to feel it."

Bodhi raised his eyes to hers. "Your knowledge seems to

be much more current than the last time I was here." It bothered him that he didn't have information on what or how much she knew, especially about him. Was she someone to be worried about?

"I have my sources. We've got to play this smart. I'm waiting for location information. They're somewhere in my Mountain, and I'll find them. The threat from Everling's wife is minimal."

"How long is this going to take? I have to get her out of here in—"

"I know. The machinery cycled on about an hour ago, so an hour to get back to the Reliquary, and that gives us twenty-two hours at most to find her." Mojica gestured him through the doorway.

This time Bodhi followed. "What is the Reliquary?" He glanced around as they walked into a control center.

"The cave with the grottos and the old man, where they're completing the configuration." Mojica walked to a console with twelve small screens lined up in three rows of four views each. She ran her hands over the halo-buttons, changing the live views at different locations.

"How is it that you seem to know exactly what's going on?" He'd have felt more comfortable being the one to have the answers. The last time here, he'd taken it for granted that because she worked for Charles Ganston, she was on their side. Now he knew segments of the First Protocol were in a power struggle. So where did her interests fall?

Mojica smiled for the first time since he arrived. "This is my Mountain. Nothing happens here without me knowing. It will be sad to leave."

"Why would you leave? Do you mean you're coming with us?"

Mojica looked up from her observations. "I—we—will be escorting your group out of here. It's time for everyone to go before it's sealed."

"Before what's—"

A shrill wail echoed across the control room. Bodhi winced. It seemed to be the right decibel to cut through his brain. His eyes darted across the screens, looking for the offense.

Mojica slapped a nearby console and killed the sound. "My day just keeps getting better and better."

"What is it? I don't see anything different on the screens."

"That alarm tells me there's a Lander child coming into the Mountain." Mojica slid into the seat in front of the farthest console and began changing camera angles with a virtual gimbal.

"Great! So you've located Selah."

"No, I said a Lander child coming *into* the Mountain." Mojica found the angle she wanted and zoomed in. She pointed to the screen. "That's the one."

The wide-angle lens panned, then faced an entrance Bodhi hadn't seen before. There was a wide area holding Air-Wagons, SandRuns, and other travel conveyances. He stared as the figures came into focus—a man and a deeply tanned woman with an abundance of curly yellow hair tied back haphazardly. The man's back faced the camera, but he was tall with dark hair. He turned slowly to face the area of the camera.

Bodhi narrowed his eyes. "Jaenen Malik—but he's no Lander child!"

"So you know Jaenen? How much do you know about him?" Mojica pursed her lips.

"I know he's a navigator and Glade hired him to find Selah's family."

Mojica slammed her fist on the console. "I knew I'd heard that name before—from Chavez." She turned to Bodhi. "Selah's family has been here a few weeks. Varro Chavez had them signed in personally by Bethany Everling."

"I need to tell Glade about this." Bodhi's head swam. It seemed like everyone concerned with Selah was winding up here at the same time. Or maybe it was the flowers he kept smelling. They seemed so close. He had looked around twice for them and neither time could locate the annoying fragrance.

"I told Glade when he left here we'd give him a briefing on the changes since he went into captivity. But he wouldn't listen. Hiring Jaenen was foolhardy. I don't understand why someone didn't warn him."

Bodhi tensed. "Warn him about what?"

"That Jaenen Malik is part of the opposition Protocol that would like nothing better than to extinguish Glade and get control of a novarium of Selah's heritage."

"But why would he be here now?" Bodhi didn't see how Jaenen coming into the Mountain could have anything to do with Selah. They hadn't come together.

"I'd say he's found a hedge of some sort. Everything he does involves money—for him. I bet I know whose child he has." Mojica led him across the control room to the gear lockers. "Let's go. Our priorities are changing faster than I can count disasters. You need to change clothes and look like one of my TFs so we can move about unhindered."

"We have to get Selah's family out too. Can we track where they are?" Bodhi worried about leading extra people, but if he could be the one to bring Selah the family she had been yearning for, he'd do it.

"I knew where they were yesterday during our immigrant briefing. But barging in there and saying they have to leave with you—a stranger, and a Lander at that . . ." She shook her head.

Bodhi had forgotten his lineage could be a factor. The outside world he lived in was accepting of and unimpressed by his mark.

Mojica directed him to the spares rack. "Here, cover your head before you cause a riot." She handed him a beret and headed back to her station.

He'd been through this before and knew how to equip himself. He hurriedly stripped and got into the one-piece suit. He slid his feet into the special boots, hooking the latches with a resounding thud. It felt good to be back in this gear again. The biomechanics of the suit tapped into his body through skin-to-material contact, regulating his chemical reactions to bring about optimum cognitive awareness.

Bodhi raised his heels to test the boots' springiness. They restored the nimbleness he'd lost in the transition. He could get used to being a TF. Securing the gear, he dashed back to Mojica's station. His internal clock counted down . . . twenty-one hours and forty minutes.

"Using facial recognition, I've established several visuals that complicate our job." Mojica pointed to the rightmost monitor on the bottom level.

Bodhi bent to get a closer look at the people hurrying through an outdoor market. "I don't know the woman or child, but that's Selah's brother—er, stepbrother, Cleon. Where are Selah and Treva?"

"Those two are from the Chavez family. I don't see Selah and Treva in this frame, but I do see something disturbing here." Mojica swept her hand over the control. The place and time stamps scrolled forward and came to a stop. She reached for the magnification screen, swung it over the frame, and zoomed in. The spot on the image magnified. "The man with the weapon is Selah's stepfather."

Bodhi's heart stuttered. Varro Chavez was pressing a pulse disruptor into Cleon's side. Bodhi pushed the magnifier aside. In this image there were two other men, one holding on to Pasha's arm and one holding on to Dane. He didn't understand how this fit—rather than a family, they looked like hostages.

He suddenly remembered how Mojica had been loath to give them weapons a few months ago. "Am I getting a weapon this time? And do you have any idea what we're getting into? It might be nice to know the combatants and the goal."

Mojica dropped her head for a minute, then looked up at him. "If we had unlimited time, I'd say no, my people could handle it. But we don't have that luxury, so yes, I'll arm you. And no, I don't know what we're getting into, but we need to go now."

Bodhi followed her to the armory. Mojica handed him a pulse disruptor. "They're silent, deadly, and don't make a scene." She cinched the leg strap. "I trust you'll be discreet in our general population. They're not accustomed to violence, and they may not understand the severity of the situation."

Bodhi cleared the weapon and laced the holster strap to several of the tabs on the suit before winding it around his leg and cinching it. He now had five other people's safety to worry about. He wanted Selah to be his first priority, but he didn't know where she was hiding. Hopefully she and Treva were headed toward the western end of the Mountain. Since Treva knew about her parents' tunnel system throughout the Mountain, perhaps she also knew of the exit tunnels.

"How do we get to Cleon's target area?" he asked.

"I'm impressed that you would eliminate the closest threat first rather than take up a fruitless search for Selah," Mojica said. She looked over at Bodhi and hitched a wry little smile. "You have a mind like a soldier."

Bodhi glanced at her, then looked away. Then glanced again. "Thank you. I think. Is that significant?"

"No. Not at all. It's just soldiers know if they were soldiers."

Bodhi frowned. "I'm not following you."

"Do you remember being a soldier before you came here?"

"No, the thought never occurred to me. I do remember—

did remember—some flashes of things but never full thoughts, and definitely nothing about any military involvement. Why?"

Mojica leaned on the sidearm strapped to her hip. "Just wondering. But watching you dial the load, mount the weapon, and the way you strapped it on—that's field assassin style."

20

Selah traipsed behind Treva through a series of tunnels made of little more than shoulder-wide corridors. A light rope ran down the center of the ceiling, which held air vents and panels strategically inserted at spaced intervals. The constant hum plaguing her for the last few hours had changed pitch. Her head felt better, but claustrophobia crept closer. The space felt warmer. The walls pressed closer as air became harder to pull into her lungs. The space . . . She grabbed Treva's sleeve, jerking the girl to a stop.

Bending over and lowering her palms to her knees, she sucked in deeply. Selah closed her eyes and tried to think of Bodhi and better times, but all she saw was Varro seething at her reluctance to do his bidding with that evil woman.

"Are you all right?" Treva leaned against the wall and rubbed Selah's back. "I wondered how long it would take these corridors to get to you."

"Can we get out and get some air?"

Treva bit her lip. "In here we're safe and can make it to the back of the Mountain in about nine hours. But out there—I don't know. We have to travel through some pretty hostile areas. The Mountain is miles of towns and courts, and not all of them get along with one another. It could be dangerous and really slow going, and it might even take us a couple of days."

"Can't help it. I have to get out of here." Selah leaned back against the wall and rubbed her forehead to wipe away the sweat stealing the last of her moisture. Nothing else mattered at the moment except breathing.

※

Selah gulped the refreshing air and relaxed on a bench to the right of a cascading fountain of angular stone and metal. It wasn't as strange in the Mountain as she thought it was going to be. They'd come out of the tunnels in an area similar to Dominion. The flower and plant landscaping around the fountain showed much care, and even the noon sun, as Treva called it, gave off a pleasant enough warmth. But with her keen eye Selah still noticed stark differences between this fake world and the outside.

Treva hurried around several stalls of hanging vegetables in the nearby marketplace, and trotted to Selah carrying some blue cloth draped over her arm and a container of water.

"Here, put this on, fast." Treva shoved one of the long blue coverings at Selah. She slipped the other one over her head and tied the belt at her waist.

"What's the matter and what are these?" Selah held the royal blue garment up for inspection.

"Of all the places you could have pulled me from the tunnels, you chose the Blue Court. If you live here, this month you're wearing blue in solidarity for the strike against the Water Consortium, and if you're not wearing blue you're either in top management or you're one of the enemy. They really don't see a distinction between the two, but that's another story. So I grabbed these from someone's laundry as I went by."

"Then let's go back in and come out somewhere else." Selah wrinkled her nose at the dirty cloth but slipped it over her head, glad that her own clothing was between her and the material.

"Can't do it. The system only has entry at certain places where they can control nearby traffic. Where we came out doesn't have an opener on this side." Treva took a gulp of water and handed the container to Selah.

She drank, then pulled a piece of the material up for a whiff. She wrinkled her nose again. "Next time try the clean pile. Let's go. I'm feeling better."

"We've got to follow the streets to Green Court, so it should take an hour or so to get out of this section—"

"Hey! You two." Six young men marched toward them.

Selah moved to stand beside Treva. The boys looked to be about Selah's age of eighteen.

"Let me talk," Treva said in a light voice without moving her lips.

The group surrounded them. Though noisy and boisterous,

none looked particularly menacing. Those on the far end of the group appeared relaxed, but the body-speak of the boy closest to Selah was hostile. She turned, putting her back against Treva's and preparing mentally for a confrontation.

Treva spoke evenly, showing no fear. "What do you rowdy men want?"

The boys seemed flattered at being called men and puffed up their chests.

"We haven't seen you in this part of the Blue, and we want to know who you are," the front boy said calmly. He wore a blue sweat scarf tied around his neck that matched the blue of his pants.

Selah felt Treva tense. "We transferred in from Green Court to work on hydroponics."

"So you're a pair of scummers who think they're coming here to do our jobs, take bio-coin from the Blue, and then report back to the Water Consortium that the bacteria is our fault." A shorter guy with a blue long-coat stepped closer.

Blue Scarf fingered Selah's cover. "Hey, Rip. Isn't your sister's name Steva B?"

"Yeah, so what?" A tall, skinny blue pole of a boy looked at them.

"This here girl is wearing her jump top." He held up the corner. "Her name is right here."

Not waiting to be grabbed, Selah pushed off Treva and they burst through the group, scattering the boys like bowled-over balance sticks. Both girls darted and dodged in different directions through the marketplace. The boys couldn't organize fast enough to catch them but still seemed determined to search.

Breathless, Treva caught up to Selah. "We need someplace to hide. We can't outrun them and they might herd us to a blind spot."

They could hear the boys coming closer. Selah eyed a row of blue-skirted tables in front of them. Grabbing Treva by the hand, she crawled under the closest set. The boys stormed around the corner. The girls sat huddled, shielding their noses and mouths from the dust filtering under the cloth as the boys scrambled around them, kicking up dirt where foot traffic had trampled the grass.

A pair of booted feet attached to leather-wrapped legs appeared when a chair was pushed under the table on the back side. The girls scooted toward the front, out of range.

"Stop running around kicking up dust," the muffled voice of an old woman yelled.

"Mind your own business, old woman," one of the boys yelled back. Their voices faded in and out as they searched around stalls and tables.

"If you come near my stand, I'll pelt you with apples. I'm as good a shot as ever. So steer clear," the old lady said. Suddenly a hand appeared under the tablecloth with two halves of a cored and peeled apple.

Selah looked at Treva, who reached out and took the offering. Selah hadn't realized how hungry she was, but it took all she had to choke down the tasteless apple with the stringy texture of a branch. She looked at Treva, who didn't seem to notice the unappealing fruit.

Next came an offering of jerky, which they both devoured, and a container of water. Selah was trying to decide how they'd escape when the cover lifted, and a soft-faced old lady with long, loose, white hair cascading over her shoulder and a full-toothed grin peeked under at them.

"You girls got a chance of skedaddlin' if you move now. The boys moved on to the next row. It will take them at least ten minutes to work their way back around," the old lady said.

"Do you have a Blue Court map we could borrow for a few minutes?" Treva asked in a soft voice.

"Before you come outta there, take off the Bentley girl's clothes and put these on." She shoved blue clothing under the cloth. "They're mine. And I don't have the modern shades like all you young ones, so you'll just have to wear old-lady blue, but at least no one will be chasing you to take your clothes."

Selah and Treva scrambled to change and gave the other clothes to the old woman.

"Now I want you both to come out, walk straight ahead for five feet, and climb the single step to my unit. I'll buzz the door open and be right in as soon as I see you didn't draw any undue attention."

Selah looked to Treva. *Should we trust the woman?* Treva shrugged. Selah pressed her lips tight. *Better to be inside than out in the open. More time to think.*

"Let's go, ladies. Time is evaporating," the old lady said with a hint of impatience.

They crawled from under the tablecloth, shielded their eyes from the bright sun, and hurried up the single rocrete step to the narrow living unit. A mechanical lock sounded and the door swung open as they reached the threshold. It closed behind them with a resounding click.

254

Selah and Treva slowed once the door closed and they were safe. *Better look around rather than storming any farther in.* Treva motioned her to the first room on the right. Selah pulled up short. The furnishings were old-lady fluffy. She wondered if all old people needed extra padding for their bones when they got old.

Treva interrupted her thoughts by pointing to a Blue Court map on the side wall. "This is a stroke of good fortune. We can be—"

The front door burst open. Accompanied by two of the six boys, the old lady charged in, brandishing a pulse disruptor. "Now back over there against the wall and tell me who you are!"

Selah inwardly slapped herself for being so gullible. Being distracted by the rowdies, she'd never stopped to read the woman's body-speak. Too late now. There wasn't much use fighting against a weapon. *Never trust old ladies offering apples, especially when they turn out to be that bad.* She raised her hands in surrender and backed up.

Treva did the same but talked all the way back. "We didn't come here to steal anything from anyone. We're leaving as soon as we get a look at this map showing how to get to Green Court." She pointed behind her head.

"I may be old but I sure ain't stupid. You expect me to believe two girls, as well manicured and clear-skinned as you two are, are just roaming around in Blue Court to *pass through* on foot?"

Selah gave a little nod to Treva. *Answer her. I don't have a clue what to say.*

Treva fisted a hand on her hip. "Our transportation broke down near Dutch Station, and someone said this was a pleasant market to visit. I'm beginning to think they were robbing me for the bio-coin I gave them for the information."

One of the boys charged forward. Treva threw up her hands to ward him off, but he stopped inches from contact with her. "So you did no wrong and have nothing to hide but stealing a girl's clothes. I see the fine quality clothing you have on under our clothes. Is this a sick pleasure for two highborn girls?"

"No! We'd never steal—" Selah stopped. They had stolen clothes. It embarrassed her now that it was framed as someone else's loss and not just her gain, no matter how necessary.

"Yeah, that lie won't work, will it, missy?" The old lady still pointed the pulse disruptor.

We can't tell them about the tunnels. Think!

"We did break down, but no one told us we were in a Blue protest. We thought it was Red Court's turn. We realized the mistake after we were too far in to turn back safely." Treva batted her eyelashes at the boy still breathing in her face.

Suddenly there was a banging at the door.

Everyone jumped. Selah kept her eye on the disruptor in case of a misfire. A commotion in the hall, the door flew open, and three more boys spilled in, slamming the door behind them. "There's TFs coming. Everyone down."

The boys scrambled to close the window panels and threw themselves flat on the floor. The old lady dove for cover.

Selah and Treva took that opportunity to run to the door. A shimmering wave seeped through the walls and door, vibrating a slow and rhythmic pulse as it spread out into the living unit. They backed away swiftly. Treva stumbled down the hallway while Selah lurched into the room they'd just left. The wave accelerated, shot through them, and was gone.

The percussion slammed into Selah's back, pushing her forward against a stuffed chair. Her arms and legs flopped on the floor as she fought for control of her own movements. Warmth spread over her, then confusion, then searing heat . . . then blackness.

21

Bodhi listened to Mojica bark orders, moving squads of TFs around to hot spots throughout the fifty square miles of the Mountain. She tapped off her earpiece and navigated the wide pedestrian roads below the MagLev tube trains, which ran on the frictionless magnetic rails winding through the Mountain.

Bodhi worried that so many incidents going on seemed to pull Mojica's sense of duty back to her Mountain. "Are we still headed toward Cleon's last known location?" He counted the time in his head—twenty-one hours to extract.

"The coordinates on the surveillance log are in the Green Court sector. I called for a backup team, but we have to wait an hour or so. They're spread too thin in there now." Mojica maneuvered expertly around stalled traffic and bottlenecks.

Bodhi winced at some close calls. There were many more people in here than he'd realized, and all of them were in the streets. He was hoping that tracking down Cleon would lead to revelation about Selah's whereabouts. This seemed too convenient a time to get stalled waiting for a backup team. "Are you trying to slow me down for some reason?"

"Green Court has been a recent hotbed of scandal because the local government was proven corrupt and removed from office." She raised the AirSkid to the same level as the MagLev trains but on the opposite side of the road, then shot forward, pressing Bodhi back into the seat. The lane marker on side poles read SECURITY. "But local enforcement backed the fallen administration and won't help the interim government with security. And GC enforcement gives Mountain security a hard time for coming into their sovereign court."

Bodhi stared out the side as the cities buzzed by. It didn't seem to matter where he went, there was always corruption. Glade had mentioned the Protocols and some long-ago government involvement. He wondered if the Mountain had more to do with this situation than he could see. He'd never gotten a chance to get back on the subject with Glade.

Mojica's DashCom squawked. Bodhi blinked to clear his thoughts as Mojica spoke in clipped sentences and tapped off the earpiece connection. "Please don't yell inside my closed vehicle, but . . . we have to make a detour." She steered to an adjacent lane bending around a curve to the right and punched the throttle.

The hairs at the nape of his neck stiffened as his frustration mounted. "You know how much time we have left to find all of them?" Had he chosen wrong in staying with Mojica?

Maybe he'd find an opportunity to sneak away and start searching on his own.

"I know, I know. But since we can't get a backup team in Green yet, the detour won't cut into our time."

Bodhi leaned over. Stress made the pounding in his head match his heartbeat. He had to trust someone in here, and it would make his life easier if he chose Mojica, at least until a better circumstance came along. Then he could stop guessing at her reasoning.

"Let's go. If you're sure we won't lose time." Bodhi raised a hand. "I'm dressed and armed for the part. Where are we going?"

Mojica glanced at him and shook her head. "There's been a TF action in Blue Court. The Mountain is in charge of this investigation, and we've finally run up on one of the baby extortion rings—"

"Baby extortion? You mean they're selling babies?"

"No, by *baby* I mean young. 'Like father, like son' sometimes has validity. These young men are taking after their disgruntled parents, and it's leading them on the wrong path away from the court spirit."

"What's court spirit?"

"This is Blue Court. A group of communities banded together to create a governing entity whose board decides everything from the court economy down to personal freedoms, and everyone happily agrees—ergo, court spirit."

Bodhi narrowed his eyes. "Are we going to have resistance from Green Court about looking for Selah? Is that why you're getting backup?"

"Yes. I didn't want to tell you. Green Court doesn't want any Mountain TFs in their territory. They want to conduct the search for Cleon and his family."

Bodhi lurched in his seat. "They don't understand the situation—"

"And we can't tell them. Let me handle it. I've got the right team." Mojica slowed and dropped down to a street-level side lane.

The crowd separated to either side of the market area, allowing Mojica's AirSkid to set down in front of a multiunit row of residences where MedTec and TF units had gathered. Pulsing blue lights on the official units bathed the area in a strange, almost icy glow. A long, lanky teen lay stretched across the rocrete walkway with his head on the single step to the incursion unit.

Mojica hopped out and looked back. "Do you want to come see how we work?"

Bodhi looked at the splayed-out kid and shook his head. "No, I don't need to see any more death in the name of peace."

"Death? What? No, that kid's not dead. He's just immobilized for an hour by a pulse cannon. Very effective new weapon. With one shot from out here, everyone in the house is incapacitated for an hour."

Bodhi waved her off. "I'll be here when you're done."

He watched Mojica stride up the walkway, check the boy's biometrics, and then angle into the house around a couple of other TFs congregating in the doorway and hall.

Bodhi sat up. This was a perfect opportunity to strike out on his own. He bolted from the vehicle and dashed through a square grouping of trees and a fountain. Clearing the other side, he turned left and back west to Green Court.

He jogged down the long, wide road, staying close to the buildings. His armband vibrated. He stared down at it and stumbled to a halt. His heart thudded. He'd forgotten to take off the gear. Mojica knew where he'd gone. The armband buzzed again.

Bodhi started to unlatch the device but stopped. Probably every bit of gear had a locator, and he wasn't willing to give it all up, especially the weapon. Besides, if he was out of uniform someone might notice faster than if he just ignored her. When she was ready to give help she could catch up.

He slowed. People had stopped on the street and were staring at him like he was naked or something. He walked down the road and his armband buzzed again, spreading the vibration up to his shoulder. He walked faster, passing slower-moving people. He could hear feet behind him. They were following him.

Bodhi wheeled, ready to fight. Two little boys of about eight or nine tripped over each other getting out of his way. They plopped to the ground with mouths hanging open and hands outstretched as though to ward off blows.

"We're sorry, sir, please. You're a TF, aren't you?" the one on the right said. Bodhi noticed he looked just like the one on the left—twins, just in different shades of blue clothing.

Bodhi kept moving, trying not to notice the vibrations shooting up his arm. He glanced at the quickly thinning crowd, then up at the few still coming down the stairway from the MagLev. He could take the train to Green Court.

The other boy hopped up and ran after Bodhi, grabbing his arm. "Wait, please. You're from the Mountain. Our brother is being attacked and no one else will help."

"They all walked by," the other boy said. "Please."

The boys pulled him by the arm. Bodhi opened his mouth to protest, but then he heard a child's wail echo off the underside of the MagLev tube.

Bodhi tensed. His eyes darted across the structures. "Where is he?"

"There!" The boys ran and Bodhi followed. His arm vibrated and he almost answered it to get help. They darted around the building closest to the MagLev. A row of trees blocked a container area in the back. A short, stocky man with a shoulder-length mop of dark hair was dragging a boy, who mirrored the other two, up a set of outdoor stairs. First he had him by the arm. The boy wiggled free, and then the man snatched him by the hair. The boy clung to the railings, kicking all the way.

"Help me!" he screamed, clawing at the hands dragging him up the stairs backward.

Bodhi clenched his fists and charged the stairs. "Let him go!"

"This is none of your business. I didn't call for Mountain security. You got no jurisdiction," the man yelled. "He owes me ten hours' work to pay for my destroyed product."

The boy's eyes pleaded. "It's his fault—the machine doesn't work right and he won't fix it. No one will listen to me. I'm only a boy."

Bodhi pulled the boy free. "You will have to take that up with the proper authorities if you want to make a complaint, but you can't drag children around by their hair." The boy scrambled down the stairs, and the sound of his footsteps disappeared around the building.

"Why, you—" The man swung a right.

Bodhi pulled back and dodged the fist. As the man's shoulder passed in front of him, Bodhi gave him a shove into the building. Maybe he pushed the guy harder than he needed to—his face smashed to the wall with a thud. Bodhi almost apologized, but the guy was a menace, dragging a kid that way.

The guy came away from the wall, leaving a spray of blood on the surface. He touched his nose and looked at the blood on his hand. He clenched his fists without a word and charged.

Bodhi captured the man's outstretched hand in a scissors hold with his arms, used his leverage to rotate the man, and pushed him onto the hard rocrete surface of the stairs. Strange. It felt natural to make those restraining moves. Where had he learned that?

"Stay there and don't try that again!" Bodhi said, moving his hand to his sidearm.

The guy held his nose and suddenly became all smiles. "I see you're a new one here. For your well-being, you'd better go back to this section's unit command and find out who you're dealing with. Tell them you met JB, and then take the reassignment." The man plastered on an evil smirk, pushed off from the stairs, and slowly went up to the next floor.

The man had never questioned Bodhi's authority, but he had practically dismissed it. What was going on in this section that little children were working any hours, let alone long hours? He shook his head. Not his problem—he'd be gone in less than a day.

The cords in his neck tightened. Time was running out. His armband buzzed.

Bodhi's shoulders sagged. He punched the button. "What do you want? There's nothing you can say that would make me come back. You're slowing me down."

"*I'm* not slowing you down. You seem to have stopped in the same area for quite some time," Mojica said.

"There was a problem with a shop owner and an employee, I guess."

"Oh, so a deviation got in the way of your plan and you actually stopped to do something, hmmm?" The lilt in Mojica's voice indicated she was smiling.

"I don't have time for sarcasm, Mojica. What do you want?"

"How about if I say Selah." Mojica's voice lowered. She must have turned away from her unit to speak to others around her.

Bodhi stared at the armband. "What about Selah?"

"I have her. And Treva."

He stiffened. "How is that possible? Are they all right?"

"They were in the incursion unit. Apparently they were just netted."

"What's netted mean?" He dashed back in the direction of Mojica, but holding his arm up cramped his speed.

"Basically kidnapped. We were very lucky. They might have never turned up if this gang had gotten them sold off during the night."

"I'm almost there. How are they?" Bodhi didn't wait for the answer. He dropped his arm and ran full-out.

⊛

Bodhi knelt on the hard-pad floor between the two bio-beds in the MedTec unit. The other occupants of the incursion unit and their old lady leader had been shipped off to security. Mojica promised him that Selah and Treva would be fine in a few minutes. By the time he got there, they'd worked through most of the cell displacement from being shot. Since it was such an effective method for taking down a riot, MedTec had great remedies to restore cell organization once security gained control of a situation.

He brushed the hair from Selah's fluttering eyes and then rubbed the back of her hand. Just that small physical contact ran a bead of warmth through his tightened chest. She looked so peaceful.

A soft sigh escaped her parted lips and her eyelids fluttered again. This whirling fireball about to wake from being riot-grade pulsed was going to hit a new level of anger. Did he really want to be the first person she saw when her eyes opened?

22

Selah's vision rippled in and out as though being stretched and folded like the ribbon candy Mother made for celebrations. *Mother . . . Mother is here. Our hands pressed to the surface—*

Her eyes opened a slit. Her vision cleared. Bodhi? Was she actually seeing him, or just wishing it? Selah willed away the gray covering clinging to her brain. Heat radiated from her head down to her toes. Her mind cleared. Bodhi held her hand. She wanted to smile but feared the feeling might evaporate if he knew she was awake.

Bodhi leaned on the side rail of the bio-bed and stroked her cheek. "Selah? Wake up," he said softly. His voice hitched like he was anxious. It hurt her heart to see him worry for nothing.

She liked the warmth of his fingers on her skin. Her cheeks

betrayed her by lifting into a smile, so she opened her eyes. "Bodhi, you're really here. How can this be?"

He pulled her to his chest and wrapped her in his arms. She felt the tremble in his hug.

"It's a long story, but Glade is in Stone Braide and I have to get all of you out of here. We've only got twenty hours left," Bodhi said.

Treva's eyes opened at his words. She rubbed her head and sat up on one elbow, squeezing her eyes shut several times. "What in the name of electrons hit me?"

"A pulse cannon. You walked into a TF capture operation," Bodhi said.

"I should have listened to my gut. I knew something was wrong with that old lady. My brain feels like a cooked egg trying to congeal. I did catch your twenty hours comment, though. We can get out of here in an hour now that we've got your help. But why the time limit?"

"Glade accidently started a countdown. But we don't know to what."

Treva's eyes widened as she scrambled to her feet. "We have to get out of here now! Before the Mountain closes. That's the hum I felt in my head!"

"What does the hum have to do with this?"

Treva edged around Bodhi and pulled Selah to her feet. "It's the machinery dispensing the chemicals and sealing the Mountain."

"Sealing it for what? What does this have to do with Glade?" Selah ran her hands through her hair and lifted the old lady's blue coat flaps. She stripped off the coat and threw it on the bed.

Treva sighed. "My parents' Keeper journals said something like, 'At the appropriate time a transitioned novarium will bring the three parts of the Stone Braide together to activate the key to the Third Protocol.'"

"But that's good. The Third Protocol is necessary to keep Selah from fracturing," Bodhi blurted out. His face turned crimson.

Selah turned to him. "What do you mean to keep me from fracturing? And why do you know it and I don't?"

Bodhi's mouth opened and closed. "Glade entrusted me—"

Her eyes narrowed and she glared at him. "Oh, so now you and Glade are cohorts? It's bad enough my stepfather is a master manipulator, but then I get my brains scrambled by magnetic pulses and now find out my father and my boyfriend are plotting out my life—"

"Look, I hate to change such an interesting subject, but Bodhi said we have twenty hours. We can make that easy. Let's get out of here now." Treva motioned toward the doorway. "Thank goodness I directed Cleon and your family out of here."

Bodhi pressed his lips tight. "Cleon, Pasha, and Dane were caught by Varro and a couple of his men."

"Where are they?" Selah felt the blood drain from her face. She moved to grab his arm. "How could you possibly know this—"

"The same way he knew about you—through me," Mojica said. She filled the open doorway of the MedTec unit.

Selah held out her hand. "Mojica, I've been trying to find you." They clasped each other's wrists and smiled.

"How do we track down where he took them?" Selah looked between Bodhi and Mojica.

"You're not going near any fighting. Glade pledged me to protect you," Bodhi said, his stance defiant.

Selah gritted her teeth. "You don't get to tell me what to do about my own family." Then, facing Mojica, "And who in the names of all my horses hit me with a pulse? I thought we learned in Study Square that those things are only used when there are clear unimpeded targets."

Mojica appeared a shade flushed. "Since Noah Everling is no longer de facto head of the Company running the Mountain, the Politico Board took over. A lot of things are different now."

Treva moved toward the doorway. "Where were Cleon and the others last?" she asked, her face ashen.

"You can't get there. It's in Green Court," Mojica said. She moved away from the doorway for the exiting women.

"We've got the Keeper system. We get in there and we can get a lot closer without being seen." Treva hopped down to the street.

Bodhi put his arm in front of Selah to keep her from following. "You didn't say what happens when the machine seals the Mountain."

Treva looked at Mojica and then back at Bodhi. "We need to be far away before that happens."

Bodhi took Selah's hand. She didn't pull away. He faced Treva. "Tell us what happens."

"The Mountain is going to be sealed from the outside, forever," Mojica said.

Selah tightened her grip on Bodhi. "How is it going to happen?"

"This community is a bio-dome built inside the Mountain, which is going to collapse, sealing off the paths in and out with enough stone that it will take a thousand years to clear it," Mojica said.

"The ancient government of this land made preparations to have an event such as we're about to experience happen at a given period of time—after a series of events such as the Sorrows," Treva said.

Bodhi locked eyes with Treva. "How . . . where did you get all this?"

"Oh, please! Have you ever met a child who didn't snoop in their parents' things? Mine had secret rooms, passages, and a collection of ancient documents. I read everything." Treva grinned.

"So the Sorrows were engineered?" Selah asked.

"There are a lot of facts that have never been uncovered," Treva said.

Selah felt a lightning spike cut through her head. She closed her eyes and then opened them to quickly vanishing sparkles of light.

"Are you all right?" Bodhi gripped her arm.

Selah recovered and nodded. "Yes, I was thinking. What's the event that's going to happen?"

Mojica pressed her lips together. "The Mountain has started the process of mixing millions of tons of stored chemicals that will seed the clouds over this range and bring rain."

"And that rain will wash away enough of the ancient ash

from the super volcano explosion in Yellowstone to open the paths to the West," Treva said.

"How much rain?" Bodhi pulled his eyebrows together.

"A deluge. Like the worst of floods. We need to be away from here," Treva said.

Mojica looked up at Bodhi in the doorway. "I've only got one problem. I've got my TFs rounding up those we need to get out of here before the Mountain seals, and I can't afford security to safeguard Selah's travel back to the tunnels. She has to come with us."

Selah grinned. Now she wouldn't have to fight Bodhi to find her family. "Are you sure Varro had a weapon on Cleon?"

"Yes, I have the video stream log here." Mojica pulled up the frames on her ComTex. She scrolled through the collected file. Bodhi and Selah hopped down out of the MedTec unit.

"Wait!" Selah grabbed her wrist. "Go back a couple of frames."

Mojica fingered the frames a single move at a time.

"Stop!" Selah and Treva gasped at the same time. "Mari!"

Selah stared at a picture of Jaenen and Mari coming into the Mountain.

"Jaenen Malik rode with us all the way here, he's being paid by my father, and then he does this?" Selah winced at the pain of his betrayal.

Bodhi's eyes widened. "Wait! Jaenen came down here with you? Who's the woman?"

Selah's glance darted away and back again. "Mari Kief, the regent of WoodHaven. We stayed with her last night."

Bodhi's face seemed to pale as he averted his glance. Selah stared at him. "Is something wrong?"

He snapped back, "I was just thinking we now have someone else to save and nineteen and a half hours to get out of here without being killed or maimed."

Mojica finished manipulating the screens on her Com-Tex. "I don't know if it's good news or bad news, but I just checked Jaenen's log-in. He was entrance-validated by none other than Varro Chavez."

"So they're going to be congregating in the same place," Selah said.

"I have to find a way to get you and Treva to the staging site in Green Court. I can't transport civilians in Green without drawing suspicion, and we're going into a high-risk situation with their security to begin with."

Selah took a deep breath as sweat beads dotted her forehead. The tunnels. She had to get over it. They needed the speed. "We can get there faster than you can by using the Keepers' tunnels."

"Then we could all use them." Bodhi brightened.

"No, your shoulders are too wide to go straight on, you'd slow us down. And Mojica, sorry, but you're just too tall," Treva said, her face flushing.

Selah clapped her hands. "Let's go. Which way to the next Keeper entrance?"

"It's at the other end of Blue, right before Green Court," Treva said.

"I can take you that far. I have jurisdiction in Blue to have you in my vehicle." Mojica led the way, and the three followed.

☥

Selah sat next to Bodhi in the rear section, while Treva sat up front with Mojica.

"I've been violated," Selah said, her head bent.

Bodhi jerked away and held her by both arms. "Who hurt you? What happened?"

"Bethany stole a bunch of her blood," Treva piped in without turning. "In reading my parents' files, I surmised that something like this might happen. The ancients wanted these people sealed away until they had forgotten about Landers and the like. That's the reason the Mountain is sealing."

Mojica navigated to the upper lane for security travel, causing Selah to jump. She just wasn't used to high-speed traffic where there were others to maneuver around.

"What is so special about my blood?" Selah settled back in the seat beside Bodhi. Some of these things no one could answer were frightening, but she'd have to save them and be scared later. Right now saving her family took priority.

"I don't know that anyone here has the exact answer," Mojica said. "They know components of your blood can increase longevity. They don't know for how long, or why. The complete answers are 150 years old. They've gotten muddled with lost or omitted data, old wives' tales, and in some instances, just plain inaccuracies. When we find the Third Protocol we'll get the answers." She pushed the speed limit and hurled them across Blue Court.

Selah looked up at Bodhi. She moved closer and felt his warmth. It made her finally feel safe and gave her shivers all at the same time. She wondered if her brain had been permanently scrambled and this was a made-up scene from her dreams.

Bodhi touched his index finger to her nose and smiled. "Hey, firefly."

Selah felt prickles throughout her chest. This was real. Her head moved closer to his, and she suddenly felt self-conscious that those in front would hear their business. "I thought you were done with me."

"Please don't start fighting now. Wait till we get home or at least free from here."

Selah started to move away. "So, are you faking being close to me?"

Bodhi snatched her back to his side. "No," he whispered. "You were right. It was Glade making me say that, but I'm not doing it anymore."

Selah dropped her glance. "So . . . we're a couple?"

"If you'll have me." Bodhi took her hand and touched his lips to the back of it.

Selah slowly brought her eyes up to meet his. "And why should I have you?"

Bodhi lifted her chin with his fingers. He gently touched his lips to her right cheek. "Because I love you."

A shiver rolled up her back, making her shoulders jerk. Selah closed her eyes and took it all in, savoring how she felt. "Tell me again."

Bodhi tipped her head, kissed her left cheek, then looked at her. "I love you, and I want you to know in case something happens to me and I don't make it out of here."

"*We'll* make it out of here. And I love you too." Selah smiled softly.

Bodhi touched his lips to hers. His breath was warm on her face, and with his tender lips pressing hers, Selah responded. She closed her eyes and drifted a mile away.

23

H ey you two, we're here." Treva banged on the console without turning.

Selah swung her legs out of Mojica's vehicle as Bodhi ran over 107 dos and don'ts. She tuned out the commands as she drank in his features. Those she would remember in great detail. Mojica shared tactical advice with Treva on Mountain technology and what she could supplement in their travels.

Mojica turned to Selah. "I'm sorry I can't give you weapons. They're traceable, and it would set off alarms for them to be on someone out of uniform. If something happens and we don't meet you in Green at our Duncan and Marrow substation, I've told Treva where to find enough equipment to get you to the tunnels and out of here."

"But we have to find my family and we can't leave Mari.

I feel like she's here because of me." Selah would never be able to live with herself if they were sealed inside.

"I promise I will get them, but you have to listen," Bodhi said firmly. "We've synchronized time with Treva. She needs to get you out of this Mountain by ten tomorrow morning—"

"But what if we—"

Bodhi grabbed her by both arms. "No buts. Please, Selah, no buts this time. Those tunnels took me an hour at a good jog to get here. Your life is at stake, and you have to be in the Reliquary with Glade at eleven when this goes off. Please. I love you." Without warning, Bodhi pulled her into his arms and kissed her deeply.

The intensity of his kiss made her knees quiver, and her fingers trembled as she clutched the fabric on his sleeves. But at the same time, Selah felt a lightning surge of strength and love . . . she felt loved. Their heartbeats turned into one synchronized sound that pounded in her ears. She drew power from their closeness, but she knew she had to be the one to pull away. A smile played at the corners of her lips. She slowly separated herself from the warmth of his arms. "I will be there, I promise."

◬

Selah jogged alongside Treva, who led the way through countless streets and past several tree-lined areas along the outside edge of the Mountain community. She noticed the landscaping had sparse tree stands along these edges, supplemented with a three-dimensional hologram of rolling hills that appeared to continue to the digital horizon.

They stopped in front of a multistory building surrounded by holographic trees. Its upper levels disappeared into the clouds floating in the bright blue sky. Selah stared. She'd never seen a building reach high enough to disappear into clouds. Maybe the top levels were an illusion too.

Treva pulled on her arm. "This is the place." A slight tremor shook the earth.

Selah stretched out her hands for balance. "What was that? I didn't know the Mountain had earthquakes."

Treva scrunched her eyebrows together. "I've never felt one here before." She led the way through the building corridors to a lower level and swung open a camouflaged stone door. A narrow slot swished open. Treva inserted her hand, and her biometrics turned the light green. An interior door clicked open.

They slid in and closed the entrance behind them. Lights brightened, and a ventilation system kicked on. Selah welcomed the cooler air. They leaned against the wall for a minute to catch their breath and take a drink.

"Are you going to be good in here?" Treva handed her the water flask.

"I have no choice." Selah took several sips. "My family is more important than my comfort."

"Do you blame me?" Treva fingered a random spot on the wall.

"Blame you for what? Bringing me into these death traps?"

Treva hitched a half smile. "These tunnels have been around much longer than we have, and I don't remember anyone ever dying here. No, I mean about Cleon and your family getting captured by Varro. If I hadn't sent them to the tunnels—"

"Don't you dare think that way. You couldn't have anticipated the level of evil coming from my stepfather. I still don't understand why he wants to keep them."

The tremor vibrated through the wall. They stepped away.

Selah glanced at a few wisps of dust filtering down from the ceiling. "Could this get serious?" Her concern clearly mirrored Treva's.

Treva looked around. "We'd better get going. Just in case." They started to jog.

Another tremor. This time harder. Treva bounced into the wall and broke her stride. She stumbled to a stop. "This is starting to worry me. I've never felt anything like this in the Mountain."

"Maybe—"

"Shh . . . do you hear that?" Treva held up a hand.

Selah heard it too. Voices. "These tunnels have thin walls. Where is that coming from?"

"We don't have time to stop every time we hear a voice."

Selah raised her hand to say something, but Treva jogged away. Selah didn't understand her sudden attitude change.

They jogged for a full hour without stopping other than to pass the water bottle back and forth, but it wasn't the same as being on an open surface. The going was tough. They'd maybe traveled only a few miles. Selah kept her mind occupied to avoid worrying. She counted green dots and then blue dots along the walls—seventy-eight green and thirty-seven blue dots on little raised pads spaced along the wall.

"Do you know where we are?" Selah pushed her fists against her sides. The lightning flashes in her head were draining her, and they seemed to come on more frequently since the run-in with the pulse cannon.

Treva stopped and pivoted back, still pumping her legs to stay warm. "We're maybe another hour from the coordinates Mojica gave me. We're somewhere close to the back entrance where we came in. Security buildings are on the other side of this tunnel wall. They service the back gate where we came in."

"It would be nice to just walk out this tunnel door and out of the Mountain right now," Selah said. Voices drifted toward them again.

"Good thinking, except Bethany gets to monitor this gate— long story—and only citizens are supposed to be using it. That's why I could get us in. She will definitely be monitoring it, and if we try to get out—"

"Okay, I get it. I was just thinking out loud." Selah sighed. "Please, I need a little break."

This time Selah knew the voice she heard. Her back stiffened. Bethany Everling.

Selah's voice rose in pitch even though she tried to be quiet. "How can that be Bethany? Does she know we're in here?"

Treva shushed her. "No one knows we're here. This system has been secure for 150 years. I told you the rooms on the other side of this wall are security quarters. I think she's here because of Jaenen and Varro. Listen."

Treva laid her hand against one of the small green plates on the tunnel wall. A foot-high plascine rectangle in the wall turned clear. Selah ducked down against the wall, clawing to pull Treva down. "They'll see us."

"These are one-way acoustics. On their side it's a solid black noise panel. They can't see us."

Both girls peered into the opening.

A tremor began under their feet, small like the buzz of invading bees. The shaking increased as it radiated down the tunnel and crept up the walls, filtering silt down on them. The sound grew louder.

Treva had to shout. "We need to go now. I don't like being in a tight space with this happening."

Selah steadied herself against the wall. "We have to see the male she's talking to. I think it's Varro."

"It won't do us any good if this place comes down on us," Treva said, grabbing Selah by the wrist to pull her down the tunnel.

"Can we mark these coordinates—even that blue spot—to know where this is on the outside?" Selah resisted moving.

The tremor slid into a rumble, and the filtering silt turned to pebbles then chunks of rock.

Treva yelled, grabbing Selah's arm. The tunnel roared behind them, and a cloud of dust rushed along the floor and billowed to envelop them. Despite the light rope buried in the rubble, the sections above their heads stayed lit.

The haze thickened, invading Selah's eyes. The grit and her tears blocked most of the light.

Treva started to cough. She covered her mouth with her hands, then pulled up her tunic to use as a shield against the invading dust particles.

Selah hacked, trying to suck in air. Tears flowed down her cheeks. She rubbed the back of her hand across the wetness and felt the grit on her face. She didn't know if she should be frightened and believe this was happening. After all, she'd been through this same thing just yesterday morning, and it hadn't been real.

She coughed hard, wheezing through burning lungs. Her mouth felt gritty and her throat burned raw. She bent over, leaning against the wall. This felt real. She slid down the wall till her knees were level with her chest. She tried to hug them to her chest to stop the pain in her lungs. *No air.*

Suddenly dirt rained down on top of her. She pushed herself from the center of the dirt storm and pulled her way to the edge. Dirt poured up to her knees, trapping her. She cried out. She could barely make out Treva's silhouette in the haze.

Treva dropped to the floor. Her coughing spasm ended in gagging and retching. She labored to suck in air.

The tremor stopped.

Selah clawed at the dirt around her knees, trying to free her legs. Her movements were hindered by the lack of oxygen. She fisted the dirt from in front of her, pushing it to the side. The musty smell of the wet earth pressed in around her.

Treva groped along the floor on hands and knees, crawling to Selah. She reached the edge of the dirt and started frantically digging to free Selah. Her labored wheezing made Selah dig faster to reach her. She broke through to Treva.

They hugged, trying to cover their faces with their arms and clothes. Selah felt herself drifting. Lack of air. She faded to black.

◈

Selah heard it before she felt it. The cycling of the ventilation system. She could breathe. Her lungs burned like seared meat when she inhaled, but the air was fresh and clean . . . and cool. She didn't want to open her eyes. She wanted to lie down and rest—

Treva! Selah's eyes shot open.

Treva lay beside her with her arms draped across Selah's back.

She shook her. "Treva. Wake up. Are you all right?"

Treva moaned and coughed up a bunch of phlegm.

They both rubbed at watering eyes. The tunnel air was as clear as before the earthquake.

Treva labored to clear the dirt she'd inhaled. "We can't stay in here for another hour to get to the meeting point. But we can get to the next exit about a half mile away."

"But Bethany is—"

"Back behind that slide," Treva said, pointing behind them. The falling earth and stone had filled the tunnel. "That security section could be cleared out. We don't know how extensive this slide is." Treva scrambled to her feet.

Selah crawled herself up the wall to a standing position. Moving required a little more oxygen than she could take in at the moment. But a few more deep inhales and a couple of productive coughs, and she seemed stable.

They came out of a doorway in a wall covered by a three-dimensional holographic forest. The doorway was cleverly hidden behind several real trees. They scooted out onto the road and walked away, trying to brush off the dust and dirt they'd accumulated. Selah felt stronger. Air had never felt so welcoming.

"How much time did we lose?" she asked.

"We have seventeen hours to be at the tunnel. We should have met Bodhi and Mojica right about now, and we're still an hour away from them—by tunnel—which I really don't want to go back in." Treva grimaced.

Selah winced. "I'd prefer if we didn't. How should we get to Bodhi?" This was one of those times when she'd have preferred to deal with Bodhi barking orders and her reluctantly listening. When things like the cave-in happened, she doubted her abilities. Not that she thought the tunnel collapse was her fault, but she should have been able to reason it was going to happen and avoid the situation. Bodhi wouldn't have made that mistake. The flashes—her mind was a jumble of sensations.

"Will that communicator reach him?"

"Sure. Do you want to tell him why we're late?"

Selah screwed up her lip. She didn't want to explain the delay after he'd made her promise not to be late, though technically she was off track because of the earthquake. "I've been yelled at enough for one lifetime. Can we delay it?"

"I could just keep communications turned off. They still have our bios, so they know where we are." Treva looked sheepish.

"No. You'd better contact them. Up to this point it isn't our fault that we're late." Selah laced her fingers tight so she wouldn't rub the spot where her scar had been. After having that memento for many years, she'd wakened one morning as a novarium to find the scar was no longer there. It bothered her to keep tracing an empty spot.

Treva keyed the ComTex. Her brow furrowed and she pushed the link again. "We have no signal on any channel."

Selah looked down at Treva's wrist. "Did it get damaged in the cave-in?"

"I don't think so. There'd be damage to my wrist if it got hit hard enough to kill the signal."

"Could it be jamming? Would Bethany have the ability to disrupt Mojica's communications?" Selah felt fear trying to take root and stomped on it.

"I truly don't know what all has gone on in here since we escaped. Looks like we're on our own until we meet up with Bodhi." Treva frowned.

Selah's chest constricted. *What's wrong now?* No response. She tried again and touched Treva's arm. "Is it my imagination, or did I get hit too hard on the head? I can't seem to mind-jump with you in here."

"No, that's another thing I found out when I left you with Bethany. She's got her blocker system running as though she expected some kind of Lander attack. Why? What did you mind-speak?"

"I was wondering why you're looking like that."

"Because I was contemplating whether to tell you I marked the coordinates to Bethany's office location while we were in the tunnel, or whether to just keep moving you toward Bodhi."

Selah grinned and put both hands on Treva's shoulders. "Look into my eyes. What do you think you should tell me?"

⚛

Selah and Treva stopped at a small shop and bought a change of clothing. Treva explained they were too dusty to walk around unnoticed. Green Court was the hard-working class, but when they came home, they did so clean and polished, and in nice clothing. These families were the miners and oil riggers who operated the laser equipment in the energy fields. They were called builders because when they had exhausted an energy field on the outskirts, it was turned into community housing space and they just drilled farther into the mountain range to create new energy fields and more communities.

"I'm glad Mojica slipped us bio-coin. At least now we can survive without stealing," Treva said.

"It should be right around in here, shouldn't it?" Selah asked. They'd been walking for ten minutes, back in the opposite direction.

Treva fingered her ComTex navigation, then looked up. "It's over there." She nodded toward a sandstone structure that stretched along the inside of the Mountain, molded to the wall.

"Do you see any damage?" Selah checked both sides of the security gate area. Nothing.

"No. That's a good thing. Everyone should have remained where they are. We're going to C-35."

Selah pulled back on Treva's arm. "How are we getting into that area?"

Treva stared at her. "I thought you'd have that answer

by now, since you're the crazy one who wants to go in there rather than leave and return with Bodhi."

Selah slowed her steps. "If Varro's with Bethany, then Mother and Dane or even Mari may be there. We can't miss a chance to find them. And we're late now. Going back and forth may evaporate too much of our time." Selah watched an AirTrans-type vehicle stop and pick up several women. Several others walked away up the street. They all wore hats and one-piece tan coveralls belted at the waist, with a logo on their left shoulder that Selah couldn't read from her position.

"Who are they?" Selah pointed discreetly.

Treva glanced up from her communicator. "They're cleaners." She looked down again.

"If we get a couple of those uniforms, could we walk in there or do we need security clearance?"

Treva looked up and smiled. "No, cleaners don't need security clearance. These are temporary gate inspection meeting spaces. No one leaves their documents here. Come on. I think I know where we could find uniforms."

Selah followed Treva down and around corridors. The next door she opened proved to be a storage closet with uniforms hanging on a rack. Selah found one close to her size. "How do you know all this stuff?"

"It's the curse of being a child with a photographic memory and limited stimulus to commit to memory. I don't think there's a place in this Mountain I haven't been at least once." Treva smiled and raised an eyebrow. "Ancient passageways abound."

They dressed quickly, putting the coveralls on top of their

regular clothes. They each pulled on a hat. Selah twisted her hair and shoved it up under hers. Treva grabbed a cleaning center cart and led the way through the corridors to the office area. They peeked around corners to avoid Bethany.

"This next set of offices is where we heard her," Treva said.

Selah pursed her lips. "I was hoping one of the doors would be open or there would be a window. But I've got an idea. I'll pull my cap down tight and stick my head in, pretending I want to clean the space."

Treva looked at her without speaking.

"What do you think?"

"I'm trying to think of ways this could go wrong, but we won't know until you try."

Selah pulled her cart up to the door and reached out her hand.

"Wait!" Treva yelled in a hoarse whisper.

24

16 Hours to Egress

Selah tensed and her eyes widened. She snatched her hand back from the palm reader and pulled the cart over to the corner where Treva hid. "What'd you do that for? You could've gotten me caught."

"When I stopped running my mouth, I remembered that the next office shares a utility closet with hers. We can listen from in there."

"But we can't see who it is," Selah said.

"You know Varro's voice, and I'm sure you remember Jaenen's voice. If it's anyone else, we don't care, so it won't matter," Treva said.

Selah agreed. Treva held the door as Selah wheeled her cart into the darkened office. It took a half minute for her eyes to adjust to the darkness. Closing the door cut off all but the LED pin lights on the base communications grid attached to the desk.

Treva felt her way along the wall to the closet opening. She slid the door open and used her ComTex light to see the space. Selah peered over Treva's shoulder. A muffled voice filtered in from the other side of the door they faced.

They crouched low with their ears to the door.

"Are you going to loop to that subject again? This is the third time in an hour. I'm tired."

Selah whispered, "Bethany."

Treva nodded.

"Don't you turn away from me. This whole operation was my plan," Varro said.

Selah made a *V* sign with her fingers. Treva mouthed, *OK*.

"Don't you forget it's my technology that's going to unlock this code," Bethany said.

"So you've got the technology. Well, I've got the transitioned novarium. Without me, all you still have is just your technology. I can sell my novarium to the highest bidder. There are other Protocol factions looking to crack this also."

"You're bringing me an unknown commodity, and you want compensation I'm not willing to give." Bethany sounded like she was walking away as she spoke.

"I've fulfilled our original commitment," Varro said.

Selah scowled. "How?"

Treva shrugged.

Bethany snorted. "I don't have Selah now."

"You took a large enough blood sample to do every experiment you wanted a hundred times over," Varro said. "Jaenen

Malik arrived on time with Mari Kief, and now that you have her back in that cell, I've fulfilled our second agreement. I expect to be paid accordingly."

Selah didn't understand why Varro and Jaenen had involved Mari, but she sure wasn't going to leave the woman behind with these crazies.

She leaned back and closed her eyes. "We have to save Mari too," she whispered.

Squatting for so long had stiffened her legs. She lost her balance and slammed against the closed door.

"You've been here—"

The door burst open and Selah, with Treva trying to stop her momentum, rolled into the room. Bethany jumped behind the desk while Varro pulled a weapon from under the back of his tunic. "Nice to have you back. Your mother's been fretting something awful about your whereabouts."

"I don't think she'll be too happy about you pointing a disruptor at me." Selah talked calmly as she assessed their escape route.

Treva attempted to creep away behind her. Bethany rushed from behind the desk and grabbed her by the hair. "Oh no you don't, you ungrateful wench. To think I felt sorry for you."

Treva clutched at Bethany's hand as the woman pulled her to her feet. "I know you were part of the operation that executed my parents," Treva said.

Bethany's expression froze.

"And I can't prove it was you personally, but I will avenge my uncle. His condition is definitely your fault," Treva yelled. She threw a punch at Bethany but it grazed her shoulder.

Selah round-kicked the pulse disruptor from a startled Varro. The initial shock kept him anchored where he stood. Her heart thudding, she swung back the other way and swept her leg under him from behind. His feet flew into the air and he crashed to the floor at the same moment Treva shoved her elbow into Bethany's solar plexus.

Bethany grabbed her stomach, gasped for air, and collapsed to her knees.

Treva darted to Selah and scrambled to gain footing as they charged out the door.

Selah turned to the right. Treva grabbed her overalls and pulled her left. They ran like mice working a maze. Finally, breathless, they stopped.

"We're safe. They'll never find us here." Treva paced, hands on hips, trying to regulate her breathing.

Selah inhaled great gulps of air. "How can you be so sure?" She leaned against the wall.

Treva pointed. "They're on the other side of that wall."

Selah jumped to her feet and stepped away.

Treva snorted. "They can't get at us and we've got an advantage. I pushed Bethany far enough back in the room to get a look at the holding cells. She's only got Mari in there."

Selah nodded. Better. One less. "How do we get her out?"

"That's why I came around here. If I counted right, we should be on the other side of her wall." Treva fingered the edges of the individual wall panels.

"We're breaking into the room? Won't there be guards in there?" Selah stared at her.

Treva pulled out the panel, unlocked the other side, and

peeked in, then most of her body disappeared into the opening. She emerged, frowning. "Either I counted wrong, or they moved her already."

"Which do you think?"

"I counted wrong." She hurried to relatch the panels and count off a few more. "They wouldn't have sent guards for Mari, because from what I read in my quarters when Bethany first sent me there, they've pretty much banned her from everything but her husband's lab. So the only security she has left is in the medical containment."

"You mean her jail," Selah said. That encounter had involved more captive people and violence than she'd ever experienced in her life.

"Yes, but they're private security. They can't come out here and throw their presence around. And Mountain security thinks she's a joke. They purposely wouldn't arrest an actual criminal if she was the one dropping him in the station."

Treva finished counting and again removed the wall panels. This time her effort was rewarded by the shocked look on Mari's face. "What in the name of Jupiter is going on here? I've been drugged, dragged, gagged, and starved. This is not the way that Jaenen is supposed to treat someone when he first meets them. Not a good first date." Mari stepped through the opening and hugged Selah.

Treva replaced the panels and stood up. Mari wrapped her in a hug too. "Thank you."

Selah smiled as Treva awkwardly extracted herself from the smothering hug.

"C'mon, ladies, we have to get out of here before those

two find reinforcements." Treva darted them around another corridor and through two hallways. They turned the last corner to the triple-glass door front and ran for the exit.

From the other end of the hall, Varro and another man with a laser dart came into view.

Selah knew they wouldn't shoot and risk injuring her or Mari. The three girls charged to the doors. The men tried their best to outdistance them, but they were out the door before the men got halfway up the hall.

"Run into the neighborhood over there and hide in someone's fenced yard. They wouldn't dare open a gate to search," Treva said.

Selah spun, panic filling her. "Where are you going?"

"Go! I'll try to slow them down." She pushed a large street canister in front of the doors, then took off running behind Selah.

Selah ran halfheartedly, looking back the whole time, until Treva caught up with her. They turned a corner and Mari popped up from behind a tall bush. "Where are we going?"

"Nowhere until they stop looking for us. In here." Treva opened a tall gate made of real wood. The hinges squeaked but no boards were missing, and the fence was too high to look over.

Selah glanced around at the strange little white house set back in the yard. It had cone roofs on two rooms jutting from the second floor on each end of the building. The first floor had a porch wrapped around three sides with spindle railings. From the ground there were four steps to reach the first floor. Very strange. Selah had never seen anything like it.

"Do you think we'll be safe here?" Mari crawled over to Selah.

Selah wondered herself but nodded. "Treva lived in the Mountain. She knows what's safe."

They huddled in the grass behind the gate. Voices approached. One sounded like Varro. His footsteps and communications faded from hearing. The other one answered a call from a voice sounding like Bethany. Selah balked at the idea of being caught and hauled back to her mad science headquarters.

Treva signaled them to move closer to the house. A row of tall evergreen bushes butted up to gardens on either side of the stairs. They slid in behind the fragrant evergreens. Mari sat on the ground and leaned against a pile of leaves to see the gate. She cried out and jerked her hand back from the pile, exposing a dead plant stalk with sharp barbs, one of which was anchoring the stalk to her palm. Mari winced and pulled it free.

Suddenly the gate slammed open. Selah recognized the uniform of Bethany's security force. Her heart seemed to quiver. A bulky man dressed in all black and carrying an evil-looking weapon Selah couldn't identify strode in through the gate.

He planted his feet and took aim. "You're all under arrest. Drop to the ground and put your hands over your heads."

Mari looked at Selah and Treva. "I'm sorry. This is my fault." She moved from behind the bush and laid herself prostrate on the ground.

Selah stared at the security guard, wondering how much

she could get away with. He motioned her out from behind the bush. She stood and came around it, slowly raising her hands. Running wouldn't help. She looked up to face the guard.

A large black metal pan swung around the side of the gate and caught the guard square in the back of the head. His eyes rolled up. The weapon slid from his hands and he fell over.

Selah's jaw dropped open. She stood still, transfixed by the way the extremely large man had been brought down with a cooking pan. Mari and Treva rushed over.

A little old woman with skin the color of a roasted chestnut, a weathered complexion, and a severely tight hair twist on top of her head marched into the opening. She pulled the guard's legs out of the way and locked the gate. "You children git on in the house. He won't invade my home looking for you."

"But ma'am, he's awfully big and he already saw us," Mari said.

"No, she's right." Treva smiled. "They won't come in her house." She herded the other two up the steps and into the haven.

Selah stripped off the cleaner coveralls and plopped into the plump old-people furniture. Sinking into it gave her a comforting sensation of being surrounded and protected. The day had been hard, and it was seven in the evening, meaning fifteen hours left before they ran out of time to get safely out of the Mountain. Her body wanted rest, her mind wanted her family, and her heart wanted Bodhi. All drained parts of her, but curiously, at the same time she felt stronger. She'd been naive and immature when she started this journey, but now, even though bruised and battered, she felt secure—a confident young woman had taken the child's place.

The old lady shuffled in, wiping her hands on the long apron covering her skirt that went almost to the floor. "Are you children ready for some food? I haven't had to cook for a family in a long time. It was quite a treat. Come on in." She motioned them into a dining area. Like the front room, this one also had bold colorings. Selah marveled at the colorful walls covered in old artwork framed with golden-colored edging. She had only seen this much clutter in historical imagery during her studies.

As Selah walked into the room, wonderful aromas caressed her senses. "How soon will we be able to leave?" She wanted an idea of how long she'd have to digest dinner, and thus how much of this wonderful assortment of fruits, vegetables, and meats she could sample.

Treva looked to the old lady. "How much longer? Maybe an hour?"

The woman nodded. "Yes. I pulled him outside the gate and locked it again. I heard him stumbling against the fence about a half hour ago. So I'm assuming he left. Give them a little more time to clear the area and move on."

"If you don't mind me asking, why were you so sure they wouldn't come in your house looking for us?" Selah took a seat along with the others. Mari handed her a bowl of aromatic roasted vegetables.

Treva cleared her throat. "Because she's a descendant. She has a direct familial line to a worker of the original Mountain project."

"I'm ninety-nine years old. My mother lived to be a hundred and three, my grandmother lived to be ninety-seven, and my great-grandmother lived to be a hundred and four. That was G-G-maw's cast-iron frying pan I hit the guard with. That pan is as old as the concept of people living in this Mountain," the old lady said with a chuckle. "I still got a swing after all these years."

"It means she's like royalty in here. She doesn't pay for anything she needs, and her house is like a free point, a sanctuary, if you will, that no one can trespass." Treva sopped up the gravy on her plate with a fat sourdough biscuit.

Selah's mouth watered. She grabbed a biscuit and a ladle of gravy. "Is that why you stay in the Mountain when you could go outside and be free?" she asked.

"Selah!" Treva's eyes widened. She stopped with the bread halfway to her mouth. "It's rude to ask a citizen that, especially an elderly one."

"Now, now. She asks a valid question, and the answer is . . . not just because I'm an old lady, but you must look at it as a revolution of sorts. My whole existence has been a life of privilege and convenience. Why would I go outside where I'd have to take care of myself? I'm a little too old to take on an occupation. Must say, though, I'd be much happier if they weren't always giving us needles." The old lady shivered. "I hate needles."

Selah pulled her eyebrows together and glared at Treva.

You ask the questions then. Treva got the hint and laid the half-eaten biscuit on her plate. "What kind of needles are you being given? I didn't know of any such thing when I lived here."

"They started a few months ago. We get them regular as clockwork now. Said they're inoculating us against some germs they think got in the Mountain when there was that big assault a few months back."

Selah stared at Treva. Her mouth started to open. Treva waved her off.

"What kind of assault? I must have been gone by then."

"Heard tell it was a big incursion of bandits wanting to steal Mountain technology. They beat poor Dr. Everling to within an inch of his life. The sweet man may never come out of the coma." The old woman shook her head. "And his poor wife, Bethany, is a wonder, just such a wonder. She's been able to secure all kinds of help from business in the Mountain to refit her husband's lab after so much damage was done to it by those savages."

Selah opened her mouth to speak and Treva gave her a sharp kick under the table, startling her. Selah squeaked and jumped. Treva gave her the look to keep her mouth shut.

Selah pursed her lips. "How do you know the inoculations are safe?"

"The Mountain wouldn't give us anything that would hurt us. We're the citizens."

Selah wanted to scream at her, but she knew it would fall on old, deaf ears and do nothing but upset this beautiful meal. She started paying more attention to what was going in her mouth than what was coming out of it, for once.

The thought crossed her mind that if she didn't have some providence, this might be the last meal she'd ever eat.

Suddenly there was a loud banging on the front door. "Open up!"

25

14 Hours to Egress

Selah's chair scraped back from the table at the same time everyone else's did, creating a great screeching groan that vibrated through her feet to her very core. The biscuit turned to a lump of coal in her stomach.

"You children git on down to the cellar. First door on the right, the shelf with the canning jars swings away from the wall. Open the door and travel through the tunnel." The old lady ushered them into the kitchen and through a doorway leading to her underground storage.

They scrambled down the stairs with Treva leading the way into the room. Mari pushed the shelf away, and Selah pulled the door open. Voices drifted through the wooden floorboard.

Selah stopped. "Wait! They're in the house. They might hurt the old lady."

"They wouldn't dare," Treva hissed. She tried to motion them to the tunnel, but Selah stood her ground, listening.

"There've been citizen reports that fugitives broke into your house," a man's voice said.

"Does it look like anyone has broken into my house? You're the only one breaking anything, and that thing is my peace. Now be gone with you," the old lady said in a stern voice.

"I think we still better have a look around," another male voice said. Footsteps creaked the boards above their heads.

Selah clenched her fists, but her teeth chattered. If the guards touched the old lady, they would need to be ready to fight. Her glance darted around the room. The long oak handle of a push broom leaned in the corner where it guarded a pile of floor dirt. She stepped on the broom and unscrewed the handle.

"What are you doing?" Mari whispered loudly. "They've got a lot bigger weapons than a stick." She grabbed Selah's arm.

She shook her off. "We can't leave that old lady to defend herself after she took us in."

"It's okay, listen!" Treva pointed up. Selah and Mari stopped to listen.

The old lady had apparently used a threat that worked. The guards were retreating. The last one's boots cleared the doorway at about the same time the door slammed shut.

⚚

Selah ran along the side road between Treva and Mari. Her breathing had leveled off about a half mile ago, so she glided along with little effort. Treva held up a hand, and they ran in place to cool down. She called up their present coordinates on her ComTex and smiled.

Selah looked at the map. "We're much closer than I thought."

"Someone is on our side." Treva nodded.

"I wouldn't have thought so when we ran into that old lady's cellar. Do I look like I've aged five years from the stress?" Selah asked, her heart thudding hard against her chest.

"I thought we were caught for sure. I had a vision of staring at a dozen lasers painting red and green dots on our faces." Mari shook out her hands from running with her fists clenched.

"Do you think they came back to her house?" Selah frowned, thinking the woman may still come to harm for helping them.

"I seriously doubt it," Treva said. "They were trying to flush us out onto the street. I glanced out her back window before we headed downstairs and could see armed security waiting on the outside of her other gate. When we didn't come out the other side of the house, they probably figured it was a false lead."

"We were lucky she had an escape route behind that wall rack. You seemed to know a lot about her, Treva. Was she a bandit or something when she was young?" Mari asked.

"No, you couldn't find a more upstanding citizen. I'd always heard rumors that her house, being one of the originals in the first colony, had secret passages that led to multilevel underground operations even more secret than the Mountain's projects." Treva finished cooling down. She planted her feet and fisted her hands at her hips. "We've just found credible evidence to support that. Too bad we'll never be able to explore the possibilities."

"Why not? You could come back when all this settles down," Mari said as she took the water flask Selah handed her.

Selah and Treva looked at each other. Treva shrugged.

Mari glanced at the two of them. "What am I missing?"

"We can't come back. That's why we needed to rescue you now," Selah said.

"The Mountain colony is going to be inaccessible in about fifteen hours . . . forever," Treva said.

Mari's face first registered concern, then fear. "We need to get out of here now! I don't want to stay in this smelly place forever. Which way gets us out the fastest?"

Selah realized Mari must smell the same odor she did. "We still have my family to find. Remember my brother Cleon? My mother and little brother are here too. They've been kidnapped by my stepfather, who is also responsible for bringing you here."

"And I can't leave without Cleon." Treva's voice hitched.

Selah gazed at her.

"Why are you staring at me?" Treva shoved the flask back in her belt holder.

"No reason." Selah patted her shoulder. "We'll get to them." She was glad to see some emotion from Treva after worrying that she harbored resentment about her uncle and the rabbits, even though she'd said she didn't.

"So you know where they are?" Mari looked relieved.

"We're headed in that direction. We only had a few miles to go when we were at the old lady's house," Selah said.

"Was it my imagination, or did we come out of that tunnel about a mile from her house?" Mari asked, looking around at the scenery.

Treva looked at her with approval. "Very good. It was exactly a mile. How did you know that?"

Mari shrugged. "I've always been good with time and distance. When I was little, my father used to tell me I didn't have an excuse for being late."

Selah liked seeing the two of them get along. "Speaking of late, Bodhi will probably be giving Mojica fits because we're so late."

"I'd say we're only about two miles from our point. The old lady's tunnel brought us through Green in a straight line instead of zigzagging through the neighborhood roads."

"Hey, what are you girls doing here?"

The three spun to face the soft baritone voice. A man in his late twenties with flat-top hair stood in the middle of the road. He did not look or sound like someone people could ignore. A well-toned chest filled his tight shirt, and the tattoo of an exotic bird with long tail feathers extended from the fingers of his right hand, up his arm, and under the rolled-up sleeve at his large bicep. He strode toward them with long purposeful steps.

Selah deliberated if they should run but decided there might be an advantage to being lost. "We seem to have lost our bearings on how to get to—"

Flat Top abruptly stopped toe-to-toe with Selah. His steel-gray eyes drilled into her. "Don't talk. Just nod to what I say, and do what I tell you."

Selah's lip curled. "Excuse me, but why should we listen to you?"

"Hey, Conti, what've you got there? How come so many women for one man?"

The harsh voice spun the girls again. A large group of militant-looking young men exited the area the girls had been jogging toward. They were dressed in dark clothing and heavy boots, their chests crossed with leather strapping adorned with knife sheaths and looped lengths of chain. Two of them wore a large weapon bandolier slung over their shoulder, but many spaces for the cartridges were empty.

Selah tensed. The girls had almost walked into the middle of them.

"No, citizen, these are my sister's friends. I was just asking them what they're doing here when they should be on the next road over to get to our place."

"We're so sorry." Selah pasted on a contrite look and raised a pained smile. "We started talking and just weren't paying attention."

The group of men surrounded them, taunting and looking them over. Selah shivered but planted her feet to keep from visibly trembling. She realized if Flat Top—Conti—hadn't intervened, they'd be the prey right now. Treva moved in closer on her left and Mari on her right. Her heart thudded fiercely.

"Come on, girls, Teena is waiting for you." Conti gestured back the way he came.

Two militants stepped in their way. Conti jerked to a stop before the one on his right. The guy wore a sadistic scowl and had an ear-to-ear scar across the front of his neck.

"Do you actually think you'd get out of my Trac if anything happened to someone under my protection?" Conti slid his hand to the knife hilt resting on his right hip. Selah hadn't noticed the blade strapped to his leg. It ran from hip to knee.

"Do your best, Conti, but I know where most of your crew are defending your Trac at the moment, and I'm willing to bet that you don't have the manpower to stop me." A bearded guy with a green bandana drawn tight around his head grabbed Mari by the hair.

She turned into an angry cat. "Let me go, you tree borer!" Mari clawed at the hands gripping her hair.

Selah and Treva lunged to her rescue but were held back by the others.

Conti drew his knife. "Buck, let her go, or I'll hunt you down myself." He advanced, but the two in front of him blocked the way, brandishing their own knives.

Buck tried to kiss Mari on the neck. She head-butted him hard, and as he backed away she stomped on his foot, throwing him off balance. He skidded to a sitting position on the street.

Mari bounced around like a feline with its claws out, daring him to come closer.

All movement around her stopped. Selah watched transfixed as Mari challenged the guy.

Buck scrambled to his feet and pulled a long blade from a sheath draped across his shoulder. He had the same kind of sword tattooed on his right bicep, with a lightning bolt woven into it. "Now it's time to mess up that pretty face so it matches your disposition."

"Mari, don't be foolish. That sword could slice you in half like a hot wire through wax," Selah said. She didn't expect Mari to listen. The look in her eyes was too intense, and Selah felt helpless to do anything but beg. Buck attacked. Selah gasped. Her breath turned to short, shallow draws, making her dizzy. Treva gripped Selah's shoulder and moaned in fear.

Mari hopped to the side like a rabbit and swung around in time to kick him in the backside and send him sprawling again. She bounced back and forth on her feet, fists raised, and motioned to him again. "If you've had enough, you can just leave."

Buck wasn't completely steady on his feet, but he charged Mari with his head low like a bull. She stood her ground until the last second, spun away from him, and continued around, bringing both of her elbows down hard on his back. He collapsed to the ground. Mari jumped on his back, grabbed a handful of his hair, and slammed his head to the road. He stopped moving.

She rose and stepped over Buck's unconscious body. No one had moved during her display. Conti stood with knife in hand. Treva remained motionless, gaping, and Selah wanted to clap and encourage Mari. But that wouldn't help with the rest of the militants, so she too did nothing but stare.

A hand grabbed Selah's arm and jerked her around.

"Nooo!" Selah screamed, thrusting out both palms.

The militant flew back four feet and skidded to the roadway. That broke the spell of Mari's moment. The rest of the militants hurled obscenities as they grabbed their fallen ones and scurried back into the night.

"Selah, did you hear me?" Treva walked around in front of her. "You did it again!" Her eyes were wide.

"Did what?" Selah felt a tingling in her arms. Her eyes narrowed. She looked at her hands. So did Treva, Mari, and Conti.

"How can I learn to do that move?" Conti returned his blade to its sheath.

"Is that what you were telling me happened with the bandits?" Mari grinned. "I like that!"

Selah looked at Treva. "I don't know how emotions make it happen. This time it was being startled that did it."

"Remind me to never sneak up on you," Treva said.

Selah smirked. "I just think it's funny that I've been training in hand-to-hand combat for months, and now, when I figure out how to use it . . . I'll have built-in hand-to-hand."

"I think you ladies should follow me to my place on the next block." Conti held up both hands. "No funny business. Promise."

The girls agreed and trotted behind him down the road and over to the next street. Conti didn't speak a word until he stopped in front of a sandstone single-story unit.

He wheeled around to face them. "What do you think you're doing? Three women, real nice-looking women I might add, have no business walking around here this late in the evening unescorted."

"We don't have a choice," Selah said. "We have to get to Duncan and Marrow."

"Do you know how far that is from here? You're just asking for trouble." Conti paced in front of his doorway.

"It's two miles, and we're three hours late as it is. Now that it's dark, I'm getting worried," Treva said.

Conti threw his hands up. "Worried! You find the dark worrisome? So stay in my sister's room until daylight. Do you know what could've happened if I hadn't been leaving a friend's place down the street? You almost got . . ."

"We almost got what? I think we handled ourselves pretty well," Mari said.

Selah understood what he meant. They'd have to be more vigilant. She was surprised that living inside the Mountain mirrored the outside world. The only difference was the air in here stank.

"We understand. Thank you for coming to our rescue, but getting to our destination is more important at the moment," Selah said.

"You don't seem to understand," Conti said. "Green Court is in a state of emergency. Our court security team is on its last legs. They took a big hit taking on Mountain security forces earlier this evening. But they did succeed in beating back a TF team trying to enter Green. The Mountain apparently panicked, and the Politicos are jamming all air communications in Green."

Selah looked at Treva and frowned. "That's probably why we have no communications with them."

"We may not have a *them* to meet," Treva said. "Conti, we'd be grateful if we could get a few weapons, though I don't think we'll ever have the opportunity to give them back."

Conti frowned and then sucked air between his gleaming white teeth.

"We'd be even more grateful if you could point us in the shortest direction." Selah's hope had to stay on Bodhi. He said he'd be there when she got to the Green coordinates, and she believed him.

☖

Selah strode along with the broad knife slapping the side of her leg. From hilt to tip it must have been twelve inches. All Conti could offer them were knives, and the girls were glad to get them, except now they resembled some of the scary people they were trying to avoid.

Treva looked at her ComTex. "I figure we'll be there in about fifteen or twenty minutes—"

A yelling echoed between the buildings. Selah motioned Treva and Mari to a hedgerow in front of a multistory building. They watched a hooded figure loping down the road, then the noise started—the running feet of cursing men. Selah's chest tightened. She recognized them, but there were only five this time. It sounded like they'd had too much mash.

"It's them again. What should we do?" Treva whispered.

"We do nothing. Let them go by so the way ahead is clear for us," Mari said.

Selah pressed her lips together. "We should—"

The hooded figure ran back up the road. Something about the way he ran . . . He turned his head to look back.

Cleon!

He kept running.

"Cleon!" Selah yelled as she darted from behind the bush,

her legs pumping to catch her brother. Treva and Mari ran behind her.

"Selah, stop yelling. We'll get caught," Treva warned.

Selah continued to run. "Cleon, stop! It's me, Selah." Her voice echoed through the stone caverns the buildings created. The sound bounced three times before Cleon came to a complete stop.

Selah ran into his arms, crying. "Where are Mother and Dane?"

Treva piled on his other side. "How did you get away from Varro?"

"The guards watching me were distracted by their meal, and I took the opportunity to get away. We're not far from there," Cleon said.

Mari stood guard for the reunion. "People, I think it's time to go," she said. "We've got company coming." She pointed down the road at the running group, but this time there were only four.

"Come on," Cleon said. "I know the way back to where Mother and Dane are."

They ran for a section and didn't hear shouting or footfalls for a few minutes.

"Can we walk for a little?" Mari breathed heavily through her nose. "I'm not used to this strange air or this much running. In our woods the pace is slower."

Selah pulled up beside her and slowed to a fast walk. "Cleon, talk to us. What's going on?"

"Father brought Mother and Dane to the Mountain, and he hired Jaenen to grab Mari. Apparently he'd been trying to find her long before we showed up in TicCity, and had stopped in her woods many times but could not lure her to show herself."

"And I came out for you and Selah," Mari said.

Cleon ran his hand through his hair and nodded. "Yeah, because of us, you and your people were found."

Treva put her arm on Mari's shoulder. "Thank you for risking yourself for Cleon and Selah. They are my family."

Selah felt her face flush. It hit her much deeper than she'd expected to hear those words from Treva. She rested her arm on Treva's shoulder, and the three girls kept their arm-to-shoulder link for at least ten steps before laughter overtook them.

Out of nowhere they were surrounded by seven militants brandishing weapons—knives, clubs, and a pulse disruptor with a TF insignia. Selah swallowed hard but her mouth had gone dry. That weapon had come from one of Mojica's TFs. Selah slipped her knife from its sheath.

The four of them stood in a square pattern—Mari positioned on Selah's right, Treva at her back, and Cleon to her left, where he kept them moving toward the hideout.

"Selah, do you see the disruptor?" Treva asked.

"I sure do," Selah said. "I think we have a bunch of Green Court security here."

"Should they be out this late at night without their mothers?" Mari waved her knife slowly in front of her, as if carving patterns in the men's chests.

"If you ladies wouldn't mind," Cleon said, "I don't have a weapon. Let's not agitate the already agitated sea slugs."

Selah snorted, bringing a hand to her mouth to cover her smile. Maybe it was nervous laughter or she was really tickled because her brother used her favorite descriptive phrase for annoying people.

The men moved closer. They were not the men from before.

Mari bounced from her place and rolled under one of the militants. His head hit the road, knocking him out. She snatched up his knife and jabbed at the guy trying to cut her off from Treva and Selah.

Mari rejoined the square. "Here, now you have a weapon. I hope you know how to use a knife for more than skinning rabbits." She handed it to Cleon.

"Thanks, I think," Cleon said.

Five of the militants charged, while the one carrying the pulse disruptor stood guard. One man with a club swung at Selah. She dodged the swing and stomped on his Achilles tendon as he turned. The man roared in pain and crashed to the road, clutching his leg.

Selah, confident of Mari's skills, turned to help Treva with the men holding knives. The man in front of Cleon had the other club. Selah thought about swinging around and trying to take that one out too, but it occurred to her . . . he was *allowing* them to move up the street.

Her pulse soared. "Stop! There has to be a trap up there. We fight here."

The guy with the pulse disruptor was still just standing there, not joining the action. Wary of when he'd start firing, Selah thought of two ways to tackle him. At the moment she wanted the guy with the club gone. He had the least damaging weapon, so if she took it out they could fight in teams of two against the three knives they were fending off.

She came up beside Cleon. The guy with the club swung it. They easily avoided it. He moved swiftly enough the second time that Selah misjudged his bouncing distance, and he hit her in the hip with a huge swing and a solid thud. She screamed out in pain and crumpled to the road. Cleon threw down his knife and went crazy on the man, knocking the club from his hand and beating him with his fists. Throwing punches was an apt description of Cleon's childhood.

Selah saw stars and felt lightning shoot from her head, down her torso, and out her toes. Fiery heat radiated from her hip. It felt like her pelvis had split in half. She pressed her hand to the pain, trying to will it away, begging her body to heal itself so she didn't die here.

Cleon and the club man were still throwing punches and occasionally rolling around on the ground without the pulse disruptor man getting involved.

Selah tried to get up from the ground, but her leg refused to hold her weight. It felt like her hip had been dislocated. She turned to crawl toward Treva. Maybe she could trip the guy for her.

One of the knife men knocked Treva to the ground. The one helping him turned his attention on assisting the last militant as he took down Mari.

Treva struggled with the man and knocked the knife from his hand. He rolled her over and straddled her with his knees pressing her to the road. Holding both her hands with one of his, he sought the dropped knife with his free hand.

Selah dragged herself toward them, trying to reach the knife first. She slumped from the separating pain wracking her hip.

The man grabbed up the knife. He let go of Treva's hands, clutched the knife in both hands, raised it over his head, and started to plunge it into Treva's chest.

Selah screamed. An arrow zipped through the air and landed in the center of the man's chest. His eyes widened. He looked down at the arrow protruding from his chest as though he didn't believe it. The barest dribble of blood spread out in an ever-growing circle around the arrow. His eyes closed and he slumped to the side.

Treva scrambled from underneath him. Arrows thumped the ground all around the attackers. Another militant was shot through the arm by the arrows raining from the nearby buildings. The other men dodged arrows for only a couple of seconds before they promptly ran away and left their dead friend. The one carrying the pulse disruptor dropped it in his escape from the road.

Selah still had her hands up covering her head. Later she would realize how useless an exercise that was. Cleon and Mari ran over to her while Treva retrieved the pulse disruptor. She hurried back.

"They're coming! I see a lot of people, guys and girls with crossbows coming out of those buildings over there," Treva said.

Selah grabbed the pulse disruptor and aimed it at them as they strolled closer, crossbows slung over their shoulders. They casually walked right up to Selah despite her holding the weapon at the ready.

"Hello. Let me guess. You don't belong in Green Court." The girl talking was fit and tall, with about a yard of black hair. Her tattoo was identical to the bird Selah had seen on Conti.

"No, we don't belong here. We're passing through to—"

"Yeah, I know, Duncan and Marrow," the girl said.

Selah and the others exchanged startled glances.

"I noticed your tattoo. Are you related to Conti?" Selah asked as she winced in pain. Just trying to move in any position caused the stabbing rush to consume her thoughts till she wanted to scream.

"Yes, you can say we're related. He told us to get you to the station without incident. Our Trac ends right before your station but we're always itching for a fight, so we wouldn't be averse to taking on those boys for you if necessary. We were a little late catching up to you. Sorry you got hurt." The girl leaned down and looked at Selah. "It looks like your hip is dislocated. I can put it back in, but it's going to hurt like all get-out."

Selah didn't care about the pain. She needed to get to the rest of her family and find Bodhi. "Yes, please do it. Then it can heal," she said.

The girl looked at her oddly for a second and then sat on the ground in front of her. "I need you to lie flat, and don't fight the way I'm going to turn you."

Selah nodded.

"Someone give her something to bite on," the girl said.

"I don't need anything."

"Trust me, you do," the girl said.

Cleon stripped off his jacket and gave her the rolled sleeve to bite on. Selah sniffed at the pungent aroma and made a face.

"Let's go, people. We don't have all night," the girl said.

Selah held her nose and bit down on the sleeve. The girl positioned her feet on opposite sides of Selah's left hip, cradling her leg in between. She grabbed Selah by the foot, made her stiffen her leg, and rotated it back and forth. Sweat beads broke out on Selah's forehead as she moaned in pain.

Her hip clicked back in the socket with a sharp sound. Selah screamed a guttural cry that bounced from the buildings in such a fashion that the returning sound scared even her. She dropped her head to the ground in exhaustion. *Bodhi.*

Within fifteen minutes Selah's body had healed enough that they could stand her on her feet.

The girl looked at her, uncertain. "Are you sure you're ready to go? It usually takes a couple of days to feel strong enough to walk. We were going to litter-carry you if necessary."

"I'm going to be fine, but we have to leave." Selah tested her hip. It held her weight. It was quite sore, but she was standing. She bent and picked up the pulse disruptor.

"Oh, that won't work for you," the girl said.

"Why not?" Selah asked as she pulled the trigger. Nothing happened. She pulled it again. Nothing.

The girl smiled. "That's why that idiot holding it didn't use it. He could have done better using it as a club."

"Why won't it work?" Selah looked it over for any obvious damage but saw none.

"They're keyed to TF technology. If you aren't wearing a uniform or accessories with TF signatures, it won't fire."

"Give it here," Treva said, motioning with her hand. Selah handed it to her.

Treva fired off four pulses at an evergreen bush, making it ever dead.

The girl's mouth opened in a perfect circle. "How did you do that?" She looked genuinely excited at the prospect of firing the weapon.

Treva held out her ComTex. "TF technology. We're supposed to meet our support team at Duncan and Marrow, but we heard TFs had a showdown with Green security. Do you know if it was a unit at Duncan?"

The girl thought for a second.

Selah's pulse pounded in her throat. *Please don't let it be Bodhi who was hurt.*

26

12 Hours to Egress

Selah still worried about Bodhi even though the girl said his team hadn't been the one attacked. With all the firepower she'd experienced in the Mountain, she still feared the worst. His safety came high on her list of wants. Without Bodhi and Mojica, she had little chance of saving her family from Varro and Jaenen, especially if Varro had the backup forces from Bethany Everling that Cleon had seen while in captivity.

"Help me understand," Selah said to Treva as they walked. The limp from her hip had slowed them down considerably, but the pain diminished steadily. "I grew up believing the Mountain was some idyllic society that achieved utopia and we peasants should learn to emulate it. From what I've seen this time, in some ways it's worse than the life I had in Dominion."

"The Mountain has achieved perfection as far as no one

going hungry or without a job, housing, or essentials, but that's where the wall comes down. Class distinction is a part of life," Treva said.

Selah took note of where they were. At night with no fake sun for illumination, it was hard to get her bearings. Yes, there were fake stars and a moon, but they were in the wrong place according to the sky outside. She had noticed most of the inside mimicked the outside, including time of day and weather. So this difference in star charts was jarring.

"So there are rich people and poor people?" she asked.

Treva snickered. "Not so much rich and poor as occupationally challenged."

Selah stopped and looked at her. "What does that mean?"

"It means that people with jobs like scientists and top-school instructors don't usually hang around with oil and gas drillers or farmers," Treva said.

They turned the last corner of the section and stopped. When they crossed the road, they'd be out of Conti's Trac and into someone else's domain. The girl wouldn't tell them who the boss was because she said he would rather kill outsiders than talk to them.

Cleon had been walking ahead, but he stopped when they did. "Are we crossing or waiting for traffic to go by?"

Selah sighed at his humor. "We had a chance to relax the last couple of sections with our shadows watching over us, but when we cross this road, we're back on our own."

Cleon looked up at the buildings surrounding them. "Are they really up there? Or did they just tell us that to get rid of us?"

Selah raised a finger. "Watch." She put two fingers in her mouth and emitted a whistle shrill enough to wake a dog in Dominion. An arrow streaked by their location and thunked into a nearby tree. The fletching on the arrow vibrated to a stop.

Cleon ducked and moved ten feet away. "That's why you and that girl had your heads together. You could have warned me first."

"Yeah, that would have saved me a lot of vigilance," Mari said. "I didn't trust they would be there for us."

"I confess, I thought the same way. That's why I didn't say anything. I was hoping but not convinced. Now that we're about to leave their territory, I'm convinced." Selah shook her head, raised her hand to wave goodbye to the air, and limped across the street with her crew.

"Before we start getting shot or attacked again, tell me why all these people are so hostile. They live in utopia, for crying out loud," Selah said.

"Do you remember the history of the United States?" Treva stayed close to Selah and watched her surroundings.

Cleon groaned. "Don't we have enough problems without you teaching Study Square?"

"Study Square?" Treva wrinkled her nose as though she smelled an odor.

Selah waved a hand. "Ignore him. He's talking about school. Yes, I remember the history. That was my favorite part of our studies."

"Think of the Mountain as the United States, each of the Courts as a state, and each of the Tracs as a town. History showed most of the United States never got along." Treva waved her hands. "And neither do any of these. They're just stuck a little closer together, space-wise."

"When people don't learn from their mistakes, they're sure going to make them all over again. I guess that could go on—" Mari gasped and pointed to a figure halfway down the next section. "See the way that man walks?"

The other three slowed and observed.

"With his right arm much farther away from his body," Selah said.

"Security people walk like that because they're used to keeping their arm from brushing the weapon on their hip." Cleon started moving a little faster toward the man.

"It's a giveaway because it becomes a habit, and they do it even when they're not wearing their weapon." Mari pulled Cleon back. "Stop." She turned to Selah. "That man is one of them. He was with Jaenen."

"He's probably one of Bethany Everling's security, out of uniform so he doesn't get spotted by the Politicos," Treva said.

"We have to keep up with him," Cleon said. "I know where I was held, but Father split me and Mother up when he saw us talking too much. If this man goes where Father is, then Mother must be nearby."

"We have to use stealth, like when I'm tracking deer," Mari said as she motioned them to the other side of the road. "Keep a tree between you and him at all times, whether on our side or his side of the road."

Selah watched Mari work the hunt like Varro had taught her and the boys. She reached Mari and slowed her advance.

"Varro taught us the same, so this guy might be ready for that approach."

Mari stopped. "Straight point. Anybody got an idea of something he wouldn't think of doing?"

"With it being dark, let's follow along from this distance for a while." Selah limped slowly down the other side of the street, staying against the buildings. "As long as the man is still in view, we're not losing—"

A hand motioned to her from a doorway three feet ahead.

Selah tried to stop but was stepping forward with her bad hip. She missed the step and nearly threw herself on the street. Bodhi darted from the doorway and caught her mid-fall, cradling her in his arms.

Every moment of the day crashed in on her at once. Selah burst into tears.

Mojica herded them into the open doorway and closed it behind them.

"I didn't know if you were alive, and we couldn't call you because of the stupid Politicos—wait, we saw a guard!" Selah pulled away from Bodhi and tried to run to the door. He held her arms and she tried to pry his fingers off. "We have to go! The guy is walking down the other side of the street. He'll get away."

"I know," Bodhi said, still holding her arms. "We've been here since five o'clock this afternoon when you were due. We're watching the commerce rental spaces Bethany Everling loaned Varro and his crew for trading inside the Mountain. We couldn't converge because no one knew when you'd show up or what we might cause you to walk into."

Selah grabbed his arm. "You found Mother?"

"Better than that. We found all of them in one spot. Apparently all is not happy in Bethany-land, and she's told Varro to get his crews out of the Mountain in twenty-four hours."

"We probably know why," Selah said sheepishly. "We rescued Mari from Bethany and Varro, and we sort of dropped into their laps and had to beat them up and run away."

Selah watched Bodhi and waited for the explosion. It was like he'd sucked all the air from the room.

Bodhi ran both hands through his hair. His face went crimson. He bit down on his lip, probably to keep from yelling, and walked away.

Mojica grinned and shrugged, giving Selah a wink. "News story of the hour—Varro is planning on moving his operation to another part of the Mountain. Seems he found a new benefactor." Mojica motioned for Mari and Treva to accompany her to the operations layout.

"Why would he need a new benefactor? He's paid back my dowry. This should be over," Selah said to Cleon, grateful to Mojica for trying to defuse Bodhi.

"Mother was afraid for you to know the whole story because it might lead you into more danger. But I don't know how much *more* danger there could be," Cleon said.

Selah kept an eye on Bodhi's location so she'd know when it was safe to talk. She didn't need him hearing of her recklessness. "I need to know it all. We're leaving Varro and Jaenen in this Mountain. I want to leave this pain here too. Tell me!" She stood straight, noticing that most of the pain in her hip joint had dissipated.

"She's just coming to grips with it herself, but she told me what she found out about Varro's past." Cleon ran his hand through his hair and looked at Selah with a pained expression. "He's been planning to sell you since your birth. He knew Glade was your real father this whole time. Somehow they gave Mother leads on Glade's direction that would bring her across Varro's path after Glade was captured in the Mountain."

Selah tipped her head. "Who is *they*?"

Cleon dropped his eyes. "Father, Simeon Kingston, and a bunch of their friends are a renegade faction of the First Protocol, and they're trying to use this power you have for themselves."

Selah stood frozen to the spot. Her whole life. He had lied her whole life. Tears puddled in her eyes. She pushed them back defiantly.

A whiff of Bodhi's fragrant soap drifted to her. His arms wrapped around her waist from behind. She leaned back into his broad chest and crossed her arms, sliding her hands over his.

"I'm so sorry," Bodhi whispered in her ear. "I didn't have any idea this could date back that far."

Selah squeezed her eyes shut. He'd heard. She hoped he would understand that she had to see this through and not be off in a corner, protected. She turned, burying her head in Bodhi's chest.

"Okay, folks," Mojica said, "I just got a communication that our kidnappers are all down for the night, and lights are out. I think we'll give them a sleepytime reality that they'll wish was a dream." She tapped the appliance in her right ear.

Mari and Treva walked over displaying Mountain hardware. Selah lifted her head. "Are we going to raid them?"

"*We* are not doing anything. You are staying here. Safe," Bodhi said.

Selah looked around. "Who's going to stay here to make sure I stay here?"

Mojica patted Bodhi on the back. "She's got you there. Listen, I've been hearing the chatter all day. These four have been giving Bethany and Green Court fits. You should congratulate each of them. They've earned the right to be part of this operation." The other three crowded around, explaining to Bodhi all at the same time.

"How have you been communicating?" Selah asked Mojica. "We thought all communications were cut off in Green Court."

Mojica turned her back to Bodhi and spoke low to Selah. "I have a special frequency for just my team that the Politicos can't control."

"But we couldn't contact you," Selah said.

Mojica looked embarrassed. "Listen, I'm sorry I cut Treva's communications, but my spies told me you were acting up and taking down Bethany's crew and the militants. I didn't want Bodhi to demand your presence until you were able to save your friend."

Selah smiled softly. "Thank you."

Mojica cleared her throat and turned to address the group. "Let's get this game under way. There are six of us, and Bethany Everling moved her underlings to the other end of the Mountain. So Varro's only got Jaenen and the four men operating his shops. He gathered them together after he got back from Selah and Treva teaching him how to clean the floors."

Finally things were turning in their favor. Cleon and Mari whooped it up while Treva and Selah smiled broadly and clasped arms. Bodhi remained quiet, but Selah was sure he was working hard at trying not to smile.

Mojica tapped her appliance and turned her head away from the group. She talked for a minute and then turned back to the excited group.

"We have a problem."

27

Day 3
10 Hours to Egress

"Your family was here," Mojica said to Selah. "But Varro moved them closer to the center of his shrinking operation. I hear Bethany is pushing her team to reduce his rental space until she squeezes him out of the Mountain like a pus bubble."

Selah gagged. She closed her eyes for a second.

"Are you having flashes or dizziness?" Mojica stared into her eyes.

"No. It was just the visual of what that would look like." Selah grimaced.

"I was a little graphic. Sorry." Mojica handed out ear appliances and a ComTex to each of them. "Keep these on your arm, and keep those in your ear and turned on. They will give us instant communications in case there's trouble."

"How do we find my mother and brother now?" Selah put

on her equipment, checked it, and walked to the floor plan laid out on a table in the center of the room.

"This is where Bethany is squeezing the rental space. See for yourself." Mojica pointed to the holo-map.

Selah looked down at Varro's diminishing area. Each area that had been closed off to him recently turned from black to red on the map.

"This last section is where they are now. It means we'll have to go in the same door as you instead of using the side entrance to the other space," Mojica said. "Bodhi and Cleon will come with me for search and seizure. I'm putting you three ladies in as the extraction team. I've observed all three of you and your abilities, so I won't tell you or your team how to fight. But if I give an order, please follow it. I want all of us to get out of here." She turned to the group. "Ladies and gentlemen, it is twelve thirty in the morning. We have nine and a half hours before we reach critical mass and have to be on our way out of here or risk being sealed in the Mountain forever. So let's make sure we are nowhere nearby when it happens."

Selah felt odd carrying a pulse disruptor. Like Mari and Treva, she was better with her hands than a weapon, but Bodhi wouldn't hear of them being unarmed. Not a sound other than their footfalls, and every so often they synced into one sound before slowly falling out of rhythm again. They crossed the road single file and continued to the end of the section. They took a quick right, and fifty yards in, the first building to the left led to a number of passages, offices, laboratories, and living units that spiderwebbed along and up the inside wall of the Mountain.

Everything they were doing happened at ground level, so toward the back of the building where the floors started their climb up the Mountain, Mojica buzzed them in through a delivery area with her credentials. Her logic—in a few hours she'd be gone forever and it didn't matter who knew she'd been part of this.

They cleared each room they passed, working their way down the hall. Selah stuck her head in an office and pulled back. She keyed her appliance. "Somebody needs a bedtime story."

"Be right there," Mojica answered. A few seconds later she came striding down the hall, pulled the pin on a black ball, and rolled it into the room.

Selah closed the door and they walked away as a poof sounded.

"Will those really keep people asleep for ten to twelve hours?" Selah asked. The balls were smaller than a person's palm and the sound was barely audible. How much damage could they really do?

"Yes, they will. I know what you're thinking. These people don't have a chance to get out of the Mountain before it closes. Personally, the only ones I hope get to stay here forever are your stepfather and Jaenen Malik. If it will make you feel better, most of the people in this section never ask for passes to go outside anyway," Mojica said. She passed off another bag of the sleepytime balls to Mari.

Laser dart fire sounded at the end of the hall. Mojica and

Selah ran in that direction. Bodhi and Cleon had two men pinned down in a temporary security office only utilized when the section was full. Mojica checked their proximity IDs.

"They're Mountain security from the Politico Board. They're the only ones allowed to off-zone at a second job. Don't hurt them. I'll take care of this." Mojica pulled out a ball, yanked the pin, and used a hook shot to bank the ball in their door. Considering the extra time it took to bounce off the walls on its way in, the security men had no time to toss it back before it poofed. The room went silent.

Mojica headed back and they moved swiftly down the hall, over a few corridors, and into Varro's section. The girls moved quickly through their set of rooms. The sound of weapons fire erupted from behind them. Mari looked back.

"No, we have to keep going. My mother and brother are in here somewhere," Selah said.

Mari followed Treva as she opened a door expecting an empty room, and a short man jumped her like a monkey. Selah cracked him in the head with the butt of her weapon. He dropped to the floor, limbs splayed out in all directions. They backed out of the room and Mari tossed in a black ball.

"Where'd he come from?" Treva asked as she straightened the appliance in her ear. "And why didn't you just pulse him instead of slapping him with the weapon?"

"You were too close. I thought I might hit you with the pulse. I wasn't sure whether to beat him with hand moves or beat him with the weapon, and it looked like he might get the best of you, so I just swung."

A door ahead of them opened, and a laser dart aimed out

and fired several bursts. They dove to the floor. Selah rolled to
the side and fired her pulse disruptor. It blew the door open,
which in turn hit the guy so hard it knocked him unconscious.

Mari looked in her bag. "At this rate I'm going to run out
of sleepytime balls before we run out of customers." She
rolled one in with the guy and closed the door. *Poof!*

Selah tapped her appliance to call Mojica. Nothing happened. "I've got no signal. Mari, try calling Mojica."

Mari tapped her appliance. She shook her head.

Treva tried her ComTex. "Okay, we're back to no communications."

Selah wondered if it was Mojica again giving them lati-
tude. But that didn't seem to make any sense in this situation.

"Treva, go back and get another ball bag from Mojica,
and find out why we have no communications," Selah said.

"Are you sure? We're not supposed to separate," Treva said.

"We need to know why we don't have contact, and you
know these corridors better than we do. We're doing fine.
Just get back fast." Selah moved down the hall with Mari,
and when she looked back Treva was gone. Good. She was
afraid Treva was going to disagree.

Mari yelped. Selah charged into the office without thinking. The guy behind the desk had them in his sights with a
pulse disruptor. Selah pulled up short. She knew that pain.
She let her weapon slide to the floor and raised her hands,
kicking herself for sending Treva back to the front.

"What are you doing in the building? Is this a government
takeover?" His hands trembled. He seemed to have a hard
time keeping the weapon trained on them.

Selah took a deep breath to steady her nerves. She worried he'd accidently shoot them—he didn't look like he had the willpower to shoot them purposely. "How about you put the weapon down and we talk about it." She slowly moved toward him.

"Stay back, lady, or I'll shoot you." The man thrust his weapon at her. Selah flinched.

"Selah, listen to him. Come back," Mari pleaded with her. "Stop. He'll shoot."

Selah focused her eyes on his and continued slowly toward him. "He doesn't want to shoot me." She was now close enough to see the whole area around him.

"Stop or I'll really do it," the man yelled.

Selah made contact and wrestled with him for a few seconds. The ordinary office guy didn't seem a fair match so she didn't hurt him, just put him to sleep with a handhold.

Mari rushed over and slapped her in the arm. "Why did you do something so crazy? He could have shot you."

"No he couldn't," Selah said. She held up his pulse disruptor. "I don't know where he got this but it wasn't his, and he couldn't fire it because he wasn't wearing any Mountain technology and there was none anywhere around him. I figured if he was asking if we were government, the odds were that he wasn't."

Mari shook her head. "You think fast. That's very observant."

"Sometimes. Toss a ball in there."

They continued on to the end of the corridor, but the additional rooms were empty. Selah stopped and turned back.

Her observation skills picked up something else. Why were these random men in rooms and offices that weren't actually occupied? And why was it so easy to subdue them? It seemed as though they were being manipulated—or was it her imagination?

She turned to another corridor. The door off to the right should be Mother and Dane. Her hopes soared. She motioned to Mari to watch the hall.

Selah opened the door.

Mother and Dane sat behind a plascine wall on the left, and on the right . . . Bethany Everling stood facing her with a pulse disruptor aimed at her chest.

Selah flinched to a stop, a lightning flash charged her body, and her weapon dropped to the floor. All in the space of two seconds.

"It's about time you two got here." Bethany smiled.

"I'm not sure what you're talking about. I'm alone," Selah said.

Mari's voice became clearer as she approached the door. "I was checking back there. I'm positive that was a corridor and now it's a—" Her eyes grew wide. "Wall."

Selah dropped her chin to her chest in resignation.

"Yes, you're right. That was a corridor as you came this way," Bethany said as she waved her hand above the panel in front of her. "And this controls which areas are open corridors and which ones turn into walls."

"Don't you think we've had enough of each other?" Selah raised her chin and angled her body away from the woman. She glanced over at her family. Mother looked drained and

Dane clung to her. Selah turned back to Bethany. "Let's get it over with. What exactly do you want from me this time?"

Bethany waved a hand over the right side of her panel. The door slid closed behind Mari, causing her to jump closer to Selah. The plascine wall lifted between Selah and her family. Selah started toward them.

"Not so fast. Get back." Bethany came from behind the panel, staying about ten feet from Selah.

Selah stopped. "I asked what you wanted."

"I've got it—you and Mari." Bethany laughed. "I'll bet Glade will just be beside himself when he finds out I have both his daughters."

Selah's head jerked back at the same time Mari looked up at Bethany.

"Daughters? Who, us? You're mistaken," Selah said.

Bethany pointed at Mari. "Mari Kief, daughter of Flander Kief." She turned toward Selah. "Kief left his colony and changed his name to Glade Rishon—father of Selah Rishon."

Mari turned slowly from Bethany to Selah, her voice almost a whisper. "We have the same father."

"Glade is *your* father too?" Selah's heart beat faster.

Mari nodded, and one side of her mouth lifted in a little smile.

"Oh, this is exceptional! You two didn't even know you were sisters. Great, I'll give you years to get acquainted. It's time for us to get going, though. I have to get you back to my lab." Bethany motioned the two stunned girls forward.

"But my mother and brother—are you going to let them

out now?" Selah wasn't sure what to think at the moment, but getting Mother and Dane out of here was paramount.

"Oh, them. No, sorry. Too easy for wagging tongues to bring other Protocols looking for my science. I never had any intention of leaving witnesses to this." Bethany reached down and dialed the pulse disruptor, then raised it and turned toward Mother and Dane.

A guttural scream burst from Selah as her palms thrust out with more force than she knew possible. Bethany flew through the air, slammed to the back wall, and dropped to the floor.

Relief filled Selah as Mother ran to her. She turned to hug Dane, but he stood in the cell area staring at her with wide eyes. "Come here, Dane. It's all right."

Dane shook his head vigorously. Selah looked to Mother. "Can you explain that it's okay?"

Mother hurried to Dane, bent down in front of him, and talked for a few moments. He slowly moved toward Selah. She put out her hands and he ran into her arms. She let out the breath she didn't realize she'd been holding.

"Let's get out of here," Mari said as she slid around behind the panel. "We've got to open all the corridors."

Selah quickly joined her. It was easy to spot the closed corridors marked with red lights. They waved them open, and Selah gave the panel a burst from her pulse disruptor to end its service.

"How do you know we have the right ones open?" Mari looked at the fried panel.

Selah gnawed the corner of her lip. She hadn't thought

there was a possibility the green lights could be wrong. It was too late now. "I guess we'll find out."

They cleared the room, and Mari chucked a sleepytime ball in with Bethany and shut the door. *Poof!*

Mari took the lead and Selah brought up the rear, sandwiching Mother and Dane between them.

Traveling back to the front turned out to be easier than Selah thought. She remembered the turns and they were all open. Halfway there she saw Treva turning a corridor in their direction.

"Thank goodness I found you!" Treva said. "I was losing my mind. Corridors that had turns in them suddenly became dead ends, and I couldn't find a way in." She looked at Mother and Dane. "You got them! We're leaving here."

Selah turned Treva toward the exit. "Bethany Everling was back there. We barely made it out."

"Bodhi, Mojica, and Cleon almost didn't make it either. They were pinned down when I got to them. This was all Bethany Everling's trap. Varro and Jaenen weren't there, but six of Bethany's security were," Treva said, rushing along beside Selah.

Selah tensed. "Are they all right?"

"Yes. We took all the guards to sleepytime after a *little* disagreement." Treva motioned that she didn't want to talk in front of Dane. Selah nodded.

They rushed around the last corner in the section and met up with Mojica and Bodhi coming their way.

Selah stopped. "Where's Cleon?" Her chest tightened and her hands went cold.

Bodhi raised a hand. "He's fine. He's guarding the way in. We lost track of Varro and Jaenen and don't want them sneaking up on us."

Selah relaxed. "Bethany Everling was back there, and she controlled the panels to close off corridors." She stretched out her hand to touch Bodhi's chest. Their eyes met. They'd both made it unscathed.

"Bethany has a block on our communications in here. Bodhi and I are going to run interference back to our spot so we can get active communications. I need to know how the extraction operation is proceeding." Mojica looked over the group. "Glad we've got everyone. Now let's get out of town."

Bodhi and Mojica jogged off to the streets. Selah wondered how long she should wait before she dare try that with her newly healed hip.

Dane moved to Selah's side and tried to take her hand holding the weapon. She smiled and moved him to her left side. They walked down the corridor to the last section turn that ended at the front door.

Selah felt a rush of relief. She could see the front door. They were getting out of this Mountain, once and for all.

A side wall panel slid aside. Varro and Jaenen stepped into the corridor in front of them. Both carried laser darts. Selah opened her mouth to speak.

Varro snatched Dane from her hands while Jaenen held her at bay with a red dot dancing on her chest. "You can have Pasha, but I'm keeping my son."

28

8 Hours to Egress

Selah glared at Varro. It was strange how fast her emotions for him had evaporated. She would have gladly figured out how to gather enough rage to push him through a wall if it weren't for the fact that he was holding on to a wriggling Dane.

"Let my brother go," she said.

Varro struggled with Dane. He finally cuffed the boy in the back of the head, and Dane recoiled in fear and hung his head.

"You've become quite a spitfire in the past few months." Varro smirked at Selah.

She pressed her lips into a tight line. "Well, at least I don't hide behind children, or hire traitors to do my bidding." She directed the last part of the remark to Jaenen. She wanted to rip him apart for making her trust him.

He acted like her words didn't bother him, but Selah could see a hint of sadness in his eyes. She started to plot. At this point she was willing to use that feeling against him. After what he'd pulled with Mari, she owed him no allegiance other than for his saving her life in Baltimore. Now she wondered if even that was real, or part of the setup to gain her trust.

"Varro, please. There is no need for this. Let Dane come with me," Mother said.

Varro snorted and sneered at her. "Just keep your mouth shut. You've been nothing but trouble from beginning to end."

Mother shrank back as though she had been struck.

"Leave her alone," Selah said.

"Just shut up and get inside." Varro led the way into the panel opening. No one followed.

Jaenen shoved Mari's shoulder, and she stumbled, falling to the floor. Treva helped her up and crowded in the door behind her with Mother and Selah bringing up the rear.

The area behind the wall was another large open area. Selah noticed marks on the floor where she could envision walls for rooms and corridors. This whole area was modular to be reconfigured as needed. Now she understood how Bethany could so easily move walls.

Their footsteps sounded like grit on a wooden floor. Selah couldn't see the floor clearly because of the low light. They marched single file into another corridor and into a room with illumination. Jaenen shut the door behind them.

Mother began arguing with Varro. Selah had never seen her this worked up. She guessed having Dane's life threatened had given her mother new motivation. But she didn't mind the distraction. It gave her time to assess where they were.

She glanced around the room. It looked to be some kind of laboratory except there was no equipment. She glanced at Mari, whose hair was flowing around her shoulders. Strange. This was the first time Selah had seen her hair loose since the forest.

She mentally calculated how much time they had left—about seven hours. She wasn't ready to panic yet. She figured Bodhi would start looking for them soon. But how would he find them in here? She should have put up more of a fight to keep Varro from taking them to another location. Working on Jaenen's weakness for her looked like the only alternative at the moment.

Selah lowered her eyes and spoke softly to Jaenen. "I don't know what Varro did to you to make you kidnap Mari, but I forgive you. I remember how you were on our trip. You were nothing but kind and supportive, and I know you never wanted any of us to get hurt."

Varro stopped arguing with Mother and pushed past her to grab Selah's arm.

Selah flinched and raised a hand to stop him. A lightning flash. He still had hold of her arm and she hadn't hurled him across the room or even moved him. Both horror and relief overtook her—what if she had used it all up and couldn't do it anymore? But thank goodness she hadn't hurt Varro. Although she hadn't thought about hurting him when she'd fought with him before. Maybe the difference was, before she had acted to defend herself, not be the aggressor.

Varro shook her. "What's wrong with you, girl? You faded out."

Selah jerked from the fuzziness. "You can count yourself very lucky today."

"I sure will, as soon as you stop trying to sweet-talk Jaenen. I see what you're up to." Varro smirked.

"You've corrupted him with your dirty plan." Selah tried to give Jaenen a sad look, but she didn't know if it had any effect. He hadn't spoken a word to her yet.

Varro shook his head. "For the last several *years*, Jaenen has been in TicCity, working for me to find Mari Kief."

"I've heard about your long and devious career. I would love to see what Glade will have to say about all of this." Selah relished the thought, but then realized if everything went right, Varro would get his rightful due and be locked in this Mountain to live out his life without polluting the world.

"Your snooping is what got you caught. I told Jaenen it was a wasted effort to go to the trouble of planting fake clues and a sensory pulse in the Repository file for you to open. The technology is too new and I said it wouldn't work." Varro shrugged. "What did I know?" He turned to Jaenen. "You're real good. I would have liked to observe the range of delusion the sensory pulse caused Selah."

Jaenen turned a little pink around the edges of his ears. Selah seethed. She wanted to shake him—better still, put him in a sleeper hold and then drop him in the ocean. The earthquake had been an effective delusion.

"So your offer to be our navigator coming here was all

an act?" Selah spit the words at him. "I thought you were a *friend*."

Varro patted Jaenen on the shoulder. "He really couldn't afford to be friends with you. He's a cousin to Jericho Kingston. You remember him? The man you were supposed to marry."

Selah stood up straight. "Yes, Jericho, son of Simeon, *your* friend. You're such great friends I bet you keep a lot of secrets together. I'll bet you two even made secrets in our barn." She stared at him.

Varro blinked. "Doesn't matter. None of it matters because I no longer have to work at a sham of a marriage to keep track of you. I'll just stay right here in the Mountain where the top scientists in the field can work on you. The best part is you're a never-ending source of blood that I could sell dozens of times."

Selah tipped her head. "I'd rather die."

She felt suspended between the beats of a second. No one said a word. She heard each individual's breathing and felt the seconds physically ticking off her life.

The door burst open.

Bodhi stormed in, grabbing Varro near the door. Jaenen took aim. Selah saw the red laser dot dancing on Bodhi's chest. She swung around and swept Jaenen's feet from under him. His weapon fired. The laser shot screeched and Bodhi grabbed his arm.

Varro slipped out the open door, dragging Dane. He yelled into his wrist communicator.

Jaenen struggled to his feet. Treva charged him but he

shoved her into Mari and Selah, and the three of them toppled over. He snatched up his weapon and rushed out the door.

Selah scrambled after him. In the low light she had to stop and mentally distinguish one person from another. It was a standoff. Varro had a knife to Dane's throat. Mother was begging him to stop. Now Mojica and Cleon were here with weapons trained on Varro and Jaenen. Treva and Mari charged out of the other room. Jaenen grabbed Mari around the neck and pointed his weapon at Treva's chest.

From behind Varro and Jaenen came the sound of running footsteps. Three men with laser darts came into view. Selah hoped they were Mountain security. But her hopes crashed when they stopped beside Varro.

"Don't make me kill him," Varro yelled.

Mother fell to her knees. "Why? Please, Varro, he's your son. Your blood. Why would you harm him?"

"Nothing and no one is more important than the success of our version of the Protocol. And I'm willing to bet his life on it. Either I go free or he dies."

Bodhi was missing. Selah looked around. He stood in the doorway they had exited, carrying a laser dart.

The room was dark and the scene loud and confusing as Selah slowly backed toward his position. "Where did you get a laser dart? And how did you find us?"

"We took them from Bethany's forces when we put them to sleep. They don't need them anymore. And there was a hair tie on the floor inside this corridor where sections intersected, so we checked this one first."

Selah made a note to hug Mari for that bit of genius.

She heard a scream. She pivoted to Varro. There was a tiny trickle of blood oozing down the side of Dane's neck. The boy was starting to list to one side, and Varro was having a hard time holding on to him. "Selah, come out of the shadows and show yourself. You can't get out of this maze, but I can take it out on Dane."

Selah sucked in a breath and got ready to run at him.

Bodhi grabbed her arm. "Don't. They can't see me in the dark here. Let me take the shot."

"But you can't do that. Do you even know how to shoot?"

"Apparently I was very good at it at one time, and I haven't lost my aim."

Selah turned back in time to see Treva in negotiations with Varro about hiding places in the Mountain. She moved too close. Varro pushed Dane away and grabbed Treva, knife to her throat. She put her hands up in surrender. Selah could see Treva had a good angle to deflect the knife. She hoped Cleon had noticed.

Mother pulled Dane far away and wrapped him in her arms, crying.

"Let her go!" Cleon dove at his father, knocking his knife to the side. Treva skirted away in one direction and the knife went in the other. Varro lifted the laser dart slung around his shoulder. He swung it as a physical weapon, striking Cleon, who stepped back and ducked the next blow. He punched Varro in the ribs.

Varro lurched to the side, putting Treva in his line of sight. "Live with this, you ungrateful boy." The red dot of Varro's laser dart lit up Treva's head.

"Nooo!" Cleon screamed as he threw himself in the line of fire. The laser exploded on his side. Cleon fell in a heap.

Treva screamed.

Selah's heart felt like it stopped.

Bodhi took aim at Varro.

"He's my family." Selah moved toward Bodhi's weapon.

29

7 Hours to Egress

Varro heard Selah speak and spun in their direction, taking aim at her voice, which was in direct line with Bodhi's back.

No! Selah's world stopped. She snatched the laser dart from Bodhi, pushed him out of the way, and fired.

A pinpoint of white left a ghostly trail of light from the weapon to where it slammed into Varro. A starburst exploded from his chest, particles of sparks shooting off in all directions. His mouth opened in a scream and froze. He fell to the floor.

Selah stared at the spot where he had stood. If she never lowered her eyes to his smoldering form, she might pretend that this never happened. That the ghostly form left on her vision was still him standing there. That she had somehow missed and everything was going to be fine.

But it wasn't going to be fine. It would never be fine again. Why had he aimed at Bodhi? She had to protect Bodhi. She couldn't protect Cleon. The smell of burnt flesh drifted to her nostrils. Her shoulders slumped. Was that Cleon she was breathing in, or Varro?

Bile rose in her throat, burning the back of her tongue. She tried to push it back down. *You're breathing in Varro's flesh.* She bent over and retched. Her stomach lurched, then squeezed tightly like a fist, cramping her sides.

Bodhi put his hand on her back. "Are you going to make it?"

"I just killed the man who raised me," she said, sobbing. "I think I need to have a few minutes!"

"I'm sorry, but we don't have a few minutes. We need to get out of here. Remember, sealed forever."

Selah tipped her head from side to side, cracking the tension from her neck muscles, and took a few cleansing breaths. Thankfully the flesh smell had dissipated. She straightened and ran the heels of her hands across her eyes to clear them. *It really did just happen. This wasn't a dream.*

"Where are Jaenen and Varro's men?" She spun as she searched the dark corners of the room. Were they going to be attacked as they tried to leave? She looked carefully at each shadow and corner, looking for discernable movement.

"They took off as soon as Varro hit the floor. Even Jaenen ran away. He must have made contact with Varro's other cohorts."

"Do we send someone to follow him? He's a criminal."

"We hardly have any room to talk. To most of the Mountain, we're the criminals. He'll be locked in this prison forever," Bodhi said.

"It doesn't seem fair that he'll have freedom. But I guess

they'll get what they deserve," Selah said. "Cleon! I need to see my brother." She shoved the laser dart at Bodhi and ran to Cleon.

He lay sprawled on the floor with Treva holding his head in her lap. She rocked him and cried while Mojica tried to render aid. Selah looked down just as Mojica cut away his tunic. The edges of the material were fused to the wound, making a large fist-sized crater in his stomach. The heat had cauterized the edges of the flesh to a ghastly burnt crispness. As Mojica carefully pulled away the debris, it made crackling sounds that turned Selah's stomach.

She fought the urge to retch again by swallowing hard. She moved away and closed her eyes. This wasn't happening. It was a nightmare. When she opened her eyes everything would be fine.

Mojica walked over and touched her shoulder. "Selah, I need to get back to the station and fashion a litter to carry him out of here." Her voice drilled into Selah. She didn't want to see the woman's expression. The graveness registered in her voice.

Selah opened her eyes. Mojica's face said it all. Selah burst into tears, and Mojica grabbed her to keep her from sliding to the ground. Bodhi quickly took the woman's place, holding Selah up.

"I'm sorry. He's not going to make it. It went through his intestines and capped off a piece of his lungs. The intestines are cut and sealed. We can't fix that in the field," Mojica said, blowing out a huff of air. "Frankly, I don't think that could be fixed even if we weren't in the field."

Selah pulled herself up straight. "Does he know?"

Mojica nodded. "He said not to tell Treva, though. He wants us to distract her until we get in the tunnels and can't open the door to let her back in the Mountain."

"He wants to stay here?"

"No, he wants to *die* here so that you all can make it out," Mojica said.

Selah stared at Treva rocking on her knees next to Cleon. This was going to break her heart. "Is he still lucid enough to talk to me?"

"Yes, I've given him all the painkiller I have. There is a limit to overdosing, but I figured in his condition, that wouldn't be a worry. I just don't want him to spend his last hours in pain," Mojica said.

Selah hesitated as she walked past Varro's body. Someone had removed his jacket and used it to cover his face and chest. Mother had always said nice words about people before they were burned on the cremation pyres. Saying niceties and such was supposed to make the living feel better about the passing of the dead, but she couldn't think of anything to say. Maybe later when she wasn't so raw. She felt her already weary body tighten.

She walked to her brother's side and knelt beside Treva, wrapping her arms around the sobbing girl. She rocked with her, feeling the heaving sobs wracking her body. Every fiber of her being trembled. Selah raised Treva's chin. "Honey, I need to talk to Cleon. Could we have a moment together as brother and sister?" she asked softly.

"Yes, just don't let him go anywhere. He can't go anywhere without me," Treva sobbed. Her hands trembled. Tears poured from her eyes and dripped to her shirt, leaving wet trails.

Selah motioned to her mother, who stood beside Mari and Dane nearby. "Take Treva so I can talk to Cleon." Mother nodded, tears streaming from her eyes too. Selah could tell by the pallor of her face—she knew Cleon wasn't going to make it.

Selah knelt beside Cleon. "Hey, brother dear. We'll be getting out of here as soon as Mojica gets back with a litter and transportation. Then we can go home." Her voice hitched.

Cleon gave her a pained half smile and tried to shift his position. He cried out in pain as the wound pulled with the movement of his body. Sweat beaded on his forehead and he fell back to the floor. "Don't try to kid a kidder." His breathing labored. He grabbed at her hand. "Please don't let Treva stay with me. Promise me."

"Cleon, you know what she's going to be like." Selah wanted to promise, but Treva could be a grizzly bear when she chose to be. Could she fulfill the promise? Or was she going to lose Treva here too?

Cleon clutched Selah's hand with both of his. "Promise me!" He said it so forcefully that it caused a coughing spasm. Selah could hear the gurgling fluid filling his lungs. She sat beside him and held up his back and head to help him breathe.

"I promise." Selah's lips trembled. She rested her chin on top of his head. Her tears flowed freely into his hair as the realization of the death of her family, and her role in it, sank in.

6 Hours to Egress

Selah walked beside the stretcher as Bodhi and Mojica carried Cleon back to the store Mojica had been using for her clandestine operations in Green Court. Bodhi had been lucky. The shot that grazed his arm when Selah tackled Jaenen had only been a glancing blow, and the bio properties of the TF uniform had absorbed most of the heat. All he had was a fused slicing across his arm that hadn't healed itself, which he said he found very curious.

She wanted to be happy he was safe, but at the same time she mourned her brother . . . and she mourned Varro, and what she had become. Now was probably not the time to celebrate having a new sister. None of that made sense at the moment anyway. None of this had turned out even close to the way she had hoped.

Selah hurried ahead of the group and opened the door to the storefront. Everyone piled inside. Selah knew it wouldn't matter in a few hours, but she wondered who would take over security when they were gone. It was a stupid thought. Who cared? She was just trying to keep her mind off the reality of the situation.

Coming back to the storefront was much different than when they'd first gone out after following Varro's man. Selah touched Mojica's arm. "Am I right that we have no one chasing us anymore?"

"Correct. Unless we run into Green Court security. Once we're in a TF transport, we'll be safe. All we need to do is get to the tunnels and—" Mojica tapped her appliance and held up her hand. She turned away and turned back with a very different expression.

"Transportation is ferrying the last of our people out. To get a unit large enough for all of us displaces a Mountain family. I'm sorry, but we have to wait." Mojica's expression said it all. She was staying here with the group, no matter if she wound up trapped.

"We'd better tell the others," Selah said. "But I think we'll leave out the part that vehicle size is a factor. It might make them feel like they're holding each other back."

She walked to where Treva kept vigil over Cleon. Every few minutes Selah noticed her checking to see if he was still breathing. The pain in her eyes was unbearable. Mother sat with her, holding her hand.

Selah felt bad for thinking it, but if Cleon died here, they wouldn't have such great difficulty getting Treva to leave. But when she found out he wanted to be left behind, there'd be a steep price to pay.

Moving next to the litter, Selah closed her eyes. *Cleon, I'm sorry for wishing you away.*

⊗

5 Hours to Egress

Selah pulled Mojica aside to talk. She and Bodhi had been discussing the travel back, and there were timing milestones they had to meet. Bodhi said it had taken him an hour to get through the tunnel. Selah didn't think everyone was up to his level of stamina and fitness. Time was their enemy. They needed to enter the tunnel by nine thirty in the morning. She was beginning to worry.

"Before you say anything, I've asked for an ETA on our ride." Mojica shook her head. "There're still several families to go, and some unforeseen consequences of trying to keep a move like this secret. I can get smaller vehicles but they'll only hold three, or a squeezed fourth, and the driver. We couldn't all go at the same time."

"Once we get transportation, how long will it take us to get to the tunnel?" Selah asked.

"A half hour at the most," Mojica said.

"So we have to leave this building by nine in the morning at the latest," Selah said, setting the times in her mind.

Bodhi and Mojica agreed.

"I think we'd better give everyone the opportunity for smaller vehicles, if they want it," Bodhi said. "Some of them, like Mari, Pasha, and Dane, could probably go out a regular gate and get out now."

Selah wanted to push them from the Mountain and keep them safe, but with her mind so jumbled at the moment, she didn't trust her own thinking. She was starting to second-guess herself by imagining vivid scenarios of what could happen with each of her choices. She tried to banish the thoughts, but the *what-ifs* kept haunting her.

"It wouldn't speed the rest of us up, because with five left, we'd still need a large transport. But you need to give them the facts and let them each decide for themselves," Mojica said.

"Everybody, can we have your attention?" Selah said.

Mari had a nervous energy from being in the Mountain

that she couldn't seem to control. She darted over from her position at the front of the store. "You need to come see this. I think there's someone watching us."

Mojica followed her to the front, and Bodhi and Selah trailed behind.

Selah peered out. She didn't see any movement. "What did you think you saw?"

"I didn't *think* anything. We're being stalked," Mari said. She pointed to several buildings across the road. "Look at the roof of that building. Watch the top right corner."

Sure enough, a couple of heads bobbed up and then out of sight.

"But couldn't that just be random people?" Bodhi asked.

"It might be under different circumstances, but it's five in the morning. There's no reason for that many people to be up and about on a normal day," Mojica said.

"And over there." Mari pointed to a building near the corner where they had crossed into this section. "Watch there."

Mojica stared at the spot, then muttered under her breath. Selah didn't catch the words, but to see Mojica show even a hint of stress was jarring. The woman was a pinnacle of strength that never wavered.

Mojica turned away from the window and tapped her appliance. Selah looked between Bodhi and Mari. "How many weapons do we have?"

Bodhi brought a hand to his forehead. Mojica turned back. "Okay, bad news and worse news."

Selah's throat tightened. Nearly all who remained of her family were in this room. How could she protect them?

Mojica waved a hand. "Years ago the plascine building fronts in this area were all made riot-safe, and since this is one-way, we can see out but they can't see in."

"So is there anything they could shoot at us that would break this front?" Selah looked around the large open room. There was nowhere for anyone to hide. Even the benches didn't offer much protection if the storefront was breached.

"Yes, but Green Court wouldn't have access to that technology," Mojica said. "The bad news is that there are none of my fighting squadrons left in the Mountain. We never anticipated having to fight our way out."

"I just asked how many weapons we have," Selah said.

"That's where the news gets worse. I checked the storage here. Unfortunately, I had the TFs who were regularly stationed here take the weapons when they left at the time Green security overthrew Mountain forces." Mojica shrugged. "I didn't want them getting hold of our weapons. We have the two pulse disruptors Bodhi and I brought, and we gained three laser darts from Bethany's security who we put to sleep."

Selah thought about the weapons she had left lying in the building. Second-guessing again.

"You need to see this," Mari yelled from the window.

Selah and Mojica joined her and Bodhi.

"I've seen at least a half dozen moving shapes hurrying into the side of that building on the corner," Bodhi said. "It's still too dark, but I'm pretty sure they were carrying weapons."

Mojica gritted her teeth. "I was hoping that they were

just making their presence known since they took over their own security, but I have to face the fact that we're going to have a problem."

To punctuate her statement, an explosion rocked the front of the store. Selah's mother screamed. Gravel and bits of the composite roadway slammed against the plascine front as a billow of dark smoke expanded and then dissipated in front of the window. The building vibrated, and a tile dropped loose from the ceiling, crashing to the floor in front of where Cleon lay. Treva threw herself over his body, which brought a sharp cry of pain from Cleon.

Selah and Mari hurried away from the front. Mojica held up a hand. "That will hold, and they can't see you, so they're shooting blind. I never should have brought this many people back here. I'm afraid that's what attracted the attention. I think they're assuming we're going to attack them."

"If that's all it comes down to, can we negotiate?" Bodhi asked.

"I don't advise it. They've never been known for their honesty in dealing with the Mountain," Mojica said.

Another explosion. Sprays of rocrete and stone peppered the front of the building. Everyone ducked. For a minute the outside was obscured by the smoke until a breeze pushed it away.

Dane started to sob. Mother wrapped her arms around him and tried to soothe him. Another blast. The whole building vibrated with the percussion.

"We can't just sit here and let them bomb us. We need to do something," Selah said. Her hands had started to shake.

She clasped them together to force them still. She had to be strong for Mother and Dane.

"There's nothing we can do. If I open the front to fire back, it will give them a way in, and it will also prove that we're combative," Mojica said.

"We can't just sit here!" Selah said again. She started to pace.

Another blast rocked the building.

"Stop!" Selah screamed. Bodhi rushed to her side. She fought him off. "They have to stop! We didn't do anything to them." She slapped Bodhi's hands away as he tried to comfort her. "They have to stop! Make them stop."

Bodhi wrapped his arms around her tightly, restricting her movements. Her breath came in fast, ragged jerks. He tried to soothe her but she pushed against him and tried to squirm free.

"I killed my stepfather!" she yelled. "Make them stop!" She slid to the floor.

Bodhi lowered himself with her, still holding her tight. "It will be all right. I promise you. It will be all right."

She shook her head and dropped her voice to an anguished whisper. "No, it won't. Varro is gone. Cleon is going to die. You're lying to me to make me feel better. I had to do the same thing with Cleon."

Another explosion. Ceiling tiles collapsed to the floor, raining down debris and dust. Cleon started to cough, then suddenly went quiet. Selah ran to his side. Liquid oozed from the blast site on his torso. Each time his lungs tried to fill or expel air, the gurgling pushed bubbles of air out the wound.

They'd grow large and then pop, spraying the blackened flesh with a glistening coat of moisture that under better circumstances an aide would have been removing. Mother looked at Selah and shook her head.

"They threw that last one on top of the building," Mojica said.

Bodhi looked up. "Is this building able to withstand that kind of beating?"

Mojica nodded. "It's never been tested, but we reinforced it about ten years ago, in anticipation of such an event. At the time we figured we'd be fighting to help the Green, not against them."

"I thought this was just a store that you took over to wait for us," Selah said.

"No, this was a standard Mountain security outpost before this last insurrection," Mojica said.

"So they probably think we're here to take back control," Bodhi said.

"Yes, I suspect you're right. I've called for backup. But the chances of getting it grow dimmer with each hour. I can't pull people back to help rescue us when it might mean they become trapped," Mojica said.

"So we just sit here and let them keep bombing us?" Selah asked.

Mari looked at her. "Do you have a better idea?"

Selah frowned. "I'm trying to protect my family. Don't make smart comments. I know you're looking down your nose at me. I'm not as good a tracker or hunter as you are, but I do love my family."

Mari looked hurt. She opened her mouth to speak, but Bodhi touched her arm and shook his head.

"So now you're on her side too," Selah said. She struggled to get out of Bodhi's embrace. "Let me go!"

"Not until you calm down and start acting rational again. You're talking crazy," he said.

She leaned her head against his chest. "I can't do this. I can't be this strong. Just let me die. I'll go out and give myself to them. Maybe they'll go away."

Mojica patted her arm. "That's just the stress talking. Take some deep breaths and try to pull yourself together. I need you to help me. You have abilities that could decide who wins or loses this fight, especially if they break in here."

"But you said they couldn't get in." Selah began to hyperventilate.

Mojica raised a hand. "I was just saying *in case*. I didn't mean they could. Look at me. Focus."

Selah pulled at every string trying to unravel from her being. *Focus*. Mojica's words penetrated the veil. She struggled to crawl from the pit in her mind where she had retreated.

"Pasha and Dane need you," Bodhi said softly. "You have to be strong for them."

Selah blinked. She looked at Mother cradling Cleon and trying to soothe Dane. She envisioned her nerves smoothing out the craggy, broken edges that stabbed at her brain. She breathed deeply, focusing her eyes on her family. She had to take care of them.

The tension drained from her limbs. Bodhi relaxed his grip. "If you need me, I'm right here."

She tried to smile, but it wound up being more of a quiver. She looked at Mari. "I'm sorry. I didn't mean any of what I said. I don't know what came over me."

Mari rubbed Selah's hand. "I think we've all been tested with what could overcome us in the last twenty-four hours. I've already forgotten it."

Mojica peered out the front. "I don't think they'll try to break in. They probably think we're heavily armed like normal, so as long as the building holds up, we'll be safe."

Bodhi fingered one of the weapons on the counter. "Will we have firepower to help us get out of here when our transportation arrives?"

"I've got two of my best coming with the armored transport," Mojica said.

Selah wasn't sure, but she thought there was a note of hesitation in Mojica's voice. She passed it off. She was not going to lose herself again.

1 Hour to Egress

Selah paced near the front of the store. She had bitten every one of her nails. The Green forces outside had not tried to contact them, but every half hour or so they lobbed another bomb at the front of the building. Even Dane had gotten used to the mind-numbing percussions and wasn't crying anymore. Selah looked around at everyone in different states of rest. She had regained her own momentum and marveled at how easily the mind became used to a constant state of stress.

But it was time to leave. They needed to be gone from this insane place where people didn't even try to talk but preferred to just keep bombing, apparently for fun. She imagined being trapped in the Mountain. Her feelings of claustrophobia threatened to overwhelm her. She tamped those things back down. *Focus.*

Mojica hurried over. "Everyone get ready. Our transportation is on the way."

Selah helped her mother and Treva get Cleon ready to travel. His color had turned to a pasty gray. Selah could see him slipping away by the minute. She didn't know how he was holding on, but she knew why. Treva herself was ashen and almost unresponsive except to throw herself over Cleon when an occasional bomb caused dust to filter down from the ceiling.

Mari had been keeping Dane occupied. She knew of Cleon's wish to remain behind, so she casually brought Dane over to talk with him for the last time. Selah watched with a broken heart. She had lost half of her family to this Mountain.

Twenty minutes later Selah was getting anxious again. Had the transport fallen victim to Green security?

Bodhi rushed over. "They're here. Let's go home." He snatched up a pulse disruptor. Mojica grabbed her weapon, while Mari handed laser darts to Selah and her mother.

A huge armored unit stopped in front of the store, blocking it from the militants. Two sharpshooters hopped out and laid down suppression fire while Mojica and Bodhi hauled Cleon's litter into the vehicle. A few random shots pinged off the armor plating.

Mojica and Bodhi darted back inside. "It seems they get the drift that we're leaving and not trying to overthrow their new regime. I think they'll let us leave, but keep your heads down just in case."

More suppression fire came from Mojica's sharpshooters, but everyone was able to get inside the armored unit without incident.

Selah sat back against the seat and put her head on Bodhi's shoulder. He patted her knee and smiled. "We made it."

Egress

Selah counted the time in her head. It was ten in the morning. Their unit had lacked enough power for the weight it was carrying and needed a charge replacement. They still weren't to the tunnel.

Bodhi held her hand. "There won't be any problems getting in, will there?"

"We're here." Mojica piled everyone out and hustled them into the access corridor. Selah tried to keep Treva's attention from Cleon, but she stayed right beside him.

Mojica motioned Bodhi to stand by her and called the group to attention. "We're entering the tunnels two at a time to avoid setting off any alarms in the Mountain. We will stagger leaving by two minutes. First Bodhi and Treva, then Mari and Dane, then Selah and Pasha. I will bring up the rear with Cleon and the two TFs carrying the litter. Remember, people, always bear to the left in all tunnels and junctions.

That is of paramount importance. We don't want anyone lost in these tunnels."

Treva protested. She refused to leave Cleon. When Selah told her she was endangering everyone's life, she reluctantly agreed to go with Bodhi. Selah kissed him goodbye and hugged Treva. They went through the door. Selah realized Mojica had set it up this way to keep Treva far ahead where she wouldn't know Cleon had been left behind until it was too late for her to go back. She felt bad having to deceive her this way. But it would save her life.

Next Mari left with Dane after he'd gotten copious kisses from Selah and Mother.

Selah and her mother spent their last minutes with Cleon. He barely had a wisp of breath left. He could no longer open his eyes fully. Selah kissed him goodbye. Tears fell from her cheeks and rolled down Cleon's gray face. Selah brushed them away and moved to the side to wait for Mother.

Mojica assured Selah that Cleon would be left where he could be found for a decent burial. Selah's lip quivered as she talked. She turned back for one last look, then allowed Mother to pull her into the tunnel.

Selah felt the strength in her mother's hand. "Mother, I'm so sorry about Varro and Cleon. It's all my fault."

"None of this is your fault, my daughter. Varro chose his own path a long time ago, and we were just part of the many ripples," Mother said.

Selah ran for the first ten minutes, tears clouding her eyes, but drawing strength from her mother. She saw nothing but a halo of light from the ribbon down the center of the ceiling. The farther she got from the Mountain the better she felt, and the more her head seemed to clear. She remembered what Bodhi had said about the tunnel curving, but she didn't sense much of that. Strange.

The tunnel straightened out and she could see Mari and Dane up ahead. That wasn't right. They were supposed to be two minutes ahead. Dane appeared to be limping. Selah and Mother caught up.

"Mother, I fell and hurt my ankle," Dane said when he saw her.

"We will make it better when we get out of here. Come, we have to hurry," she said. She grabbed him by the hand and tried to pull him along, but Selah felt them lagging. Dane wasn't moving well, and Mother seemed to be winding down too.

Mojica and her TFs caught up. "We need to move, people. This is not good. We're only through about half of Bodhi's hour-long travel time, and my ComTex says there's fifteen minutes left before the Mountain seals."

"What would happen to us in here? Would we be sealed in the tunnel?" Selah's eyes darted around. This was not the place she wanted to use her last breaths.

Mojica's lips twisted. "I don't know what would happen, but I don't want to have to find out either. Let's move it." She turned to the TFs. "You two take Dane."

The boy started to protest leaving his mother, but one of the TFs threw him over his shoulder and started to run. The other one followed.

If this had been any other day, Selah could have kept up. Little food and no sleep had brought her to the end of her reserves. A cramp stitched her side near her bad hip. She winced and tried to ignore it until it radiated up and stabbed her in the diaphragm. She breathed through the pain.

They were quickly wearing down. Selah desperately needed water. Her mother fell behind, and twice Mojica had to put an arm under hers to hold her up. Mari held her up on the other side. They made a little better time with Mother's feet barely hitting the ground.

They turned a corner that Selah didn't expect. She stared in disbelief.

30

Could she really be seeing an open doorway? Was this a mirage? Yellow light poured into the tunnel just as brightly as sunlight streaming through a window. The TFs herded them into the cavern. Bodhi restrained a screaming, clawing Treva. Selah's mother, breathing heavily, limped to her side. Still Treva screamed.

Bodhi yelled to Selah, "When you're all inside, close that door or she's gone."

"Is this the old man's cave?" Selah glanced around.

"Yes! Quickly, shut the door! I'm losing my grip," Bodhi said as he struggled with Treva.

Selah counted heads, leaned into the door, and pushed the massive slab shut. The seams around the doorway disappeared as though they'd never been there.

She turned. Taraji walked toward her and embraced her.

"I wanted to see that you were safe before I left to lead the Mountain people away from here."

"Wait! I need you with me for security! Jaenen Malik was a traitor, and I don't know who else we have to watch out for," Selah said.

"We know." Taraji pointed at Bodhi. "You are in fine hands with Bodhi. I'll see you over the Mountain."

Bodhi released Treva and nodded to Taraji as she turned to walk through the cavern.

"Why did you leave him in there? He was your friend!" Treva screamed, slapping and punching him.

Bodhi didn't strike back, he just defended himself from the blows.

She raced to the door. "Selah, open it, please. Let me go back. I need to go back." She clawed at the edges where the door had closed. "Cleon, my Cleon, I love you," Treva wailed as she slid to her knees. Her fingers bloodied, leaving angry crimson streaks on the solid stone wall.

Selah's mother bit her lip and bent to console her.

Tears pooled in Selah's eyes. She couldn't go to Treva or she'd break down too. She walked to Mari and Dane. Mari looked at her and gave her a hug.

"Where's Cleon?" Dane's eyes were fearful as he watched Treva scream and rage.

Selah bent down in front of him. "Cleon said for me to tell you that he loves you, but he was very tired and he had to go to sleep."

Dane squeezed his eyes shut. They glistened when he opened them. "Forever?"

Selah nodded. Her heart broke into little shards that stabbed and cut her to pieces.

Dane pressed his lips together. "Do I have to go to sleep like that?"

Selah hugged him, kissing his head. "No, my sweet. You don't have to go to sleep like that." *Not until you're very old, I hope.*

A commotion stirred on the far side of the cavern. Glade and the old man whisked into the room and rushed over to Selah. Glade stopped abruptly, looking from Mari to Selah and back again. His mouth dropped open. "Mari? Is that you?"

Mari smiled and stepped forward to caress his hand. "Yes, Father, it's me. Selah and I need to have a little talk with you about sharing family stories."

His mouth had closed but dropped open again. Selah bit her lip to keep from smiling. She had never seen him so flustered.

"Glade," a soft voice said.

His eyes came alive—a special kind of love. Selah knew he recognized the voice. He turned slowly to face Mother. His shaking fingers touched her cheek as a single tear slid from his eye. She took his hand and kissed his palm. They touched foreheads and remained that way for almost a minute. No words spoken.

Glade lifted his head. "You look well."

She smiled. "As do you."

This was the only time Selah had seen Glade display this level of vulnerability. It warmed her heart. It was curious to see how natural the two of them were together, as though they'd never been apart. It was like a feeling of peace had spread upon the chaotic sea, calming the storm.

The old man rushed out the door, then back into the room a minute later. "It is time. We need Selah." He grabbed her by the hand. "And the rest of you need to clear out of here and seek higher ground." He waved them away. "Shoo, go on with yourselves now."

"Why higher ground?" Mari asked.

"I'll explain on the way," Mojica said. "We have power sleds for our Mountain people. Taraji took charge. They've already left. They know the drill."

"But we don't know the drill," Selah said. "What's going on?"

The old man hurried over to the far table and came back with a leather bag stuffed to brimming. He handed it to Mari. She sagged under the unexpected weight.

"The Stone Braide Chronicles. They tell all you will ever need to know. Read them carefully. I put the Keepers' journal back in there because it has things you will need, in addition to all of Glade's documents. The digital trail was compromised a hundred years ago, so these are the majority of the ancient papers that survived. Take care of them and commit them to memory." The old man took Selah's hand again.

"What will it matter? What will committing the past to memory do for us other than impress some bad memories?" Selah wanted to forget most of the last few months and go back to being innocent and ignorant of the real world.

The old man patted her hand. "It will matter . . . yes, it

will matter—in about a thousand years, or eight hundred and fifty to be exact. There will be tumultuous times. They'll have to prepare to do battle."

Selah tipped her head. "You'll need to explain that to me."

The old man smiled and patted her hand again.

She pulled free. "Wait a minute." She turned to Bodhi. "I thought you told me it took an hour to travel that tunnel. How did we just make an hour trip in a half hour?"

The old man grabbed her hand again. "That's the way the tunnel is designed. Shortcuts, shortcuts. People always want answers instead of accepting what is right in front of them, tsk-tsk."

Selah pulled away again. "Well . . . next time please communicate better." She realized that sounded stupid but considered it part of being overtired. She sighed and put her hand back in the old man's. He led the way into the Reliquary with Mari and Bodhi following.

The old man pointed to several spherical grottos carved into the wall. "We are going to prick your finger and put a couple of drops of your blood on the first, second, and third pads. The fourth one gets the stone from the necklace, and when they have activated the cycle I will press the button to start the last phase. As soon as the grottos finish turning, remove the stone and take it with you. You will need it for the completion of the Third Protocol. There will be a very short period of safe time after you remove the stone from the grotto, so leave quickly. I will say my goodbyes to you all here. That security lady Mojica knows how far away you need—"

The old man clutched at his left arm. His coloring paled as

his complexion turned ashen. His mouth opened and closed like a fish trying to gulp water.

"Glade! I think there's something wrong here!" Selah yelled. She didn't get a response. She heard the sound of machinery cycling up. The sound hammered at her ears and she winced.

The old man bent at the waist and clutched his chest. He coughed. His face contorted in agony.

"Glade, something's wrong out here!" Selah repeated with ragged breaths. Her voice echoed from the pocketed stone walls. She didn't know what to do, but she was trying not to panic.

Bodhi darted to the other room to retrieve Glade. The old man collapsed in Selah's arms. She tried to loosen his collar so he could get air. His hand patted hers then slid off to the side. He expelled a sigh and went still.

Mari clutched the leather bag to her chest. "What happened?"

Selah brushed back tears. "I don't know. I think he died."

Glade rushed in and dropped to his knees next to Selah, feeling for the old man's pulse. He shook his head. "He hasn't looked good for the last few hours. He said he was glad it was almost over. Poor man, he lived his whole life waiting for this single moment in time, and he's going to miss it." Glade sat back on his haunches with a resounding sigh. "Selah, Mari, I had so much I wanted to tell you two about each other, but you'll have to learn the old-fashioned way, by being friends."

Selah frowned. "I don't think this is the time for a speech. You can tell us when we get home."

Bodhi frowned. He ran his hand through his hair.

Selah looked at him. "What's the matter with you two?"

Glade dropped his gaze. "Tell Pasha I never stopped loving her. I gave my private journals to Bodhi to give to her."

Selah looked from Glade to Bodhi and back again. "What are you two up to? You're scaring me."

Glade looked up at Bodhi and motioned him over. He smiled softly and took Selah's hand, placing it in Bodhi's. "You are to take care of my daughter with your life."

Selah opened her mouth to protest but shut it. This had to be some strange hallucination because she was so tired.

"I will take care of her as long as we both shall live," Bodhi said solemnly.

Selah wanted to laugh at how they were acting. "Will you tell me what's going on?"

Glade kissed Selah's forehead, then he grabbed Mari close and kissed her forehead. "I'm staying behind."

Selah looked at him. "No. You can't stay behind. We have to go home. I need time to get to know you."

He sighed. "Someone has to lock in the switch. It's a failsafe to keep the cycle from happening by accident."

"But no, it can't be you. Who else can do it?" Selah's breathing quickened. She looked to Mari, who had tears streaming down her cheeks.

"He's lying over there dead." Glade reached inside his tunic top and pulled out a triangular stone on a chain.

"That's the same necklace Treva has," Selah said.

Glade nodded. "Good, good, then you're set. Touch them together and then find the third stone. It will lead you to the

381

right path. You will be complete and safe. Bodhi, take care of my daughters."

"No!" Selah clawed at his sleeve. "You have to come with me, Father. I need you." Tears flooded her eyes. She blinked them back so she could see his face—remember his face. She hadn't had enough time.

Glade took Selah in his arms. "I've often lamented that I got to spend years with Mari but none with you. And even after I had you with me these past few months, I was so caught up in trying to find this path to the West to keep you safe—I thought there'd be much more time. I'm so sorry."

A new cycling level sounded. He turned and looked back through the other doorway. "We have to do this now. Time is running out. The poor man—he must have realized he might not make it, that's why he taught me the sequence."

Glade moved a protesting Selah over to the grottos. He used the old man's ceremonial knife to prick her finger and she flinched. A rivulet of blood ran out and grew to a great drop. Selah stared at it. Her blood looked the same as everyone else's.

Glade turned her finger over the pad in the first grotto. As the blood drop touched the surface, it was sucked into the spot and the pad glowed red. A little pedestal raised the pad and spun with the blood drop securely encapsulated in the center.

He moved Selah to the next pad and the sequence repeated, except the pad glowed blue before the pedestal popped up. For the last one, he had to squeeze her finger to get a complete blood drop without pricking her again. That pad changed to green.

With all three pads glowing and spinning, Glade mounted the triangular stone from his necklace into a matching crevice. A hum grew from the tiny sound of a single bee to a vibrating crescendo. Selah heard a new pitch. Another machine cycled on somewhere.

Glade looked to Bodhi. "When that stops spinning, grab the necklace and get them out of here."

Bodhi nodded. Glade hurried back through the other area and into the far room.

"But Glade! Father! I need to tell you I love you!" Selah yelled.

Glade looked through the door and smiled. "I love you too, and I've always loved both of you, my daughters." He closed the door, and even over the sound of the machinery, the clunk of the heavy latch echoed in the large cavern, making it final.

The gem stopped spinning. Bodhi snatched it up, shoved it in his pocket, and grabbed Selah and Mari by the hands. They both protested, but he was stronger. By the time they had reached the main tunnel and could see the sun, the Mountain had started to rumble, making the ground vibrate.

They broke out into the daylight and fresh, real air. Small stones bounced down the hillside, accompanied by small amounts of dirt and debris. Selah wanted to run away and back in all at the same time. Bodhi kept a grip on her hand and Mari's.

Mojica stood by with an AirWagon with its top up, covering the vehicle. They piled in and she slapped the throttle. "Hold on, folks. We have to try to outrun this thing."

The AirWagon quickly rose and shot off away from the

mountain range. The acceleration pushed Selah back against the seat, startling her, and she grabbed onto Bodhi's hand.

She glanced around. "Where are Mother and Dane and Treva?" she yelled over the sounds of the AirWagon and the rumbling of the Mountain. She suddenly felt panic. Did they get left behind?

Mojica worked at pressing the machine higher and faster than Selah had ever seen one travel. "They're safe with Taraji and the rest of my people. They had enough of a head start to reach the high point of the mountain range."

Selah looked down at the land passing by at a dizzying speed. She could see the road into Stone Braide. Off to the left, a steam vent opened between two scraggly, dead bushes. A huge jet of steam shot toward the sky with a rushing hiss loud enough to be heard over the rumbling. A burst of white vapor billowed over the road like sea foam.

Mojica had both hands on the stick, fighting the jerky movements caused by the increasing percussion of explosions on the mountain range. Selah was transfixed looking back at the mountain range. All along its length, small stones and pebbles bounced and danced down the slopes. They turned into an onslaught of larger rocks and boulders rolling down the side with waves of dirt and debris. Trees tipped over and were carried down the hillside. The vibrations slowly increased to an urgent pounding as the eruption grew closer to the surface. The boulders bounced with the pounding, making it almost seem surreal. One boulder crashed into an evergreen, shearing it off. The tree continued down the slope with the rest of the debris.

The pounding turned into an earthquake. The ground they flew over shook with great jerking movements, dislodging everything possible. Trees were falling, and on the ground she could see animals running up the hill. All sorts of animals. Ones that an hour ago would have been trying to kill each other were now running together to save themselves. But from what, Selah wasn't sure.

The tallest peak on the range collapsed in on itself, sucking in all the rocks and trees in a fifty-foot circle, as well as any living thing that hadn't gotten out of the way fast enough. The sunken center rose again. A gray-colored peak formed and split in the center. For a few seconds only steam escaped from the crevasse. The earthquake stopped.

Selah tapped Bodhi and he turned to look, as did Mari. They were about two miles away now, but as they rose on another mountain range, it afforded them a perfect view of the event.

The top of the gray peak expanded and contracted several times like it was puckering up for a kiss. The last time, in slow motion, it continued to expand.

When it blew, almost an eighth square mile of Mountain and what looked like ash exploded into the air. The gas accompanying the explosion was hot enough to melt any remaining minerals in the soil and incinerate any living thing in the area.

The percussion of the explosion rocked the AirWagon, throwing Selah, Bodhi, and Mari from their seats and into a pile on the floor. Mojica wrestled with the stick, trying to get more speed.

Selah grabbed the seat and pulled herself up. The explosion was still climbing high into the air as they flew away from it. A black column of dust and chemicals rose out of the breached opening. Sprays of lightning from the friction of the escaping particles shot out in all directions.

The dark, ominous cloud at the top of the column billowed and rolled as it expanded to the east of the eruption. As Selah watched, it seemed to circle around the top of the mountain range and head toward them.

"Mojica, that cloud is coming after us!" Selah yelled.

Mojica slapped more circuits, trying to boost output, but the faster speed made the magnojets suck in more air. The black cloud enveloped them. Mojica fought with the stick as the AirWagon bucked and lurched. One of the magnos sputtered and cut off. The AirWagon listed to the right. She tried for more altitude. The dragging side clipped an ancient pine tree that would not yield its dominion to a piece of metal.

The AirWagon spun flat out into a large grouping of trees where it balanced precariously about twenty feet from the ground. Over their heads, lightning shot across the sky as though from a hundred directions at once. The air changed. Selah tasted it before she saw it. Ozone.

The darkened sky raged with a light show. First a large plop of rain landed on Selah's upturned face, then another great splash on her arm.

Mojica recovered from the impact and looked over the side, then up at the sky. "We need to get on the ground." As though the world agreed with her, the sky opened up and it started to rain. Not soft pattering rain, but hard, pelting, stinging rain.

Mari climbed over the side of the AirWagon. "Follow me!"

Selah didn't think it the least bit odd, but Bodhi and Mojica both stared over the side at her as she began climbing down the tree with Mari. "You better come on before that fills with water and pulls itself out of the tree," she yelled up to them.

That seemed to register with both of them, and they came over the side in the same manner. As they reached the grass, they heard a cracking sound, and Bodhi had just enough time to rush everyone out of range before the AirWagon crashed to the ground.

They stood there in the pouring rain looking at the wreck.

"That could have been us," Bodhi said loudly enough to be heard over the roar of the rain.

"But it wasn't, is the important part," Mari said. She brushed the wet hair out of her eyes and crawled over the seat wreckage closest to her.

Selah looked at Mojica. "What's she doing?"

Mojica shrugged.

They were beginning to resemble the litter of puppies that Mother had saved when the creek flooded their barn.

Mari crawled out of the wreckage hauling the leather bag. "I figured since Father entrusted it to me, I'd better not lose it," Mari said.

Selah hugged her. She still felt guilty about yelling at Mari earlier. After all, the woman was her sister.

"We need to get to higher ground," Mojica yelled.

"Can't we just find some shelter from this rain and let it blow itself out?" Bodhi asked.

Mojica shook her head. "This isn't going to blow itself out. It's going to run itself out."

"What does that mean?" Mari asked.

"Flood. This is going to end in a massive flood," Mojica said. "What you saw blow from that Mountain was five thousand tons of chemicals." She directed them up the side of a hill. Selah was glad it wasn't too steep. Her legs were throbbing with muscle aches that hadn't recuperated yet, and her hip was still not quite right.

"What are the chemicals for?" Bodhi must have seen Selah favoring her hip and put himself on that side for support.

"Seeding the clouds to make it rain." Mojica slung the leather bag over her shoulder so Mari could climb the hill.

Selah shut her eyes and let the rain wash her face for a minute. "If it's going to end in a flood, how much good can the rain be?"

31

T he rain is going to create a specific and engineered flood that will wash away the ash from the mountain pass to the West," Mojica said.

Selah stopped and stared at Mojica like she'd stared when the farmer next door had a two-headed calf. It just didn't register in her consciousness what the woman had said.

"When Treva mentioned that before, I thought she was exaggerating, but you're saying this water event is real?" Selah leaned on Bodhi and traipsed across the ridge. "How is something like that even possible? It's been raining for 150 years and it hasn't washed away the ash."

Mojica hoisted the leather bag higher. "I'm sure your copy of the Keepers' journals will tell you how the chemicals would work on the ash. I'm not scientifically interested enough to remember all of those extensive words. But yes, this flood will cut through the ash."

Bodhi helped Selah over a fallen tree. She sat on the trunk. "So does that mean we're going to go to the West?"

Mojica turned back. "You won't be going anywhere if you don't come on. Remember—flood. We need to get to higher ground, much higher ground."

Bodhi looked back down the slight hill. He lifted Selah off the thick log. "You mean it's going to fill in those hills?"

Mojica snorted a little. "It's going to cover all of here."

This time Mari stopped too. Mojica turned around to the three of them and threw her arms out to her sides. "Come on, folks. We don't have time to dawdle."

Selah touched Mari's back. She knew the story of Wood-Haven, but Bodhi didn't. It made them kindred of sorts besides being sisters. A flood had been in her ancient past, and another one would be part of her future. "How are you feeling about this coincidence?"

Mari smiled and dropped back to walk next to Selah. "Father used to say there are no such things as coincidences. That everything happens for a reason, and it all works together for a future."

"After all the things I've been through since I got here, I have to agree with that," Bodhi said.

Selah nodded. "How much higher do we have to go?" Her hip was starting to sting.

"I don't know, but I'd say if we got from this hill to that part of the mountain range over there, we'd have plenty far up that we could go to escape water," Mojica said.

Selah slipped on the soggy, wet leaves and Bodhi caught her in his arms. For a second she closed her eyes. The rain pelted her upturned face, but she wished for this moment of peace always. She hopped up and trudged on.

They made it to the base of the mountain. Just looking up made Selah wince. This angle was much steeper than the slight hills they'd been on.

Her thoughts were interrupted by a crash. Maybe an explosion. They stopped and looked back down the hill.

Mari saw it first. "Look at the valley, over there on that side." She pointed at a natural canyon between two hillsides. Water had started running between them. Enough water that it could be seen from where they were standing on the mountain. It turned into a major torrent faster than Selah anticipated.

"That crashing sound must have been the dam breaking upstream from here. That would explain such a rush of water at one time," Mojica said.

Bodhi pointed. "What explains that water?"

In the opposite direction, a second flood was doing battle to converge with the first.

"I'd guess that when those two meet up, they're going to come this way," Selah said.

"You would be correct on that. I was just calculating how fast I think it's going to get to this spot," Mari said.

"You mean here where we're standing?" Bodhi asked.

"Probably above where we are. We'd better get going," Mari said.

Selah sucked in a breath and started walking faster. The stabbing in her hip brought tears to her eyes, but she couldn't stop. A thundering sounded behind them. She turned just in time to shout a warning as a herd of deer fled up the mountainside.

Rabbits, bobcats, and smaller creatures were all streaming away from the water. It had taken over the valley. It was a river of swiftly moving water, churning and destroying everything in its path. The sound was coming closer.

Bodhi now was practically carrying Selah along by her arm. Her hip had become almost useless with the stabbing pains. Mari propped up her other side. Mojica's strength would have been ideal, but her height difference made it awkward for her to lend Selah a shoulder. But she was strong enough to carry the leather bag that had to weigh at least thirty pounds.

"We need to go faster," Mari said. "At the rate it's rising, the water will overtake us before we get another four hundred feet. This just isn't steep enough." She stopped, looking around.

"We really need to keep moving," Mojica said, a sense of urgency in her voice.

Selah raised a hand to stop her. "Hold on a minute. I think I know what she's thinking."

Mari turned and smiled.

"Okay, ladies, we need to go somewhere, and soon," Bodhi said.

Mari and Selah pointed together. "Up!"

Bodhi raised a hand to his forehead. Rain poured down his face, making him furrow his brow, or Selah was sure his eyes would be as wide open as her mother's saucers.

"Up? You mean like in climb a tree, up?" Bodhi said.

Mari nodded.

"Yes! That's exactly how Mari's people survived the tsunami during the Sorrows. They climbed the ancient trees in their forest."

"That could work!" Mojica smiled. "Brilliant! That could work."

Bodhi looked at her as though she'd just called him a girl. "Are you serious about this idea?"

"Up is the perfect way to go. Most of the trees in this part of the forest are from before the Sorrows. They will surely hold a couple of people and hold back the water."

Bodhi shook his head. "I guess I don't have a choice, and rather than argue and waste time, let's get up there. Mari, which ones?"

Mari and Mojica conferred on their best options. Nearby were two huge trees that you could drive an AirWagon through if they'd had holes. Bodhi and Selah went up one, and Mari and Mojica went up the other one.

The pain each time Selah stepped up was excruciating. "I need to stop. I can't keep going." She looked down at Bodhi below her. For the first time she could see water lapping below them. Her hands kept slipping. Her foot slipped once, but Bodhi was there to catch it flailing in midair and direct it back to a nearby branch.

"Can you see the water over there?" Mojica asked.

"Yes," Bodhi said. "I admit, you ladies were correct about this. Can we make it high enough?" He and Selah were about four or five feet below where Mojica and Mari had climbed. They were moving up the tree like a pair of squirrels.

Selah felt like crying. Maybe she was already. So much

water was running down her face that she had to keep her nose pointed down or she'd sniff in liquid. If she could just rest a minute, the needle pains might stop. She was shaking from the sharp, pointed pain, and it kept causing her hands to tremble and miss the branches. *Climb, Selah.*

Mari and Mojica were now ten feet higher.

"Why don't you climb past me and get to the top. I need a little rest," Selah said to Bodhi. She leaned her head against the rough bark. Water slid between her and the tree.

"Do you really think I'd leave you now, after all I've gone through to be with you?"

"My hip hurts too much. It's been less than twenty-four hours, but it hasn't healed properly. The blood loss must be weakening my system." Water was lapping at the tree, all around. She looked up to call out to Mari. They were at least fifteen feet higher.

"Come on, firefly, you can do this, please." Bodhi pulled himself up to Selah. She reached out a trembling hand and touched his hair. He lifted her left foot. It was easier not needing to flex the muscle, but she cried out in pain from the distance he had to push it for her to reach another branch.

"I'm trying." Selah's pain turned to shivers. In the cold rain she could barely breathe. Bodhi lifted the other foot for her. She clung to the tree. From above, she could hear Mari and Mojica calling to her, telling her she could make it. She raised her bad leg. At the place where the pain became unbearable, she stopped. Bodhi pushed her foot the rest of the way up. She scrambled, clutching at the rough bark. Her hands had bloodied, but the rain kept washing the evidence away.

She looked down. The water was climbing the tree. It would reach Bodhi soon. She forced every muscle in her body to move. She screamed at herself. She screamed at her hip. She screamed at Varro, because it gave her strength.

One foot after the other. She looked up. Mari and Mojica had reached as far as they could go. The treetop swung lazily back and forth as they tried not to move. She was still at least fifteen feet below them. The water was almost to Bodhi's feet.

"I've got an idea," Bodhi said. "Let me come up under you, and you sit on my shoulders."

"No, no." Selah shook her head. "You can't. I'm too heavy. You won't be able to climb."

"I'm not climbing at the moment anyway, and it's getting a little wet down here," Bodhi said.

Selah tried to raise her leg. Pain shot through her hip as though she had just been hit with a weapon. She screamed, and Bodhi slipped up under her, seating her firmly on his shoulders.

Selah grabbed for the tree and hung on. "You're crazy. We're going to fall off and die."

Bodhi climbed one step at a time, but much faster than they'd been going. "Better to die moving than sitting still waiting for it." He grabbed the next branch and hoisted them up as Selah clung to the tree for stability.

She dared to look down. Bodhi was in water up to his ankles. He'd step up and the water would be higher by the time he moved.

"Let me off your shoulders. You could get up there much

faster without me," Selah said. "Please, I love you. I don't want you to die."

Bodhi pushed up faster. They covered two steps that time. "But I'd die without you. So if you're going, I'm going with you."

Tears and water filled Selah's eyes. "Mari! Tell my mother and brother that I love them." She pulled up as hard as she could, willing her arms to move faster to pull Bodhi from the water.

"Selah? What's the matter?" Mari yelled.

"Selah, I can see you. Keep climbing. Just a little farther," Mojica called out.

Her voice was nearly drowned out by the pounding rain. Selah looked down again. The water was up to Bodhi's waist. He was struggling to get footholds on the waterlogged branches in the swift current.

She screamed and clawed at the tree, trying to reach a branch to help Bodhi pull up. When she could take her weight off his shoulders, he could climb. The water was up to her own feet now, passing Bodhi's waist.

"Climb, firefly, climb," Bodhi said.

He was exhausted. Selah could tell by the heaving in his chest. She stretched her fingertips to reach the next branch. The water was lapping at her thighs, near his head.

"I can't reach it!" Selah shouted. "It's too far away!"

She felt Bodhi's hands under her legs. With a burst of strength he thrust her up in the air. Selah passed the branch she had been reaching for and went two above that. She found footholds and pulled herself up another three steps. Sitting on his shoulders had reset the socket and she got four more steps up.

"That was wonderful. You gave me just the right—" Selah looked down. The water lapped at her feet. Bodhi wasn't there.

"Bodhi!" she screamed.

She tried going back down. Her hip popped out of joint. She froze in place. She yelled at the water lapping at her feet. She kicked at it. Pain shot up her leg. She held the tree and screamed.

"Selah, I can see you. Where's Bodhi?" Mojica shouted just across from her. She'd come back down her tree.

"Go back up. Go back up. My hip won't make it."

"You can do it. Think of Dane and your mother. They need you," Mojica said.

"I can't. I tried to go back down and my hip popped. The leg is useless. I can't move."

The water was rising up her calves. She knew she was going to die, and she was ready. After all, she had seen three members of her family die today. Bodhi was the last one. She couldn't take anymore. The heart pain and physical pain were too much.

The cold, swirling water was reaching her hips now. *Let go. Just let go of the tree and let the water take hold.*

She wasn't shivering.

She wasn't scared.

Selah let go of the tree.

32

The water made her buoyant. She started to drift backward. She was slammed against the tree and held there. Warmth on her back, around her sides.

Bodhi popped up out of the water, gasping and spitting. Selah almost fell off the tree again to hug him.

"Hold the tree, firefly. Hug later. All I can do is hold us here. My arms don't have much more strength."

"Bodhi!" Mojica called and pumped her fist. "Woo-hoo! Mari, Bodhi made it." A greeting came down, but Selah couldn't make it out with the rushing water and her heart thudding in her ears. If she was going to die, she would do it in Bodhi's arms. They clung to the tree, his body providing the warmth to keep her returning shivers at bay.

The rain stopped. It didn't stop slowly or in little degrees. It just stopped completely. They looked up at the sky. The churning mass of black clouds that had supported the storm dissipated to mist and then was gone. The sky was clear beyond the clouds, as though the rest of their world was having sunshine while they were under a cloud.

Mari yelled from the other tree when the rain stopped. Selah clung to her tree with her head resting against the unbelievably rough bark and smiled. "Where does she still get the energy to yell after all this?" She was doing her best just to hang on to the tree.

"Some people just have it all." Bodhi leaned his head on Selah's shoulder. "Is it my imagination or is the water going down already?"

Selah lifted her head and tried to discern if the water had receded any. "I believe you're right. We may live to fight another day. Do we go down as the water does?"

"Yell over and ask Mari," Bodhi said.

"I'm too tired."

"Can you climb down?"

"We could just stay up here forever."

"I don't think that's very practical."

Selah started to laugh. She clung to the tree and laughed until tears came. She didn't think she had any tears left, but she was probably just waterlogged from the flood. "I have to take you to WoodHaven."

"What's that?"

Selah laughed again. "A bunch of impractical people."

Selah was happy to finally get down from the tree before evening fell. Five hours clinging to a tree gave her a whole new respect for those of her people who had survived the Sorrows in WoodHaven.

"Good news!" Mojica said as she slipped and slid her way back down the mountainside. "All of our group made it safely out of the designated area. Your family is fine and looking forward to seeing you."

Selah leaned back against Bodhi's shoulder. She had finally begun to dry and the warmth felt cozy. "I can never thank you enough for helping us and my family. You were the answer to many calls. Where are you going from here? I'm sure you'd all be welcome in TicCity."

"Some of our folks are going to settle there, but my team and I belong to you."

Selah frowned. "I don't understand. How can you belong to me?"

"You are the novarium. When you start reading the Stone Braide Chronicles, you'll see what our role is to be in your future. It's our sole mandate to unite you with the Third Protocol."

"We don't know how to find it. And what about the fracture thing?" Selah waved a finger in the air.

"What fracture thing?" Mari sat on a high boulder out of reach of the slippery muck that remained.

Bodhi looked down. "I guess I can tell everything now that Glade is gone."

Selah sat up.

"You—we—need to find the Third Protocol within nine months or you will fracture. Your mental and physical functions will degrade until you're no longer functional," Bodhi said.

Selah rubbed her forehead. "So when were you going to tell me more about this?"

"I figured I'd wait until we found out if the passages to the West had actually opened," Bodhi said.

"My crew has already flown over the pass. It is open and free of ash," Mojica said. "We can start exploring as soon as you've recovered some. They should be here in an hour or so. They're tracking our coordinates and have sent out AirWagons."

Selah slumped back against Bodhi, more tired than she ever knew possible.

Bodhi looked over at her and tweaked her nose. "What's the matter?"

"My father is gone. I fought all that time to find him, and my cause is what killed him."

"It's not your fault that old guy had a heart attack," Mari said.

"I know, but still. Father kept telling me I was the future."

Bodhi shrugged. "He told me the same thing."

"I don't know what that means."

"It means that you have an army of your own traveling with you day and night, and we're going to the West."

"I've also taken the liberty of contacting Taraji and Tic-City. She and a host of her security will be traveling with us," Mojica said.

"So do you know why I'm here?"

Mojica looked at her as though she had a lot to say, but

the mask fell again and her face became serene. "You will find out all in good time."

"Father said I was the answer to good and evil."

Mojica looked away, then directly at Selah. "A lot of people have died to give you this chance to unite with the Third Protocol."

Selah sat up straight, her body aching at every move. "Then I have to succeed."

Read an Excerpt

Book 3 in the Stone Braide Chronicles

COMING FALL 2016

1

S elah launched herself out the back of the AirWagon, landing crouched behind the large barrier. Her breathing played catch-up with her runaway heartbeat. She didn't fear for herself but was scared stupid for Mother and Dane hiding inside this lead vehicle. She slowed her breathing and concentrated on the sounds. The serenity of the sun-drenched morning fled with the songbirds.

A barrage of weapons fire sliced the side of a nearby boulder, lighting the area with trailing starbursts and scarring the surface with white furrowed streaks that propelled a barrage of chiseled stone bits in her direction.

"They're using bullets! These aren't TicCity security. They're splinters," she yelled to Mari in the AirWagon. Selah remembered the familiar smell of sulfur from gunfire back in Dominion.

They'd been worried about an ambush on the way back

to TicCity, and they had just begun to relax as they reached the last mile to town.

A bullet ricocheted off a tree stump. Selah flinched. It bit the dirt in front of her feet and sent up a burst of dust. She pulled back. "Somebody tell me where they are and give me a weapon!"

Multiple bullets zipped by from at least two directions in front of them. Shots echoed behind her where Bodhi and Mojica brought up the rear, with Taraji and Treva in the middle. They were surrounded.

Mari slid a crossbow over the back edge of the AirWagon. "Here. I've got your mother and Dane secured."

Selah slid the quiver over her shoulder and nocked an arrow. Mari dropped down beside her and retrieved her own crossbow from the AirWagon bed. A shot sliced the side of their vehicle. They pulled back.

Selah lay flat on the ground and edged around the side, away from the shooting. The bullets hit the vehicles behind her, where Bodhi and Mojica returned fire with laser darts. Elongated bursts of heat and fire belched from two rapidly shooting guns hidden in the tree line across the road. She listened for the echoes of the shots and took aim at the deep foliage beside a wide oak. Taking a deep breath to steady her shot, Selah let it fly.

The arrow sliced silently though the greenery, and she heard a solid thunk. Mari sank a second shot into the bushes on the other side of the tree. They were rewarded with silence. Selah released her breath.

She turned to the other side of their vehicle, listening for more gunshot echoes to home in on their direction.

Bodhi crawled along the back side of the convoy to reach Selah. Even though her abilities outpaced his at the moment, she was overjoyed to have him at her side.

"I knew I should have made you keep Mojica up here with you. You could have been killed with just crossbows to protect you," Bodhi said, his laser dart at the ready and still keyed to Mojica's frequency for her special squad.

Selah, trying to distinguish between two different gun sounds, patted his arm. "Mari and I have taken out two of the guns on our left, and before you interrupted my train of thought I was about to get another one. Excuse me a second." She rolled away from Bodhi and peered out between the airlift mechanisms. She could see the flash from the other shooter, but these weapons confused her. They fired much faster than the guns she was used to. Her hands started to shake, but she gripped her weapon to steady them. She watched a half minute longer than normal when spotting.

Selah nocked the arrow. Just then a huge weight slammed her to the ground and her crossbow skittered several feet away. She adjusted her center of gravity, flipped the direction of the arrow she was holding, and swung back hard, stabbing her assailant in the leg with the arrow. He roared in pain as she propelled him off her back. He flipped over and slammed his middle into a tree, knocking the wind from him.

Bodhi was locked in hand-to-hand combat with a dark-clad figure. Bullets peppered the dirt on the far side of the vehicle. Selah clawed at the ground and reached Bodhi's laser dart. She flipped over and pulled the trigger before registering that she wasn't an authorized user. Nothing.

She scrambled to her feet and grabbed the barrel like a club, raising the laser dart over her head to hit the figure fighting Bodhi.

Suddenly the weapon jerked out of her hands from behind. She gasped. She pivoted to face the assailant and threw up her arms in a defensive posture as he swung at her with the weapon. Bodhi was too close for her to use an energy thrust on the man. She would have to fight.

Mari fired an arrow that clipped the assailant's hand, jerking the weapon from his fingers and over Selah's head. She tackled the man's legs, propelling them both against the boulder. He came up swinging and his gloved fist clipped her in the chin, slamming her to the ground just as the assailant she had stabbed grabbed Mari from behind.

Tiny stones ripped at Selah's palms. Her hands clutched at the dirt and she saw sparkles in her vision. She threw up her arms to ward off another blow, but just in time Bodhi grabbed the guy, pulling him around into his waiting fist. Selah scrambled to help Mari.

An ear-piercing sound split the air. Selah pulled her chin to her chest and shielded her ears. The pain weakened her knees. She and everyone else dropped to the ground. When the brain-rattling sound ended, they were surrounded by TicCity security forces. The assailants rose to their knees and raised their hands to their heads in surrender.

Taraji and Mojica marched forward with the three assailants they had caught. They met up with Selah just as the head of TicCity Council security reached Bodhi and Mari.

"Hmm, this does not look good," Taraji said. "The head

of Council security never comes out on an operation. Her job is a ceremonial assignment."

"We were warned at the last stop that we might find some resistance. So I guess it's better for them to meet us on the road when we need to be saved," Selah said. They walked over to meet the Council woman and deliver the last of the assailants.

The tall woman removed her head gear as she turned toward them. Blonde hair spilled from her helmet. "Well, finding you together saves me a trip," she said to Selah and Taraji.

"Thank you for coming to our aid. My father, Glade Rishon, would have been pleased at your assistance," Selah said. She didn't like this woman. Glade had faced opposition from her at every Council meeting. But she had saved the day, so respect was in order.

The woman pursed her lips and looked down her nose at Selah. "Yes, well, it was purely circumstantial. This will be the last assistance you get from Council security. With Glade's death, the regime has finally and permanently changed in TicCity."

"Congratulations on your new job, but the fact remains I'm still the novarium, and the legends have been proved true. We're going west to search for the Third Protocol," Selah said.

"Good, then you won't be upset at my announcement," she said.

"What announcement is that?" Selah watched the security forces gathering up the assailants in the TicCity transport.

A wry smile spread across the woman's face. "Out of respect for Glade Rishon, I'm giving you forty-eight hours to clear out of TicCity or be sold to the highest bidder."

Bonnie S. Calhoun has retired from being a clothing designer and seamstress to write full-time. She also has mad skills at coding HTML and designing websites.

Bonnie lives in a log cabin in the woods with fifteen acres and a pond full of bass, though she'd rather buy fish at the grocery store. She shares her domain with a husband, a dog, and two cats, all of whom think she's waitstaff. *Thunder*, the first book of the Stone Braide Chronicles, was her first YA novel. Learn more at www.bonniescalhoun.com.

Get to know

BONNIE S. CALHOUN!

• • •

BonnieSCalhoun.com

Join Selah on the Journey That Will
Change Her Destiny . . . **AND HER WORLD**

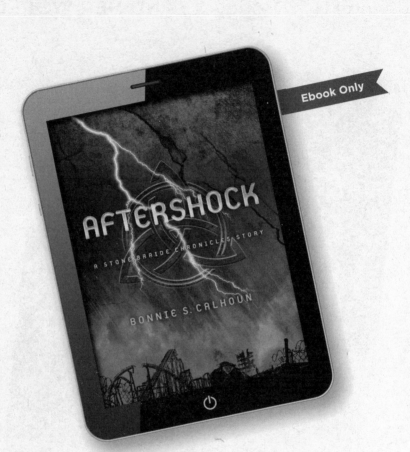

Don't miss *Aftershock,*
the prequel to *Lightning*